THE HEART OF IT ALL

BOOK 2

I0566076

Wormwood's

Water

Michelle Heisel

Published by Michelle Heisel

ISBN: 978-0-9986935-2-1
Ebook ISBN: 978-0-9986935-3-8

Cover art by Extended Imagery
Cover design by Extended Imagery and Cody Heisel

Printed in the United States of America

www.michelleheisel.com

Praise for Michelle Heisel's
Wormwood's Water

"Again, like in book one, I could not put this book down…It keeps you on your seat and wondering what will happen next."

- Andrea A.

"Fully engaging. Interesting and meaningful - on many levels. Love the creativity, and especially the relatable characters."

- Wendy E.

"If you like a book that intrigues you right from the beginning with mystery and love and a search for the truth, you will love Wormwood's Water. I couldn't let go of this book! I can't wait for the next one! Michelle Heisel is an exceptional writer that will appeal to many age groups!"

- Amazon Customer

Chapter 1

Mira sipped out of the scratched teal colored aluminum tumbler that she'd gotten from the Locators – the exploration group that recovered pre-war artifacts. The group was one of many that had popped up in the city of Pillar over the past year. So many changes…yet she still felt the same.

Letting the glass drop to her side, Mira frowned. One year ago today, she'd been staring out her dining room window, much like she was doing right now. She'd craved more out of life and had actually done something about it. With the help of her prophetic visions, she'd embarked on the most exhilarating adventure. The retrieval of the object of her quest, the Enchiridion of Emmanuel, had prompted the LifeChip Obliteration Movement, giving the citizens of Pillar their emotional freedom. Pillar's passion and creativity had exploded because of it – an amazing thing really, since they'd lived for thirty years with embedded nano-chips that had dulled their senses and spirit. She squinted toward the town that seemed to glow with vibrant energy and purpose. Why did she feel so restless?

Bringing the glass to her lips, Mira tilted it back, only to find it empty. Lowering it to eye level, she spotted one droplet hugging the metal edge. She licked it, but it was much less than satisfying. She wanted more, and not only of the water.

At the sound of a light knock, Mira turned. Her mother, Addison, stood in the doorway that led into the foyer. "Hey, mom," she said.

"Hey, yourself," her mom said as she came to stand next to her. "You doing okay?"

Mira could feel her mom studying her. "I'm fine."

"Even though it's only a week and a day until Vaughn and I leave for Enab?"

Mira didn't like to be reminded that the parents she had just started to get to know were leaving her. She lifted her chin ever so slightly. "I'm almost nineteen, remember? Of course I'll be okay." She shrugged. "Besides, I'm sure starting a church on the island will make a huge difference, and it will be very rewarding for you and dad, too."

"I believe it will, but I'm still worried about you." Her mom ran her finger over the dust that had gathered on the windowsill.

"Don't worry about it. I can handle being on my own."

Her mom let out a long, slow breath. "I just thought you'd have some direction by now, like when you were searching for the Enchiridion." With a deep frown, she brushed her hand across her flowing purple gauchos, leaving a trail of dirt behind. "But all you've done since then is float around. You've had various jobs, a business of your own, several different college majors - none of it makes you happy, honey."

What she said was true. Gripping the tumbler in front of her, Mira said, "I sprained my ankle when I was working with the Locators." It had been hot and grimy work anyway, she reasoned as she moved to the table. She set the glass next to her final project for art class, which at the moment consisted of a blank piece of canvas and several nearly full tubes of paint. "And getting fired from the Grub Station because I had a miscalculation with the money a time or two, doesn't actually count." She breathed in through her nostrils, trying to control her anxiety. "And half the majors they offer at the university are stupid. The other half have professors who are either ancient or clueless," she said, shoving the canvas and paints in her backpack.

"What about the store you opened…Bags & Beverages? That seemed so perfect for you, but you quit that too!"

"Two months of that business was way too long," Mira huffed. It had cost too much money to run. Strike one! Her customers had only wanted to drink excessively and gossip, which was fun at first but became annoying and depressing. Strike two! And packaging purses to ship to other cities had been extremely tedious. Strike three! Mira zipped up her backpack. "I haven't found my niche, but at least I have figured out some things that won't make me happy."

"So how are you going to find what *will* make you happy, Mira?"

I don't know!! her mind snapped, but she said nothing.

After a few long moments of silence, her mom pinched the bridge of her nose. "I think Vaughn and I should postpone our extended trip to Enab."

"Don't." Though uneasy about staying in her childhood home alone – the house was spooky at night – Mira didn't want them to change their plans because of her. She'd really feel bad about herself then. "This is just something that I have to figure out on my own," she said, slipping her backpack over her shoulders. "And I actually have a new plan of action that I'm working on." It had just popped into her head.

"You do?"

Mira nodded. "I'm going to be a prophetess." She'd given messages through her prophetic paintings, why not through another avenue? "Prophetic word, to be exact."

Her mom raised a brow. "Do you mean prophesying as in using the Enchiridion of Emmanuel to preach and encourage?"

Quite honestly, she hadn't read much of the Enchiridion, but felt she had a good handle on its message. "No. I want to make a difference by giving people the messages I hear from the Spirit of God – like they do at the Prophet House." She just had to learn more about how to tap into it. Shoulders straight, Mira strolled into the foyer.

Her mom followed. "But that's like a psychic hotline undercover!"

"Well, it's been accurate for me…and it's so much more than that." Mira turned to face her mom. "Look, I've been going to this place for several months now and I know how it makes me feel. God speaks to me through these prophetic words – and He can speak *through* me to others who need to be encouraged." Mira noticed how wide her mom's eyes had gotten, so she tried to reason with her, even as she tried to convince herself. "If I rely on the Spirit's leading, I won't be limiting God. Instead, I'll walk in the same power that Christ was given and do even greater miracles than He did. What could be better than that?"

"You seriously think you'll teach more clearly and heal with more power than the Son of God?"

Her mom's incredulous look affected Mira more than she wanted to admit. Shrugging off the surge of doubt, Mira focused on what she'd learned yesterday about herself at the Prophet House. She really hoped that once she figured out how it all worked, she'd be able to hone in on the prophetic power that would bring goodness and healing to the world. "Well the Spirit leads us to the truth - and I'm just following Him off the map."

"But the Spirit brought us the map – and that's the Enchiridion of Emmanuel," her mom said, frowning deeply. "And its power is NOT dependent on us using religious experiences to escape its boundaries."

"Well, the couple of times I tried reading it, I didn't feel anything." She shrugged. "On the other hand, the prophetic words from the prophetess make me feel alive, like I am truly experiencing the love of God."

Her mom grabbed onto the dark wooden pommel that marked the end of the staircase. "You risked your life to find the Enchiridion, why not give it more of a chance? Get to know Christ intimately!"

"I already know about Him, mom. And have you ever thought that maybe my calling was only to find the Enchiridion of Emmanuel, not necessarily to study it? Besides, I feel I gave it chance enough," she said, lifting her chin. "And I'm starting to think maybe faith is different for different people anyway."

"But knowing *about* Christ is not the same as *loving* Him. And God is God – He is unchanging."

"So *you* say!"

Before her mom could respond, the front door of the house whooshed open, revealing a whistling Vaughn with a picnic basket over his arm. The smell of croissants and coffee filled the entryway. When Vaughn saw her mom, he grinned mid-whistle. "There are my two favorite women in the world," he said, yet he only had eyes for her mom.

Mira felt an envious squeeze of her heart, wishing Nash would look at her like that.

"Want to join your mother and me for a picnic?" her dad asked, glancing down at the basket. "I think I have enough for the three of us."

As her mom reached up on tiptoes to kiss his cheek, Mira said, "Thanks for the invitation, but you two enjoy. I have to head to class." Needing to escape the loving pair, she hurried outside, winding around to the back of the house. She didn't stop until she got to the gate. Pausing there, she took several deep breaths. She remembered standing in that very spot with Nash before they'd risked their lives to recover the paintings that led them to the Enchiridion of Emmanuel. Even though she and Nash hadn't trusted each other totally then, they'd at least managed to work as a pair. And they'd been good together. Now it felt like they were little more than acquaintances, not where she'd anticipated their relationship would be. She was not where she'd thought *she* would be, either!

A deep, burning pang threatened to overwhelm her as she dug into her front pocket for her phone. No missed calls. Nash hadn't called like he'd said he would. She bit back her hurt and called him anyway…even hoped he would answer, with an apology of course. If he'd reassure her they were meant to be, that would be even better. But instead, she got his voicemail.

She clutched the phone, pressing it tightly to her ear as she waited for his long recorded riff to end. By the time he said *leave a message*, her throat seemed too tight to speak. After a few seconds of painful silence, she managed to tether her emotions enough to push out the words through her gritted teeth. "You didn't call. We need to talk. I'll stop by your store after class." With the ache in her chest heavier than ever, she stashed the phone back in her pocket.

Closing the gate behind her, she unlocked the bike she had chained to the fence and started walking down the hill with it. She couldn't see Pillar Peace University from there, but as usual, the Center of Operations to the north of campus stuck out like a beacon in the dawning light, taunting her. The lit-up wall mural - redone by the Art Reborn Club - was still a tree, but instead of gnarly vacant branches, it had thousands of leaves and various bright fruits hanging. In its branches were many different colors and kinds of birds and nests. *Pillar Transformed*, it was now entitled.

Mira trudged her way toward the Prophet House, the rhythmic click of her back-wheel sprocket barely heard over her mind-ramblings. She had evolved over the past year, too, but instead of becoming something vibrant and uniquely beautiful like the tree and the rest of the people of Pillar, she was a lonely misfit without direction. Today, though, she vowed to change that.

Chapter 2

Showered and starving after his run, Nash dashed down the stairs of his loft into the music store he'd opened about six months ago. He took a moment to survey Spectrum Music with pride. A year ago, this hadn't even been a blip on his radar. In fact, he hadn't even been introduced to music at all, and now it was so ingrained into his life, he couldn't imagine it any other way.

Nash's phone beeped to let him know he'd missed a call. Mira. He'd forgotten to call her. Glancing at the metal guitar clock, he opted not to call her back. It was already 7AM and he didn't have time for another complaint session on how he didn't measure up to her expectations. Besides, he couldn't let Hayes beat him to Eldorado's Eatery. Whoever showed up last had to pay. Nash hurried out into the cool morning. Out of the corner of his eye, he saw Hayes park his truck in the lot next to the cafe. Racing across the street, Nash swung the restaurant door open and slipped onto the scraped log couch with its animal print cushions. Trying to catch his breath, he managed to feign nonchalance when Hayes stepped inside.

"It's about time you showed up," Nash said with a smile as he got to his feet.

Hayes' good nature never seemed to leave him. The deep grooves that framed his smile deepened as his eyes crinkled to mere slits. "I saw ya sneak in here." He slapped Nash on the back. "But a deal's a deal." He turned to the hostess. "We can just seat ourselves, darlin'."

Buffalo Alys, or so she called herself, shook her head, her brown, curly hair staying in place, but her golden loop nose ring jiggling. "Your table is taken this morning." She leaned in close to them, her voice as gruff as usual, but her eyes sparkled with excitement, replacing her typical bored look. "She seems like someone who might be famous, so I just had to give her the best seat in the house."

"Well, then. We'll take the table right across from her," Hayes said. "Maybe we'll recognize her and you'll be able to post it on yer wall that someone famous ate here."

Alys grinned, something she didn't do often. Adjusting her vest, she strolled to the table, her heeled cowboy boots a soft rhythmic thud against the roughly hewn wooden floor. "Here you go, gentlemen," she said, splaying her hand out toward the two-person table topped with a denim tablecloth. "Do you need menus?" she asked, looking askance at the interesting visitor.

"No, just give me the usual," Nash said, letting his gaze slide to the table they'd used nearly every morning over the past year. The woman sitting there was one of those people who seemed like she could be twenty…or forty. Her hair was jet black, rolling down her back in waves of glistening perfection. Her dress was sleek, hugging her curves, and she wore heels with tall spikes, making him wonder if she would ever be able to walk in them. As she brought the copper-lipstick-smudged coffee mug to her lips, her right hand sparkled with four diamond-laden rings. Setting down the coffee mug, she turned the page of her magazine, clearly absorbed.

"See what I mean? She has to be *someone*," Alys said.

Hayes cleared his throat and unzipped the bag tucked between the wall and his left leg. "I'll have the special," he said, taking out a copy of a book from the Enchiridion of Emmanuel. Leaving the bag open, he put the stapled pages on the table. "And coffee, black, and some tomato juice."

"Got it," Alys said, and after one final look at the visitor, headed back to the kitchen.

"Do ya recognize the broad?" Hayes said, running his hand over the top of his note-filled pages.

Broad? Nash shook his head at his friend's strange vocabulary. "She doesn't look familiar, but I agree with Alys. She looks like she's important."

Right at that moment, the woman glanced over at them. Her eyes locked onto Nash's with a look he couldn't quite explain. What he *did* know was that his interest was piqued.

"So what did ya think about this passage?" Hayes asked.

"What?"

"The passage from Revelations eight that we're discussin' today."

One morning a week, Nash debated Hayes concerning different passages from the Enchiridion. It was something he thoroughly enjoyed. As it turned out, he quite liked to play devil's advocate. He drew Hayes' paper close and reread the verse from chapter eight that, for some reason, had stuck in his head since he'd read it. *Then the third angel blew his trumpet, and a great star fell from the sky, burning like a torch. It fell on one-third of the rivers and on the springs of the water. The name of the star was Wormwood. It made one-third of the water bitter, and many people died from drinking the bitter water.*

"The book of Revelations seems like someone with a great imagination wrote it."

"That's one way to see it," Hayes said.

"So this verse," Nash said, pointing to it. "What does it mean?"

"I suspect it's both literal and figurative." Hayes smiled and took the paper from him. As his eyes scanned across the words, Alys swooped in with an overly bright smile and set their drinks on the denim pocket coasters.

Leaning in close, she whispered, "I found out who she is." The skin exposed in the scooped neckline of Alys' shirt turned splotchy and crept upward as she cast a quick glance over at the woman.

"Well, who is she?" Nash whispered.

"Her name is Porsche Grant. She owns Driven Records, the biggest record label since before the war." Alys scampered over to the woman and, breathy voiced, asked her if she needed anything else, half-bowing as she did so.

Nash's stomach tensed even as it fluttered. He'd heard of the record label, and of the successful Porsche Grant. Half of him wondered why she'd come to

Pillar when the city of Bolinbroke, where her business was located, was chock-full of burgeoning musicians. The other half didn't care. This was the opportunity he'd hoped for. His leg began its jittery dance, bouncing under the table as he tried to think about how to approach Ms. Grant.

Hayes laid the paper down and hooked his index finger through the handle of his cup. "I think we can learn a lot from these verses," he said, inhaling the steam from his coffee, "like that the star is Satan – the absence of good, the definition of evil." He took a swig of his brew. "And wormwood is actually a poisonous plant and if it's found in water – water we all need to live…"

Alys wandered back to the kitchen, giving Nash a wide-open view of Ms. Grant. A thought quickly passed through his mind…was she married? Hayes waved his hand in front of Nash's face. "You listenin'?" Hayes asked.

Nash looked across the table at his friend, his mind still buzzing with thoughts of the mysterious woman and what she could do for his career. He frowned. "Not really. Sorry."

Again, Alys traipsed in, this time with their food.

Nash looked down at his eggs - which were supposed to be over-medium, but looked like snotty globs. Hayes' pancakes looked equally unappetizing with their variety of sizes, each nicely burned.

"Um, these look kind of burned, Alys." Hayes crinkled up his nose.

"Hmm." Alys frowned down at the stack, then she smiled as she flipped the top one over. "There. Now they're perfect."

Hayes chuckled. "Can't argue with that, I guess." Instead of complaining, or demanding new pancakes, he doused the stack with butter and syrup and dug in. "As I was saying," he said, talking between chews. "We need to focus on the water part of this verse. We have to make sure the water - ," he circled his fork in the air, "the information we drink in…the paths we take - are good and true."

"That makes sense." Nash swiped his toast across the glazed yoke. "But what if, for example, the Enchiridion of Emmanuel isn't true? And what if my dream of becoming a famous musician isn't a good path?"

"What I believe is…" Hayes paused to look over at Porsche Grant who had gotten up and was approaching their table.

Neither Hayes nor Nash spoke. They only watched her move regally over to them. She stopped at their table.

Nash stood up and stretched out his hand, and in the process, bumped into his plate…which knocked into his glass…which spilled the orange juice onto his food and splashed onto his jeaned thigh.

Ms. Grant laughed and handed him a napkin. "I'd say that it's too bad you ruined your food, but by the look of it, it might have made it more edible."

Nash smiled, the nervous cinch on his chest easing a bit.

"Can we help ya with somthin', ma'am?" Hayes asked.

"I overheard something you said," Ms. Grant remarked as she glanced at Nash, "the part about your dream of becoming a famous musician?"

He swallowed, wishing the orange juice was in his suddenly dry mouth rather than on his jeans. "That *is* my dream. I own Spectrum Music, a music store right across the street. I record music there, too, and I'm actually almost done recording my album. And my songs seem well received in the area," he rambled. He chanced a look into her eyes. They were encouraging. "I have a lot of passion, a lot of talent, and I'm not afraid to work hard."

"That's what I like to hear," she said. "And that's just the kind of person Driven Records is looking for."

"It is?"

She nodded, flipping open the magazine she held. "Tell you what. Read this article I wrote on the motto of our company. See if it's something you'd really like to get into." She handed him her business card. "If it *is* what you want, give me a call and I'll stop by to check out the album you've put together."

Nash tucked her card into his back pocket then took the magazine from her. "Thanks, Ms. Grant. I really appreciate the opportunity."

She smiled warmly. "And I'm really looking forward to working with you. I *love* new recruits. It makes life…interesting." She stepped away from the table. "You gentlemen have a nice day," she said.

"Thanks. You too, Ms. Grant," Nash said, dabbing at his wet jeans.

In her circuitous route around the puddle of orange juice on the floor, she paused to look over her shoulder. "By the way, I'll be in town for only a week or two, so if you're going to make a move, keep that in mind."

"Of course, Ms. Grant."

"And one other thing. Do call me Porsche. Ms. Grant seems much too impersonal."

"Thanks, Porsche," he said with a shaky smile.

She smiled again and with a wave, strolled out the door. She *could* walk in those heels after all, Nash thought. And she did it well.

Hayes frowned as he stabbed another bit of pancake.

Nash glanced back at the door through which Porsche had disappeared. He recognized the gift he'd been handed. The owner of Driven Records wanted to give him a shot. The door to his dreams had just been opened – and he needed to walk through it. He stood up, feeling a powerful sensation driving him to grab his chance.

"You're leaving?" Hayes asked.

Nash nodded.

"What about our discussion? And our breakfast?" Hayes asked.

"Sorry." Nash glanced down at the magazine article clutched in his hands. The company motto listed there was *Play hard and make an impact*…which was just what he wanted. "I've got to get to composing."

Chapter 3

A plume of dust followed Mira as she rolled into the driveway of the stately white house called the Prophet House. After leaning her bike against one of the five giant pillars that held up the roof of the front porch, she jogged up the steps. Hopefully, Eleanor would have time to pray with her and share with her how she, too, could get the gift of prophetically ministering through the spirit.

As Mira approached the door, she again read the sign next to it. *Experience God's love in the glory. All are welcome to receive inspiration and healing through prayer. Open 7am-10pm, Monday through Saturday.* She checked her watch, smiled and went inside.

The sizzle and smell of pancakes pulled Mira's attention to the kitchen where Eleanor's husband, Elroy, stood in front of the stove, spatula in hand. Eleanor sat beside an elegantly set dining table, her head bowed in prayer.

As Mira closed the door softly, Eleanor opened her eyes and smiled. "Mira. I'm glad you stopped by."

Mira smiled back at the woman who was old enough to be her grandma. "Me too," she said, shifting from one foot to the other.

Eleanor stood and motioned Mira to follow her. "I sense you are in need today," she said, opening the door to the study where they held their private prophetic-word sessions.

Mira followed her inside and sat down on the Victorian-style chair that was curvy and floral, but not very comfortable. She tried to relax, but it wasn't possible. Legs bouncing, she wondered if Eleanor would answer her question before she asked it.

In the matching chair, across from Mira, Eleanor leaned back and crossed her hands in front of her. It was the pose she always had as she waited for the Spirit's word to come to her, the words of insight and healing that she would share with the wandering, restless souls that sought out a personal connection to God through her.

Sitting up straighter, Mira stared at her, trying to catch a glimpse of how she managed to hear the prophetic word. A calm, stoic face was the only thing she saw.

Finally, Eleanor spoke. "I'm sensing you are searching for who you are."

"I am," Mira admitted, her nervous legs bouncing even faster.

"The Spirit is telling me that you are very special and that you are a person who enjoys adventure."

She was spot on! "Yes, I do like adventure."

"But I also sense you are afraid to embrace adventure on your own, and that maybe there is a relationship you need to let go of."

Was she talking about Nash? A sharp pain zipped through Mira's body. "Go on."

"I can see, too, that another relationship is around the corner, one that is adventurous and fulfilling if you will take the chance."

Breathing in slowly through her nose, Mira released it even more slowly. Let go of Nash? She didn't think she could do it...even if she wanted to.

"The other strong feeling I'm getting here," Eleanor said, "is that you are gifted and that God has big plans for you. You only need to follow where He is leading."

Mira clutched the edge of the chair, nodding. "Yes...yes."

"The key is that you need to open your mind and heart."

"I think God wants me to do what you do," Mira blurted. "Can I learn how to do it?"

Eleanor smiled. "Anyone can do it, dear." She grabbed a pamphlet from the end table and offered it to Mira. "We still have a few openings in our summer classes," she said.

As Mira perused the information concerning the Prophecy Training Workshop – How to Hear God's Voice...Receiving the Gift of

Prophecy…Interpretations of Prophesies and Dreams…Practice Sessions, she asked, "Do you have a class starting today, perhaps?"

Eleanor chuckled. "No, but I can give you something to get you started." She went to her shelves. Withdrawing a book from a row filled with identical paperback spines, she handed it to Mira. "When you are applying the instruction from this book, keep in mind that prophesying takes time and practice." She glanced at a clock hanging next to the room's open screened window. "But we'll have to talk more about it on your next visit. I have someone coming in a few minutes."

Mira glanced at the book's title. *Interpreting the Voices That Reveal God's Purposes.* "This is perfect. Thanks," she said with a smile. Tucking the book beneath her arm, she headed toward the door. "And thanks for revealing this to me. It's just what I needed to hear," she said, turning the knob as she swung the door open.

"The Spirit is working powerfully!" Eleanor grinned, nodding encouragingly.

Excited, Mira bolted around the corner and slammed right into Eleanor's next customer, knocking her down onto the living room floor.

"Oh…Kya? I'm so sorry!" Mira reached her hand out to the woman she hadn't talked to for almost a year. That Kya had withdrawn from their group made sense, she supposed. The Enchiridion of Emmanuel, which was what had united them as a group in the first place – and Vaughn – the man Kya loved – had reunited with her mom.

"Hi, Mira," Kya said, taking her hand and getting to her feet.

"It's been a long time." Mira said, feeling awkward and lonesome for her at the same time.

"Yeah. It has." Kya straightened her lacy dress.

"You look nice." Yet even though Kya's make-up was pretty, it didn't quite cover the dark circles beneath her eyes.

"Thanks." Kya ducked her head. "I better go inside." As she wandered slowly into the study where Eleanor was waiting, she said, "It was nice seeing you again, Mira." Then the door closed between them.

Mira stared at the door for a moment, listening to the muffled voices. Then Elroy cleared his throat behind her, prompting her to move. She peeled herself away and strode to the front door, raising her hand in farewell. "See you soon, Elroy."

"Glory to God and Godspeed," he said, repeating his usual good-bye.

"Thanks," she said, and slipped outside. Skipping down the steps to her bike, her hands trembled as they stashed the book inside her backpack. Her dilemma was solved! But poor Kya. How hard it must have been to work with Vaughn all those years, to have loved him, only to lose him when their group accomplished their goal. Mira wasn't surprised that Kya hadn't kept in touch with her. After all, Vaughn was busy making up for lost time being her dad…and being her mom's husband.

Mira walked with the bike to the side of the house, then paused when she felt an urge to listen in on Kya's prophetic word. Was God prompting her in that direction? She had to find out. Leaning her bike against the white cement board siding, she crept to the back of the house. The window was open, giving her the perfect opportunity to learn a thing or two about her new profession. After all, she wanted to help people like Kya, and she'd never heard any prophetic words besides those Eleanor had given to her.

Quick steps brought her directly to the over-sized office window. She sat down on the perfectly clipped grass so that her head wouldn't show through the window. She tilted her ear upward, straining to hear what Eleanor would reveal to Kya, the excitement of it even making her hands quiver.

Eleanor spoke. "I'm sensing that you are searching for who you are, Kya. The Spirit is telling me that you are very special and that you are a person who enjoys adventure."

"Yes, I do."

"But I also sense you are afraid to embrace adventure on your own, and that maybe there is a relationship you need to let go of."

What?? That was exactly what Eleanor had just said to her!

"I can also see that another relationship is around the corner," Eleanor continued, "one that is adventurous and fulfilling, if you will take the chance."

Mira pressed her lips tightly together. The same…it sounded the same!

"The other strong feeling I'm getting here, Kya, is that you are gifted and that God has big plans for you. You only need to follow where He is leading."

Mira's hands clenched. Eleanor's prophetic word for Kya was identical to hers! Unbelievable! She leaned against the house, feeling a burning in her eyes and a painful twist in her gut.

"Yes…yes," Kya said. "There is this guy I met…"

The rest of the conversation was drowned out by the ringing in Mira's ears. *This can't be!* her mind screamed. Crawling away from the window, she scrambled to her feet. She ignored the grass stains on her knees as she trudged toward her awaiting bike. As she approached it, her eyes glazed, and for a moment, all she could do was stare through her tears at the backpack slung across the handlebars. The clasp of the zipper waved back and forth in the breeze as if to taunt her. It said, *Hello, fool.*

After running her sleeve beneath her nose, she snagged the backpack and whipped it open. "Very special…my butt!" she spat. "I'm just the same as everyone else to you, Eleanor." She jerked out the book. "I'll show you *interpreting voices. Hmm, let's see. Ah yes, I hear it now. Yes. I sense, very clearly, that this is a bunch of bunk!*" She tore out a clump of pages and tossed them on the ground. "And revelation? Let me reveal how I really feel!" Her mom had been right, Mira thought, ripping out the rest of the pages. The book, now an empty shell, she tossed to the ground. She kicked her foot at it and missed. *Could her life get any worse?* Jumping on her bike and pointing it toward campus, her mind answered. *Probably.*

Chapter 4

Nash hurried through the front glass doors of Spectrum Music. Tory Brookfield, his store manager, had already unlocked the doors to open it up for business.

"Mornin', Ms. Brookfield," he said with a bright smile. His heart beat overtime as he jumped over the desk. His foot snagged an "I 'heart' Music" mug filled with pens that had been sitting right next to the till. "Oops," he said, ignoring the scattered pens as he reached for a new composition notebook.

Tory bent to pick the pens up. "You sure seem chipper this morning." She stood, and after shoving the bridge of her glasses back in place, calmly stuck the pens back into the mug.

"I am," he said, grabbing a freshly sharpened pencil. "You aren't going to believe what just happened."

"Try me." A tiny curl of the edge of her mouth was the only hint that she sensed, or shared in, his obvious enthusiasm.

"Porsche Grant...you know, the record producer...she was at Eldorado's." He grinned, still rushing from the experience. Last year at this time, he'd never dreamed all this was even possible – or to be desired. But he *did* want it, big time. "She wants to hear my stuff."

Tory's smile grew infinitesimally. "That's good." She opened a package of sheet music they'd gotten in last night.

"Good?" He shook his head. "It's awesome! I could be a star in a week." His heart fluttered again, the paper itching in his palm. "Can you hold down the fort for the rest of the day? I've got some music to create."

"Of course."

He winked at her. "I knew I could count on you." Because she oozed responsibility and intelligence, he'd trust her implicitly...with both his business and whatever he confided in her. As he hurried back toward the studio, she called out to him.

"What if Ms. Grant doesn't want to market your work?"

His steps slowed, his heart squeezing at the thought. "I'll have to live with it, I guess." He looked over his shoulder. She stood behind the counter as she frowned down at her clasped hands.

"And what happens if you succeed? What about the store? And your..." she said softly, but clearly, "your relationships?"

He hadn't thought about any of that, nor did he want to waste time on what-ifs. "I'll deal with it when and if it happens. Don't worry," he said, taking the last two steps to the door of his studio. He opened it and let himself inside the room that felt more like home than anywhere else.

"I'm not worried. I'm just being logical," she said.

Nash laughed. As the door began to shut behind him, he called out, "I've had enough of being logical for a while." Although the old Reformer in him popped up occasionally, over the past year he'd thoroughly enjoyed letting his emotions come into play. Not that Tory hadn't had to rein him in a time or two, but today wasn't that day. He had a song inside of him waiting to be put onto paper – a song the world would never forget.

Nash opened his case and pulled out the Rave guitar Mira had shown him at the compound. It was the first time he'd realized what music was, and that music was an innate part of him. Now, he wanted nothing more than to create music, to be surrounded by it, to build a career from it. What if Mira hadn't introduced him to an instrument, he wondered, running his hands over the strings? *Mira*...he'd forgotten to call her! Pulling his phone from his pocket, he saw she'd left him a message. He punched in his code and cringed, his face contorting more with each accusation as he listened to the message she'd left him. So he hadn't called! Why was she making a big deal of it? Irritated, he punched in her number. He knew she wouldn't pick up because she was in class, but that didn't mean he couldn't leave *her* a message.

"Mira. This is Nash. I'm *sorry* I didn't call you like you'd *told* me to." He sucked in a deep breath through his nose. "I've been busy lining up a record deal." It hit him, then, that she hadn't been the first person he'd wanted to call to share his great news. It made him feel horrible. He softened his tone. "I'll tell you about it later, okay?"

Nash turned the phone off, tossed it into his guitar case and shut the lid. She wouldn't be out of class for a while and he didn't need any distractions. He strummed a chord, did a few scales, and then played the riff he usually played to start his day. It was soothing, inspiring, and got his heart and head into the zone. With the final chord still vibrating in the air, he looked down at the empty page on the music stand that sat next to the soundboard. He scribbled a title, hoping to work from there. *Discover Me*. Yeah. That was perfect.

Chapter 5

Mira busied herself with rearranging the folders and notebooks in her backpack until the last of the students filed out of the classroom. Breathing a little easier now, she wandered up to the professor's desk. *Finding Your Inner Artist 101* had proven to be a class in which she had discovered, not her inner artist, but rather her lack of having one.

"You wanted to see me, Ms. Lovejoy?"

"*Divinya* Lovejoy, please. Ms. is so regular and, well…old sounding." Professor Lovejoy's mouth curled slightly to soften her chastisement.

"Okay." Her teacher *was* old, but she wasn't about to mention that!

"How's your final project coming?"

"Well, um," Mira scanned the artwork littered room. Next to the window stood a slab of marble sporting a crystal ball. Inside the glass orb was a hand reaching out of a calla lily. Near the desk, a doll laid in a wicker crib, the surface of its face like glued together puzzle pieces. In the far corner atop a shelf sat a metal pole holding up an over-sized white balloon wearing a fabric-less bustier. The white latex protruded from the breast opening and the leg holes, giving one the feeling that the person was fat and spilling out of their confines. One painting in particular claimed her attention. A beautiful woman's face peered at her through a leafless tree, her loneliness palpable.

"Mira?"

Mira tore her gaze away from the painting to look at her teacher. "What was your question again?"

Divinya raised a brow. "Your final project…how's it coming?"

"The artwork is…it's coming along," she said, trying to forget the empty canvas in her backpack.

Divinya pulled a portfolio off the stack of papers on her desk. Mira recognized the cover. It was hers. The teacher opened it to the first page. "This one is, shall we say, nice." The painting was of a field of flowers, all different kinds, colors, shapes and sizes. Ms. Lovejoy turned the page. "And this is very similar to the first painting."

Mira frowned at what had been her second assignment, which pictured a field of flowers as well. "But the flowers are in a different pattern, and they are different colors, and…" her voice drifted off because Divinya had turned to the third page, then the fourth, fifth, and sixth.

"I think we have a pattern here," her teacher said, then grinned as she turned to the last page. "Except for this one."

Mira held back a groan. She'd tried to come up with something different, but all that had come to mind, and therefore onto paper, was a cantaloupe. "At least it's not an apple."

"I'll give you that one," Ms. Lovejoy said with a chuckle. "But I can't give you a good grade with this portfolio," she waved the booklet in front of her, "unless you wow me with your final assignment."

A sinking feeling threatened to consume her from the inside out. Looking down at her sneakered feet, Mira whispered, "Truthfully, I can't figure out what I even want to do for the project." And it seemed to be the same for everything in her life.

For a moment, the silence between them was stifling. Then Divinya said, "As with all my students, I want you to succeed, to find your own creative spirit. So I'm going to give you a little advice."

Mira looked up into Divinya's light eyes that seemed to sparkle beneath her silver brows.

Professor Lovejoy, with her pleasant expression and fluid movements, shifted a wire screen model of a naked woman closer to a stone-carved chalice filled with graphite pencils to make room on her desk. "What I sense is that you need something to release the energy you have inside you. Creative energy…life energy," she said, sitting on the edge of the desk with legs spread wide. Her skirt sported an image of a rooted red tree, its branches spiraling, a dark moon casting an odd light behind it. As she sat, the skirt's long jagged slit exposed too much tan, weathered skin as well as a tattoo of the same red tree and moon on her inner thigh.

Mira looked away, hoping her expression wasn't giving away her repulsion. "What do you mean by that, exactly?" Her advice sounded like gibberish to Mira.

Divinya Lovejoy stood up to wrap an arm around her. A tuft of underarm hair tickled Mira's bare shoulder, but she powered through the uncomfortable interaction. Her grade depended on it.

"See that picture there?" Divinya asked, pointing to a portrait entitled *Look Upon Your Inward Eye*. Two women sat beside a fireplace, a table between them.

"It looks like the one is about to blab her secrets," Mira said.

"You're probably right." Her teacher smiled. "The woman wearing the high-necked rather shapeless dress…that's Vashti Argent," Divinya said. "She owns a place downtown called Cofa's Tree, and she has a way of opening a person's eyes to opportunities they don't even realize they have."

"So Cofa's Tree isn't a coffee shop?"

Professor Lovejoy's laugh trickled around the artwork-filled room like water splashing over a glass of ice cubes. "She sells coffee there, but it's much more that just a coffee shop." She wound around the desk and opened the top middle drawer. Taking out a misshapen business card, she wrote something on the back of it. As she handed it to Mira, she said, "Give this to Vashti and you'll get a free session. I guarantee that she'll spark an idea for your final project if you give her a chance."

Mira looked down at the card, which read *Vashti Argent, Midwayer, inspired revelations that point you to your life's energy and promote spiritual progress*. On the back was a quick note from Divinya that said, "This girl has a lot of potential!"

"Is she a therapist, then?" Mira asked, feeling good at the written compliment.

Ms. Lovejoy slid the drawer shut. "I guess you could call her that."

"What else would you call her?" Mira tucked the business card into the back pocket of her jeans.

"I'd call her a very talented woman," Divinya smiled, "who has a knack for helping people unlock doors."

I could use an open door right now, Mira thought. "In that case, I'll stop by her store later today."

Divinya grabbed a stack of papers and shoved them into her bag, which was painted with various heart shapes and a star within a circle, book-ended by two moon slivers. "I'm looking forward to hearing how it all works out," she said. "Or rather, seeing it."

"Me too," Mira said, excited about the direction her life was taking.

Chapter 6

A flat tire...*big surprise there*, Mira thought. She walked with her bike down B Street. Well, it wasn't really B street anymore, but had been renamed with a weird symbol instead of an actual name. A ridiculous idea in her opinion, so she still called it B Street. Street name changes were just the start of the creative explosion in her city. Downtown now teemed with people all in a hurry to do, see, and express themselves in their own ways. Billboards, signs, stores, organizations, clubs...all seeming to advertise ways to fit in even while they fought to be the most unique and different. One thing from Pillar's past remained somewhat the same, though – an altered version of their government. Since the Benefactor had died falling out of the Center of Operations' top floor window last year, posters of candidates running for his governing position hung on light posts, garbage cans, benches, and windows.

Sighing, Mira trudged up the sidewalk, shutting out the noise of the bustling popular strip. She glanced at the new billboards that had popped up over the past week. They advertised everything from baby art therapy to DNA testing as identification of a person's past, present, and future. The ad for the genome testing looked especially interesting to her. If Vashti didn't work out, maybe she'd give it a shot.

Mira continued down the sidewalk, pausing in front of the Essential Living store. Its diffused oils permeated through the screen door and made the warming spring air smell even better. Closing her eyes, she inhaled the scent of lavender and felt a little calmer about everything. She still had a week to get her art project done, and if she took her teacher's advice, she'd probably do alright in the class. Not that a good grade solved any of her other problems. As she continued to walk, her mind wandered to Nash. On a good note, he had called her back. And he'd had great news, too - he was on his way to stardom, just like he'd dreamed.

Yet, why wasn't she all that excited about it? Actually, she knew why. She couldn't help but picture him famous and her being left behind.

"Stop it, Mira," she muttered, irritated with herself and with the numerous people milling about the sidewalks like bouncing atoms. Looking in through the window of the dance studio as she passed didn't help either. The class in session displayed lithe bodies of beautiful dancers - a work of art in themselves. She glanced down at the baggy t-shirt she'd picked up at Electra's Originals and pulled at a stray thread hanging from the bottom hem. The shirt didn't look that great on her, but the shapeless form hid the ten pounds she'd gained eating the fabulous food of Chef Ricki. The college hiring him to cook for the campus cafeteria had been a mistake, in her opinion. His alfredo sauce was to die for - an entrée she'd most definitely have to cut from her diet if she wanted to get back in shape for the new summer wear that had been popping up in Pillar's clothing stores.

She continued the route she'd taken many times over the past year and stopped in front of the pet shop with the sign that sported a wagging tail. After a quick wave at the hedgehog that was never awake to notice, she moved on to the Book End, the bookstore on the corner of Glee and B Street. Before she turned the corner, she glanced across the newly paved road toward Cofa's Tree…the coffee shop that wasn't exactly a coffee shop. Visiting with Vashti would have to wait until she'd talked to Nash. He'd be expecting her right after class, and she really needed to hash it out with him before she could even think about concentrating on her future and what she needed to do.

As she hurried around the corner, she smacked right into a girl wearing a ponytail that hung to her waist. She stood at the end of a line of young and old waiting to get into the bookstore.

"What's going on?" Mira asked her.

"Amaryllis Star has her new book out. *The Creatrix* is going to be so awesome!" The girl grinned, her fluttery movements giving away her excitement. "I can't believe she's really here," she squealed, "signing copies."

Mira had heard of the newly emerging author, but she hadn't read any of her work. "Maybe I'll stop back after lunch and grab a copy for myself."

"Oh, I doubt there will be any left," the girl said.

"I'll keep that in mind." Mira continued on and peeked in through the bookstore's open door as she wound around the line. The woman behind the desk had to be Amaryllis. She wore layers of silver gauzy material, which accentuated her bright red lips and black hair. Her short, blunt hairstyle surprised Mira. After all the years of being forced into wearing short hair, most women had grown theirs out. Amaryllis wasn't all that pretty, but something was pretty about her. Maybe it was the smile directed toward the older woman she was talking to. Whatever it was, she seemed magnetic. As the fan said good-bye and wandered away, Amaryllis caught Mira's gaze. Her eyes were as silvery soft as the gauze she wore. The corner of her mouth curved up as she gave Mira a quick nod. Before Mira could react, the author turned her attention to the teenaged girl who was blabbering almost incoherently in front of her.

Mira moved on to Nash's music store. Standing in front of the double doors with electric guitar simulations for handles, she said, "Time to make some changes." Heading inside, she searched the retail space. Bob, aka Banjo, was busy flipping his long bangs off to the side as he spewed all the information he knew about the guitar he was trying to sell to a kid with hair spikes as long as a flute. And Tory was there, of course, standing behind the counter. She pushed up her horn-rimmed glasses as she relayed the price total to a mother distracted by her two kids who kept pulling out guitar picks. Nash was nowhere in sight.

"Did I miss Nash?" Mira asked over the squeal of delight of one of the kids who had raced away with a handful of picks.

"He's working on his new song," Tory said, nodding back toward the studio. She laid change on the counter as she watched the woman try to catch her thieving child.

Mira headed to the back of the store. She peeked through the soundproof glass of Nash's studio. He sat on a metal barstool, guitar in his hands, headphones on. His eyes were closed as he strummed, and she swore she could even see his heart beating at the base of his throat. Nash knew music, he loved it…he *was* music. And he wore it well, as he did his v-neck shirt and jeans, both of which fit him to perfection. She tugged at her own shirt, thinking about the changes she needed to make in so many areas of her life. Man, she hated feeling like this!

Nash strummed a chord then scribbled something onto the paper in front of him. Her stomach twisted with longing. What was he writing about, thinking about? They used to talk about their dreams for hours and about the new world they'd experience together, but they hadn't been spending much time together at all. She missed him. A lot.

After a deep breath, Mira hit the trumpet key turned doorbell Nash had installed. The strobe light immediately flashed on the wall in front of him. He swung around. Mira waved through the window and smiled, only instead of a welcoming smile in return, she got a scowl. "It's open," he said, flinging the headphones across the room.

When they hit the soundboard, reality struck her hard. He didn't want her to be a part of his life. "I don't need this," she muttered and turned to walk away.

The studio door opened before she got too far. "Mira. Don't go."

She slowed, but didn't stop.

"Please. It's writer's block, not you. I'm sorry."

He sounded sincere. She stopped, but couldn't bring herself to look at him.

Nash came up behind her and put his hands on her shoulders. "I'm sorry. Will you forgive me? Please?"

Tears welled in her eyes, but she refused to let them fall. "Well, *I'm* having artist's-block for my final project," she sniffed, "but *I'm* not treating *you* like crap."

He turned her around. "You still don't know what you're going to do?"

Her heart thumped as she stared at his cross necklace. "This isn't about me or my class. It's about how *you* aren't putting any effort into *us* anymore. You don't call when you say you will. You never seem to have any time for me."

"But we *do* spend time together!"

Her rapid breaths took a moment of conscious effort to slow down. "Not enough."

He growled as he looked off to the side. "I think you need to find some more friends or a new hobby. I can't fill every free minute of your day, Mira."

Rubbing her hand across the base of her throat as if it could ease its constriction, Mira squeaked out what her mind insisted but her heart resisted, "You know Nash…I think you're right."

"You do?"

She shifted her feet before firmly planting them. "I need someone that will spend time *with* me…and take up hobbies *with* me " Heart squeezing painfully, she propped her hands on her hips and blurted, "I guess you're not that person."

Nash grabbed her upper arms, frowning fiercely. "What are you saying?"

She should repeat what she'd said and then tell him point blank that it was over, but she couldn't get the words out. Instead, she tried to pull away, only his grip tightened, holding her in place.

"I want to do life together with you…only you," he said forcefully.

"Well," she said with a humorless chuckle, "forgive me if I don't believe you." She tore out of his hold, turned on her heels and marched toward the exit. As the distance grew between them, her heart ached more and more. Secretly, she hoped he'd run to stop her, or at least call her to come back. He didn't. With a hurt so deep that it was almost impossible to breath, she let herself out. Once she was outside, she couldn't help but glance back to see how he'd responded. He was watching her, a deep frown on his face. What that meant, she didn't know.

Mira was a mix of emotions – none of them good. She snagged her bike and marched alongside it toward Cofa's Tree, desperation driving her. With a growing dark loneliness shadowing her, she stole past the line of women by the bookstore and hurried across the street. As she stepped up onto the sidewalk, a man on a bike whizzed by, barely missing her. A brown paper bag from the basket behind his seat flipped onto the ground by her feet. She grabbed it. Holding it up, she yelled, "Sir…you lost a package! Hey…hey you on the bike…"

He looked over his shoulder and grinned. "Go ahead and keep it," he called out.

"But…" she let the package drop to her side, watching the sharply dressed guy as he disappeared around the corner.

Mira looked around, half-dazed. Although the sidewalk was busy, no one said anything to her about the strange exchange. In fact, they didn't seem to notice her at all. Finally, she peeked inside the bag, glimpsing a straight part in the blonde strands of a doll's head. Why would an attractive, grown man have a doll? Weird.

As she reached inside to pull it out to examine it further, she heard the chime of an opening door. She looked up and into the doorway of Cofa's Tree. The woman looked identical to the one in the painting. It was Vashti, the owner.

"I've been waiting for you. Come on in," she said, motioning for her to do so.

"Did Ms. Lovejoy tell you that I was coming?" Mira asked, not moving from her spot.

Vashti chuckled. "No. I just had this feeling that someone new would be gracing my doorstep, so I opened my door and there you stood."

Mira glanced down at the bag she was holding and then up at Vashti. Both had certainly added depth to her day. "Maybe…" Here was the spark of hope she'd been wishing for, and yet, she still felt hesitant to go into the store. "Maybe some other time. I have some things I need to work on," Mira said.

"No problem." Vashti smiled. "But if you could spare a few minutes, I would really appreciate your opinion on the drink I want to add to my menu. Would you be willing to try my new tea?"

Mira glanced over her shoulder toward Nash's music store. What did she have to lose? "Sure," she said, "I'd be glad to give it a try," and, after locking her bike onto the bike rack out front, stepped inside Cofa's Tree.

Chapter 7

The door closed with a jingle behind her.

"Welcome to Cofa's Tree," Vashti said, leading her through the entryway into an open area with a kitchen on one side and a living room on the other.

It wasn't the business look Mira had expected. Between the two couches stood a coffee table filled with reading material – magazines, books, newspapers, pamphlets. Off to the right was an eat-in bar made of the cross-section of a tree. Three bar stools stood beneath it. On the wall behind were shelves of teapots and cups, none of them matching. A scarred wooden table sat beside the front window overlooking the main street of Pillar. In the back corner was a set of steps next to a his/hers bathroom.

"This *had* to have been a house," she remarked.

"Not exactly," Vashti said, looking around the place herself. "It was what they'd called a sanitarium back in the day." She shook her head. "They were misunderstood souls, locked away, tortured for being different. But…" She raised a finger and smiled. "We have transformed it into a place where we honor people for who they are and encourage them to embrace their imperfections. This mindset frees us all to live fully and creatively unfettered."

Oh, the stories this place could probably tell! "Interesting," Mira said, focusing on the back wall covered with uneven plaster. In its center was a circle of stones that looked like they'd been melted into place. On either side of the circle were shelves, one containing art pieces even more bizarre than the ones Professor Divinya had in her art room. One sculpture looked like a centaur, only it was half fat man, half pig; another was a wooden puppet, misshapen in form with a ghostly face and hollow eyes, its strings the tendrils of the tree it was attached to. She looked to the other display. On these shelves was a doll collection, a few of which looked similar to the ratty thing she'd just inherited.

"What do you think of our Enchanted Garden?" Vashti pointed to the enormous window shedding sunlight on the dolls – and the rest of the room for that matter.

Mira moved in front of the spotless glass to get a better look. The heat of the sun felt soothing and warm. "It looks really nice," she said of the courtyard enclosed by a vine-covered wood fence. Various benches blended in with the natural surroundings, but the art pieces did not. One that especially stood out was a stone statue of a man on one side of a wall, reaching around a corner to hold the hand of a woman. Their fingers were entwined yet on the verge of letting go. "I'd love to check it out." Maybe she could get some ideas for her final project.

Vashti chuckled. "It's not open to the public, I'm afraid."

"It's not?"

"We want it to be an intimate sanctuary for those who can truly respect it."

"I can respect it – and it looks like it could be a good spark for my creativity." Mira looked at her hopefully.

Vashti chuckled. "Tell you what." She moved into the kitchen to put a teakettle on the two-burner gas stove. "Since Divinya sent you this way, I'll make an exception for you and let you explore the garden - with a chaperone, of course."

Like she'd need a chaperone…but whatever! "That would be great!"

Taking out two teacups, Vashti set them on the bar and then waved her over. "I'm calling this tea *True Destiny*. Come and have a taste."

Mira walked over to the bar and sat down on one of the smooth wooden chairs that had stone chiseled bases. They didn't look comfortable, but surprisingly, they were.

"Are you a tea drinker?" Vashti reached into a ceramic jar and dropped a pinch of tea leaves into the bottom of the cups.

"I like tea, both hot and cold," Mira said.

Pouring boiling water over the leaves, Vashti commented. "Then you'll probably like this."

Mira smiled, noticing that the tightness in her chest wasn't so tight anymore. "Thanks," she said, swirling the hot water that was deepening in color, wondering how to drink it without ending up with tea leaves stuck in her teeth.

Vashti must have read her mind because she handed her a metal straw with a flared end that had small holes in it. "This is a bombilla and it's a straw and sieve in one. It blocks the tea leaves," she said. "But be careful. It can be pretty hot on your lips."

"Interesting," she said, twisting the ornate tube before dipping it into her cup. "What *is* your business here, exactly?" she asked, looking around again.

"Well, life and spirit balancing I would say sums it up." Taking a sip of her own tea, Vashti added, "Our motto here is this: Life & Spirit balance is attainable if one is willing to have an open mind and search for it." She smoothed her hands over the bar's thick varnish coat as if clearing debris from a pond's surface to glimpse her reflection. "We enlighten our clients how to look inward so they can not only live fully in the present, but also be free to find their truly individual pathway to fulfillment."

Mira thought about what that meant as she watched the tea leaves swirling around the drinking stick. "On the way over here," Mira said, "I saw this billboard ad saying that if I tested my DNA, I could find out a lot about myself - like a filter that gives me the knowledge to understand what makes me, me." Mira twisted her cup around. "Is your service something like that?"

Vashti chuckled. "You don't want the past, or your family's history, or a DNA sample to tell you who you are!" She leaned ahead, her eyes sparkling. "We take an entirely different approach – one that focuses on the liberty to become who you *want* to be."

Now that she said it that way, it sounded perfect! Mira pulled the card from Divinya out of her pocket. "Do I need to use this to sign up?"

Vashti took the card from her and read Divinya's writing on the back. "Are you available right now? My next appointment isn't for another hour."

It was time to make a change. Mira could just feel it. "Sure."

"Well, alright then."

Vashti tossed the business card into an old beat up tea tin that had other business cards in it. Before taking a seat at the scarred table, she patted the cushion next to her. "Have a seat."

Mira took her tea to the table and joined her, half leery, half hopeful. Could she really know the answers to her problems?

Vashti closed her eyes as she placed Mira's hand into her palm. She said nothing. Mira waited, and waited. Her leg began to bounce in double the time of the ticking clock.

"Well?"

"You are not patient, are you?" Vashti asked, opening her eyes.

"Patience has never been a word that describes me."

Vashti smiled. "Maybe that's part of the reason I'm sensing trouble in your life…relationship trouble."

"Maybe." Mira turned from her gaze to glance through the sheer-curtain covering the front window. She frowned. "But you could say that about anybody. Many people are impatient, and have relationship troubles, too." And many people fall for generic words, just as she had at the Prophet House.

"Oh, I'm not done yet." Twirling the cup of amber liquid in front of her, Vashti continued. "This relationship trouble is centered in something deeper. I'm sensing it has to do with a loss – I feel you lost something important."

She'd lost the ability to connect to the source of her prophetic dreams, a fact Vashti couldn't know. Mira closed her eyes and let the insight and truth of the woman's words sink in.

"It would seem you are holding on to this, but it's stifling you," Vashti continued.

Mira hadn't ever thought of it that way. "Yes. I suppose it could be stifling me."

Vashti paused, then she said in a tone that would calm the most frightened child, "You need to let go of the past in order to have a life where you make things happen for you."

"I don't know if I can," she said in a hush.

"You can," Vashti squeezed her wrist. "And if you do, you'll discover who you really are, deep down in your soul, and then you'll know what it takes for you to find true happiness."

The woman looked so sure of herself. "How do you know or sense these things?" Mira asked.

Vashti smiled. "I guess I opened the 'sensation' door long ago when I became in tune with my own nature." She took a swig of her tea.

Mira studied the woman she knew nothing about except that she was friendly and her expression was that of sympathetic understanding. "What else do you sense about me?"

Tilting her head, Vashti said, "You don't fit into any mold." She folded her hands on the table in front of her. "And you're on the edge of learning life's most important lesson: how to tap into your inner power."

Mira took a big gulp of the tea, tasting more of the spicy earthiness than she had with her first few sips. A growing inner restlessness prompted her to ask, "How do I tap into my inner power?" One that could give her something to paint for her final project among other things.

Vashti grinned. "Here's what you are going to do: First, I want you to repeat this every day for a week." She went to the coffee table and tore off half a piece of paper from inside a book. Taking it back to the dining table, she flipped it over and wrote on the back, then pushed it in front of Mira.

"I am a pioneer of a new season of life returning. I can feel it, and I am in charge," Mira read. She looked up from the page into Vashti's confident eyes. "But I don't feel in charge...of anything."

"That's because you need to free yourself to do so."

Finishing the rest of her tea, Mira set her cup down. "And how do I go about doing that?"

Vashti pointed at the front window. Through the sheer curtain panels, Mira could make out the shapes of people walking by. "There's a guy out there, on a bench," Vashti said. "He's in your art class. Talk to him…and whatever his proposition is, say yes."

Mira didn't know what she'd expected her to say, but it hadn't been that! "What if he asks me to do something I don't want to do?" Her heart revved up into a hardy beat.

"He might." Vashti stood up. Gathering the teacups and teapot, she strode with them over to the sink. "But think about it this way…one yes will be the beginning of a new adventure, and many more to come." She walked back over to Mira, grabbed her hands and squeezed. "Can you feel the energy inside of you, waiting to be released? I know I do."

Mira *did* feel it, more than she had in a very long time. And as she glanced out the front window at the silhouette of the guy on the bench, she felt she was ready to take the risk. Maybe this was what she needed to figure out her final project – and her life. Maybe this was what she needed to be happy and content. "I'll talk to him," she said finally. Mira grabbed her doll package and headed to the door. As she turned the ornate iron knob, Vashti asked softly, "But will you say yes?"

Mira took a deep breath and answered with a shaky smile, "I will."

Chapter 8

Mira stepped out of Cofa's Tree with the intention of marching right over to the guy on the bench to introduce herself. Yet her feet felt like they'd melted into the sidewalk, so she took a moment to gather her courage…and to observe.

The guy looked to be about her age. His hair was a wavy blend of wheat and rye. It almost looked like a tiger's fur faded by the sun. His eyes were a cognac brown, his jaw square and scruffy. His nose was a bit broad but somehow it made him more strikingly handsome. He was staring at his hands, which were clasped between his knees.

"Do you like what you see?" he asked, slanting a glance her way.

While part of her wanted to run, the other was compelled to stay - and not only because she'd told Vashti that she'd see this through. "Yes," she said breathily, thinking he was even more attractive when his gaze was directed on her. She moved to the bench to sit next to him…not too close, but not on the opposite end either.

He smiled. "Good."

Mira was having a hard time catching her breath as her mind scrambled for her next words. "So, um, Vashti told me you're in my art class."

He raised a brow at that. "It's almost the end of the semester and you just realized that now?"

"I…I'm sorry." She frowned. How *had* she missed him? He wasn't exactly a forgettable kind of guy.

"Not a big deal." He held out his hand for her to shake. "I'm Tanger Hardy."

She shook it and found that his hands were softer than she thought they'd be. "Mira Kinneson."

"Everyone knows you, sweetheart," he said with a teasing grin. "Why don't you tell me something I don't know?"

Again, she found it hard to catch her breath. She rubbed her hands up and down the tops of her thighs. "Let's see…something you don't know." She looked back into Cofa's Tree through the gauze curtained window, trying to think of something interesting yet not too personal. "I was nearly run over by a bike and ended up with a weird doll as a parting gift," she said, holding up the paper bag.

Tanger laughed. "Can I see?"

She handed him the bag. He peeked inside. "What did the guy look like?"

"He had slicked back dark hair and wore a pin-striped suitcoat…" She glanced at Tanger. "And he had a cigarette hanging out of his mouth."

"Ah. That's Houser."

"You know him?"

"Where have you been living, woman?" he said with a shake of his head. "Houser is not what you'd call a normal sort of guy, but he's got a kind heart."

"Not normal in what way?" Mira asked.

"He lives in a house made out of all the bottles and junk he's collected over the years, for one."

Mira felt a little better about the doll, but worse about herself for missing so much of what had been going on all around her. She was no better than those in Pillar before they'd gotten rid of their LifeChips. "So now it's your turn, Tanger. Tell me something I don't know about you?"

"Like that I've been sitting down the row from you all semester?"

"That's not all that interesting." Mira grinned. "Tell me something else."

He chuckled. "Okay. I'll play." He crossed his foot over his knee, his eyes seeming to glaze over. "I grew up in a small town called Bolinbroke. I saw my family die at the hands of madmen. I survived all on my own until Vashti found me. Now we're here."

"Bolinbroke?" She'd never heard of it.

"It's a…unique town."

She wanted to ask more, especially about what happened to his family, but before she could figure out how to ask it delicately, a child came running past them, crying.

"Mama! Mama!" he called out through a mouth distorted by emotional pain.

Tanger grabbed his dirty little hand. "Hold on there, cowboy. We'll help you find your mom."

The kid looked up at him with wide eyes.

Tanger knelt down in front of him. "How about I lift you up on my shoulders and then you can take a look around to see if you can spot her. Deal?"

The chocolate ice cream smudged face nodded. Tanger took him in his arms and stood. Swinging the boy up onto his shoulders, he turned him in a slow circle. "Do you see her?"

After a few turns around, the boy squealed. "I see her!" He waved wildly. "Mama! Mama! Look at me!"

A terrified looking woman in a floral print dress sprinted toward them. She skidded to a stop in front of Tanger and raised her hands up to her child, whose legs were swinging wildly. "I've been looking for you for a half hour, Josiah. Where did you go?"

"To get ice cream," he said with a broad grin. The mother's glare turned soft and glassy. "Not without me next time…promise."

"Promise," Josiah said as Tanger handed him over to his mother, who thanked him profusely before taking her son into a nearby flower shop.

"That was really nice of you," Mira said.

"It's no big deal. Most people would do the same." He shrugged. "So do you have any plans for the rest of the day?"

Here it was…the proposition she had to accept – or so Vashti had told her. The funny thing was, although she was a little apprehensive, she was intrigued – and game, now that she and Nash were on the outs. "I don't have any plans…besides coming up with something for the final project for art class."

"You're kidding," he said, sitting down on the bench again.

"Unfortunately not." She sat beside him. "I suppose you have yours done."

"Yeah. Creating things, expressing myself through art is easy for me," he said, "But I guess that's probably because I didn't really have anyone around to listen to me growing up."

Mira pictured the little boy he'd probably been – maybe a kid like Josiah. The last of her unease drifted away even as her heart drifted closer. "Well, I haven't been able to really paint since…" she locked down at her paint-free fingers.

"Since you found the Enchiridion?"

She nodded.

"Well, I think what we have planned today will help spark your creativity," he said, waving at a couple about a block away, heading in their direction.

"We?"

"My friends and I are going to our favorite outdoor hangout." He tilted his head to the side as he looked back at Mira. "It'd be great if you came along with us. Want to come?"

She was supposed to say yes. She wanted to say yes, and yet something in her head was telling her no.

"I'd really appreciate not being the third wheel for once," he added, nodding toward the pair that approached them hand in hand.

"Okay. I'll come with you," she blurted before she could change her mind.

Tanger's face split into a wide grin. "Seriously?"

"Seriously," she said with a nod.

He took her hand and pulled her to her feet, whooping so loudly, several people turned to stare. It felt really good to be embarking on an adventure with someone who actually wanted to spend time with her.

Tanger introduced her to his friends, Claire and Hunter.

"We brought food. Deli sandwiches with a side of chutney," Hunter said, holding up a picnic basket.

"We didn't get the chutney, remember? We decided on sriracha and mayo," Claire said, and then whispered to Mira behind her hand, "The chutney is made with too much garlic."

"There isn't garlic in the chutney, Claire." Hunter launched into a detailed summary of what was in the chutney, and was interrupted several times by Claire, who seemed to enjoy irritating him.

Tanger winced. "I hope this yammering hasn't changed your mind about coming along." He pointed his thumb toward the arguing pair.

"Not a chance," Mira said.

"I'm happy to hear that," Tanger said, pulling a key from his pocket. "Very happy."

Mira was happy, too. And she could hardly wait to embark on her new adventure, one that would make her feel like she was finally getting somewhere.

Chapter 9

Nash pressed the heels of his hands against his eyes. *I can do this. The song will come. It has to.* But the garbage can was stuffed full of his crumpled attempts at lyrics, and every tune he'd come up with sounded a lot like other songs he'd written.

Swinging the strap off his shoulder, he laid his guitar down. As he rubbed the back of his neck, he dragged himself off the bar stool and went over to the arm chair in the corner. Grabbing a bottle of water he'd set on the end table, he took a swig to relieve his raw throat. After replacing the lid, he put it back and sank into the chair and propped his feet onto the leather footstool that looked like a tortoise.

"This is ridiculous," he whispered, softly drumming his gouged and throbbing fingers on his thigh. After several long minutes, he reached into the end table drawer and pulled out a tiny printed book. Hayes had told him to read it often, especially when he was struggling - and that described his current situation perfectly. As he opened up a copied chapter of the Enchiridion, he saw the piece of paper tucked inside. He knew what it was – the painting of him and Mira in the future. He stared at it for several moments, a deep ache seizing his chest. Grabbing his phone, he punched in Mira's number. It rang four times, but she didn't pick up. Before it went into voicemail, he disconnected. What had he done? He rehashed his words and hers and realized he didn't even know if they were a couple anymore. His fingers shook as he hit redial. This time it went right into voicemail, meaning she'd probably turned her phone off.

Nash threw his phone across the room. He didn't have time for this! Laying his head in his hands, he tried to grasp the feeling he'd had that morning, but the inspiring energy was gone.

The doorbell to his studio rang, interrupting his hovering despair. He glanced over, hoping to see Mira, but it was Tory. He waved her in with a half-hearted sweep of his hand. "What's up?" he said as she closed the door behind herself.

"I was just wondering if you needed some food…or some help maybe?"

Nash wasn't hungry, nor did he think she'd be any help – she was too logical for this kind of thing. On the other hand, he was at an impasse, so what could it hurt? "Actually, I do need some help."

Her hazel eyes blinked behind her glasses. She smiled. "What do you want me to do?"

"My song title is *Discover Me.*" He looked at her…really looked at her. "Tell me one thing about yourself that I don't know. Who are you behind those glasses?"

Instead of removing them, she shoved them up on her nose. But she did keep her grin, albeit a half one. "If I tell you, you won't be discovering it."

Nash leaned back against the chair with a growl. "You're not helping me here."

"And you're trying too hard," she said, reaching into the garbage can for one of his rejects.

Nash vaulted out of his chair, sending the excerpt copy of the Enchiridion from his lap onto the floor. The painting floated to a spot near Tory's sensible shoes, distracting her enough that he could grab the rejected song from her hand.

"None of these are any good," he said, tossing the wad of paper back into the garbage can. "And they belong right where they are."

Tory frowned, but as always, remained completely calm. She bent to pick up the stray paper and unfolded it. "So how are you and Mira doing?"

"We're fine."

"I saw her when she left." She looked at him. "Why don't you try telling the truth?"

"We're not fine," he admitted. He looked through the studio window toward the door Mira had exited less than two hours ago. "But I don't have time to worry about it right now." He snagged the painting from Tory's hand, tucked it back into the booklet and stashed them both back into the drawer.

"But you *are* worried about it – about her."

She had a point. "Doesn't matter. I have a song to write, and either you're going to help me or you're not." He plopped onto the bar stool and grabbed his guitar again, strumming random chords with voraciousness.

"I'm not sure that's quite the sound you're looking for," she said.

"I'm just trying to work up some creativity." He strummed harder, but he couldn't get the painting of him and Mira out of his mind.

Tory suddenly grabbed his strumming hand to still it. As the twang of strings continued to echo around the room, she said, "You know, you can be dumb and sit here all day and strum the heck out of the guitar, or you can go set things right with Mira and then try again to compose something"

He didn't know what to say, but it didn't seem like she expected a response. Tory dropped his hand and went to the door. Looking over her shoulder, she said, "Hayes came by a few minutes ago and said he'd seen Mira in front of Cofa's Tree, talking with friends."

Friends? Nash wondered who they were. As he watched the door close behind Tory, he realized she had a point about making things right. He needed to find Mira.

Chapter 10

"We'll let Mira taste the chutney and see who's right about the garlic," Hunter said, digging into the picnic basket.

Mira didn't want to get in the middle of it, nor did she particularly want to eat chutney solo, but Claire chimed in before she could gracefully decline. "*If* the chutney is in there, it's a deal," she said.

Tanger shook his head and slipped the key into the padlock. "The chutney doesn't matter," he said. He swung the gate open, revealing the Enchanted Gardens, the area Mira wasn't supposed to go into without a chaperone. Since Tanger had a key, she assumed he qualified as one. "And what it's made of doesn't matter," Tanger added.

Hunter's rifling stopped as he moved into the gateway. "No chutney," he said.

Claire grinned. "Told ya."

He shoved the basket into her hands with a slow grin of his own. "No sriracha either. Ha!"

"What?" Claire peeked inside, doing her own digging. "Looks like we're stuck with naked sandwiches!"

Hunter made a face, to which Tanger said, "Why don't you two head down to Wormwood? Mira and I will get some sandwich toppings and meet you there."

Claire and Hunter glanced at each other. "Works for me," Claire said, and walked into the garden, picnic basket slung over her arm. Hunter followed, frowning as he mumbled, "I swear I put the chutney in."

Tanger locked the gate behind them. "Sorry about that."

"Not a big deal," Mira said. In fact, she actually enjoyed their interaction. "I'm looking forward to getting to know them better."

"Be careful what you ask for," he said with a smile. "Come on. Let's go raid Vashti's refrigerator."

Mira followed him back into Cofa's Tree, where Vashti greeted them with an overly bright grin. "So you said yes?" The question was directed toward Mira.

She felt strangely uncomfortable. "I did."

Tanger's perplexed look accompanied his softly spoken words. "What did she say yes to?"

"You." Vashti chuckled, watching them as Tanger took four labeled preserve jars out of her fridge.

"Mustard-honey sauce, sweet chili spread, wasabi-ginger spread, or garlic-avocado?" Tanger asked, not responding to Vashti.

"All of them sound good," Mira said.

Tanger grabbed two and shoved the other two back into the refrigerator. Striding to the sliding doors, he snagged a small fabric bag from one of the coat hooks beside it. "Thanks, Vashti," he said rather sharply as he shoved the jars into the bag. Then without another word, he headed outside through the sliders.

Vashti gave him a look Mira couldn't decipher, but it did make her even more curious about Tanger and his relationship with the shop owner. Mira followed him through the doors, pausing a moment to look around.

Tanger stopped beside the stone piece she'd noticed earlier. He turned around. "Are you coming?"

"Yeah," she said, moving toward him. With each step closer, the feelings of attraction, of danger, of intrigue unfolded in her chest.

When she stood right in front of him, his eyes searched hers as if looking for answers of his own. After a moment, he dipped his head to the side and whispered in her ear. "I've been sitting down the row from you all semester, wanting to get to know you – the real you, the one that isn't sheltered behind a veneer. I'd love to have the opportunity to do that…today, right now." He glanced toward the glass door behind them, then back to her.

Mira wasn't afraid of him, especially because she had her knife tucked away in her backpack, easily accessible. But what she *did* fear was that there wasn't more of her for him to discover...that this was it, the real her stuck in her mediocrity with no purpose or joy. "What if there isn't...more to me than you see right now?" she dared to ask.

Tanger chuckled, tilting his head back to upright. "Then I suspect that there are two of us needing to get to know you better."

She smiled as hope blossomed. "Sounds like a plan, then," she said. "Lead the way."

Chapter 11

Because Hayes had last seen Mira in front of Cofa's Tree, Nash decided to start his search there. He walked the short distance, reviewing in his head what he'd say to her. As he approached the small business, though, Mira wasn't there. He looked up and down the block. Except for her bike, there was no sign of her or her new friends. Then he heard what he thought was her voice, muffled by the wind. The sound had come from behind a locked fence attached to the small business. The pit in his stomach swelled.

"Everything will be fine," he whispered as he opened the door to Cofa's Tree and stepped inside. A strange feeling came over him as soon as the door closed behind him. It was like the eerie, thick-aired calmness that arrives before a tornado. He cast a desperate glance in the direction of the fenced-in outdoor area where he'd thought he'd heard Mira. Through the sliding doors he glimpsed movement. Heart dropping to his toes, he hurried over to the sliders to get a clearer look. His eyes *weren't* playing tricks on him. Mira had just followed a guy into the densely treed area toward the west. He grabbed for the handle.

"The gardens aren't open to the public," came a firm, feminine voice from behind him.

Still, Nash tried the door. It was locked. "My girlfriend is out there. I need to talk to her."

"I'll tell her you were here, that you want to talk to her…if that helps."

He turned to look at the woman who he at once hated because she wouldn't allow him to go after Mira. Stomach in knots, he spat, "What would help is you opening this door."

She shook her head, her long earrings jingling like wind chimes. "Mira has some soul searching to do. Let her do it."

Who was she to order him around? Anger infused his being and pulsed into his fingertips until they curled. "I've always given her the freedom to do that."

"Freedom, but not the support perhaps?" The woman leaned back against the bar, like she knew exactly what she was talking about.

What had Mira told her? "Then let me start now," he said through gritted teeth.

"It's too late."

"You can't know that!"

Vashti's smile was sly. "I can, and I do."

Nash felt sick. He'd really screwed up big time. But this? He didn't deserve to be tossed aside like this. "Who is the guy she's with?"

"That is something she'll have to tell you. I'll let her know you stopped by and that you want to talk to her, okay?" She moved away from the bar to adjust the dolls on the shelves.

"Whatever," he barked, and stormed out the front door. Once outside, he sucked in the cool air, trying to gather his thoughts – and to come up with solutions. Yeah, he and Mira weren't getting along so well. He thought again about how she'd left the store earlier that day and he felt his world spin. From the moment he'd been able to dream unfettered by the LifeChip, all those dreams had included her. What if…? He plowed his hand through his hair. He couldn't think of what ifs. He had to fix this.

Nash rechecked the bike parked near the store. It was Mira's for sure. He strode to the blocked-off area. The locked wooden gate stood eight feet high and he grabbed the edge of it, wiggling it to see how sturdy it was. It was solid. He propped his foot on the hinge poking out and pulled himself up so he could see over it.

"Whoa there, son. Where do you think you're going?"

Nash turned to see two police officers, both standing in a wide-legged stance, their weapons visible.

"I think my girlfriend has been kidnapped and the guy disappeared with her into here."

One of the officers shifted his feet uneasily. "Did you talk to Vashti," he said, and swallowed hard.

"I did. She seems to think Mira went of her own accord. I don't agree."

"Mira Kinneson?" the non-shifting officer asked.

Nash nodded, hoping that her notoriety would get him somewhere.

Mr. Shifty glanced toward the window of Cofa's Tree. Vashti was peeking around the curtain, no expression whatsoever on her face. "Well, we can't trespass. We'll have to get a warrant, which will take some time."

"She's in danger, isn't she?" Nash said, feeling the angst of the shifter.

"After what she's lived through, I'm sure she can take care of herself," the other said. "How about you come down to the station and fill out a missing person's report."

Nash didn't want to do that – especially because in reality, she most likely *was* out there with another guy of her own freewill. "I'll stop by after I talk to her mom and dad. We won't be able to do anything about it until she's gone for 24 hours, right?" And it had only been a couple hours since he'd seen her.

"Right." Shifty looked relieved. "Keep us posted," he said as he and his partner ambled toward their car, which was parked across the street directly in front of the bookstore.

Nash waited, hoping they'd drive away, but they stayed in their car, watching him. So he walked further down the block until he got to the corner of the fence's edge. He glanced down the sloping bank. The wooden slats continued all the way down to the lake.

The sinking feeling in his stomach got even worse. Nash rubbed his hands over his face. *Think, Nash, think.* Breaking in wasn't a good option – at least not until the cops were gone. Talking to Hayes or to Mira's parents wasn't the best bet, either. All he'd probably get was a lecture. Even though he felt he deserved it, he didn't want to hear it right now. But he could certainly use Tory's calm logic.

"I'll be back," he rasped, slapping his hand against the fence before heading back toward Spectrum Music.

Chapter 12

Mira caught up to Tanger, who'd tied the condiment bag's drawstring through his belt loop.

"How far is it to Wormwood?" she asked. She didn't know what Wormwood even was, but she didn't want to seem stupid so she didn't ask.

"It's not far, but it's kind of a maze in here, so if you get lost, it can take a long time." He glanced at her and smiled. "And the way back can be a little rough since it's all uphill – and most of the time, in my case anyway, I don't want to leave it at all." His smile broadened. "I suspect this day won't be any different."

Mira glanced back up the way they'd come. The steep incline was littered with jagged rocks amidst dense trees so she couldn't see the top anymore. The hill she could handle, but not knowing where she was exactly kind of unnerved her.

"Are you having second thoughts?"

She considered his question carefully. The answer was yes and no, but her curiosity urged her on. She was intrigued by the thought of having a place that would beg her to stay. In fact, she longed for it. And she was intrigued by Tanger's confidence. He was so different from anything she'd experienced and she wanted to learn even more. "I want to see Wormwood...with you."

"Well, alright then." He inhaled deeply, as if breathing in his glorious natural surroundings. It was like he belonged there. "It's not much further." He nodded to the right and began to walk in that direction.

She followed, almost overwhelmed by everything around her, like she couldn't seem to take it all in at once. Then she heard squealing, and splashing.

Tanger stopped. "I have to warn you. Sometimes when we feel especially one with our natural surroundings, we feel comfortable in our most natural selves."

What was he talking about? "Okay."

He slid down onto a flat grey rock that seemed like it might extend out over the water, only she'd have to go to the end of it to see. He held out his hand to her.

She took it and he helped her onto the rock. "Welcome to Wormwood…the place of mystery and discovery," he said.

The protected area was beautiful, the stone outcropping solid beneath her feet. Granite cliffs made walls on either side of them while the steep hill butted up behind and the water in front. It was like they were cocooned in this pristine area, where nothing from the world could interfere. "It's beautiful."

"Hey, you two. The water's cold, but awesome," Claire called out.

Mira inched her way to the rock's edge. As she peeked over it, she wondered how Claire and Hunter had gotten down there. But then she looked at the pair – both without a stitch of clothing. She turned away, her face red.

"I warned you," Tanger said with half a grin.

"You could've come right out and said that they were skinny dipping rather than hint around the subject."

"I could've," he said with a chuckle. "You two enjoy yourselves," he called out. "Mira and I are going to eat some dinner." His hips rolled ever so slightly as he moved toward the back of the stone floor. He sat down beside the picnic basket, which was tucked into a spot where fifteen foot stones were wedged together to make a curved wall.

"Veggie, turkey, beef, or ham?" he asked, opening up the basket.

She walked across the rock and sat near him. "Any would be fine."

"Choose one."

"It doesn't matter. I like them all."

He let the basket snap shut and crossed his arms over his chest. "If you can't make decisions about a sandwich, how can you make any big decisions?"

"Like what?"

"Like what to do for your final project?"

"Good point." She said the first thing that popped into her head. "I'll have turkey."

He handed her a sandwich, then took out one for himself. Leaning back against the rock, he grabbed the wasabi-ginger from the bag and lathered the top slice with it. After plopping it back in place, he took a giant bite. Between chews, he said, "So you up for playing a game?"

The splashing and giggling of Hunter and Claire made her wary. "What sort of game?" she asked, opening up her sandwich to swirl the garlic-avocado sauce over the turkey.

"The Know-know game." He took another bite of his sandwich.

"I've never played it," she said, smashing her sandwich back together and taking a bite. Delicious. "How does it work?"

Straightening his legs out in front of him, he crossed his ankles. "It's actually a game to help a group of people get to know each other, but since it's just the two of us, I'll have to modify it." He ran his tongue over his front teeth, working to get the bread out of the grooves. "Here's how we'll do it. We'll take turns filling in this statement, 'I bet you didn't know...'. I'll start." He cleared his throat and looked out over her shoulder toward the water. "I bet you didn't know that I like to dance." His whiskey eyes connected warmly with hers and she immediately felt a sweet burn. "Now you go," he said.

What could she say that would be interesting? He knew her past, or at least the portion of it that had been publicized. "I like to..." her mind went blank. What did she even like to do? She fiddled with her shoe string as she considered what had driven her to find the Enchiridion. "I enjoy mysteries," she finally said.

Tanger's almost feral looking teeth seemed suddenly accentuated in his growing smile. "Well then you're lucky you met me." He handed her a cup from the basket and pulled out something that looked like a wineskin. "Water?"

She nodded and he poured her a cup. As he poured one for himself, he said, "I bet you didn't know that our town was overtaken *after* the war was over. I was four." His jaw hardened and his nose flared ever so slightly. "As I hid in the bed of our family's truck, the streets around me melted from the heat of fires caused by bombs. I watched my mom - who was trapped in the middle of the street - hold my baby brother up high to save him from the flames. She cried out for God to help them, but they burned up while I watched. I couldn't get to them, or to my father and sister."

Inside, Mira felt queasy. Her fists clenched at the harsh injustice of it all. Poor Tanger! "So, you believe in God, then?" was all she could think to say.

"I believe in super-natural power, yes, but no more questions." He took a swig of water. "That's not how the game is played. It's your turn to reveal something I don't know about you."

"Oh, okay," she said. But she couldn't erase the picture of Tanger as a little boy watching his family die. "I can't seem to think of anything to tell you."

"How about what brought you to Vashti – and don't tell me it was coincidence, or that you needed inspiration for your final project."

"I *did* need inspiration for my project," she said.

"What else?"

"No fair asking questions."

"But you haven't told me something I didn't know, yet."

Mira scooted to the rock and sat next to Tanger so that she was looking outward. It had to be easier to talk if she wasn't constantly looking at him and trying to figure him out while thinking about his horrific childhood. She crisscrossed her legs.

"I bet you didn't know that I pretty much just broke up with my boyfriend," she blurted.

Tanger was quiet for a moment, then he said, "I bet you didn't know I think staying in a relationship that doesn't make you happy is useless."

A gust of wind kicked a leaf onto her lap. She stared down at the lone leaf, disconnected from its life-giving branch. "I bet you didn't know I was told to let go of my past, but that I have no clue where to go from here."

Tanger plucked the crisp leaf from her lap. After carefully laying it in his palm, he blew across it. It fluttered, caught the edge of a subtle breeze and landed on an outcropping about halfway up the stone face wall behind them. "I bet you didn't know I can show you how to get control of your life and where to get the power to make the changes that will be good for you – not for everyone else."

She looked at him a moment…really looked at him. Even with his tragic past, she couldn't see any hint of the restlessness she was feeling inside. She could hear that Hunter and Claire were approaching, given the increasing volume of their conversation.

"I bet you didn't know that I want what you're offering," Mira said, her heart beating erratically at the boldness of her statement.

Tanger reached inside the picnic basket. "I bet you didn't know that your dreams hold immense power." He handed her a small vial.

"What's this?"

"If you put twenty drops of this into your bath water tonight while visualizing a dream, you should be able to tap into lucid dreaming."

She took the vial from him. "Which is…"

"It's knowing you are dreaming while you are dreaming. And when you can control your actions within those dreams, you can explore your wildest imaginings. You don't have boundaries or limits…or consequences."

Tanger's eyes took on a look that brought heat to Mira's face. "And this will solve all my restlessness?"

"That, and more, if you let it." He grinned and leaned back against the rock. "I bet you'll even come up with a great idea for your final project, too."

Before she could ask more, the pair of friends climbed onto the rock surface. Clothes sticking to their damp skin, Hunter and Claire plopped down on the opposite side of the picnic basket and immediately dug in.

Mira quickly slipped the vial into her pocket, but her thoughts wouldn't be tucked away so easily. She couldn't quit thinking about the hot tub of water…and what she could possibly dream. A glance at Tanger said that he hoped to be in that dream. *What could it hurt?* she asked herself for the second time that day.

Chapter 13

Nash jogged down the block, barely noticing the people, the cars, the commotion. His thoughts jumbled and twisted with his emotions. How could she…? Why did she…? His anger mingled with the intense pain in his heart as he charged inside his store.

"I take it the meeting with Mira didn't go so well?" Tory's voice barely pierced through the clatter filling his head.

"I saw her and…" Nash looked around. They were alone. Locking the door behind him, he started to pace. "And she was with another guy!"

"You're kidding, right?" Tory swiped a cloth over the glass counter, watching him carefully.

"I wish I was." He pinched the bridge of his nose. "There was something weird about it, though."

"What do you mean?"

"I guess it seemed like she was being set up or something. The owner of Cofa's Tree wouldn't let me go after her, wouldn't unlock the door leading to the side lot where I saw Mira follow a guy into the trees."

"Mira did follow him, though?"

"It looked that way, but maybe she was tricked."

"Or maybe she was looking for something to work on for her final project. She mentioned it when she was here."

"She did to me, too. Maybe that's it." The option eased his heart, but just a little.

"Or maybe because you no longer have a shared goal of finding the Enchiridion, you've both gone your own direction," Tory said softly. "Think about it." She locked up the cash register. "With no quest to keep you connected, maybe you don't have anything left in common."

She had a point. "But what about the painting? You know, the one with us together in the future?" Nash asked. "All her paintings have been right on, everything happening just like she'd painted."

Tory pushed her glasses back into place. "Did you see all the paintings before they happened?"

"Only one."

"Could it have been a self-fulfilling prophecy?" She placed her hand awkwardly on his shoulder. "In other words, did you make it happen because you thought it would happen?"

He'd never thought of it that way before, but it was definitely a possibility. It didn't make him feel any better, though.

"The way I look at it, Nash, is that we need to live in the moment because it might just be all we have."

He hardly thought of Tory as a live in the moment kind of person. She seemed too controlled for that. Maybe there was more to Tory than he'd thought. "What about heaven?"

She didn't hesitate to answer. "Hogwash."

"You don't think it's a possibility?"

She shook her head. "The Enchiridion is a book of made-up stories useful only to people who need a crutch, or someone to blame, or even a way to explain things they can't control or understand."

Hayes' words prodded in the corners of his mind, but before he could grasp them, they drifted away like a dry leaf in gust of wind. *What if there wasn't a God?* Nash thought. *What if the Enchiridion wasn't all it claimed to be?* Nash glanced at the recording room, feeling strangely empty. The eerily silent room didn't help either.

"You have a glorious life ahead of you, Nash." Tory nudged him back to reality. "We have a concert booked for tomorrow night and you have an agent waiting to hear your stuff." She peered up at him. "Are you still going to be able to do that?"

Nash shrugged. "As far as writing a song goes, I just don't know if I have it in me right now."

Tory didn't even blink before she asked, "And the concert?"

"I'll manage I guess." He brushed his hand through his thick hair. "It would be a heck of a lot easier with some resolution, though. You know what I mean?"

Tory wandered toward her desk, which was located in the far corner of the store, away from all the instruments. "Let me take care of that. You get to work on your song."

He glanced at the stairs that led to his over-the-store apartment. He felt like going there, to mull things over and figure things out, but Tory pointed him toward the studio.

"Go," she ordered. "I'll look into the background of the owner of Cofa's Tree."

The tightness in his chest eased a little. Tory would take care of it. She always took care of things, him included. As he wandered toward the studio, he looked back over his shoulder. She was watching him with a slight smile on her lips and suddenly he saw her differently than he ever had. There was much more to Tory than intelligent efficiency.

Chapter 14

Mira sank into the hot, bubble-filled tub of water, goosebumps racing over her skin. She inhaled the spicy scent of the oil she'd added to the water to prompt her lucid dreaming. It was pleasant enough, but she was nervous…really nervous. She'd read a few articles on lucid dreaming. Its power would be instantaneous and freeing, although some said it allowed dark spirit entities to access the mind. Other writings claimed it to be perfectly safe, that the dreamer always maintained control of their dream world. Mira chose to believe the latter.

Staring into her room through the bathroom door, Mira thought she saw movement – a slight shift in the dark shadowed view through her bedroom window. She clutched the edge of the tub, holding her breath as she watched. Had she made a mistake? *Relax.* Mira looked around for the source of the whisper. She saw no one. Perhaps it had come from her subconscious. How could she relax? Would she feel better if she couldn't see the darkness out her bedroom window? If she got out of the tub to close the bathroom door, though, would it lessen the effects of the special oil Tanger had shared with her? She wanted what Tanger had promised, and she wasn't going to wimp out now! Inhaling deeply through her nose, she tried to relax.

"Don't think about what-ifs, just follow the instructions," she muttered, turning her mind back to what she'd gleaned from both Tanger and the articles she'd read. Step one was to memorize the details of the area around her. Carefully, she began to catalogue her surroundings. The bathroom full-length mirror sat propped against the wall across from her. It had a crack in the corner, but she could still see herself clearly. Her face looked chubby, and she had a bright red pimple in the middle of her forehead. She cringed, but moved on with her observation. Right next to the tub was the toilet and sink, both still the utilitarian white she'd grown up with, minus the auto-bot. The x-shaped porcelain faucet knobs on the sink matched the tub's - which sported the sideways letters C and H. Sealing that into her mind, she glanced out the door into her room. Next to the window sat her easel, a blank canvas resting upon it. A red brocade Elizabethan chair sat in front of it.

Mira closed her eyes as she reviewed every tiny detail. She slid lower into the tub, the water sloshing and spilling onto the floor. Chin now cradled in the water, the liquid resting at the edge of her bottom lip, she opened her eyes. The letters C and H on the tub's faucet knobs no longer sat at a slant. She frowned, trying to sit up to look at them more closely, but she couldn't move her arms or legs, fingers or toes. She could move her head, but just a little. She tried not to freak out.

"This is what's supposed to happen…I think," she whispered, her heart beating hard beneath the water's surface. The feel of the room suddenly shifted. Now shrouded in a peculiar haze, it took on the appearance of a sepia tone picture. She turned her gaze to the mirror. She looked like herself, and yet unlike herself. There wasn't a pimple to be found, her face was a perfect shape, and her lips a deep red. The oil was working! But she had to move to the next step - testing her power within the dream. She wanted it, craved it.

"One, two, three." She let herself sink beneath the surface of the water. Holding her breath, she looked up through the bubbles that had parted on the surface. If she was in a dreaming state, she could do anything and live – because it was a dream. She'd come this far. She had to try it! Relaxing her jaw, she allowed her lips go slack. Water seeped around them, filling her mouth. Then she breathed in deeply through both her nose and mouth. And she didn't choke! She was breathing water! Limbs and voice freed, she laughed as she spun in circles beneath the water's surface. It felt like a warm ocean because she couldn't even feel the tub surrounding her. After a few moments, she pulled herself up into a sitting position, a bright smile on her face.

"What are you doing?"

The deep voice startled her, as did the censuring tone. She looked toward the sound that had come from her room. Nash stood next to her easel, which was on the right side of the window now rather than the left. His features were hard with disapproval. She squeezed her eyes closed, trying to shut him out of her heart and her mind. When she opened her eyes again, Tanger stood where Nash had been. He smiled. Her heart flipped into overdrive as she watched his expression grow into one of desire. "Tanger?" she asked breathlessly.

"You knew I'd show up eventually. In your heart you knew it."

She supposed she did. She nodded.

He crooked a finger, beckoning her. But she was naked…and her naked body had at least ten extra pounds of flab hanging from it. Only…she glanced down at the now bubble-less water, seeing her body through dream-filled eyes for the first time. She was perfect. As if in slow motion, she rose from the water. Not daring to look at him, she stepped out of the tub. As she reached for the towel, he said, "Don't."

Her gaze traveled to his face – one filled with approval. Though the window was now open and a sharp breeze gusted through it, it didn't cool her hot, wet skin. Feeling confident and sexier than she had in her life, she sauntered over to him. He reached for her, but as his hand brushed her glistening skin, she pushed him onto his knees with a confident laugh. She wanted him, but on her terms. Before she could deliver her demands, though, something caught her attention. Fire…it spewed like lava out of the chair sitting next to her easel. For some reason, it intrigued her, beckoned her.

Tanger disappeared the instant she reached the chair, but at the moment, she didn't care. The chair had changed. In the middle of the brocade cushion was a large hole. She stood over it, peering into its depths. It seemed to go on forever, its layers of fire clouded with images like souls hissing as they swept through the abyss for a place to rest - and finding none. It was like the pit Pillar had been heading toward in her vision from long ago! She edged backwards as old fears set her heart to hammering in her chest. The fire burst upward again, singeing her skin. A scream clawed at her throat as she took another step back.

"It's a dream, Mira. Face your fears." The voice was Tanger's but he wasn't in the room. "It will unlock your creativity," he continued. "It will give you the freedom to find what you are looking for."

Mira stared at the chair until her eyes burned. *I'm in a dream,* she reminded herself. *Nothing can hurt me.* Squaring her shoulders, she took a step closer. The fire singed her hair as it spewed from the gaping hole. It seemed so real, as if hell was gasping through its portal. But she owned this dream and through it, she could create the reality she wanted, right? After all, she *had* breathed under water.

"*I* have the power," she said aloud. Taking a deep breath, she imagined the life she wanted and inched between the chair and the easel. The curved edge of the chair nudged the back of her knees. "And I refuse to let anything keep me back from getting what I want," she said, and sat down.

Chapter 15

Mira gasped for air as she sat upright in the tub. Clutching the sides, she tried to wrap her head around what just happened. She'd done it! She'd sat on that chair, had fallen into the pit of her imagined hell. Then she'd waken up with not only an amazing picture seared into her mind but also a sense that she could take on the world. She'd used her own power to overcome her mental roadblock!

Jumping out of the tub, she ignored the mirror and grabbed the towel off the hook. After drying herself, she hurried over to her closet. Rummaging through its contents, the image of a body reaching for the moon wouldn't leave her. She knew that it was perfect for her final project, but there was something she needed to do first, and that was to see the guy that had helped her, the guy that would be the focus in her painting. "Tanger," she whispered, the sound of his name making her jumpy inside. She grabbed a black knit dress and slipped it on.

Wanting to look her best, she took special care with her makeup. As she slipped on her knee high boots and donned her jacket with the twisted yarn along the edges, she glanced at the clock. She'd have to be really quiet. Explaining a two A.M. trek to her parents wouldn't turn out well.

Escaping outside, energy and the feeling of freedom rushed through her like never before. She sprinted down the hill toward Pillar, arriving at the edge of the town in record time. Stepping onto the sidewalk, she paused. This was the same route she and her mom had taken to escape Burt Guyver. A wisp of air scraped past her ear, the eldritch sound giving her a feeling that - even though Burt hadn't been seen since the day the Benefactor had died — he was somewhere…somewhere close. A quick glance told her she was alone, even if a part of her didn't believe it. Trepidation and loneliness peeled away the layers of power she'd felt only moments before, leaving her feeling as vulnerable as an abandoned newborn.

"I don't even know where Tanger lives," she said with a shake of her head. Her quick breaths mingled with the noise of the people and cars and loud music of Pillar as she tried to think. No - she didn't have a phone number for him, either. How dumb was that! After a backward glance at the woodsy area behind her, though, she decided that the dark shadows were more daunting than a search for Tanger, so she hustled into town.

Two blocks in, she bypassed a group dancing to bass-heavy music booming from a pyramid speaker. Not seeing Tanger there, Mira crossed the adjacent campus parking lot to B Street. Maybe Tanger lived with Vashti, she thought. And even if he didn't, she would know where to find him, right? The plan settled in her mind, Mira hopped up onto the sidewalk that would lead her right to Cofa's Tree. Within fifteen minutes, she approached the door, which stood ajar. She stared at it a moment, debating, then reached out to push it open. Only right before she touched it, the door swung open wide. Mira bit back a squeal, but couldn't help but recall that this place had been a sanitarium. Spirits weren't actually a thing, were they? Could the insane spirits be inviting her in?

"It was a draft," she whispered, trying to reassure herself. And like Vashti had said, it was time to put her fears aside. She could handle this!

Mira stepped inside the store, calling softly, "Vashti? Tanger? Anyone here?" There was no answer. Then she noticed the soft glow of a row of candles burning in the Enchanted Garden. After closing the front door behind her, she walked quietly toward the flickering light. Through the slider, she could see that the candles created a lighted pathway into the woods where she and Tanger had entered earlier that day. It was like they were inviting her to explore.

She straightened her shoulders and tried the sliding door. Surprisingly, it opened. It must be a sign that this was where she was supposed to be. Ducking into the garden, she closed the door behind her. The area looked a lot different in the darkness, the shadows taking on a sort of humanness by the light of the candles. A nearby bench tempted her to sit and observe, and yet the lit path drew her along like a rip tide. And as she stepped onto the meandering varietal stone-littered pathway, it seemed like a step to freedom. No more would her boundaries define the pathway of her life, she decided. *That* Mira was in the past. Because of her lucid dream…because of Vashti and Tanger…she felt she had tapped into the power to move forward, to create the life she wanted - one with love, purpose, meaning, and a whole lot of excitement.

A jolt of energy urged her along, her footsteps as light as her heart and moving ahead as if they knew just where to go. A hum hovered at the back of her throat, the tiny smidge of fear she still held onto keeping it at bay. After all, she didn't know what or who she would find at the end of the path. But good or bad, she was ready to experience it. She hurried down the steep incline into the trees, and slowed as she approached an area that felt familiar. Was this Wormwood's Water where she and Tanger had had their picnic? Mira paused to listen. Voices…a lot of them. She inched closer, trying to pick out what they were saying.

A calm, yet sure female voice rang out. "Hail, fair moon, ruler of the night. Guard us and ours until the light. Hail, fair sun, ruler of the day, make the morn to light our way."

"Amen," said a guy. He said something else, too, but it was muffled.

Mira took a couple of steps closer, straining to hear.

"Let's recite the Rede together."

The group said in unison, "Harm no one, do what you will."

That sounded like a good rule, Mira thought.

"Anyone have any announcements to make?"

The first person to speak up sounded like the man who'd said amen. He shared with the group about how he'd gathered three thousand water bottles over the week. When he said he'd have a mansion within a year, a few chuckled, but a strong female voice spoke over them. "There's nothing humorous about ruining the earth."

The group quieted.

"I am having dreams about the new moon celebration we are having next week. It's going to be a powerful celebration," said another member of the group.

A new moon celebration? What was that? Mira inched ahead another step.

"I'd like to talk about the election at the end of the week. We don't want to be under the thumb of another Benefactor and I think we should do something about it."

"I agree. We've had enough restriction for this lifetime."

"Any ideas?"

Many talked at the same time, which made it impossible to garner their words.

"Why don't you all write up your thoughts and bring them to me tomorrow. Then I'll pray about it and see what we should do. Agreed?"

"Agreed."

"Here's to promoting flexibility and diversity of thought and practice." The sound of clinking glasses followed.

Mira loved that they weren't just sitting around complaining and that they were taking steps to make changes. Her leg suddenly seized up with a constricting pain. She hadn't had a Charley Horse in years! She shifted, rubbing it with forceful circular motions, her teeth clenched. A tiny moan escaped, but she clamped her lips shut. Thankfully, the conversation continued and her cramp eased. She breathed a sigh of relief that she hadn't been noticed.

"Any other announcements? Tanger?"

So he was there! Mira's heart tripped into action even as her ears perked up.

"I'd like to share a poem I wrote," he said.

Mira loved the smooth sound of his voice. And he wrote poetry too? She pressed a hand against her heart and leaned closer.

"The new moon is near

It fuels my power

Nature bends to my desire

It brings me my reality

My soulmate…

I intuitively know it."

The group responded. "Make it so."

Mira moved nearer, as if gravity was pulling her toward the group. *Snap!* A branch split in two beneath her booted foot. She swung around and ran…right into the solid chest of Houser.

Resting his hands firmly on her shoulders, he smiled down at her. "Are you enjoying the doll?"

It wasn't at all what she'd expected to hear from him. Not wanting to tell him she'd hid the freaky doll away in her closet, she just nodded her head.

"What's going on?" Tanger came up beside them, his eyes hard as they zoned in on Houser's hands.

Releasing her shoulders, Houser said, "I caught her listening in - thought maybe I'd ask if she'd like to join us."

"I'll take it from here," Tanger said.

Houser grunted and wandered off. She watched him, chewing on her lower lip.

Tanger moved into her line of vision, his eyes soft as he looked at her. "*Do you want to join us?*"

"That depends on who the "us" actually is."

Chuckling, he put his arm across her shoulders and urged her ahead a couple of steps. She could see the group now, even though trees still separated them. "To put it in a nutshell," he said, "we're just a small circle of peace-loving people celebrating nature and spirituality as it speaks to us individually." He looked at her for a moment. "Sound like something you'd be interested in?"

It sounded intriguing, so she nodded.

He ducked his head to whisper in her ear. "Then you have to swear to secrecy."

She nodded again.

"You're sure?" He studied her carefully.

"I'm sure…I promise." Her nerves were jangling, but it was a good kind of jangling.

Tanger took her hand and led her over to the group. "This is Mira," he said, "the wonderful lady I met today, the one the poem was about."

She glowed with his compliment as she studied the faces of those sitting in a circle on the flat rock that overlooked the water - Wormwood's Water. She recognized Vashti immediately, but it wasn't until a cloud shifted to reveal the moon that she could identify the rest. Surprisingly, she recognized them all. Hunter and Claire were there, waving and grinning. Divinya sat across from them and Amaryllis Star, the famous author, sat cross-legged, adjacent to Vashti. She wondered if she'd scared Houser away, but no one remarked on it, so she supposed it didn't matter.

"Hi Mira. Welcome," Vashti said, scooping her hand fluidly in the air.

"Hi," Mira said, sitting down next to Tanger.

Chapter 16

Nash paused to scratch out the third line of the chorus when he heard his phone ring. Propping his guitar against the couch, he grabbed his phone off the coffee table. The number wasn't Mira's, but a call at three o'clock in the morning had to be important.

"Hello."

"Hi, Nash." It was Vaughn. "Mira wouldn't happen to be at your place, would she?"

Nash pressed the phone more tightly against his ear as he turned to glance at the door of his apartment. "She's not here. What's going on?" he asked, a sick feeling creeping up his throat.

There was a long pause as Vaughn took a deep breath. "There's no easy way to say this so I'll just come right out with it. Kya is dead."

"*What?*" He couldn't believe it! "What happened?"

"Mel found her. I'll explain the details later. Right now we need to find Mira."

"When did you see her last?" he asked, unable to erase the image of Mira following that man into the woods. He should've gone with his gut, he thought, snagging his lightweight leather jacket off the back of the couch.

"She ate dinner with us, but didn't eat much before locking herself in her room," Vaughn said.

One arm now in his jacket, Nash paused. "Maybe she left to meet someone," he said, "besides me." It was hard to admit, even harder to stomach.

"But she left a bathtub full of water and didn't take her purse or her phone." Vaughn's tone had risen to that of a young boy. "Kya died in the bathtub, Nash. We really need to find Mira!"

Nash agreed, but he didn't have time to explain his own intuition on the matter. Time wasn't on his side. "I'll be over as soon as I can," he said, disconnecting. Jacket on, he zipped it up. After grabbing his bike from his closet, he hoisted it onto his shoulder and hurried down the stairs into the cool night. Jumping on his bike, he pedaled like a maniac the short distance to Cofa's Tree. The street was quiet as he approached, but he could still hear the raucous beat of the bars and nightclubs located closer to the college. Maybe Mira was there, partying with the college kids. He doubted it. His heart thumped as he rested his bike against the storefront.

He went to the door and tried the knob. It was locked. Hurrying to the gate that led into the garden, he noticed it was locked, too. He knocked on the rough wooden panel.

"Mira." Knock, knock, knock. "Mira!"

Silence was his answer, but he sensed she was in there somewhere...with someone. Had he pushed her right into another man's arms? Or had she been taken from her room, a captive of the guy she'd followed earlier? He just had to know if she was safe – and if he found out a hard truth at the same time, so be it. Propping the toe of his sneaker on top of the gate hinge, he hoisted himself up to get a look. Candles lit a pathway that lead into the trees, which for some reason gave him goosebumps. He swung a leg over the top of the gate and rested his foot atop a wooden slat on the garden side.

"Stop right there."

Nash looked over his shoulder at the two police officers who had given him a hard time earlier that day. One had his hand on a weapon that hung from the holster belted around his waist, the other had a Taser drawn. Nash didn't have time to deal with them. He swung his other leg over the fence, only his plan to jump onto the garden path and make a run for it was halted by a loud ZAP.

The jolt that hit him felt like an electric fork had been stabbed into his spine, creating a body-wide pressure. Was he going to explode? Crying out from the intense pain, Nash lost his grip and toppled onto the ground. The impact left him flat on his back, gasping for breath…and looking up into the hard eyes of a young police officer.

"We warned you son," the officer said, and grabbed his arm to sit him up against the fence.

"But I have t-t-to…" he frowned, trying to gather the thoughts that seemed to be escaping him at the moment. Mira…yes, Mira. "I need to find Mira," he said. "She's missing." His body felt like it was on fire and he couldn't stop his limbs from tremoring.

"We had this talk earlier," the older of the two said with a grunt.

"And after doing a little digging, we confirmed our position on the matter." The young cop squatted beside Nash. "She's eighteen. And looking at her history, she's very capable of taking care of herself."

Nash muttered something even he couldn't comprehend.

"Just because you suspect something else doesn't mean you can break the law," the one beside him said with a shake of his head.

"I didn't do anything," Nash said. If only he could get up and run, but he couldn't. His body wouldn't cooperate. All he could seem to do was lay there and let the cuffs snap around his wrists.

"You were trespassing." *Click.*

"But…"

"But nothing," the older one said, finally tucking his Taser away to help his partner get Nash to his feet. "Has it been twenty-four hours since anyone has seen her?"

"No," Nash said, hating himself for not thinking his plan through - and hating them as they drug him toward their vehicle with its back door open as if it was waiting for him.

"Then she can't be a missing person and for sure we have to book you for trespassing," the younger reasoned.

As they lowered him into the car, Nash whapped his head on the edge. He took a deep breath, trying to shake off the pain and gather his wits. "She's in danger! You have to find her and save her life!" he said in his most persuasively urgent tone.

"You don't know that she's in danger – and no, we don't have to find her," the older one snapped.

"You're making a mistake!" Nash tried to focus on the fence that had kept him from finding Mira, but his eyes blurred with pain and hopelessness and his head felt like mush.

"No. You're the one that made the mistake," the older cop said as he jumped into the driver's seat.

"But don't worry," said the other getting into the passenger side. "We'll get your statement, give you your fine, then you can be on your way. Shouldn't take long."

"By that time she could be dead," Nash growled.

"Or she could be back home by then," the younger one said in much too cheery of a voice. The electronic hum of the rising separation window stopped any more conversation

As they made their way down B Street, Nash shifted, only to see that the car had another passenger, who tilted his hat off to the side so part of his face now showed.

"Hello," the man said.

Chapter 17

"First, let's take a few minutes to really feel the power all around us." Vashti paused to close her eyes as did the group.

Mira followed their lead. She rested her hands on the knees of her crisscrossed legs, but she couldn't relax. Her hands were fisted and sweaty, and her mind was elsewhere, thinking about last year, how she'd introduced a newly chipless Nash to the beauty of sound in a way similar to this. But Nash was in her past, she reminded herself. Though the ache in her heart remained, she finally managed to relax her hands and mind to pick up the sounds encompassing her. Trickling water filtered through the whoosh of rapidly running water and mingled with the rustling of leaves. An owl hooted nearby, a chorus of cicadas its supporting orchestra. Crickets mixed with the crackling of the small fire burning in the center of their circle. All the sounds seemed to work together. Even the groups' breathing patterns seemed to mesh.

"Since the Enchiridion was found, we've developed a new way of looking at the world. One thing we've discovered is that nature is power and this power is in everything, including us," Vashti said in a hushed tone. "And this power is ours for the taking."

"Should we give Mira an example?" Hunter asked.

Vashti nodded.

Amaryllis cleared her throat. "I received personal spiritual communication that guided me to write my book in less than a week."

Mira knew it was possible. After all, she'd experienced something similar with her prophetic paintings.

Vashti was quiet again for several moments. Then she said, "I sense you've had a breakthrough, Mira."

Goosebumps sprouted on Mira's arms. She knew Vashti couldn't be referring to her prophetic paintings because that ability had been lost. The only other thing it could be was her lucid dream. Mira glanced at Tanger, who nodded encouragingly.

"I guess I did," she said softly.

"Tell us about it," Vashti said.

Mira swallowed, first looking at all the people in the group. She saw interest instead of censure.

She took a deep breath. "I had a lucid dream and it was…actually, it was amazing!"

Smiles beamed from her admission, their nods prodding her to tell them the details. So she told them most of it. The group seemed enthralled, and even laughed when she told them the part about Tanger kneeling at her feet. The dream, and the experience of telling this accepting group about it - it was all so…freeing! And to top it all off, as she wrapped up her story, Tanger winked at her. Her heart was so full!

"Thanks for sharing your experience, Mira," Vashti said, and stood, raising her arms toward the moon. Claire got up as well, a flute in hand. She brought the instrument to her lips, and as soon as she breathed over the tone hole, a lilting, soulful tune filled the air.

Tanger rose to his feet and held out his hand to Mira. She took it and as he helped her up, he gathered her in his arms and started to sway to the music. His warmth enveloped her, his earthy spice drew her in. The rest of the group joined in, but Mira was only minimally aware. She felt so alive and like she was where she truly belonged. She hadn't felt that way in a long time – maybe never.

Claire's fluted melody continued, so Mira snuggled in closer to Tanger. Resting her cheek against his chest, she watched the others and found herself entranced by the beauty. Each person had their own unique way of dancing to the music yet still maintained a sort of cohesiveness - with each other and with the natural setting that flowed and harmonized around them. Just as Mira's eyes drifted shut, the song came to a close. Tanger stopped swaying but didn't let her go.

"This has been a joyous night, a night we've added to our own," Vashti announced. Tanger released Mira as the store owner approached them. Wrapping her in a big hug, Vashti said, "We're so glad you're here, Mira." The rest of the group followed suit, thanking her for coming as they hugged their good-byes.

Mira's heart swelled as she watched her new friends wander back up the hill, and it began to beat overtime when she realized that she and Tanger were alone.

"I'm sure you have a lot of questions," Tanger said.

She nodded. "Like what do we do next?"

He smiled and tapped the end of her nose. "We go where life takes us, like a spider floating through the air on a silken thread."

She felt the silken thread drawing her closer to this enigmatic man, but Nash's logical voice came at her out of nowhere. "I'm not sure that's the best idea."

"I wouldn't have it any other way," Tanger said with a shrug. "It keeps the mind and heart open for truly spiritual awakenings."

It sounded intriguing – as long as it was more real than Eleanor's prophetic words. "Is a spiritual awakening what I'm looking for?"

He tugged her into his arms, looking down at her with a mesmerizing gaze that promised more than that. "Maybe…or maybe right now it's simply swinging you closer to answers concerning your final project."

"About that." Mira grinned, taking a step back, feeling like she was walking on air. "How do you feel about taking a dip?"

Chapter 18

"I didn't know the cops had picked up someone else," Nash said, staring at the stranger next to him. He looked like a slick operator, but smelled more like lilacs than anything.

"They actually don't know it." He chuckled softly.

Nash glanced at the police officers through the tinted glass window that divided them. Neither were paying any attention.

"Why are you here?" Nash asked the guy.

"I just needed a ride to the other side of town where the cop shop is." He reached into the overly full pocket of his trench coat and pulled out a square package about the size of a deck of cards only thicker. "Care for a fag?" he asked.

Nash looked at the package. "A cigarette you mean?"

The man shook out a cigarette and held it toward him. "Fag is an old word for an old habit. I prefer it, especially on nights like tonight. Want it or not?"

"Sure. Why not?" He took the cigarette in his cuffed hands and managed to get it propped between his lips.

"Why not, indeed," the guy said, reaching out to light the end of it.

Nash inhaled as he'd seen his employee, Banjo, do. "What do you mean by nights like tonight?" He said through a cough.

The guy didn't answer, only lit his own cigarette and took a long drag.

Nash's head began to buzz and nausea settled in. "So were you around Cofa's Tree when I was arrested?" He glanced at the guy, whose attention was focused outside. He could see a faint bruising on his pale neck.

The man took another long draw on his cigarette then slowly released its toxic smoke upward and away from himself. "I was."

Nash didn't really care that the guy had witnessed his humiliation, but he *did* care if he'd noticed anything else. Licking his lips, which tasted a bit like ash and the coffee he'd chugged earlier, Nash asked, "Did you happen to see a dark-haired young woman hanging around Cofa's Tree?"

The man puffed out a couple smoke rings. "Maybe. Why?"

Nash snuffed out his cigarette on the side of the car door then threw the butt on the floor because he couldn't open the window. "My girlfriend…or at least she was my girlfriend…is missing. I'd seen her in that garden earlier today with a guy." His brows pinched together. The back of his throat seemed to do the same.

The guy shot him a quick glance. "I'm sure she'll be fine."

"Well I'm not." Nash sat up straighter, looking out the window, but not really seeing anything. "A friend of ours was found dead in a bathtub tonight – and now Mira is gone, a tub full of water and her purse and phone left behind." His heart pounded as his mind drifted to could-be scenarios he'd rather not entertain, but they remained lodged there like un-chewed steak in a diner's throat.

"Could she have had something to do with the friend you'd found dead?"

The thought appalled Nash. "Absolutely not!"

The stranger quashed his cigarette and flicked it onto the carpet, but didn't retract his accusation. He didn't say anything at all.

Nash wanted to punch him right then and there, but they'd pulled up to the station. The younger hurried to open Nash's car door.

"You have another passenger," Nash muttered to the cop as he moved out onto the sidewalk. The fresh air was a huge welcome to his queasy stomach.

The officer ducked his head into the car. "You again?"

As the man got out, he tipped his hat. "Much obliged officer," he said, and adjusted his trench coat before tucking his hands into its pockets.

"Yeah, yeah." The cop shook his head. "Whatever." He reached into the pants pocket of his crisp blue uniform and handed the guy a dollar. "Next time let me know you're riding along, okay?"

"Absolutely," he said. "Good night officers." As he turned to walk away, he took out another cigarette and lit it. As he strolled down the block, unhurried, Nash could see the tiny glowing end and the trail of smoke that followed.

"Strange guy," Nash commented.

"Yep. Now let's go get this trespassing incident taken care of," the younger one said, grabbing the crux of Nash's elbow. Nash didn't resist as the officer ushered him inside. The sooner he got this over with, the better.

As they stepped up to the desk, Nash took a good look. He'd never been in the police station before, and found himself curious. Behind the large desk sat a young woman in bright purple cop gear. She was chewing gum as her fingers flew across her computer keys. "Can I help ya, Danno?"

"We need to book this guy. Trespassing by Cofa's Tree."

She stopped typing. "Seriously?"

"Yeah."

She looked up at Nash, her face a bit paler than moments before. "I'll bring him to a consult room and take care of it." Grabbing a file from her desk, she stood up. "Right this way."

As he followed her down a dimly lit hallway, he asked, "By room you don't mean a cell, do you?"

"No, though it would probably be safer for you than the stuff you're messing with." She swung a door open, revealing a grey walled room, a table, and one chair on either side of it.

"What do you mean?" he said, taking a seat. "I was just looking for my girlfriend."

"I hope you find her somewhere else," she said, her hands shaky as she laid the file on the table. "That place is possessed. I can feel it whenever I go by it. And the rumors…" She clutched at the cross necklace she wore, sliding it back and forth on her silver chain.

"What have you heard?" he asked, sitting forward on the hard chair.

Her eyes widened. "That they are devil worshippers."

Nash held back a snort. He and Hayes had talked about the devil a few months ago, and after discussing it further with Tory, Nash had made up his mind on the subject. The devil was just a mindset, a lack of conscience persuading a person to do evil. He wasn't a real being or spirit or fallen angel. He was just an easy excuse and a label for bad behavior.

"I suppose I shouldn't mess with them, then," he said.

She visibly relaxed. He felt sorry for her - that she was so afraid of something her mind had invented.

Leaning over the desk to write on the file she'd brought, she said, "So you were trespassing because you were looking for your girlfriend. Is that correct?"

He nodded.

She wrote it down before reaching into her pocket to pull out a tiny key. "If you agree to stay off the premises, I can unlock your handcuffs. Do you agree?"

"I agree," he said. *For now*, he silently added.

After unlocking his cuffs, she slid the paper in front of him. "Sign here, and here." She pointed to two x-ed lines. "Then we'll do your prints and get you out of here."

He rubbed his sore wrists, then, even though he wasn't thrilled about it, he signed the paper that seemed pretty straightforward. It would go on his record as a misdemeanor. The fine was $200.

"Two hundred bucks is crazy," he growled. "Do you have a cash machine around here?"

"We do, but," the woman pulled an ink pad out of the desk drawer, "Your fine is already paid. Now press your index finger against the ink. And then kind of roll it onto the form in this box."

As he did as she directed, he frowned deeply. "Who paid my fine?"

"A woman that has been popping in quite a bit over the last few days." The woman helped him with inking his next finger. "She says she's some kind of music producer. Whatever she is, she's got some cash." She finished his right hand and started on his left. "You work for her?"

"Sort of, I guess." Why would Porsche pay his fine? And how had she known? Whatever the reasons, he owed her big time.

When the woman finished up his left hand prints, she handed him a wet wipe to clean his fingers.

"You're free to go, but don't be getting into any more trouble, okay?"

He nodded, but until he found Mira, he couldn't guarantee it. As he walked away, the woman rasped, "I was serious about staying away from Cofa's Tree, you know."

"I know," he said, hightailing it out of the station, knowing he'd wasted too much time. Yet as he ran down the sidewalk in the direction of Mira's place, he hoped with every fiber of his being that time didn't matter – that she'd be there, safe and secure when he arrived. And maybe they could even talk and repair their relationship. After thinking about never seeing her again, he really wanted to make it work.

Chapter 19

"So you want me to jump into the water, shirtless, and reach up to the moon with one hand?" Tanger asked with a grin.

"Yes."

He tugged at a stray clump of her hair that had stuck in the crease of her lips. "I'll do it, but not tonight."

When she opened her mouth to argue, he put his finger across her lips. "The moon isn't ready tonight." He looked over his shoulder at the glowing orb. "We will wait until it's completely full."

She rolled her eyes. "But that won't be until next week! I won't have time to paint it."

"Maybe you could take some photos instead, then."

It was an option, but she'd had her heart set on painting it...that, and, she had to admit, she didn't want the night to end. "I can easily paint a full moon into the portrait if I get the rest of it done."

Tanger shook his head. "The scene has to be completely natural to get the full effect, the right shadows and nuances, the perfect lighting. You need an A on the project, right?"

He had a point. "All right. We'll shoot for next week Wednesday, which is the night of the full moon and it will give me a day to print the pictures for my portfolio."

"It's settled then." He took her hand and started up the hill. "What are you doing tomorrow?"

She watched the terrain around her as she trudged up the hill behind Tanger. "I suppose I'll help my parents with their packing."

"Are they going on a trip," he asked, peering at her over his shoulder.

"No, they're moving to Enab, at least for a while."

For a moment, he remained silent. Then he said, "How do you feel about that?"

That he cared about her feelings made her heart sing. "At first I was upset. I had wanted a 'normal' family for so long, and I guess hearing that they were leaving me to pursue their own dreams made me feel like I hadn't been good enough for them to stick around." She shrugged. "But I've had a change of heart."

"Oh yeah?"

"Yeah." They came up to the garden where the candles still flickered. "I decided that I'm ready to figure out who I am in this world without them trying to mold me. I want to be more open-minded than that."

Tanger blew out one candle, then another. "Maybe we can be your family – one that will allow you to create your own way." Smiling softly, he leaned over a candle so the glow turned the tan skin of his face a seductive gold.

"I'd like that," she said.

"Oh…and I think you'll like this, too." Tanger reached into his back pocket and pulled out a soft-covered book. He held it out to Mira. "The author does a great job of introducing flexibility exercises for the mind and heart."

Mira glanced at the title. "*The Creatrix*…how did you…this is…" she looked up into his warm eyes and forgot what she was going to say.

"This is a gift." He took her hand and pressed the book into her palm. Mira's heart fluttered in reaction to his gentle touch. "After I met you today, I called Amaryllis and had her save a copy. It's one of the perks of having her in our group."

She hugged it against her chest. "Thank you."

"You're welcome." He looked at her a moment longer, then finished blowing out the candles. They walked in silence toward the gate. He opened it for her, his hand resting on the top edge. She could see his taut build, all the more beautiful in the moonlight.

Would he try to kiss her? Should she let him? Finally, she managed a shaky smile. "Thanks for an interesting evening," she said. The gush of feelings flooding her insides begged her to say more than that lame statement, but the words wouldn't come.

"Thank you for joining us." He kissed her cheek gently. "And I'm looking forward to many more *interesting* times with you."

His eyes sparkled with promise. "Do you want me to walk you home?" he asked, looking down the block into the distance.

She shook her head. "Thanks though." She needed some quiet time to think, to absorb everything that had happened and what it all meant.

"Okay. Whenever you want to hang out, I'll be around." He moved to close the gate. "And if you guys need extra help with the packing or the moving, let me know and I'll be there."

What a nice guy! But having him around at present would bring too many questions. Mira didn't want to have to explain Tanger, or her problems with Nash. And the last thing she wanted now was for her parents to stick around to fix her. "I think we have the moving covered, but I really appreciate the offer."

He nodded.

"Well, good-bye," she said, forcing herself to turn around and start for home.

"Good-bye, Mira."

The softly spoken good-bye seemed to promise a world she hadn't even begun to imagine. It was everything she could do not to turn around and delve right in.

As she climbed the hill toward her house, Mira concentrated on the turf beneath her feet, replaying the amazing night she'd experienced. The darkness and the shadows didn't bother her because her newfound confidence clothed her like armor. But when Mira approached the gate encircling her home and looked up, the spring in her step faltered. All the lights were on.

She frowned. "It's four in the morning." A little frisson of worry wheedled into her mind as she wandered toward the front door. She didn't know what was going on, but with all the lights on, chances were good they'd discovered her missing.

Walking up the steps, she paused, her hand resting on the knob of the front door. She listened, but she couldn't hear any crying or raised voices – a good sign, she hoped. After all, a big fight before her parents left wouldn't help anything.

"Might as well get this over with," she muttered, and swung the door open wide.

The foyer was empty. "I'm home," she called out.

Her parents, Hayes and Mel…and Nash, came running into the entryway, relief on their faces. Her mom immediately hugged her, her grip so tight, Mira thought her lungs might collapse.

"I'm fine," she finally managed to squeak out. She had to admit, it felt good that her mom had worried about her. But how had she discovered she was even gone?

Her mom squeezed her once more before stepping back. "Where have you been?" she asked, her tone harsh and accusatory.

Now that was more like the reaction Mira had suspected. "Why, what's going on?"

Vaughn stepped close enough to put his arm around Mira's shoulders. "Kya is dead."

The news hit her like a rock to the head. "But…but…she was part of the team! How? How?" The words stumbled out of her mouth even as tears rolled down her cheeks. She'd just seen her that morning!

"They found her dead in her bathtub," Mel said softly. "They scheduled an autopsy and are investigating the crime scene right as we speak."

Heart pounding, stomach sick, Mira sucked in the air that seemed much too heavy to breathe in. Could she have tried the lucid dreaming, too? Maybe she had too much of the oil, or maybe she hadn't really been dreaming and had…the thoughts were too horrifying to consider.

"You said crime scene?" Mira rasped, feeling so guilty for having an exciting evening while Kya had been close by, dying.

"They suspect homicide but are careful to label it as such until they've gathered all the evidence," Hayes said, his eyes incredibly sad. "They are trying to put together a list of the many guys she dated and the places she frequented."

"And there was a sketch of her in the tub. You wouldn't know anything about that, would you Mira?" Nash, who was standing in the far corner, shot out.

"Now hold on," Vaughn said, raising his hand. "It was an ink drawing made to look like a photograph. Mira doesn't draw like that and now isn't the time to be throwing out accusations."

"But she wasn't here, and she's the artist of the group," Nash pointed out. Pulling himself away from the wall, his stare intense and accusing.

How could he think…"I didn't do it! You know me better than that!" she railed.

"Do I?" Nash glared at her.

"I would never hurt Kya."

"Prove it. Where were you at two this morning?" Nash approached her, his eyes haunted and scared – which wasn't what she'd expected to see in them given his accusations. "Think about it," he said softly. "We need to consider that the cops are going to view you as a suspect. We need to be prepared."

He was right. She closed her eyes, trying to shut out the truth of Kya's death and the very real possibility that she could be a suspect.

"Do you have an alibi?" Nash's voice trembled as he waited for her to answer.

She didn't want to tell him, but she nodded anyway.

"Who is it?" Nash clasped her upper arm, his grip firm but not painful.

Because she'd sworn to secrecy concerning the group, her only choice was to tell a partial truth. "I was with Tanger Hardy."

Nash lurched back as if she'd slapped him. Guilt curled in her stomach, replacing the sting his words had caused. She closed her eyes, willing herself back to the place she'd felt so alive, but with Kya dead and Nash emanating hate, she couldn't latch onto even the tiniest bit of those good feelings. Why was this happening to her?

"Maybe you two should go outside and talk," her mom suggested after the silence became too much for them all. "And we'll work on a plan of action on how to handle all this."

Mira looked at Nash. He nodded, and strode outside. She followed.

Marching over to the waist high gate that surrounded the house, he clutched the top and stared out over the city. Mira moved beside him, taking the same pose.

"I'm sorry, Nash," she said, not knowing what else to say.

Slowly, he leaned forward onto his elbows. "I'm scared, Mira," he admitted.

She frowned. That wasn't at all what she'd expected him to say. "What do you mean?"

Looking down at his hands folded in front of him, he said, "This morning, I was so sure of everything…that my career was going to launch, that I'd be doing what I love, and that you'd be beside me the whole way." He looked at her, his eyes bleak. "And now here we are. A friend of ours is dead. You're seeing," he paused to swallow, "another man." He took a deep breath. "I guess I just wonder what the purpose is in all this heartache."

His frankness melted away all the trouble they'd had. Tears hovered at the ends of her lashes as she sniffed. "And I wonder why God would bring us together, then let us fall apart." She clenched her fists. "And why would God let Kya die?!"

Nash reached for her clenched hand and, bringing it to his lips, gently kissed the knuckles. "I think *we* probably let us fall apart." He smiled sadly. "Or rather *I* did." He frowned as he stared at their hands. "And maybe there isn't a God at all."

"What about my prophetic paintings? There had to be a supernatural power behind it."

He made a small noise in the back of his throat. "It doesn't really matter at this point." After a moment, he wrapped his arm around her shoulders. She leaned into him because it felt natural, it felt right.

"I was so worried something happened to you, Mira," he said, the rasp in his voice giving away the depth of his worry. "I don't want to lose you. Please tell me I haven't lost already."

Nash felt so good, so comfortable, so solid beside her. But what about Tanger? Tanger *wanted* to hang out with her and seemed to enjoy her company – and she'd had so much fun being with him. With Nash, she had to fight just to get him to spend time with her. Oh, he'd probably be willing to commit to more time, but it would be out of obligation...and then real life would butt in again. She'd end up in the same predicament.

When she didn't comment, his body tensed. "I want to give you what you need, Mira." He turned her to face him, his hands cupping her shoulders. "What is it you want from me?"

"I want this." She stood on tiptoes, pressing her lips against his, trying to show him how she felt. She craved closeness – a return to how they used to be – only with more hope, more intimacy between them.

"You don't know how hard it's been to control myself - to keep my hands off you over this past year," he said, his lips now hovering a breath away from hers.

Mira felt a thrill race through her body.

"But it would be a mistake."

His words sliced into her hope and tore it to shreds. She took a step back. "So loving me would be a mistake? Is that what you're saying?"

He shook his head. "Hayes said waiting to experience that beautiful gift inside the bounds of marriage will create an unbreakable physical, emotional, psychological, and spiritual bond. He said we would never regret it."

Her mom had told her the same thing, but what was wrong with living and loving in the present? What if more intimacy would keep them together? What if it enhanced their closeness and sealed their future? "What if Hayes is wrong? What if this is right for us?" she whispered.

Nash grasped the back of her head to draw her in closer, his kiss gentle at first, then turning ravenous. She could feel the desperation in his kiss, and felt that same desperation claw at her. But then Nash broke it off, leaving coldness and rejection behind.

"I'm sorry. I want what Hayes and Mel have, and this isn't the way to get it." He looked down the hill toward Pillar. His voice dropping to a whisper, he said, "I just don't know exactly what to do to fix this – to fix us." He reached for her hand. "Help me, Mira."

The pleading tone tugged at her heart, but his words said it all. He wouldn't consider solutions unless they fit in with his ideals. She was tired of parameters, tired of fitting into other people's boxes. She *wanted* to be that spider floating in the wind, going where life took her.

Finally, she said, "What I want is space to figure out who I am."

She could feel him tense up even more "How much space?"

"I'm not sure."

He dropped her hand, his body almost drooping as he looked at her with pain-filled eyes. "I don't want to ask, but I need to. Are you talking about freedom…to date other people?"

Oh, how she wished she hated him so that this would be easier. "I guess I am," she finally said. She touched his arm. He remained motionless.

"I don't know how I feel about that." He laughed humorlessly. "Besides horrible."

"Have you ever thought that maybe we need to grab love whenever it passes by?" she asked, repeating the words Tanger had written in the front cover of the book he'd given her.

Nash snorted in disbelief, shoving hands through his thick hair. "That's stupid, Mira. Love is a choice, not a feeling."

"Thinking of love as logical is stupid." She lifted her chin. "And only a heartless Reformer would say something like that." The moment the words came out, she wished she could take them back.

"I guess the way I love you isn't enough." He opened the gate with controlled precision. "It won't ever be enough, so I suppose I should thank you for this," he hissed, stalking away. But then he stopped a few steps out and turned back to her. She could see the tears glistening in his eyes. "You know what? Go ahead, Mira. Be free. But don't expect me to be around when you change your mind."

Mira watched him walk away. Her heart ached, but her limbs were too heavy for her to even think about following him. Either she'd made the best decision of her life or the worst.

After Nash disappeared into the shadows, Mira slowly made her way back into the house. Even though she was worried about how her mom would react to her news, she hoped that she wouldn't be too tired to talk. She really needed the support right now.

She stepped inside the house, closing the door gently behind her. The soft murmur of voices floated toward her from the dining room, so she walked to its doorway. "I'm back," she said, trying hard to keep herself from crying.

"Where's Nash?"

"He went home."

Stares of accusation bore into her, making her feel defenseless and heartbroken. Her jaw tightened, but she guessed she couldn't blame them. She was having a hard time accepting it herself. "So have you figured anything out yet?"

Vaughn nodded and threw down the pencil that he was using to write notes. "Yep. Two things, the first being that your mom and I are staying in town until they find Kya's murderer and your name is cleared."

That wasn't all that surprising she supposed. "The second thing?"

"You're grounded."

Chapter 20

Nash adjusted his custom molded in-ear isolation earphones and leaned in so his lips hovered an inch from the mike. "Testing one, two," he said. It echoed...at least he thought it had. He couldn't actually tell because his head was numb from no sleep and buzzed from his triple-strength coffee shots.

He shaded his eyes to look across the wide grassy expanse where his fans would soon be congregating. Tory stood at the far edge, looking his way. "How does it sound, Tory?" he called out.

She gave him a thumbs up.

Must be fine, he thought, and jumped off the stage. Striding over to the artist refreshment area, he grabbed the first thing they offered him that was cold and wet. He didn't know if beer paired well with all the coffee shots he'd been drinking, but what did it matter?

As he chugged down the bitter brew, Tory approached. "How are you holding up?" she said with a slight smile.

"Alright I guess."

"Hmm." Hands on hips, she said, "You don't look alright."

He gave her as much of a grin as he could muster, which wasn't much. "I'm fine."

"Well your definition of fine must be a lot different than mine. You even have bags under your eyes!"

"I stayed up all night. Got my song finished." Just thinking about it brought an ache to his throat. He'd poured all his emotions into it, every longing, every regret.

"That's awesome. Are you going to perform it tonight?"

"No."

Her brows raised in response. "Maybe you should reconsider. I heard Porsche will be in the audience." She pointed to the producer, who was talking to someone in front of a van auto-wrapped with a Driven Records decal.

Nash hadn't even been aware that Porsche was nearby. "Maybe I *should* sing it." He shook his head. "I don't know if I can."

"What's up with you?" Tory asked.

He looked down at his feet and frowned. "Mira and I are done…for good." It hurt to say it.

"Really?"

"Yeah." Before he could say more, he heard a giggle. He turned around to see two young ladies smiling at him.

"Will you autograph this for me?" the one with the hair down to her waist asked.

He tried to shake off the gloom, he took the glossy postcard held out to him. It had his picture on the front of it. As he signed the corner with the green glitter pen they'd provided, he asked, "Where'd you get this?"

She pointed to the back of the truck. "Got a whole bunch of stuff," she said, holding up her bag.

"Me next," her friend said, butting in front of her.

Nash held out his hand, but instead of handing him a picture or poster, she tugged the scooped neckline of her shirt and tucked it under the edge of her lacy purple bra. "I'm broke, so sign here please," she said, chewing her gum at high speed.

"Seriously?"

"Of course." She grinned, tilting her head back.

As he signed his name on her smooth skin, her breath hitched. When he was done, he stared at the signature a moment before handing her back her marker.

She waved her hand across it, giggling as she did so. "Take a picture with us?"

"Of course." He slid between the girls, putting his arms around both.

Tory took the picture with one of their phones. "Isn't this just precious," she said in an overly bright voice.

The girls didn't pick up her sarcasm, only continued to beam as they retrieved their phone. Checking out the picture, Ms. Purple-lace said, "Sweet. Sis is going to be so jealous!"

The girl with the long hair agreed, then glanced at Nash. "So what are you doing after the show tonight?"

The other girl nudged her.

"What? It can't hurt to ask," she said.

"Hey girls, I have something for you." Porsche Grant stepped up beside Nash as she held something out to the girls.

They took the gift and as soon as they'd read what it was, they squealed. "Backstage passes…backstage passes," they yelled, jumping up and down.

Nash didn't know if he'd be able to tolerate them being backstage. That was his 'hideout' between sets and before and after the show, where he could relax and be himself with his friends.

"Now leave us to our work, girls," Porsche said. "We'll see you later."

"K. See ya later." They waved as they walked away, identical grins on their faces.

"I don't know if I want them backstage," Nash muttered.

Porsche put a hand on his shoulder. "This is how the big time, works, Nash. Tonight is a trial run for you, which includes awing your fans, and making them love you."

He didn't know if he wanted anyone's love but Mira's, but that choice had been taken away. "Alright. I'll deal with it."

She chuckled. "If you give it a chance, you'll love it. Trust me."

He nodded. As Tory bent to pick up the marker the girl had dropped, he noticed her glower.

Porsche handed him a Driven Records water bottle engraved with his name. "Get yourself hydrated, relax, do whatever you want for a bit. Remember, you're a star."

"Yeah," he said with a small smile. "I guess I am."

"And here's your schedule for the rest of the evening."

He took the list from Porsche, frowning as he read. *Two hours before the show, feel free to go backstage and get warmed up. There's a survival kit waiting for you. Take whatever you want out of it. One hour before the show, you'll have about fifteen new fans joining you. Make them happy.*

Although he had his own performance routine, she was the expert. He tucked the list into his pocket.

"You'll do great, Nash." Porsche smiled with the assurance of someone who had never been unsuccessful.

"Thanks." Nash glanced at Tory for a nod of reassurance, but she wasn't paying attention to his conversation. She was looking at something in the distance. He followed her gaze.

"Mira," he whispered, feeling like he'd taken a punch to the chest. She sat on a park bench, a book in her lap. A guy sat next to her. It was the guy from the back of the police car! Was *he* Tanger Hardy? Had Nash actually shared a cigarette with Mira's new boyfriend? Had the guy been laughing inside at his folly? "Who is that guy?" Nash asked, holding his breath.

"His name is Houser," Porsche said. "He's working on our production crew."

Houser. It was better than Tanger, but Nash didn't like his slick look. "I don't like him."

Porsche chuckled. "We're just using him for tonight. He can easily be replaced."

Nash felt a little better knowing that.

"Well, go and enjoy yourself now so you can be ready to work the crowd in," she checked her watch as she walked toward the truck, "four hours and fifteen minutes."

As Porsche wandered off and disappeared behind the truck where the merchandise was located, Nash said to Tory, "I'm going over there."

She must have noticed the sparking daggers in his eyes, because she grabbed his arm to stop him. "What happened between you and Mira?"

He tugged on his arm, but she didn't let go. He sighed. "Well, Vaughn called me in the middle of the night with the news about Kya. He also told me Mira was missing."

"I heard about Kya. I'm sorry, Nash." Her hand on his arm softened then let go.

"Yeah. Me too. Anyway, I didn't know where Mira was, so I went over to her house. She came back a bit later. She was fine, only..."

"Only what?"

"We had a talk. She wants space. I want to give it to her, but..." he shook his head.

"That means she's not yours anymore, Nash," Tory said.

The words cut him to the core. He still couldn't believe it. "She'll change her mind. I just need to talk some sense into her." Nash started toward Mira and Houser, but a trio of girls in matching bikinis got in his way.

"Hey gorgeous. I hear you're singing for us tonight."

He didn't recognize any of them. They were all striking. Perfect. "Are you from around here?" he asked.

"No. We're from Bolinbroke. We came on the bus and are staying at Cofa's Tree."

"Really?" It could be his chance to get inside the place, maybe figure out what was actually going on with Mira! "Maybe we can get together after the concert."

The one in the middle laughed throatily. "I think we can arrange that."

The three girls kissed him…one on the lips, the other two on each cheek. "Looking forward to tonight," they said, and sashayed toward a mud volleyball game someone had set up in the park.

When they were almost to the volleyball court, he remembered his intent. Mira. He jogged over to the bench, which was now empty except for the book Mira had left behind. He grabbed it. "Mira," he called out as he scanned the area.

There was no answer and no sign of her or Houser. He yelled one more time, which earned him a few looks from passersby, but no Mira. He slumped onto the bench, staring down at the book entitled *The Creatrix*. On the cover, a woman stood with one wrist shackled to tablets made of stone, the other held a painted sign with the words, "The secrets of me." Nash opened the book. Carefully printed script had been penciled inside the cover. It said, "Dearest Mira. Grab love when it comes your way. It is a gift, the perfect way to natural love. Yours, Tanger."

That's just what Mira had said to him last night. Those were Tanger's words - words she believed! Nash threw the book into the trash and headed back toward Tory. "Let's go," he ordered.

Chapter 21

Mira glanced at Houser as they stood together on the doorstep of her house. At first, she'd thought he was strange, especially with the doll incident, but now she thought him charming in his own eclectic way. And he actually listened to her!

"I'm sorry you're sad," Houser said, tucking his hands into the front pockets of his grey jeans.

"I *am* sad about Kya."

"And many other things, no?" His soothing voice and empathetic eyes filled her own eyes with tears…again.

"Since I heard about Kya's death, I just can't help but feel like I need to live life before it is too late, you know? Only I don't know which direction to go." Seeing Nash setting up for his show had brought on its own wave of sadness, one Houser had witnessed firsthand.

"Moving into one of Vashti's rooms will surround you with the positive atmosphere you need," he said.

"Thanks for setting that up for me." She managed a half-smile. "But I'm not sure that will take care of it." She pressed her hand against her heart. "It seems to go much deeper than that." Then she shook her head. "I'm sorry, Houser. I'm sure I'll find the answers I need at Vashti's." Her voice dropped to a whisper as she added, "And with the group."

He smiled, the action making him seem all the more likeable. "Now that's what I like to hear." He started down the steps. "I'll see you tonight at Cofa's Tree, right?"

"Right," she said, but saying it made her feel guilty…guilty for skipping out on her parents, guilty for missing Nash's concert, guilty for wanting to have fun while Kya laid lifeless on a mortician's table.

"Good," he said. "I'm looking forward to it."

Mira watched him walk away. Even his stride seemed to be calm and collected. She envied it, and his self-assurance. Maybe he was right. Maybe moving out was the answer. She opened the door to the house. As she proceeded inside, she noticed her parents sitting on the steps waiting for her.

"It's quite obvious you didn't take our grounding seriously," Vaughn said softly, but with an edge to his voice that made her stiffen.

"I am an adult now, and I've had experiences most people would never have survived," she said. "It's senseless to ground me."

Both parents stood up. Her mom lowered her chin, her look one of authority. She said, "You are still under our roof and you will abide by our rules, young lady."

Inside, Mira began to shake. "I've been locked away enough in my life," she ground out. "So I'm moving out." She marched toward them because she needed to get to her room. As she'd expected, they blocked her way. "I need to get my things," she said.

"You're not being reasonable," Vaughn said. "We are protecting you. This is for your own good."

"Oh really?" She lifted her chin, meeting his glare with one of her own. "You think keeping me under lock and key until I become who you want me to be is for my own good? Do you even care that I'm miserable?"

"It's what you call parenting," Vaughn shot back.

"Parenting?" She snorted. "For the first seventeen years of my life, you were not my father. My mom wasn't even really my mom. What do either of you even *know* about parenting?"

"Just because we've made mistakes doesn't mean we should allow *you* to," her mom said, her eyes a hard marble yet pinched with regret.

"You need to let me grow up...find my own way." Mira's breaths accelerated, her face turned red, her hands fisted. She'd give anything for

Houser's calm right now. "I'm moving out and you can't stop me." She shoved past them to make her point. To her surprise, they let her through.

"But where will you go? How will you pay for it?" her mom asked, her voice catching.

"Already got it covered," Mira barked, but then paused on the top step. "I'll be living in a room at Cofa's Tree. They gave me a job in exchange for rent and food." She glanced over her shoulder, which was a mistake. Instead of anger, they held each other like they'd been given news of her death. "I need to do this," she rasped, swallowing back the guilt that threatened to alter her decision.

"We can work through this. Don't shut us out." Their pale faces and pleading expressions were almost enough to change Mira's mind.

"I need to do this," she said again before escaping to her room. She closed the door behind her. For a moment, she leaned back against it, trying to shut out the pain she was feeling. It seemed like no matter what she did, she couldn't win.

"You are starting fresh," she told herself. "And it's time to focus on the positives and to do something for *me*!" She headed for the closet. Snagging several of her favorites, she grabbed a suitcase from the shelf. Laying it on the bed, she dumped clothing and toiletries inside. It would be enough for her to get by.

As she closed the suitcase, she glanced around. This was the last time she'd be in this room, as a resident anyway. She didn't know quite how she felt about that.

A soft knock sounded on her door.

Mira dabbed at the corners of her eyes, then after clearing her throat, said, "Yes?"

"I have something for you."

It was her mom.

"You can come in." Mira put the suitcase on the floor, ignoring the green sleeve that peeked out of it.

Her mom stepped inside and carefully closed the door behind her. She sat beside Mira on the bed. Her chin trembling, her brows knitted, her mom handed her an envelope. "I know I can't keep you from leaving, but I want you to have this."

"What is it?" Mira asked, lifting the envelope as if to test its weight.

"It's a reminder of who you really are and what you're meant for. It's where you will find true joy and completeness."

Mira had an idea of what she was getting at. "Your way hasn't worked for me yet," she said, the envelope feeling very heavy in her palm.

She closed Mira's fingers around the white rectangle. "I'm not here to give you a lecture, and even if I'd prefer you stayed here, I'm not going to try to talk you out of leaving." She wiped a tear rolling down her cheek. "But I refuse to let you walk out that door without the truth. Read what is in the envelope, Mira. Keep it close to your heart and know that God is always waiting for you to come back to where you belong."

Mira took the envelope and shoved it into her suitcase. "Thanks," she said, though her tone gave away her irritation. Why was her mom always trying to fix her? And why did she think her way was the only right one? "But this has nothing to do with God," Mira said as she dragged the suitcase to the door.

Her mom stayed sitting on the bed, looking like she had just been beaten in some alleyway. "Will you come back to see us?"

"Yeah. Sure."

"When?"

She'd be back when she was ready to deal with their manipulation, but she didn't say that. Lifting the suitcase she stepped over the threshold, probably for the last time. "I'll call you and let you know."

Chapter 22

"Hey. Wait up." Tory sounded breathless.

Nash slowed down so she could catch up to him.

"Where are we going, by the way?" she asked.

"To find Mira."

"What good will *that* do?"

"I just have this feeling she's in danger."

"Because of what happened to Kya? Or because you're jealous."

"Both, probably," he admitted, thinking about the book he'd just dumped in the trash.

"Maybe we should look at this more logically," Tory said.

Nash ran a hand through his hair as they continued down the street toward Mira's house. "You have one minute."

"Running after Mira and confronting her after she wanted space...where will that get you?"

He thought about that. "Probably nowhere." He kept walking. He had to do *something!*

"Okay. At least you're thinking somewhat clearly." She glanced up at him. "So let's consider the second part of the equation...Kya's homicide."

His heart felt sick. "With the killer on the loose, Mira isn't safe." He picked up his pace.

"No one is safe," Tory said. She grabbed the crux of his arm and stopped.

He looked down at the hand that was keeping him from his goal. Drawing in a deep breath, he met Tory's eyes. "I realize that..." He frowned. "Hey, you're not wearing your glasses."

"I got contacts."

"You look great," he said, meaning it. It gave her a whole new look.

"Thanks," she beamed, "and the good part about it is that I can still think, too."

He smiled an easy smile he hadn't thought would ever be possible for him again. "And what are you thinking?"

"That we need to concentrate on looking into Kya's death."

"Great idea." His smile broadened and he kissed her on the cheek. "That would definitely help me feel better." He took her hand and led her the opposite way down the block.

"Now where are we going?" she asked, trying to keep up.

"To Kya's house. Where else?"

"But it's taped off. Only the police and forensics are allowed."

He glanced down at her and tapped the end of her nose. "I used to be a Reformer…and you're a perfect forensics person. I think that qualifies us."

"But…"

"But I don't want them to miss anything. Between you and me, we could easily pick up on some clues that might lead us to the killer."

"But it's against the law," she said, stopping at the end of the block that would lead them to Kya's house.

"Then we just don't get caught," he said.

She folded her arms across her chest and shook her head. "You can't be serious!"

"I am," he said, giving her his most pleading look. "Please!"

She closed her eyes a moment. "I know I'm going to regret this, but alright."

Chapter 23

Mira stood in front of Cofa's Tree with a backpack on her back, a suitcase in her right hand, and an overstuffed duffle bag in her left. Her anger had dwindled on the walk over, and yet she was determined to see this through. It was time for her to become her own person, not someone defined by anything or anyone else. She put the suitcase down and opened the door. Propping it open with her foot, she stepped inside.

"Mira. You're here," Vashti stood behind the bar with a welcoming smile on her face.

"You didn't think I would be?" For some reason, that stung.

"I thought you might change your mind," Vashti said, though there wasn't any censure in her voice. "Tanger!" She spoke into a speaker box attached to the wall near the sink. "Mira is here."

Tanger appeared seconds later in the doorway that opened to steps. He didn't pause, but swooped in to give her a big hug and a kiss on the cheek. "I'm so glad you're here."

How much different his reception than Nash's in the music store...or even last night in her house for that matter! "Me too," she said, her insides aflutter.

"Do you want anything to eat?" Tanger asked.

She shook her head. Her stomach was too jumpy to eat.

"Would you like me to show you to your room, then?"

The quicker she got settled in, the better. "Absolutely," Mira said.

Vashti finished toweling off the plate she held. As she stowed it in the lower cabinet, she said, "Give her the gypsy room, Nash."

"Will do," Tanger said, glancing at Mira. "I think it will be perfect for her." His sanguine smile boosted Mira's resolve.

"Then what are we waiting for?" Mira asked, suddenly impatient.

Tanger chuckled. "Follow me, sweetheart." He grabbed her suitcase and duffle and headed up the steps.

Mira trailed behind, curious about the gypsy room. What would it be like to live here, especially with someone like Tanger close by? He almost seemed too good to be true – sweet, sexy, considerate. She climbed the narrow amber wood steps. Each had a depression in the center as if thousands had climbed them thousands of times. They all creaked. The stairs opened up into a long hallway with four doors on either side and one door at the far end.

"The bathroom is there," Tanger said, pointing to the door at the end of the hallway. "My room is to the left of it, room number four. Your room will be to the right, directly across from mine. Room number five to be exact."

"Where's Vashti's room?"

He looked at her over his shoulder as he wandered down the tapestry-style runner that covered the hall floor. "She has a room downstairs…behind the store."

"And who lives in these other rooms?"

He opened the door to room number five…*her* room. "Vashti rents them out by the night. Amaryllis is currently staying in room number one. Houser stays in room eight, when he doesn't want to travel all the way back to his house. The others are rented out to some people going to the big concert tonight."

Mention of Nash's concert brought on a fresh wave of hurt. When she'd seen him earlier in the park, she'd immediately regretted how she'd handled everything between them. Yet after seeing how alive he'd looked talking to his fans, pride had kept her from groveling and going to talk to him. Oh how she missed him, even though she didn't want to! She still longed to have that same rush of love back again, just like old times. But those times were gone. Houser helped her realize that. And he'd been so nice, listening intently to all her babbling. The least she could do was consider his advice. He'd told her now was the time to live fully in the present, not the past, and he'd reassured her things were about to get better for her. He seemed so certain. She hoped he was right!

"So, what do you think?" Tanger asked, jarring her from her thoughts.

Mira stepped inside the room. The bed - littered with a variety of pillows and a quilt of many fabrics and colors - sat against a stone covered wall. Tucked into a cove, flowing earth-toned material made bookends around it. Candles sat on each nightstand, and on the desk that stood beneath the window overlooking B Street. The remaining walls and the stamped ceiling were terracotta in color. And several rugs covered the wooden floor, giving it an even warmer feel. "It's really nice," she said.

"I thought you would like it." Tanger laid her things between the oval standing mirror and a scratched up rocking chair that listed to the side. "It's our most colorful room, and…" he tilted his head as he studied her, "it seems fitting for someone who has wanderlust yet is looking for a sort of family to belong to."

She tried to keep her heart open, but skepticism won out. "You could say that about anyone."

"Yeah. Maybe."

At his easy agreement, her suspicion melted into curiosity.

Tanger opened a narrow door. "Come check out this closet. It's made out of cedar."

Mira sniffed and headed his way. As she skirted around the mirror, her foot caught on the edge of the thick rug beneath it. Her ankle rolled painfully, and she heard a slight pop. "Oh ow!" she wailed, clutching her ankle as she hopped on one foot.

Tanger was beside her immediately, and scooped her up. As he carried her to the bed, he said, "Wait here." Laying her down carefully, he left the room.

Mira's ankle pulsed. She quickly removed her shoe and groaned. Her foot was puffing up like a marshmallow in the microwave.

Tanger returned carrying a small bowl of paste that smelled like ginger, honey, cucumber, and something very pungent.

"What is that stuff?" she asked, crinkling up her nose.

"It's my secret healing poultice." He sat at the base of the bed and lifted her now bare foot onto his lap. "It's already bruising. You really did a number on yourself."

"It pretty much goes along with the day I'm having," she grumbled.

"Want to share?" Tanger dipped his fingers into the mash and layered it onto her ankle.

She sucked in a breath. "No. I want to forget."

"I can easily help you with that, if that's what you really want," he said with a soft smile.

"That would be nice," she said, squeezing her eyes shut to help her forget everything but the feel of his hands on her skin. She relaxed even more as the salve became warm beneath his touch. The pressure from his fingertips - that had at first hurt like mad - now felt soothing.

"You're beautiful, you know," he said.

She peeked at him. His lazy grin making her heart trip. Adrenalin zinged through her body. She didn't know what to say, so she just stared at him.

"How does it feel?" he asked.

Intense...hot... "How does what feel?" she asked.

He laughed softly. "Your ankle."

She circled her foot to the right and then to the left. "It feels better than before I rolled it."

"You haven't seen anything yet, doll." His eyes sizzled with promise, reminding her of the poem he'd written...the one she'd overheard. His gaze entranced her. She couldn't look away.

Tanger shifted on the bed and she thought for a moment that he would kiss her. But he didn't. After patting her ankle lightly, he stood up. "Rest that for a few minutes and I'll put away your things."

"You don't have to do that."

"I want to."

It would keep him here longer…which meant she'd have time to get to know him better. And she wanted to know everything. As she watched him pick up her suitcase, she asked, "So what do you do for fun?"

Unzipping the bag he had set on the chair, he said, "I have a lot of interests. I do like to spend time on my art the most, though."

"I'd like to see it sometime."

"And I'd like to show you," he said, opening the flap to reveal her wad of clothing. "Maybe you could model for me even."

She snorted.

"What? You don't think I'm serious?" His playful eyes met hers.

"I don't think you would really want me as a model, Tanger."

His gaze grazed her from head to toe. "I would. I definitely would."

His words made her feel more beautiful than she had in a long time. She watched as he went back to his task of carefully folding the items she'd carelessly tossed into the suitcase.

"And I'm going to make sure you know just how beautiful you are," he added. As he grabbed the next balled up shirt, the envelope her mom had given her flipped out and dropped to the floor.

He bent to pick it up.

"Give me that," she said, swinging her legs around so that her feet touched the floor.

He said nothing, but held the envelope out to her.

Cautiously, she stood up. "Hey, my ankle feels great!"

"I'm glad," he said with a knowing smile.

Mira took the envelope from him. As she stashed it in her nightstand drawer, Vashti's voice piped through an intercom hanging near the light switch. "Mira and Tanger…we have some visitors," she said.

"Are those intercoms in every room?" Mira asked.

"Unfortunately, yes," Tanger said with a shake of his head.

Mira laughed, but began to nibble on her bottom lip when he propped the doll she'd acquired from Houser into the rocking chair. She'd have to move it out of sight later – when her helpful hero wasn't there to see.

"Why don't you both come down and meet them," Vashti said.

Tanger frowned at the intercom as he zipped up the empty suitcase. "I'd say no, but Vashti usually has her reasons." He took Mira's hand. "You know, my little gypsy, I am going to like you being close by."

"I have a feeling I'm going to like it too," she said, a little breathless as she walked with him downstairs to meet the new visitors.

Chapter 24

Nash and Tory approached the ranch style house that Kya had rented. The slate blue paint was peeling, and the shingles had begun to curl under their blanket of yellow-green moss. Besides the flutter of the yellow tape that marked it as a crime scene, the house was lifelessly silent and bleak.

"You sure about this?" Tory paused at the edge of the driveway to look up the street.

Nash glanced the other way, toward the dead end, then back at the house. "I'm sure they're done gathering evidence." He lifted his leg over the tape, but Tory grabbed his arm, stopping him.

"I really think we should leave this to the authorities."

Nash wanted to say that he used to *be* the authority and that he knew what he was doing, but he was no longer that person even though pieces of his past still came alive in him at moments like these. "I don't really trust the authorities to be all that thorough." Nash pulled out of her grasp and marched up the driveway. He let himself in through the garage where Kya's van was parked. He'd ridden in that van. A powerful feeling came over him as he touched the window, looking through it as if he could see into his past.

"You're doing this for Mira, aren't you?" Tory's soft voice interrupted his mind's meanderings.

"I don't trust the new police system," he whispered, "and I want to make sure we are *all* safe. We have to find Kya's killer." Nash brushed past her and headed into Kya's house. The kitchen looked clean. There were no dishes in the sink, but the garbage was starting to smell. Obviously, the police hadn't gone through everything, just as he'd feared. "You check the garbage and then the bathroom. I'll investigate the rest of the rooms."

"Why do I get the stinky garbage and the place she was found dead?" Tory asked, but she was already opening the cupboard beneath the sink where the garbage can was located.

"Because you're better with smells…and blood."

She snorted. "Wimp."

In the past, smells and blood wouldn't have bothered him. Actually, right now, it wouldn't bother him except for the fact it was someone he'd known, someone that Mira truly cared about. "Nice vase of dead roses on the table," he said, bypassing the card-free bunch of blackened flowers. He wondered who had given them to her, and when.

Nash wandered down the hallway. As he entered Kya's bedroom, Tory yelled out, "Found an empty wine bottle."

Had Kya shared wine with her murderer? With a growing knot in his stomach, he rummaged through her drawers. Nothing strange there, but he did find one black lace stocking stuck to the inside of her wicker laundry basket. Nash filed it away into his memory then went to search her nightstands. The first was empty but for one long blond hair trapped in the spliced corner. As he knelt beside the other nightstand, his thigh brushed against the something hard. He glanced down. A book jutted out from between her mattress and box spring. With shaking hands, he pulled it out. It was a journal.

"I found drops of blood by the tub. You find anything?" Tory called out in a loud whisper.

"Yeah. A journal." He sat down on the floor and flipped to the first page.

I'm writing in a new journal today because my prophetic word told me that I needed to start fresh. Vaughn is with his true love now. I'm happy for him, but I don't know how to move on. I don't know if I can. I've had many dates with many men, and yet I feel so empty inside. I don't know how to stop the pain.

Kya's loneliness came powerfully through her words, so much that Nash found himself choking up. He wondered if she'd been suicidal. But no, the evidence pointed to murder. He flipped to the last entry.

I can't believe he's coming here and that I'm finally going to see his face. I can't wait! I even cleaned my house, if you can imagine. I'm not sure he will be able to make me forget Vaughn, but I feel he's different somehow, and that it's a step in the right direction. Oh…oh…he's here. But he's not alone.

Nash turned the page, hoping for more. It was blank. Standing up, he flipped back to her second entry.

"What are you doing here?" asked a deep voice that sounded like it came from across the hall.

Nash froze. Tory answered the guy. "I just stopped by to see my friend Kya."

"You're trespassing. Didn't you see the tape?"

"What tape?"

Tory looked smart. Her answer wasn't going to fly, Nash thought.

"Alright," the guy said with a loud sigh. "Come with me."

Nash closed the journal with care, then tucked it back beneath the mattress. His mind scrambled for a way to save Tory, but he couldn't think of anything. And he couldn't risk getting caught himself. He had a concert to perform, the chance of a lifetime…one he couldn't blow.

Off Kya's room was a small deck, he noticed. Guilt smacked him in the chest as he reached for the sliding door's handle. But heavy footsteps grew closer with each second. He had to decide now! He slipped outside, his movements quick and silent. Once on the deck, he spotted a wildly growing hedge that skirted Kya's property. He jumped the cedar railing and ducked behind the greenery. Peeking around it, he caught sight of Tory being lowered into the back seat of the police car.

"I'm so sorry, Tory," he whispered. As they drove off, he told himself she'd be fine - that she'd just be charged with a trespassing misdemeanor like he had been. Tory would surely understand and want him to get to his show and have his best performance ever.

Once the car was out of view, Nash checked his watch. He had only minutes to spare before his pre-performance began. Shame begged him to go to the police station, but he told himself it wouldn't be any help to Tory…only trouble for him – especially with the trespassing that had just been added to his record.

"I guess it's time to make it big," he said, and took off down the street. As he neared the end of the block, he looked back over his shoulder at the dismal house. "But I won't rest until I find your killer, Kya." A cool wind brushed across his clammy skin, making him shiver. Perhaps Kya's soul was thinking the same thing.

Chapter 25

When Mira stepped into the dining area of Cofa's Tree, her eyes were immediately drawn to the woman who sat beside Vashti. She had long flowing golden hair, heightened in its beauty by a crown of flowers. The golden dress she wore exposed her shoulders and accentuated a locket with the picture of an eye on the front of it. Mira couldn't seem to take her eyes off the locket, which seemed to be staring directly at her.

Vashti stood up and waved them forward, so Mira and Tanger joined them at the table.

"Mira, this is Sylvia, the founder of our group," Vashti said.

Mira rested her hands on the chair back and nodded at the woman. "Nice to meet you."

"And you," she said. She proceeded to use her fingerless-gloved hands to make circular motions about an inch above the table's surface - like she was wiping off the table without touching it. Mira had no idea what she was doing, but neither Tanger nor Vashti seemed surprised by it.

The front door to the shop opened. Three young ladies came in wearing bright smiles and very tiny bikinis smudged with mud. Mira had seen them take pictures with Nash earlier that day and felt a surge of jealousy.

"These are my three understudies…Daphne, Daria, and Tinker."

Instead of saying nice to meet you, as she felt she ought to do, Mira blurted, "Are you here for the concert?"

The three nodded in unison. "And we need to get ready," one said as she headed toward the stairs.

"Because we got backstage passes," the middle one added, following after her.

"And we have a bet on which one will get Nash Montgomery to come back here after the concert," said the last as she skated along behind the other two.

Mira's heart squeezed, but she told herself that they were just talking. Who wouldn't be dreaming about having Nash as their own? But what would she do if Nash actually came back to Cofa's Tree with one of them? How would she ever be able to handle it?

"I see what the girls said has troubled you," Sylvia said.

"I guess a little." Mira shrugged, trying not to look the woman's third eye. "Nash and I...we were a couple, until recently."

Sylvia glanced at Tanger, who then took a step closer to Mira.

"So what's the problem then? Or haven't you moved on?" Vashti asked.

"I'm the one that called it off." She frowned. "I guess I just want more than he's willing to give me." Admitting it was harder than she'd thought.

"What if I told you that you are the director of your life," Sylvia chimed in, "and that you can change the actors, the setting, or the channel any time you choose?"

Interesting concept. Mira moved to sit down on the chair across from her. "I don't feel like I'm directing anything."

"Then you should do some spiritual aerobics to help you change that," Sylvia said.

"What do you mean by spiritual aerobics?"

"It's a process...a transformation that starts with changing your perception of reality. When you do that, your reality will happily conform to your perception."

"So I can create a life I want just by thinking it?"

"Pretty much, yes."

The entire group stared at her with a confidence she craved. Was it possible? Maybe. And just think of the life she could have! "Okay. What do I do?"

"First, visualize what you want to happen with Nash," Vashti said.

Even though Tanger was right next to her, Mira said, "I'm not sure what I want to happen. Maybe that I can forget him and move on?" Yet even as she said the words, she didn't know if that was entirely true.

"That's a good start. Now close your eyes and picture him as he enters Cofa's Tree with, say Daphne. How do you feel?" Sylvia asked.

"Horrible."

"Now, I want you to think about it differently – maybe like this: Nash was just a stepping stone in your life, a love to enjoy until the next phase of your spiritual growth. He was holding you back, but you have so much to explore, so much life to live, so much yet to enjoy," Sylvia said.

A little of the pressure in Mira's chest eased. "Yes. I can picture that."

"Now envision Nash coming here with Daphne again. How will you treat him? What can you do to prove to yourself that you've moved on?" Vashti asked.

Mira still didn't want to think about it, but she forced herself to, and then she let her thoughts twist into a manageable plan. "I'll treat him with nonchalance…and then to prove that I'm over him, I'll hang out with Tanger." *Fake it until you make it,* she thought.

"That's just what I'm talking about." Sylvia stood up and offered Mira an encouraging smile. "You're off to a great start, Mira."

"I am?"

She nodded as she made her way to the stairs. "You're taking responsibility for your life, and have taken the first step in transforming your reality and yourself to match your choices and your dreams."

Something bloomed inside her, something powerful and wonderful. Mira straightened her shoulders. "I am, aren't I!"

Vashti grinned and patted her on the shoulder. Tanger leaned over to whisper in her ear. "So what do you say we give your nonchalance a test?"

A tiny ribbon of pleasure shot through her veins. "What did you have in mind?"

He reached into his back pocket and pulled out two backstage passes. "Will you join me?"

Her heart hammered in reaction and her mouth felt suddenly parched as anxiety leaped into her throat. Yet if she was going to move on, she needed to take action. "I will," she said.

Chapter 26

Nash entered the onsite trailer set up entirely for him. It looked like a house on wheels, and was filled with top of the line stuff…leather couches, granite countertops, and a complete bar with a sound system he couldn't have dreamed up. Even the bathroom was top notch and included a granite shower with multiple showerheads and a Jacuzzi tub.

He wandered into the room located toward the back. He was told he'd find his show clothes there. "Porsche doesn't miss anything," he said, rifling through the closet filled with items that were his size and his style, only more top-of-the-line in quality. He picked out a pair of skinny jeans, a white belt, and a tank top, which would look great under the white button-down shirt with rolled sleeves. After laying the ensemble on the bed, he sat down to take off his ratty shoes. That's when he noticed the art work displayed on the window shades.

The hand-painted scenes from around the world displayed a variety of people and landscapes, hinting at where his career might take him, but also reminding him that the landscape of his own life had changed against his own will. Mira…he wanted to shake her and hold her close at the same time - only he wasn't allowed either option. Getting up off the softest mattress he'd ever felt, he meandered over to the shades, brushing his fingertips along their slightly raised lines. His eyes traveled over the details, wandering to the bottom of the piece. When he saw the artist's flowing signature, he released the breath he hadn't even realized he'd been holding. It belonged not to Mira Kinneson, but to Houser.

"Figures," Nash snorted and went back to the stack of clothes he'd laid on his bed. Something about that guy rubbed him the wrong way.

Stripping down to his briefs, Nash donned his stage clothes. A glance in the mirror told him he looked the part, but he was a long way from getting excited about his performance tonight. After all, he'd left Tory to the cops and an impulsive Mira to who knew what with the people at Cofa's Tree. Not like it was his problem anymore, but the knot in his stomach grew every time he thought about her there. He had to get into that place to check it out, to make sure she was safe.

Nash shook his head. "You can take the guy out of the Reformer job, but you can't take the reformer out of the guy, I guess," he said, *or the love out of his heart*, he silently added. Sweeping his bangs to the side, he tried to think about his music. The tune to *Discover Me* planted itself in his mind, along with all the emotions it invoked. His music could not be separate from his life. Why couldn't Mira see that? With a groan, he grabbed the pair of black pull-on ankle boots sitting at the foot of the bed. The soft leather cradled his feet, the grip tape strap along the back giving them a fun, but expensive look.

He glanced at himself again in the wall-sized mirror. This was the new Nash. He was no longer in a position of authority. Instead of fighting to reign in the city's *extreme freedom mindset*, he was permitted to utilize those unclear boundaries to suit his purposes. Was this logical? No. Was this beneficial? Probably not, but if it got him what he wanted, he didn't really care.

Wandering to the stocked bar, Nash picked up the left end bottle on the middle shelf. After pouring a goodly amount into the glass, he took a swig. His eyes watered something fierce as the liquid left a trail of fire all the way down his throat. Swiping the back of his hand across his lips, he leaned against the counter and felt warmth spread throughout his body. Was this what they meant by a buzz? Unfortunately, it didn't work to numb his brain – or his heart.

"Time to greet your backstage fans," came a loud voice, accompanied by a knock on his trailer door.

Nash slapped his cheek three times. *Get out of this funk, now,* he muttered to himself. *This is an opportunity of a lifetime.* He pushed away from the counter and went to the door. "On my way," he said, opening it. *Houser.* He couldn't help but frown.

"Nice seeing you again, too," Houser said with a half-grin. He seemed totally unaffected by Nash's glower.

"Sorry. I just saw you talking to my ex earlier today," Nash admitted. "It's nothing personal."

Houser laughed. "Sounds *very* personal to me." He clapped Nash on the back. "Don't worry. I was just a listener that was close by."

"What did she say?" Nash asked, walking alongside him toward the stage.

He shrugged as he took out a cigarette and lit it. "That she's confused about her life, mostly, and was anxious to do something about it."

"Like what?"

"Like move into Cofa's Tree, for one." Houser looked at him. "I think it will be good for her."

Nash didn't comment, but the information made his stomach turn. He needed to get into Cofa's Tree! As the pair approached the door that led backstage, the sounds of excited chatter grew louder. The group waiting to spend time with him was definitely not a timid one, Nash thought.

"You'll really enjoy this if you let yourself, you know," Houser said, flicking the ash from his cigarette before taking another puff.

"I know. But I'm used to relaxing and getting in the zone before my performances."

"And?"

"It's just a big change, I guess."

"I get it, but that's half the fun." Houser dropped the butt of the cig and smashed it beneath his booted foot. "Don't forget about the emergency kit in the bathroom cupboard that Porsche left for you. It might come in really handy."

"I won't," Nash said with a forced smile. Taking a deep breath, he opened the door, determined to make a splash with his fans…and to enjoy it, too. The first groupies he saw were the bikini girls…only they weren't wearing bikinis anymore. Their skintight mini dresses, each a different color and pattern, hugged their curves and exposed just enough skin to entice a saint. He grinned at them. "Hi girls. So glad you could make it."

The one with the red hair and purple dress turned around to grab her purse off a leather chair, giving Nash a glimpse of some of the others in the backstage group. Nash felt his heart drop to his toes. Tanger and Mira…they were here! How was he ever going to get through this?

Chapter 27

"I'll grab a drink and join you all."

Nash's voice was easily recognizable in the small space. Mira peeked around Tanger and caught Nash's gaze. He quickly looked away, but she'd seen the hurt.

Like a Reformer on assignment rather than a musician mingling with fans, Nash wove through the group to the open bar with its disco light flashing overhead.

"Maybe we should go," Mira said to Tanger.

"He'll get over it," Tanger said, handing her the drink he'd made especially for her. "Drink up."

"What is it?" she asked, her eyes glued to Nash's back.

"It's called *Devil May Care*. It's to help you in your efforts to be nonchalant." He nudged her so she'd look at him. He gave her an encouraging smile. "Just trying to help."

She took a swig. The drink was cold and delicious. "I hope it works because I don't feel nonchalant at all. I feel like crap." For many reasons...all balled into one knot in her stomach.

She turned her attention back to Nash, who had wandered over to a group sitting beside a high table. He had a small glass of wine in hand. His cheeks were flushed, accentuating the overly bright smile plastered on his face.

"Say cheese," Houser said, approaching the group with his camera.

The fans huddled in close to get their picture taken with Nash.

"So what are your plans for tomorrow?" Tanger asked her.

Mira said the first thing that came to her head. "I'll probably go down to Wormwood's Water to take some practice photos." She watched Nash leave the table to work his way through the idolizing crowd. Several women hung on him, their eyes full of adoration, their lips smiling as they chattered. Even the guys laughed and joked with him. His fans loved him! *Of course they did!* Mira thought.

"Yoo-hoo." Tanger flicked the collar of her shirt. "Don't start falling for him again just because he's on his way to fame."

"I'm not. Sorry," she said, but maybe that did have something to do with what she was feeling right now. She looked up at Tanger. He didn't look upset, only amused.

"I'm not doing such a good job of helping you move on to more exciting things, am I?" he asked.

She admired Tanger's way of saying the way things were. "It's not your responsibility."

"But it *is* my pleasure," he said with a wink and a smile that would melt any woman's heart.

Mira knew she had to move on…and that meant putting her strategy into action so she could. Closing her eyes, she tried to think of Nash as a stepping stone – he was just one of those people to ride her life train for a short amount of time, only now it was time for her next stop. She imagined Tanger getting on the train as Nash got off of it. Her heart ached and begged for something to lessen the pain. In her mind, she knew what that was. She needed to take the next step and make it a reality. Opening her eyes again, she said, "Kiss me."

Tanger stared at her a moment. "Are you sure you want to go there?"

She wasn't, but she had to do something, or she'd race out of there like a coward and heart-aching fool. "I'm sure."

Instead of kissing her, though, Tanger took her hand and brought her over to where Nash was busy showing off his guitar skills to a circle of fans. Mira tried to put the brakes on, but Tanger coaxed her to a spot directly in front of Nash. Nash's hands stilled and he looked over at her with longing and regret. For a moment, she lost her breath and her nerve.

"Will you play a song for us, Nash?" Tanger asked, holding Mira firmly in place beside him.

Nash tore his gaze from Mira to stare down at his fingers that were pressed tightly around the neck of the guitar. He cleared his throat. "What would you like me to play?"

"Moving On," Tanger said.

Mira forgot to breathe. Could she do this? She had to! Would Nash bow out? The song was one of the first he had written, so there was no getting out of it due to not knowing it. But would he have another excuse?

Mira waited, forcing the thick air in and out of her constricted lungs. After several quiet moments, Nash finally nodded and started the beautiful introduction. Tanger pulled her into his arms and began to sway to the tune.

"Now look at me," Tanger whispered into her ear.

Nash's tenor voice trembled slightly as he sang the words to the song he'd written when he'd moved on from his emotionless, LifeChipped state to one of passion and excitement, hopes and dreams. The words fit perfectly for what she was feeling, yet even though she kept her eyes trained on Tanger, the connection she felt still belonged to Nash.

"Will it get easier?" she asked, trying to convince herself that what she was doing was the right thing for her.

"It will," Tanger promised. As the song neared the end, he dipped his head so that his lips were mere inches from hers. "Are you ready for this?"

She knew he was talking about the kiss, and she could see hunger and caring in his eyes. "Yes. I'm ready."

Tanger leaned in, pressing his full, soft lips against hers. His eyes closed even as cheers went up around them. Mira didn't know if they were cheering for the kiss, or for Nash's performance of the song, but it didn't matter. She'd done it. She'd taken the next step to moving on.

At the clunk of Nash putting his guitar down, Tanger ended the kiss. He smiled at her in a way that she knew he was proud of her...and that he desired her. It felt good. Yet when she turned and saw Nash, guilt stabbed her right in the heart. Nash's eyes were filled with pain...pain she'd put there.

"I'm sorry Nash," she mouthed, trying to pull away from Tanger, only Tanger wouldn't let her go.

Nash just shook his head and, raising his glass of wine, he called out, "Here's to moving on!"

"Here, here," came shouts from the fans as they joined him in his toast, tapping their drink glasses together.

Out of the shadows came an ear-splitting bang, startling the whole group. They all turned toward the sound. Houser had appeared, a cowbell in hand. "It's time to clear out and find your spots down front. Nash needs a few minutes to warm up before his performance," he announced.

Nash seemed happy about that idea and quickly took a spot near the exit. As the fans filed out of the backstage area, he shook hands with or hugged each of them. When the three bikini girls approached, though, Nash went one step further and planted a kiss on the lips of the blonde one in the middle.

Daphne. Mira's imaginings from earlier hadn't been far off. *They seemed chummy, but at least they weren't at Cofa's Tree together!* Mira thought. She didn't know if she was ready to handle that yet.

"Are we still on for tonight?" Nash asked the girl, swaying a little on his feet.

Daphne gave him a thumb's up. "Cofa's Tree for an after concert get together, right?"

What?! Mira's heart swung into a gallop.

"Yep. See you later tonight then," Nash said with a promising smile as he waved them off.

The only two fans remaining were Mira and Tanger. Tanger approached Nash. "Thanks for the song, dude," he said, and with a quick nod, moved outside.

"Yeah, sure," Nash said, his face a mask Mira couldn't read.

As she moved in front of him, he wouldn't meet her eyes. She glanced through the doorway to where Tanger now stood, on the lawn out of earshot. Knowing she was alone with Nash, Mira considered a quickly blurted "thanks-good-bye" as she escaped, but she reminded herself that she needed to take control of her thoughts and her life.

"I'm sorry if the dance made you feel bad," she said, trying to be as upfront as she could be. "I don't want to hurt you."

Nash shrugged. "We called it quits. You can do what you want."

"Good," she said, although part of her wanted him to put up more of a fight. But he hadn't in the music store, and he didn't now.

Rubbing the back of his neck, Nash leaned against the door frame. "Thanks for coming," he said. This time, he managed to meet her eyes. His were hard and unforgiving.

The distance between them seemed to grow.

"Well, good luck with your concert." She tried to smile. "I know you'll be a big hit." She frowned. "I always knew." Which was one reason, she reminded herself, that she'd chosen to go a different way. It's okay, she told herself. It's all going to be okay.

"Thanks." He looked at her coolly for a second longer before reaching behind him. The motion knocked the cowbell to the floor. He ignored it, snagging the water bottle off the chest-high speaker so he could take a big swig. "Anything else?"

She didn't know what else to say, so she shook her head. "Goodbye, Nash."

"Goodbye, Mira."

Mira hurried down the steps to where Tanger waited, forcing herself to not look back. Pasting a bright smile on her face, she said, "So where do you want to stand?"

Chapter 28

Nash stared at the growing crowd on the lawn through the trailer door. Even though Mira had told him last night that she wanted space, he hadn't dreamed of her immediate – and obviously serious - involvement with another guy. How could she do such a thing after all they'd been through together? How could she move on so easily – and then flaunt it too?

Nash shut the door and leaned his forehead against it. It just didn't seem like something Mira would do! Could she have changed that much without him noticing? Or maybe Tory was right...maybe he and Mira had become a team only because they'd been on a mission together. But did that mean Mira and Tanger were working on something together? The thought rankled.

"You okay?" Houser said, laying a hand on his shoulder.

Nash turned around and sniffed, trying to ignore the bubbling acid in his stomach. "I'm fine." He wasn't, but Houser didn't need to know that. "I just need a pick-me-up before I go on stage." Nash brushed past him.

"I understand," Houser said, giving him a knowing look.

Nash shoved away the feeling that he was a weak idiot and headed to the bathroom. It was small, but clean, with a built in vanity mirror, which he opened. The emergency kit sat on the top shelf. Wanting a cure, or at least something to kill the pain, he reached for the white metal container. Opening it, he stared at the pills stashed inside. Popping one of them would probably make this night easier. Only he knew better – knew the risks...*and* the results of taking these, but was it worth it? Could he, without the numbing effects of the drugs, bear to see Mira, swaying in Tanger's arms to music he couldn't even perform without thinking about her?

He clutched the kit, sweat popping out on his forearms as his head fought with his heart. He took a deep breath and then another. No...he'd get through this on his own. And he would get himself into Cofa's Tree tonight to find out what was going on with Mira. It wasn't too late! It couldn't be too late! There had to be something more…something he was missing. Stashing the kit back into the cabinet, he polished off the remainder of his water and escaped the tiny bathroom with only a twinge of regret at his decision. Houser was waiting beside the curtain that divided the back room from the stage.

"No opening band tonight. It's all you," Houser said, holding out his hand.

Nash approached him, frowning down at his outstretched hand.

"The water bottle," Houser said, eyebrows raised.

Nash gave him the empty plastic water bottle, expecting him to throw it away. Instead, Houser put it into his backpack – which Nash noticed also contained a doll.

"I'm building a mansion with these, in case you're wondering," he said with a smile.

He *had* been wondering. "I'm more curious about the doll."

"I collect them, study their history." He shrugged. "It's surprisingly interesting, especially because we lived for over thirty years without them."

Pillar had gone without a lot of things for thirty years. "Whatever rocks your socks, Houser," Nash said, picking up the electric guitar that was propped against the wall. As was his routine, he plucked the strings, listening carefully to see if each was in tune. He couldn't help but remember the first time he'd seen, and played a guitar. It had been shortly after becoming chipless. He'd been at The Compound, and Mira had shown him the instrument. She'd played it so horribly, he felt himself cringe, then smile. No, he couldn't let himself go there.

Even though his heart reacted by hammering a bruising rhythm, he aimed his eyes on Porsche, who was in the middle of announcing him on stage. The way she made him sound was fantastic. If he hadn't known it was him that she was talking about, he'd be pumped to hear the musician she was describing. But it *was* him. And he was going to be a super star. He could feel it.

The drums started their plodding rhythmic beat that slowly increased in speed. His heart did the same.

"And now, let's bring out that special someone who if you don't know and love him already, you will. Nash Montgomery!"

As Nash stepped out from the curtain, he swayed a little, but managed to stabilize himself and jog onto stage, front and center. He looked out at the sea of faces, yelling, screaming, taking pictures He lifted his guitar high and tilted his head back, drinking it in. They were all there to hear him! He allowed the smiles and the cheers to transport him to a new world where he was king over a country called Euphoria. This was who he was meant to be. He was made for this! And he was going to enjoy every minute.

"Hello Pillar!" he called out.

Another cheer rose up.

"Thank you. Thank you," he said with a grin that, for the first time that night, was genuine. As he waited for the noise to die down, he glimpsed Mira in Tanger's arms and vowed he wouldn't let her ruin his night. Better yet, maybe he could prove to her that he was more than just a mission partner. "Hey you…" he pointed at Daphne who sat right down the row from Tanger and Mira, "the blond in the animal print dress. Come on up here."

Daphne pointed to herself and raised one eyebrow.

"Yeah you." Nash glimpsed Mira's reaction. It had definitely affected her.

As Daphne made her way to the stage, the crowd hooted and whistled. Nash reached for her outstretched hand and helped her up the steps and onto the stage. "Tell the crowd your name, sweetheart," he said.

"You already know it, handsome, but it's Daphne," she said.

He smiled. "And Daphne, are you ready to get this party started?"

"Oh yes I am, sugar," she said over the thunderous cheers.

Nash put his arm around her shoulders. "What do you say we perform a song for Daphne?"

The crowd screamed. Mira remained still, staring at the stage.

He had to play this just right. "Alright, but I'm going to let you in on a secret first," Nash said.

The crowd quieted enough that the blender at the Smoothie Cart sounded blaringly loud.

"It's the first time anyone has ever heard this song since I've completed it. And I want to dedicate it to Daphne." His fans exploded with a loud and steady chant of *hoot, hoot, hoot, hoot.*

Nash couldn't spot Mira as he ushered Daphne back toward the edge of the stage, but he had to see this thing through. As he helped the girl back down the steps, he said, "See you later, doll," and kissed her cheek before giving her a pat on the butt.

The audience loved it. Filled with an energy and a rush he hadn't known possible, he strummed the first chord of *Discover Me,* and let the flashing cameras and idolizing crowd absorb and revive his crushed soul.

Chapter 29

To think that alcohol would help her cope seemed ludicrous now. Mira adjusted her pillow and stared at the painted ceiling above her bed, willing it to quit spinning and her mind to quit looping through the events of the evening. She swiped a hand across her sweat-dampened forehead. When she'd left backstage, she'd thought her new power had worked quite well. But misery had glommed onto her like dirt on a dropped sucker.

After seeing Nash put the moves on Daphne, after seeing how he relished his new fame, Mira realized a door of her past had closed. Why did she feel so horrible?

"I'm okay with this," Mira whispered, trying to believe it. "I have new friends, an inclusive group to belong to, new ways to think, and new opportunities to be the me I want to be. What could be better than that?" *Less after-effects of too much to drink would be better*, she thought. She kicked the covers to the side and sipped in tiny breaths of air to help relieve the nausea of overindulgence.

"Focus on the positives of tonight," she rasped, trying to shift her thoughts to those less miserable. Only one stuck out...Tanger. He was unlike anyone she'd ever met. Not only had he been sweet and understanding, but his kiss goodnight had nearly melted her on the spot with its promises. It would be enough for now...a step in the right direction.

Finally, the vertigo eased and her eyelids grew heavy. Yet just as her lashes lowered to meld into a peaceful rest, she heard something that sounded like a baby crying. Her eyes popped back open. The sound came again. Had Vashti rented a room to someone with a baby? Mira edged up onto her elbow, the movement unsettling her stomach. There it was again! It was a mewling pathetic sound, as if the child had been abandoned to a cold dark room with no hope of comfort or reprieve. Tucking the blanket around her ears, Mira tried to shut out the noise. It didn't work – and the cries became more insistent! Didn't anyone hear the baby's crying? After a few minutes, she couldn't stand it anymore.

A new sense of purpose - spurred by irritation - overshadowed her earlier distress and refreshed her mind and body to full alertness. Mira turned on the lamp and got out of bed. She wore short shorts and a flimsy t-shirt so she went to her closet to grab the robe she'd brought. As she reached for it, she heard another cry. She froze. It sounded so close! Heart slamming against her chest, she reached for the closet's light switch and flipped it on.

"This can't be real!" she gasped and dashed out of the closet, slamming the door shut behind her. She ran to her room door, intent on escape, yet when she reached for the knob, she paused. Tanger would think she was out of her mind if she'd told him what she'd just experienced! Seriously…who would believe that the doll sitting on top of the trunk in her closet had actually cried? Could the alcohol she'd drunk have caused her to hallucinate? She didn't think so – especially because her stomach had settled and the spinning had stopped.

"But it can't be real," she reminded herself. She had to be imagining things and taking a second look would prove it. She crept back toward the closet, her mind going in all kinds of directions. She truly hoped it wasn't some lost soul left behind during the place's sanitarium days! Opening the closet door, she held her breath and stepped inside. Her gaze swept over to the creepy doll. It wasn't crying. Although relief washed over her, the thought that her mind could be playing tricks on her was almost worse than it really being true. Snatching the creepy figure off its perch, she stuffed it into the old trunk and locked it inside with the tarnished metal key, which she stashed high on the shelf above her hanging clothes.

Backing out of the dark closet space, she paused, listening. All was silent, but she'd never be able to sleep now. Maybe a splash of water on her face or a snack would help. She escaped into the hallway. As she closed her door behind her, she heard a shrill female voice.

"Stop."

It was Daphne and she was standing by the door to her room, swatting at Nash's hand as he tried to use her belt loop to get himself off the floor. When he managed to stand with the help of the wall, he turned. His glazed eyes locked onto Mira.

"Hey babe. Care to join us?" he said loudly.

Babe?

"You're not invited," Daphne piped in, fumbling to get her key into the lock.

Mira's nausea returned full force, forming a knot of hate, jealousy and hurt that wanted her to lash out – or to curl up in a ball and weep. She refused to do either. This was her real test. Mira knew she needed to implement the reality she had created in her mind only hours ago. "I'd have said no anyway."

Daphne managed to get her door open. As Nash moved to follow her inside, he lunged to kiss her but the sloppy kiss landed on her ear. Daphne only laughed and kissed him right on the mouth. He seemed more than happy about it.

Mira rolled her shoulders back and sucked in her queasy stomach. She really had to force herself to let Nash go…now. "I guess I'll say goodnight, then."

Nash's head whipped around and, for a moment, he looked perplexed. As he stared, his glassy eyes turned wondering and wanting while challenging Mira at the same time. "Don't go," he said, shoving Daphne away from him. "I need to talk to you."

Even though her heart considered it, Mira grabbed at ways to wound him and to help her break it off for good. "Actually, I was just going to see Tanger. You and I will have to talk another time." She reached for Tanger's doorknob, hoping it was unlocked and that she wouldn't look like a fool.

"Well enjoy," Daphne said, trying to tug Nash into her room. But he was holding onto the doorframe as if his life depended on it.

With Nash still watching her, Mira took a chance and turned the knob. It was unlocked! Don't hesitate, she told herself. She stepped inside the room and before she even looked around, she blurted brightly, "Hi Tanger, I hope you haven't been waiting too long." Then she snapped the door shut behind her. The moonlit room afforded her just enough light to make out Tanger's raised brows.

"Mira. What's up?"

"I'm creating my own reality," she explained with a shrug and a sheepish yet miserable kind of smile. At his bemused look, she pointed her thumb toward the hall. "Nash is out there with Daphne."

"Ah." Tanger, who stood in front of his dresser wearing only boxer briefs, lit the four candles atop it. "I'm glad you're here."

She smiled, thankful at least that she was wanted. And wasn't this her chance to override the reality she didn't want? Creating an experience with Tanger could be her ticket to true freedom. Shoving all thoughts of Nash aside and focusing on the artistry of Tanger's fluid movements, she asked, "What are the candles for?"

"They represent the four elements of the earth," he said, adjusting the stones surrounding them. "It's a spiritual thing I do every night. It helps me align my mind and my emotions with my soul."

Was that why he seemed so confident in who he was? She craved that feeling in the worst way, yet there was always a part of herself that seemed elusive, like she was missing a piece of the puzzle. "Does it actually work?"

Holding out his hand, he brought her to stand beside him. The flickering of the candles and the heat of his arm resting against hers enveloped her with a heady combination of serenity and excitement. A little of her hurt over Nash dimmed.

"This actually works amazingly well," he said softly.

At the thump in the hallway, she knew she needed even more of a distraction. "*How* does it work?"

He continued to stare at the candles. "First, I close my eyes and go deep into my mind and heart, using the reflective time to polish away what is false in me, things like my past beliefs and my history." He gently brushed his fingers along her hairline and tucked a strand behind her ear. "Then I feel myself shift into the space between the physical dimensions and the non-physical and I imagine a loving spirit that opens a door to another world."

Mira let her eyes drift shut, trying to picture that loving spirit – and the door to another world.

"Once I step through that door, I can see things more clearly." Tanger's soft voice relaxed her. "And my soul is able to tap into the natural energy of the universe that belongs to each one of us."

It sounded intriguing, but a little confusing. Mira opened her eyes to look up at him. "What good does it do to tap into your natural energy?"

He smiled down at her. "For one, it helps me align myself with my divine purpose so I can fulfill my potential as an artist of Life."

Yes! That was exactly what she needed. And she needed it right now. Mira nodded toward the setup on his dresser. "So should I set something like this up in my room? Will you show me how?"

He looked at her thoughtfully. "Maybe you'd like to join me to see what it's like first."

She heard a crash and laughter from somewhere down the hall. She pasted on a smile, trying to control her spinning thoughts "Anything to get my heart, soul, and mind going in the right direction," she said. She glanced at the candles and then up at Tanger's face. The way he looked at her melted her anguish and her confusion, leaving behind hope and a feeling of power.

"Anything I can do to help," he said, and pulled her one step closer to the dresser. Keeping their hands clasped between them, he raised his free hand up toward the ceiling and closed his eyes.

Mira mimicked his pose, but kept peeking so she wouldn't miss any details.

"Oh God and Goddess of the earth," Tanger said after a few long silent minutes. "We know that our souls are what is most true about us, and that what is true is the divine. Help us to see that truth, and to become who we are meant to be."

Mira frowned. What was true about her? Although she'd seriously loved having visionary power, she didn't have that skill anymore. But she did enjoy taking on new challenges, especially if she had someone to do it with. Only what did that new challenge look like? Did a powerful experience await her?

Tanger lifted their entwined hands and turned slightly toward her. He said, "You have a strong energy of your own, but this connection between us," he pulled her hand to his lips and kissed the top of it, "is undeniable."

She nodded, swallowing against the thick lump in her throat.

Tanger continued. "I feel like the gods want us to journey together. Do you feel it too?"

Equally important to finding her place in the world was to have someone to do it with…someone to love her, understand her, and encourage her to be the best Mira she could be. She wanted that joy and peace that Tanger had already obtained, and she wanted it in the worst way. "I *do* feel it."

"That's my girl," he whispered, granting her with the most glorious smile she'd ever seen.

"So what now?" she whispered. "Does this mean we're, like, dating?"

"It's deeper than that," he whispered, then lowered his lips to hers.

They tasted like honey, and she suddenly craved him like she'd craved nothing else in her life.

"Mira," he rasped, "will you join me tonight?"

"What…what do you mean?" She looked into his smoldering eyes, mesmerized by what they seemed to promise. Hope wound itself with her longing as she waited for his answer.

"Be with me, Mira - heart, soul, body, and mind."

His words enticed her. His gentle sway soothed her. His spicy scent hypnotized. Was she actually considering this? Even though a part of her brain begged her to put on the brakes, to leave before she did something she'd regret, the other part of her brain along with her heart begged her to take the chance. Could he be the essence of her divine purpose? Would an entwining of their hearts and bodies gift her with a true, soul-deep love that would make her whole again?

"Yes," she whispered, feeling cherished in the cradle of his arms.

"Are you sure?"

"Yes," she said, "I'm sure." She moved to the bed to prove she was serious. It wasn't as graceful as she'd hoped, but she was determined to continue. Tanger would ease the longing inside her, she just knew it! She laid down, resting on the soft pillow.

Tanger blew out all but one candle, then joined her on the bed. When she met his unfamiliar gaze, insecurity struck. She frowned.

"Having second thoughts?"

"Maybe," she whispered.

Laying on his side, he propped himself up on his elbow to face her. "I don't think you realize your beauty," he said, his deep honeyed eyes caressing each inch of her body, leaving a trail of goosebumps in their wake. "And you underestimate your power."

She looked down at his six-pack and felt a twinge of disbelief, yet his obvious pleasure in her presence overcame her self-doubt. The power surged inside her and made itself known as she reached up to touch his face with trembling fingers. He was perfect...for her. That's what she kept telling herself.

"Life continues through love's energy. Mira. Share it with me," he said, taking her hand and pressing it against his beating heart.

He sounded so certain...and she felt like she needed this deep connection like she needed food to sustain her. This intimacy would be like a seal to the promise of living and loving life together. It was the only way...the best way...to move on.

"It sounds...divine," she finally said, staring at his sure hand as he reached for the edge of her t-shirt.

Chapter 30

Nash woke to pounding…insistent, loud pounding. He grabbed his head, pushing in on his skull with his palms to try to ease the pressure.

"Nash! Open up."

Nash opened his eyes a slit and groaned at the sunlight streaming into his room. "Go away," he said, but the knocking continued.

He shoved the pillow over his ears, wanting to ignore the incessant clatter – but he couldn't. "Are you a fricking woodpecker?" He yelled, then cringed.

"Open up."

They weren't going away. "I'm coming," he growled, "if you'll just stop knocking!" Ouch! Why did even talking hurt like the devil? Thankfully, the banging stopped. Nash swung his legs around and slid off his bed. Slowly, like a creeping bug after being doused with bug spray, he made his way to the door.

"This had better be important," he said, opening the door. Hayes was there, staring back at him.

"It *is* important," he said quietly. "Can I come in?"

"Will you go away if I say no?"

Hayes shook his head.

He stood aside to let him into his apartment. "How'd you get in here anyway?" He knew he hadn't buzzed him up, and it was Sunday, so Spectrum Music was closed.

"The store doors were open," Hayes said, taking a seat on the overstuffed sofa.

Nash frowned and regretted it. The hot poker-like pain was almost unbearable. "That doesn't make sense," he growled out. "Tory always makes sure they're locked." And then he remembered. "Have you seen Tory?"

Hayes nodded. "She's part of the reason I'm here."

Nash wandered over to his favorite chair, the one without armrests that sat next to his favorite guitar. He didn't reach for the Rave as he normally would. He wasn't in the mood…his head wasn't in the mood…and for some reason, just looking at it made him feel uneasy. Stashing it behind the chair, he sat.

"Are you going to extrapolate on that, or do I have to guess," Nash grumbled. "Just so you know, I don't really have it in me to guess."

Hayes stared at him a moment. "Yer worse off than I thought. I'll go make us some coffee first."

As Hayes went into the kitchen, Nash rested his head back against the chair.

"So I got a call from Tory a little bit ago," Hayes said, flipping cupboard doors open and then closing them. Each bang made Nash's skull feel like it would split apart at any moment. "It turns out she needed someone to get her from the police station and she needed bail."

Nash cursed beneath his breath. "Was she mad?"

"Hoppin' mad, more like it. But she still cared enough to send me over here to check on ya." He poked his head around the corner. "Where's the coffee?"

"First cupboard to the right of the sink."

"Then yer out." He grabbed his cell phone and punched in a number. "We need two double caf espressos, delivered." Hayes gave them Nash's address and then slipped his phone back into his pocket. "So what were ya thinking, going to investigate Kya's murder?"

That seemed like a lifetime ago. "I don't trust this new law system…and with a killer on the loose…" Nash tried to pull his thoughts together, but his head was really fuzzy. The crazy thing was he only had a beer, one partial glass of wine, and a swig of that brown burning liquid before his concert. It was hardly enough to make him feel like this! Something weird was going on. "Mira isn't safe," he said.

"Well there are legal ways to go about these things." Hayes handed Nash a couple of ibuprofen and a glass of water then sat down on the couch across from him again. "Tory said she'd found a dark hair beside the tub, and with Kya being blonde, it probably belonged to the perp."

"Makes sense. So our killer has dark hair. Did she find anything else?"

"Just the cops and that her friend had ditched her."

Guilt tugged at his heart and churned up his already queasy stomach. Before he could tell Hayes about the journal, Nash's phone rang. He snatched it up before it could ring again.

"Hello?"

"Hi Nash. This is Porsche. Awesome concert by the way."

"Thanks." Unfortunately, he didn't remember much of it. He *did* remember seeing Mira with Tanger, something he'd like erased from his memory…pronto.

"Well, because you were such a hit, I've decided to sign you on with Driven Records," she said, "All I need is your John Hancock on the contract, then we'll get to work mapping out your tour and producing your album."

It was exactly what he'd been wanting, only somehow the news fell flat. "Thanks," he said again.

"You don't sound all that excited."

Nash pinched the bridge of his nose. "I'm just not feeling all that well. Maybe we can meet this afternoon sometime when my head isn't so messed up."

"It *is* afternoon." She laughed. "You had quite the party after the concert."

"I did?"

"You don't remember breaking Vashti's tea cups?"

"Vashti's tea cups?"

"At Cofa's Tree? You shattered her sliding door, too. That didn't sit too well with her."

Nash groaned, half wishing that he could remember, half glad he didn't. "Any other things I should know about last night?"

"Nothing to worry about. I covered the damages and had Tanger take you home so you wouldn't get into any more trouble."

He didn't know how to respond to that. He vaguely remembered an image of Mira going into Tanger's room. He didn't know if it was true or imagined, but puke surged into the back of his throat anyway. "When do you want to meet with the contract and where?" he said.

"Tell you what. I'm heading out of town soon so I'll just send Houser over to your place with the contract. That way you can check it over at your leisure, then get it back to him by the beginning of next week."

He didn't know if that was enough time, but he didn't have it in him to negotiate right now. "Where does he live?"

"He's staying at Cofa's Tree for a while, so you can find him there."

Cofa's Tree? His breath hitched. "Will they even let me back in the place?"

She chuckled. "I'll make sure you're welcome there."

At least he'd have one more chance of getting into the place. "That'll work," he said, and hit the off button before slinging his phone onto the floor.

"So you're going to be a star," Hayes said.

"Looks that way."

"You're not happy about it?"

Nash sighed and closed his eyes. "I just thought it would be with Mira."

"I don't think it's too late for that."

Nash snorted. "If you knew what I knew, you wouldn't say that."

"Have you tried praying about it?"

Nash shook his head. "If there was a God, I wouldn't be going through this misery. Love sucks." And he did love her…even though it was apparent she didn't love him in return.

"Actually Christ gives us the perfect example of what true love is – and that includes whether to accept that love or not."

"So you say." Nash didn't want to hear it. "Where is that damned coffee?"

Chapter 31

Bang!

Mira's eyes popped open. Holding her breath as she clutched her blanket up to her chin, she listened.

Bang! The noise had come from her window. A bird maybe? She jumped from her bed to check it out. Swinging open the curtains, she looked out and then down. No bird lay lifeless on her sill, but a rope lay there, draped across the thick cement ledge. Cracking the window open, she leaned out to get a better look. Her eyes trailed down the braided hemp. She screamed out in terror…only she made no sound. Heart beating erratically, she stared at the dead woman – Kya…it was Kya hanging by a noose from her windowsill! Should she try pull her up? Or call the police? Just as Mira reached for the rope, Kya's eyes popped open. Mira pelted out another frantic cry, but again, it was soundless. She tried to turn around so she could run for help, but her feet seemed to be glued to the floor. Looking over her shoulder, her mind begged someone to walk through her door to help her. Someone *had* come into her room…a hooded figure with a blank face, and he was heading her way.

Her silent, pathetic attempts to scream only added to her helplessness, and a fear so unimaginably horrible gripped her as she tried to pry herself away from the window. She couldn't move! She couldn't make a sound! The hooded figure laughed.

Help me God, her mind shouted. And as though God had listened, the glue released and she fell backwards onto her butt. With the jarring, her dimly lit room immediately changed. It wasn't her room. It was Tanger's. And she was in his bed, not on the floor.

For a moment, Mira lay still, trying to calm herself. "It was only a dream," she said aloud, happy to hear her own voice. She knew the power of dreams, though, and her body continued to shake as she considered what hers had meant. It couldn't be prophetic. Kya was already dead. Was it somehow related to her lucid dream, then? Had she opened a portal to the abyss she'd thought she'd mastered? Though the flickering fire of evil spirits singed her thoughts, she refused to believe her lucid dream had been anything but a harmless attempt to manipulate her imagined world. She had been in control, right?

After a few minutes, she managed to lock the images from her dream behind the doors in her mind…but that left her with the reality of her present. She looked down. The shirt she wore buttoned on the wrong side and the sleeves hung to her fingertips. Tanger's scent clung to her. What had she done? *You gave away a beautiful gift to a stranger,* a voice in her head said. Dumb, dumb, dumb! She glanced around the empty room, a deep heaviness filling her.

As she rose from the bed, tears she didn't want to cry dripped from her lashes. She wiped them away angrily. It was her body, her life! She could do with it what she wanted. But why did she feel so bad, then?

Because it wasn't Nash…and because you're still alone a tiny voice inside said. But maybe Tanger had just gone to get breakfast. Maybe he'd come back with promises of the soul-deep love she longed for – to continue this beautiful adventure they'd started. "It doesn't matter to our souls that we didn't know each other that well," she said softly. And she had taken love when it had come to her, right? "It's just something I have to get used to." Unfortunately, her reasoning wasn't all that convincing. Guilt and sadness gripped her like a leech on bare skin, sucking away the happiness she wanted to feel.

As she looked around for her clothes, she caught sight of a lovely pot of flowers atop the dresser that had held the candles. She wandered over to them and plucked the note stashed between their stems. "Love and passion belong together and we are those from the depths of our newly entwined souls. Thanks for last night, Mira. Love, Tanger."

Her lips slowly curved up into a soft smile, the sharp sting of her anxiety now a dulled ache. It was going to be okay. It had to be. Wanting to freshen up before Tanger returned, Mira went back to her room. The first thing she did was to look out the window. She released the breath she'd been holding. There was no rope, no Kya hanging from it, and no evidence of it being there. Burying the gruesome image in the back of her mind, she grabbed her favorite shirt and jeans, intent on getting herself back into good spirits.

"This is going to be a great day," she told herself and headed to the bathroom.

After a nice hot shower and a swipe of her newest lipstick, she slipped on some shoes and went downstairs. She hoped that the store would be empty. Although having people around would distract her, she feared they would see the change in her – and that was something she didn't want to talk about.

Mira peeked through the doorway at the bottom of the steps. Vashti carried a plate of caramel rolls to the table where the bikini girls and Sylvia sat, waiting expectantly. Mira turned to go back up the stairs.

"Ah Mira. Do join us," Vashti called out. "Everyone is leaving after our coffee break."

If she escaped, she'd look like a coward or that she was too good for their company. Neither was what she wanted them to think of her, so she stepped into the room, telling herself that she was proud of who she was, of what she'd done, and that everyone would love her. "Hi everyone," she said with a bright smile.

"Hi," came a chorus of voices.

Mira glanced at the clock as she headed toward the group.

"That clock can't be right!" Mira said.

"It's right. You must have needed the sleep after last night," Daphne said, a smirk on her face.

Mira could feel her face flush, but chose not to respond. She sat down between Vashti and Sylvia.

"I didn't get much sleep either," Daphne said with a grin.

"That's because Nash was making such a ruckus that Vashti had to get Tanger to escort him home," one of the others said

What?? Was Tanger still with Nash? Mira's stomach churned.

"I don't know if I'd call breaking teacups and destroying the sliding door an actual ruckus," she said with a laugh. "Just a fuzzy-headed outburst."

Mira glanced at the sliding door. The glass on one side, though shattered, was still intact. How did I miss all that? Mira thought of what might have been distracting her and felt her face redden.

"This is amazing!" Daphne said, taking a giant bite of her caramel roll. "Mira…you better get one of these before I eat them all."

Mira hoped Daphne would get fat from it. Sucking in her own gut, Mira said, "I had something to eat in my room." It was true, if that leftover bite of candy bar she'd eaten counted.

"So how did creating your reality go last night?" Sylvia asked, "The girls mentioned that you'd gone with Tanger backstage."

Mira wondered what they'd all told her, but she didn't want to be analyzed or advised at the moment. "It went well. I'm great…and I'm really anxious to get to work. Do you have anything for me do, Vashti?"

"Actually, could you take care of a delivery for me? I thought Tanger would be back by now, but he isn't, and it needs to get out."

"I can do that." It would give her some breathing and thinking room.

Vashti went back behind the counter and, after slipping something into a bag, folded the top over and used a little wax stamp to seal it shut. "Don't tilt this," she said, handing it to Mira. "The address is written on the edge of the bag."

"Got it covered," she said, holding the package carefully. It smelled like coffee.

Vashti followed her to the door and opened it for her. "Thanks Mira."

"No, thank you," she said. As she stepped outside, Mira looked over her shoulder. "Do you know where Tanger went?"

"I'm not sure. He said something about protecting his interests." Vashti smiled. "Don't worry."

But she *was* worried. Protecting his interests? What did that mean? Did it have anything to do with her, with Nash? Mira placed the bag into the basket on the front of her bike. She peeked at the address. Her stomach plummeted even as her pulse raced. "This can't be right," she rasped, reading it again.

"It doesn't matter. Do your job. Get in get out…it'll all be good," she told herself. Unless…she had a whole lot of unless-es running through her brain. She glanced through the window at the table where Vashti sat with the vibrant group. Mira was NOT going back into Cofa's Tree with coward stamped on her forehead…especially not in front of the bikini girls and definitely not in front of Daphne.

Jumping on her bike, Mira pedaled across the street before she could change her mind.

Chapter 32

Knock, knock, knock.

Nash cringed, rubbing this throbbing temples as he stood.

Hayes grinned from his spot on the couch. It was a "you deserve this" kind of grin.

"Be right there," Nash called out in a tone not much louder than a whisper. Barefoot and shirtless with his hair still sticking out at all ends, he made his way to the door. He swung it open before the delivery person knocked again. "Coffee is just what..." His words drifted away. "Mira?"

"It'll be fifteen dollars," she said, not looking him in the eyes.

"Fifteen dollars? Are you kidding me?" He reached a trembling hand into his pocket. His wallet wasn't there.

"It's great coffee – and it includes the delivery fee," she said, holding it out to him.

"It smells awesome." He reached for the bag holding his coveted coffee, and though he didn't know what drove him to do so, he purposefully let his hand brush against hers. She looked up at him, then. He frowned, overwhelmed by the feelings that rushed through him. "I miss you," he rasped.

She looked away. "It'll be fifteen dollars, please."

Nash opened the door wider and sighed heavily, trying to ignore the throbbing in his brain and the ache in his heart. "Come in a minute while I round up some cash for you." He didn't wait for her to respond, but went back to his room. As he opened his top dresser drawer where he stashed his rainy day fund, he heard Hayes say, "Mira. I didn't know ya worked for Cofa's Tree."

He heard her light footsteps and held his breath. "I'll be working there for a while, anyway," she said, her voice sounding closer. "Gotta pay the rent, you know?"

"Cofa's Tree has great coffee and tea," Hayes said. "Do they sell anything else there?"

"Artwork," she paused, "and advice I guess."

Interesting, Nash thought. When the questioning moved on to school, Nash popped back out of his bedroom. Mira stood near the wall that separated the living room and the front entryway. "Here's a twenty. Keep the change as a tip," he said as he approached her.

Mira took it from him. "Thanks, Nash. I appreciate this."

They stood together a moment, just looking at each other.

Hayes interrupted the silence. "Nash paid a visit to Kya's place yesterday."

Nash shot him a look. The less people that knew about it the better.

"And he was just about to tell me what he discovered, besides the new information about a dark strand of hair found in Kya's bathroom." Hayes smiled. "I figured since ya were her friend, too, that ya'd want ta know."

"I *do* want to know. What else did you find, Nash?" she asked, her eyes wide and curious. Nash wondered if this could be his chance to win her back, to make everything right between them. They could be a team again and do this together. His music career was suddenly only a vague tickle in the back of his mind. "I found a journal, but only had time to read a little of it before the cops stormed in. From what I read, though, she'd been anxiously awaiting a visitor, one who she thought was the answer to her prayers. But he arrived with another person. That was her last entry."

"That information will definitely help things along," Hayes said. "Where'd ya put the journal?"

"Back in its hiding place beneath her bed, only I left it poking out further than she had."

Hayes nodded. "The investigators should be able to find it, then." He swiped his finger across the dust on his coffee table. "Maybe I'll mention to the new PI, Detective Richards, that Kya used to keep a journal and ask if they'd found one. If they haven't, I will make sure they have a second, more thorough look."

Mira frowned, her hand pressing against the wall as if it was holding her up.

"Something wrong?" Nash asked.

"Yeah, um, I saw Kya the morning before she died. She was at the Prophet House. Eleanor has long dark hair." She pressed her hand over her mouth. "No. Eleanor couldn't..."

"This is an important clue that could really help Detective Richards in the investigation." Hayes got up to leave. Grabbing the light jacket that he'd hung on the hooks near the entrance, he said, "I'll mention it to him without saying any names, but if he asks where I got the information, I'll have to be truthful." His serious gaze included them both. "Ya realize that, right?"

Mira nodded and so did Nash. Although Nash wasn't particularly happy about it, he knew Hayes. He didn't back down from his principles.

As Hayes opened the door, he added, "In the meantime, the two of ya put yer heads together and see if ya can come up with anything else that might lead us to Kya's killer." He held up his phone. "Call me anytime." And then he was gone, leaving Mira and Nash alone.

Mira looked ghostly, and Nash really wanted to take her in his arms, but he didn't dare – and he didn't know if his heart could take another rejection from her.

"So you saw...Eleanor was it...at the Prophet House?"

She nodded and took a seat on his couch. "I left right after Kya had gotten there."

Nash sat in the chair across from her, relieved that she had stayed. Man, even though the tension sizzled between them, it somehow felt right with her being there. "Do you remember if either Kya or Eleanor said anything strange or acted in any way that was out of the ordinary?" he asked.

Her nose scrunched up in that cute way of hers. He couldn't help but stare. Oh how he wished he could just gather her in his arms and start over.

"The only weird thing," Mira said, "was that Eleanor gave Kya the exact same advice as she gave me."

"What advice was that?" Nash held his breath, thinking it had to have something to do with Mira giving up on them.

Mira looked down at her clasped hands. Right as she opened her mouth, there was another knock on his door.

Nash cursed beneath his breath. "Hold on a sec, okay?" He hurried to the door, wanting to quickly get rid of whomever was behind it.

"Oh hi, Houser. I didn't think you'd be here so quickly," Nash said, taking the contract he held out to him.

"I have other things to get done today, so I wanted to get this errand over with." Houser shook his head. "For some reason, that woman loves having me run her errands."

Nash chuckled, the action sending another punch of pain through his head. "Well, I'll bring it back over to you sometime between now and tomorrow evening, okay?"

"Perfect."

Nash closed the door. As he walked into the living room, he quickly paged through the contract.

"What's that?" Mira asked.

He lifted the papers. "A contract."

"For producing your music?"

He nodded. "And for going on tour."

She frowned. "When does the tour start?"

He flipped to the second page. "She wants me to head to Bolinbroke a week from Friday." He could see her jaw working and he wondered what she was thinking. "I'd love it if you'd come with me," he said softly.

She paused a moment, which made his heartbeat triple. But then she shook her head. "I have other things I need to take care of here."

Thinking about Hayes' advice, he didn't give in. "What things?"

"School I guess," she shrugged, "and figuring out who I am and what my *own* purpose is."

"Could that ever include me?" He hated to beg, but with his heart and his eyes, he did.

"We've talked about this." She stood up.

He sensed she was leaving him for good. The air felt too heavy for his lungs.

"We've both moved on," she said. "I'm sure you'll see Daphne in Bolinbroke anyway, and I have Tanger and…" her voice trailed away. "You need someone who won't get in the way of your career." She turned away from him and walked to the door.

Nash followed. "That's just an excuse."

"No, it's reality."

He snorted. "I need you…*that's* reality!

"Do you need me enough to tear up that contract?" she challenged.

He glanced at the paper in his hands. It was everything he'd worked for, everything he was. He honestly didn't know if he could walk away from the opportunity of a lifetime. "I can't believe you'd ask me to do it!"

"That's not the point." Tears welled in her eyes as she stepped across the threshold into the hall. "Goodbye, Nash."

As Nash watched her walk away, he called out, "Don't go, Mira."

She paused and said, "I have to do this, not just for you, but for me." She cleared her throat. "Have a great tour."

"Unbelievable," he spat as she disappeared around the corner. Muttering under his breath, Nash stormed back into his apartment. He grabbed a pen and slapped the contract onto the table. "I deserve better than this," he said, "and it starts today."

Chapter 33

Mira's legs and heart were heavy as she biked back to Cofa's Tree. She peeked through the window of the front door. Thankfully, no one remained except for Vashti, so she went inside.

"Oh, Mira. There you are. I was beginning to worry about you," Vashti said as she dried the pan that the caramel rolls had been baked in.

"It was Nash's place." She squinted at Vashti. "I assume you knew that."

Vashti nodded. "It's all a part of the growing process. How did it go?"

"Fine." Mira didn't want to say anything more about it. "Is there anything else you'd like me to do right now...I mean work wise?"

"Actually, yes." She dried her hands on a towel and reached into her pocket for a key. Bringing it over to Mira, she said, "Since most of our guests have left, I need you to clean their rooms and the bathroom." She handed her a list with the room numbers and what they needed to have done – put on fresh linens, clean mirrors, dust, and run the sweeper over the rugs.

"No problem," Mira said, glad to have something to do. She took the key. "This will get me into all the rooms?"

"Yes. The fresh linens and the cleaning supplies are in the upstairs bathroom closet. You'll find a laundry basket there, too. Put the dirty sheets and towels in that and bring them down here so I can launder them."

"Got it," she said and headed toward the stairs.

"Mira?"

Mira paused and looked over her shoulder. "Yeah?"

"You can do great things. Believe in yourself."

She didn't, but she was going to fake it until she *did* believe it. "Thanks Vashti." She forced a smile as she headed back up the steps. Once in the hallway, a feeling came over her - like someone was watching her. She looked around.

She was alone. Shrugging it off, she continued to the bathroom. Grabbing the laundry basket, the sweeper, and the dusting rag along with its earth-friendly spray, she headed to the first room on the list. Daphne's room.

Mira set out to work quickly, trying to shut out any thoughts of Daphne and Nash together, but his lingering scent made it impossible. And as she tore off the covers and sheets of the bed, a sick feeling crept up inside her. "I don't even know if anything happened between them," she muttered through her thickened throat. Maybe she should go talk to Nash again. No. She couldn't go back now. Last night had solidified their course. She and Nash had each chosen to go their own ways — even if the decisions had been impulsive or swayed by alcohol. She sped through the rest of the duties and dashed out into the hallway, closing the door behind her. Instead of going to the next room on the list, she escaped to her own.

Once inside, she plopped down on the edge of her bed and let the tears fall. She hated to admit it, but she missed Nash intensely — and she regretted last night in a way that reached deep into her soul. She swiped at her wet cheeks and sniffed. "I did the right thing for me," she said, only it didn't *feel* right at this moment. An empty chill swept through her and the loneliness settled in. She stared out across the room toward her window, the image of Kya hanging there bringing another surge of emotion...hopelessness. She didn't know what to do with it.

She growled out, but it sounded more like a pathetic whimper. Had this been how Kya had felt in losing Vaughn? And what had she done that ended up aligning her with a murderer? She shivered, remembering the last time she'd seen her. Could Eleanor have actually killed her? As far as she knew, the woman wasn't an artist skilled enough to sketch Kya in the tub, but maybe her husband was — and maybe they were the pair who had shown up at Kya's house. With those possibilities came another — that she, herself, was in danger because she'd witnessed not only that their business was a farce, but that they had been with Kya earlier that day.

Mira stood up. No…she wouldn't believe it! Eleanor and Elroy were impostors, yes, but they couldn't be murderers! Going to her nightstand, she paused. Slowly, she opened the drawer. Taking out the letter her mom had given her, she held it in her hands, her eyes glued to the careful script. She could almost guess what was inside the envelope – that the answer to all her problems was a relationship with God. That was her mom's answer to everything.

"But I don't want that lifestyle…reading the Enchiridion of Emmanuel, submitting and sacrificing and turning the other cheek," she whispered. It just didn't feel right – at least for her. And she truly doubted it would solve any of her problems. Mira tucked the note back beneath her folded clothes and shut the drawer.

Okay. This was ridiculous. She needed to get herself figured out so she could get on with her life and not live with a balled up bunch of anxiety and remorse. At every turn, she seemed to feel like she'd come out the loser. That needed to change. She wanted to feel confident in who she was and where she was going. The first step was to get her mind in the right place. Going to the closet, she grabbed a shirt that absolutely yelled confidence. Sequins ran along the low scooped neckline of a bold turquoise fabric. The shoulders were cut out, the flowing bodice giving it a seductive feel. It was daring…just like she wanted to be. As she pulled off the tags, she caught a glimpse of the antique trunk sitting at the far end of the closet.

"No way!" The doll…it was on top of the trunk again! She stumbled backward into her room. "Okay. I'm not going to freak out," she said, staring at the closet door. At least she didn't hear any crying! After a few silent moments, she slunk ahead, chancing a peek around the corner. The doll was still there, and the key had found its way back into the lock! What in the world was going on? Had she dreamt that she'd stashed the doll inside the trunk? She didn't think so. Maybe someone was playing tricks on her.

Slinging the shirt over her shoulder, Mira tiptoed over to the doll, careful not to wake it…just in case. With shaking hands, she stashed the ratty-haired thing inside the trunk again, and this time, shoved the key into her pocket. Tonight, when everyone was asleep, she'd throw the doll in the dumpster. Then she wouldn't have to worry about it anymore.

After donning her new shirt, she grabbed the laundry basket and cleaning gear and headed back into the hallway. She turned toward the next room on her list, but as she went by Tanger's door, she hesitated. His sheets...she needed to change them before he came back!

Mira let herself into his room and closed the door behind her. Her face burned and shame threatened her choke her. "It's not a big deal," she ground out. But it felt like a big deal – like she was here to clean up her own mess. She stripped off the sheets and stuffed them into the basket. Her arms trembled as she hurried to put on the new linens. Bed made, she propped the cleaning gear by the door and, leaning against the jamb, took a deep breath. The room felt strange to her, suffocating. She closed her eyes and tried to recreate the feelings of magic she'd had last night. She could imagine herself there, yet all that had happened seemed surreal. Maybe that was normal. And as Sylvia had suggested yesterday, she needed to refuse to accept she was anything less than joyful about the situation.

"This is my reality. I love Tanger and we are going to take on the world together, one art piece at a time," she whispered. She opened her eyes and wandered through his room, trying to capture the essence of who he was and how they fit together. When she came to the windowed section where he created and stored his artwork, she was reminded of her art studio at The Compound. Trying not to let the past and her regrets bubble up again, she began to peruse through his pieces.

Tanger was a brilliant artist. He had used several mediums...from pencil sketches, to metalwork, to sculptures. And they were all extraordinarily beautiful. Even though she felt like she'd never measure up to his talents, she was curious about the subjects he'd chosen. She flipped through one stack of paintings. The grouping had several pictures of naked women – all shapes and sizes, none with perfect bodies. She didn't know if that made her feel better or worse.

Beneath the nude art, she found a canvas piece wrapped in brown paper. Tanger had written in the corner, Final Project – title to be determined. She turned it over to see if she could somehow peek inside, but it was taped securely.

"Like what you see?"

Mira gasped as she swung around, holding the wrapped artwork in front of her. Tanger sat on his freshly made bed, watching her. How hadn't she heard him come in?

"I do like what I see," she said, quickly putting the package back on the easel and smiling brightly at him. "But I'd like to see more. Can I see what you did for your project?"

Tanger laughed as he stood up. He was looking at her in a way that made her feel giddy…and desired. "I'll show you soon." He stepped very close to her. "I really want to kiss you," he said.

She laughed nervously. "Then why don't you?" Maybe it would make her feel like this was more real…that they were the real deal.

"Because you're having regrets. I can feel it."

Was she that transparent? "I just don't trust my feelings right now…or really believe that what happened, really happened."

"It did." He lowered his voice as he cupped her cheek with his palm. "It definitely did." Instead of kissing her, as she had thought he was going to do, he said, "I have some good news."

"You do?"

He nodded. "I went down to the police station and told the cops all about how you were with me the night of Kya's murder."

That's what Vashti had been referring to! Although she felt great that he'd done so… "But the time of her death was before I met up with you that night…it happened while I was lucid dreaming," she said, biting at her lip.

"They don't know that. And I fully trust you didn't do it...so from now on you were with me all night. Your name has been cleared."

Relief flooded through her veins. She hugged him hard. "Thank you. Thank you."

He smiled at her. "It's the least I could do." He did kiss her then, and it was filled with promise and hope. She'd made the right decision. And that's what she was going to keep telling herself.

"So do you still want to go to Wormwood's Water and practice your photography before tonight? We are still on for tonight, right?"

She nodded and glanced at her watch. At the rate she was going, she'd barely be able to get in any practice shots at all. "I just don't know if I'll have time. I have to finish cleaning these rooms and the bathroom first." She frowned. "What if it doesn't come together right?"

"The moon won't disappoint us. Don't worry."

"That's not what I meant. What if I stink at taking pictures?"

"You'll fail the class?"

She hit him. "Thanks. That makes me feel a whole lot better."

"Would it make you feel better if I helped you clean so that you could get some practice time in?"

"You'd do that for me?"

"Absolutely."

A big chunk of her tension floated away. "Thanks Tanger." She handed him the cleaning supplies before grabbing the basket and the sweeper. "I think this is going to be an awesome day after all."

Chapter 34

Nash scratched his name at the bottom of the ten-page contract with a flourish. Mira wanted him to move on, to follow his dreams, and that was what he was going to do!

A loud knock at the door interrupted his inward turmoil.

"Go away," he yelled.

"I will...after you accept my resignation."

"Tory?" Nash rushed to the door and swung it wide. A disheveled Tory stood glaring at him, her arms crossed over her chest.

"Can I come in?" she asked, her scowl firmly set.

"Of course." Nash stood to the side.

Tory marched past him and into his kitchen. "First, I really need to get this off my chest." She paused to inhale deeply through her nose. "I just spent the night in jail because of you, and I'm not happy about it."

This was the most riled up he'd ever seen her. He couldn't help but smile just a little. "I'm sorry, Tory."

She glared at him. "You better be more than sorry...you better be solving this case pronto."

"Why is that?"

"Because they accused me of tampering with evidence, and so now I'm one of their suspects. Can you imagine?"

He could, and he felt really bad about it. He pulled her into his arms for a hug and she started to cry, something he'd never seen her do. "I'm so sorry. I'll fix this." He hoped he'd be able to. He didn't have much time.

"It was so horrible, Nash. They got my finger prints, frisked me, interrogated me, took my picture after they put me in prison garb...I look horrible in orange!" she wailed.

Nash ran his hand down the back of her hair. "You look fine in orange."

"Don't lie to me Nash Montgomery." She sniffed loudly. "And that's not the worst of it. I had to spend the night with a drugged up guy that was puking his guts out into the steel community toilet. Not like I'd go to the bathroom in there anyway. And then there was this woman who smelled like she hadn't bathed in years. She kept shooting toilet paper spit wads at everyone. And…" she gulped in a breath.

"It's over now." Nash pulled a spit wad still clinging to a strand of her hair. "Can you ever forgive me?"

Her voice trembled a little, but the words were clear. "I can forgive you, but forgetting is another matter." She stepped out of his arms and headed over to his kitchen sink. "I really need a cup of coffee," she said, looking in the cupboard to the right. "You're out and we're out in the breakroom, too. I'll add coffee to the list."

So she wasn't quitting? Nash was more relieved about that than he realized. "If you want to heat this up, you can have it," he said, holding up his coffee cup. He hadn't been able to drink any of it.

"Cofa's Tree? I didn't know they sold coffee." She took the cup from him and put it into the microwave.

"I guess they do."

She turned to look at him, and he knew she could tell there was something more. "And it comes with someone to share it with?" she said, pointing to the other cup.

"That one was for Hayes." He frowned. "Mira showed up, however."

She cast a quick glance his way, then opened the microwave to retrieve her coffee. "That had to be hard."

"Yeah." He sat down at the kitchen table, suddenly exhausted.

She took a seat across from him. "Anything happen that I should know about?"

He smiled at the question. "Just that my music contract came today and I signed it."

"What? No way?" She grinned. "I knew you'd be a big hit after last night."

He felt a twinge, regretting Tory hadn't been able to be there because of him. "It's a tremendous opportunity," he said. "I'll be touring and everything."

She looked almost sad for a moment, then she looked away. "So when do you leave?"

"Next Friday."

"That's fast!"

He nodded his head, still unsure he was doing the right thing.

Running a finger across the lip of the cup, Tory said, "I could be your business manager."

He considered it. "You'd be great at that." And having a friend along would be nice, only who would run his store?

She pursed her lips. "Unfortunately, I can't go anywhere until I've been cleared…you know, that being a suspect thing because you talked me into going to Kya's."

"Maybe we can solve the case before I leave," he said, trying to be positive for her. He really *did* feel horrible about getting her into trouble.

"I don't have much hope for that! All we have to go on is that the hair fiber I found was synthetic…probably from a wig."

He hadn't known it was synthetic, only that it was black. "We also know she'd had two visitors that night and that she'd gone to the Prophet House that morning."

"How do we know that?"

"I found Kya's journal," he said, not wanting to mention that the Prophet House information had come from Mira. His protective instincts where she was concerned were still strong, whether he wanted them to be or not.

"What else was in the journal?"

"I didn't get a chance to read much else. I had to get out before I got caught too."

Tory's eyes squinted at that statement. "Do you still have it?"

"I left it there for them to find."

Her sigh was long and drawn out, like he'd truly disappointed her again. She went to his desk and got out a pen and piece of paper. It only took a few seconds for her to write down all the clues they had. "So where should we start?"

"*We* are not going to start anywhere," he said, ushering her to the door. "I am *not* going to get you in trouble again."

"But...I need to clear my name."

"Let me take care of that," Nash said. "You go home, take a shower, have a nap, whatever you want to do. I'll get someone to cover the store today."

"I guess I am pretty exhausted." She stopped just outside the door. "But promise me you'll call me and let me know if you find out anything else."

"I promise," he said.

———————————————— ✦ ————————————————

Nash stepped outside the store, wondering if he should take a taxi to the Prophet House, or if he should walk. That's when he noticed Porsche standing beside a sleek, black motorcycle. That woman rode in class!

She waved at him.

He took a step toward her, tucking his hands into his back pockets. "I thought you were leaving town?"

She smiled. "I just couldn't leave without giving you a token of my appreciation, first."

"Oh, yeah?" He was a little surprised that she hadn't sent Houser.

"Yeah." She approached him, her spiked heels clicking in sophisticated prowess. She held out her hand. In it was a key. "This is your bonus for last night." She grinned. "You did well...very well."

He stared at the key resting on her palm. "This motorcycle is for me?"

"Yep. No strings attached."

Even though he'd already signed the contract, he still had time to tear it up. Time to test the waters. "So it will be mine whether I sign the contract or not?"

"Yep."

He snagged the keychain sporting the Driven Records logo. The weight and feel of it in his hand made it all the more real. This was truly happening! And he suspected it was only a hint of the world of fame and fortune that awaited him! He smiled. "Thanks Porsche. I really appreciate this." He had wanted a motorcycle ever since he'd seen the ad for the new Fireride crotch rocket. Fast, sleek, sexy...what could be better than that?

"The gift is my pleasure," she said, stepping back to give him a closer look. "Why don't you take it for a ride?"

He moved to stand beside the machine. His hand brushed against the smooth metal as he imagined his first ride...the stream of air across his face, the feeling of power beneath him and the freedom before him. "I think I will!" He swung his leg over the seat and slipped the key into the ignition. As he turned the key, he couldn't help but think the machine had been made just for him. He loved it, loved the purr of the animal beneath him, loved the possibilities it represented.

With a small nod to Porsche, he took off down the block. He was cautious at first, but as he neared the edge of Pillar and saw open road before him, he kicked it into high gear. Yet as he approached a familiar bend in the road, he slowed to a crawl. The Prophet House was just off to the right, down a gravel road. How had he forgotten his objective so quickly? Well, at least he hadn't forgotten altogether!

He turned, taking the corner slowly. After silencing the engine, he rolled the bike across the gravel and into the trees. His bike now hidden from view, he took off on foot, jogging through the tree line until he stood across the lawn from the Prophet House. All was quiet. He waited a few minutes, contemplating his next move.

"There's no time like the present," he finally said, and made his way to the house. Jogging up the steps of the porch, he knocked on the front door.

Within moments, a lady opened it. "I'm sorry. We're closed for business today."

"Why is that?"

"Because a dear friend of ours died, and we're in mourning," she said, with a long drawn out sniff.

"Your sign says something about prayer. Shouldn't you be open to pray for people?" The anger in his voice wasn't feigned.

She peeked up at him through her puffy eyes. "You're right. Would you like to come in?"

He nodded and followed her inside. He didn't see anyone else around. "So where's your husband? Shouldn't he be here with you during this difficult time?"

"He's out on his hike. He does it more when he's stressed." As she went into an office, she turned to him and said, "You are full of questions. What's your name?"

"Nash. And yours?"

"Eleanor."

"Nice to meet you, Eleanor." Although he didn't know if he actually meant it yet.

"Nice to meet you too, Nash. Please, have a seat." She sat down on a couch across from him and folded her hands in her lap. "So what can I do for you today?" she asked after taking several deep breaths.

"I'd like a prophetic word." Whatever that really was.

She stared at him for a moment, then her eyes filled with tears. "I can't do it! I'm sorry." She sniffed and grabbed a tissue. As she wiped her eyes and then her nose, she said, "The last person I gave a prophetic word to is dead!" she wailed. "I should've predicted it," she added in a high-pitched tone. She leaned forward, hands pressed against her cheeks, sobbing.

He stood up, and placing a hand on her shoulder, said, "I'm sorry, Eleanor."

She looked up at him, her eyes pinched with distress, her face blotchy. That's when he noticed the bobby pin right next to her ear, and that she wore a wig. His first thought was to tear it off and demand the truth. Yet thinking about what Tory had just endured because of his impulsiveness, he kept his words locked in his mouth. Looking for clues and motives was a better idea. And putting together a strategic line of questioning could lead him to answers more efficiently than ones off the cuff. He needed time to plan.

"Why don't you get some rest Eleanor," he said carefully. "And I'll let myself out."

"Okay." She immediately curled up on the couch and closed her eyes as if she wanted to shut out the entire world. Guilt or grief? He wasn't sure, but in this state she was hardly a threat at the moment.

Nash left the room, closing the door behind him. He scanned the living area, not really seeing anything out of the ordinary. Spotting a door off the kitchen, he hurried to open it. It was a bedroom. The master, it looked like. After a quick glance told him he was still alone, he slipped inside. Rummaging through the drawers, he found nothing unusual. He opened the closet door to have a look and whistled softly. Ms. Eleanor had several wigs piled up in a basket on a shelf. Had she just put on a good show for him? She was a great actor, if that was the case. Nash pulled strands out of each of the various wigs, and grabbed a tissue off the nightstand to wrap them in. Gingerly, he stuffed the potential evidence into his jacket pocket.

As he rifled through the rest of the junk on the shelves, he heard a loud clank. It had come from the kitchen. And now water was running! Wishing he'd been paying more attention, he debated between jumping out the window or facing Eleanor with the excuse that he hadn't known where he was going. If she had anything to do with the murder, he suspected she wouldn't buy his being lost story, so the window won out.

Nash carefully opened the double hung window. Thankful there was no screen, he slipped outside, doing his best to pull the window closed from his spot outside. Once in the fresh air, he waited. No alarm bells went up, so he crouched low, running past the living room window and the office. That's when he noticed the impression in the mud print beneath the office window. He knelt down to get a closer look. There was no mistaking the misshapen heart in the "M hearts N". It was the exact design that Mira had melted into the bottom of a pair of her favorite shoes. He pressed his palm against it, wishing things were different between them. But all he could do right now was make sure Kya's killer was found so that he knew Mira would be safe before he left on his tour.

Nash followed the prints to the side of the garage where he found bike tire prints beside a book, which he picked up. *Interpreting the Voices That Reveal God's Purposes.* The pages were ripped out of it and a few loose sheets remained scattered, marooned by the mud. He had to smile. Mira must not have liked what she'd read! But then his heart lurched as he realized he might never experience her erratic piques again.

Blowing out a long breath, he squatted to trace the divot her tire had made. That's when he noticed the other set of footprints. These were much larger, and the heel of the shoes was unusually large and square. He took a picture of them with his phone then headed back through the trees to where his new motorcycle was hidden. Hopping onto its molded leather seat, he rolled the bike out onto the road, then started it up. It hummed beneath him like the quiet rumble of thunder long before a storm. Nerves jangling, he shifted into gear and drove toward the area of town where the sharp-angled, practical houses stood.

As he wove through the pristine neighborhood, he found the street he wanted. Mid-block, Nash pulled onto the asphalt driveway and looked toward a house shingled with a solar-paneled roof. Maybe he shouldn't be here. Maybe he should take this information to the new PI. But he didn't trust any of the police force. They were inexperienced, inconsistent, and a bit jaded in his opinion. He was none of those. Add to that his desire to protect Mira, and only one viable option remained - to continue this investigation, at least until he had to leave for his tour.

Leaning the bike over so that it rested on its kickstand, he hurried up the sidewalk to Tory's front door. He knocked.

After several moments, she appeared in the doorway wearing a spaghetti-strapped, silky, knee-length nightgown. She rubbed her eyes beneath her glasses, blinking up at him. "Nash?"

"I, ah…" He glanced away from the impractical Tory he wasn't used to.

As if she'd read his mind, she said, "This is an organic cotton nightgown, practical and cozy, so get over it." She crossed her arms over her chest. "What are you doing here?" Before he could respond, she answered her own question. "You found more clues."

He nodded, his eyes finding hers. "And I need your help."

She hesitated only a moment before letting him inside. "What do you want me to do?"

"Get dressed – in black preferably. I think Mira is in big trouble."

"Why is it always about her?" she snapped. "Don't answer that," she added, blowing a breath through her puffed lips. "I'll go change."

When she disappeared into her room, she called out, "If this gets me into any more trouble than I'm already in, I'm going to quit."

"As a friend?" he asked.

"As a friend *and* as an employee," she said as she came back through her doorway, dressed in black as he had requested. "Is it worth the risk?"

That, he could answer easily – at least for himself. "It is," he said, his drive to assure Mira's safety overriding everything else. Some things never changed!

Chapter 35

Mira stepped out of the shower, feeling refreshed and more than a little anxious. The cleaning was done, thanks to a very helpful Tanger, but he'd insisted on preparing a meal for them to share in the Enchanted Garden before heading to Wormwood's Water to take pictures. He said she needed to practice patience – a quality just as important for getting that perfect shot as taking practice pictures was. Judging by the photographs she'd seen mixed in with his other artwork, he obviously knew what he was talking about, and she trusted him.

Slipping into her room, she hurried to the bed where she'd laid out her clothes for the evening. She'd chosen a black jumpsuit made of a stretchy fabric with an elegant sheen. The sleeves were short, the legs tight around the ankles. It would give her a classy look yet would allow her flexibility to do the shoot. The strappy red sandals bumped the outfit up to striking, but they also made it less practical. She'd just have to ditch them when she was working. Moving to stand in front of the mirror, she grabbed a comb. Teasing her hair at the roots, she made a low, loose, imperfect knot and then pulled at a few strands to make messy loops. The modern knot framed her face which, after applying her makeup, really made her eyes pop.

Satisfied with her appearance, she headed downstairs. Tanger stood looking out the sliding door, his camera bag hanging over his shoulder. She paused a moment to stare. He had changed into dark denim jeans and a tight black t-shirt. Perfect. Handsome. Mysterious. *And mine,* came a thought out of nowhere.

He glanced over his shoulder, his eyes meeting hers with an intensity that took her breath away. "Everything's ready," he said, holding out his hand to her.

She took it. "Where's the food?"

He grinned. "Already set up." He pointed toward the garden.

Mira squinted through the clear side of the sliding door, but instead of seeing the product of Tanger's hard work, she could only picture Nash trying to kick in the door. What had he been thinking? Did it have anything to do with her?

"Don't you like it?" Tanger asked.

Blinking to rid herself of the anxiety that came with her thoughts of Nash, she focused her attention outside. A cloth covered table stood just beyond her favorite garden sculpture – the one of a man reaching around the corner for a woman's outstretched hand as if they would at any moment truly cohere and find rescue in their connection. A candle flickered in the middle of the table, two wine glasses sitting on either side of it, already filled with a deep burgundy liquid. "It looks beautiful," she said, "and I'm starving."

"I hope you'll enjoy the food as much as the presentation," he said with a lop-sided grin. The fractured glass stayed in place as he opened the door. He led her outside to the table. "I'm not the best cook – even if I did get a few pointers from chef Rickie."

"Well, you can't be good at everything." She took a seat in a chair that beheld an old world elegance. Its richly carved wood design was enhanced by its gold and red upholstery. She loved it and felt like a queen sitting in it.

Tanger sat down across from her in a similar style chair, only with a taller back, and a brushed black and silver fabric. "Well…dig in!" he said.

Her mouth flooded with anticipation as she lifted the dome covering. She frowned at the unexpected dish. On her plate sat what looked like a man's face. Pita bread made up the face portion. She straightened one of the hard-boiled eggs, which had been sliced, with olives placed atop the yolk, to create his eyes. Half an avocado sat between two tomato halves, which gave the appearance of a nose and chubby cheeks. Shredded cheese lay in a scattered mess beneath it to form a beard. A single row of corn kernels sat between two slivers of carrots, creating a yellow-toothed smile. And to complete the presentation was a red pepper tongue.

"I'm supposed to eat this?" she asked with a laugh.

"What? You don't like it?" Tanger removed his own dome and dug into his food.

"I *do* like it," she said, thankful for his light-hearted presence. Her earlier tension had lowered from boiling down to simmer Shoving all the ingredients into the pita shell, she took a big bite of the sloppy mess.

Tanger went for another bite. Holding it just in front of his mouth, he asked, "So what do you think?"

"It's terrible," she said with a laugh and took another bite, this one full-on rubbery egg. Tanger watched her, his eyes taking on a strange gleam as he did so. She wiped her mouth with her napkin and swallowed. She looked down at her plate. "Thank you for this," she said.

"For what? I can tell you don't like it."

"I know, but it fills me up and made me laugh and relax. It's perfect." She smiled over at him, noticing he'd already finished his entire plate.

"Before we go out to take the pictures," he said, swallowing a sip of wine, "I wanted to talk to you about something."

He looked serious. Her chewing slowed. "Okay "

"I've never felt about anyone the way I do about you, Mira."

Her chewing stopped, but the beat of her heart ramped up. "And how is that?" she dared to ask.

He got up from the table and stood at the edge of the trees, his back to her. "I just feel like there's something different about you." He clasped his hands tightly behind him. "Something I can't put my finger on."

"I hope that's a good thing," she commented, tossing the napkin on what was left of her food.

"Differences are a gift," he said and nodded as if to convince himself. He turned to smile at her. "And they're a variety of life to be discovered and explored."

"I agree," she said. She didn't know quite what he was getting at, but the sun was waning and time was wasting. She stood and, grabbing his camera from the stump he'd put it on, headed to the pathway that would take them down to Wormwood's Water. "And it starts with our pictures tonight."

Tanger glanced at her as if surprised. Had he thought she'd sit and wait at their table while her chances of passing her class dropped like the sun on the horizon?

"You're coming, right?" she asked, her bravado slipping. What would her picture be without him? Crap…it would be crap!

"Of course I am," he said. Only instead of heading toward her, he went to the opposite side of the garden. "But it's this way," he said with a chuckle.

Embarrassment flooded her face, yet she worked up a smile. "I can't be good at everything," she said with a playful shrug.

He laughed as he led her down the path and through the trees to the rock shelf where they'd picnicked a mere week ago. "I think you will get the perfect angle from over there," he said pointing to a spot right on the edge that overlooked the water.

"Are you sure?" she asked.

"Yes. I'm sure."

She didn't like the idea of hanging out on the elevated point, but he was probably right about the angle. *I can do this*, she thought. *And it will be fun!* She told herself. "Ready for some practice shots?"

He nodded. "Do you know how to use my camera?"

"Not really."

He took it out of the case for her and showed her the features she'd want to use. It was intoxicating as he worked to explain. His warmth grazed her often, his gentle voice was like a song to her heart. Could he be any more perfect? She didn't think so.

"Any questions?" he asked.

Even though she only remembered about half of what he'd told her, she said, "No. I think I can handle it." Swinging the camera around, she snapped a picture of his face. After taking a peek at the results, she smiled. Maybe she wasn't so bad at this after all…especially not with the photogenic Tanger.

"Take all the practice shots you want," he said as he peeled off his shirt.

Oh, my! Click. Click. Click.

Chapter 36

Nash patted his chest to make sure his contract was still tucked inside his inner jacket pocket. From his spot in front of the pet shop, he could see Tory saunter up to the entrance of Cofa's Tree. Though it was dusk, the streetlights were already beaming, giving him a clear view. As she reached for the door handle, the light glinted off her now jet-black hair and gave her naturally bright white skin an eerie glow. Her lipstick and fingernails were black, as were her eyeshadow and nose ring. He hoped she'd forgive him for insisting on that little addition to her disguise. It was so NOT Tory that even if Mira was in the store, she wouldn't recognize her.

Tory entered Cofa's Tree, as planned. Nash could see her through the window, talking to the store owner, Vashti. The woman pointed up the stairs. After a nod, Tory tugged on her nose ring - the signal they'd agreed on.

Waiting a few more seconds for them to disappear up the steps, Nash hurried across the street, and as quietly as he could, slipped inside Cofa's Tree. He closed the door softly behind him and took a moment to listen. Tory's overly zealous laughter from upstairs sounded ridiculous. He shook his head. She should definitely not go into acting! Nash scanned the room, cringing when he saw the damage to the sliding door. Not wanting to think about it, he opened the drawer of an end table. Inside it was a book called, "Finding the Right Spirit Guide." He debated on whether or not to take it, to see what it was all about, but being the only book stored there, he didn't dare. Besides, the little hairs on the nape of his neck were standing on end. He took a picture of the book with his phone and shut the drawer before moving into the kitchen area.

As he rummaged through the cupboards and drawers, laughter floated down the stairs again. Tory was quite the trooper, he thought. Finding nothing suspicious in the kitchen, Nash continued his search. He snapped a few quick pictures of the doll collection, the artwork, and the stone circle, wondering what significance they had, if any. He opened a door that had been built into the wood-slat wall to the left of the stairs. Inside the small room was a toilet and a single sink. As he bent to open the vanity door, he heard someone come into the store.

Nash quickly closed the cupboard and peeked out the door. "Oh hi, Houser. I was just going to go to the bathroom while I waited for you."

He looked at him suspiciously, but only said, "Do you have the contract for me then?"

"I do." Nash reached into his jacket pocket and pulled out the papers. He held them out to Houser.

Houser reached for the papers, but Nash didn't let go of them.

"Having second thoughts?" Houser asked.

"And third and fourth," Nash said with a slight chuckle. Out of the corner of his eye, he caught a glimpse of flickering light in the Enchanted Garden. Why were they so protective of the place? What did they even do there? Did he really want to know?

"You'll be able to have anything you want if you align yourself with Porsche, you know." Houser's direct gaze showed no hint of deception. He believed what he said.

Nash had his own belief. If he signed the contract, he most likely wouldn't be able to make it work with Mira. *That*, Porsche couldn't promise him. "If we can have anything we want, I guess you must want to be her lackey?"

Houser's mouth curved into a half-smile. "It suits me…for now."

Footsteps trouncing down the stairs interrupted their conversation. As Tory and Vashti appeared at the bottom of the steps, Nash let go of the contract. Houser took it in hand.

"Oh, I didn't realize I had a customer," Vashti said. She looked at Tory. "I guess I didn't hear anyone come in because I was showing Flora the rooms available for rent." She looked Nash up and down. "I see you've recovered."

Nash ducked his head, not because he was ashamed really, but because he didn't like the woman and he didn't want it to show. "Although I don't remember it, I'm sorry I caused a ruckus."

"I bet," she said, and went to the kitchen.

Houser folded the signed contract in half and shoved it in his back pocket. "I have some things to get done before I leave tomorrow. If you'll excuse me," he said. "Nash - I'll let you know if she has any questions." After a curious glance at Tory, he disappeared up the stairs.

"So Flora," Vashti said, reaching into a drawer near the till, "Are you interested in renting a room?"

"Yeah. Actually I am."

Nash hid his shock. They hadn't planned this! And Tory was a person who thought things through, except for the time he talked her into investigating Kya's murder. Now she was moving into this crazy place on a whim? It didn't make sense.

"That's great! I have some paperwork for you to fill out here," Vashti said, laying a stack of papers on the table and positioning a pen right next to it.

Tory…or Flora…sat down and began reading through the contract. At least she still had enough logic to do that!

"Is there anything I can help you with, Nash?" Vashti asked.

"No. I just brought my contract to Houser."

"Well, I assume that's done since he's gone." Her smile had a passive aggressive slant. "So goodbye then." She opened the front door for him. As he stepped through it, she said in a low whisper, "I promised to let you in here today, but my hospitality ends there."

"You were reimbursed for the damage I caused," he said, wondering why hate for him seemed to be seeping out her pores.

"Let's just say that I'm preventing more damage that you might cause." With that, she shut the door behind him.

Though uneasy at leaving Tory with Vashti, Nash had to trust she knew what she was doing. He wandered past the two neighboring, adjoined stores – The Baby Boutique and The Dairy Depot - and turned into the side lot where he'd parked his bike. Pacing in front of the cycle, he waited…and waited. No Tory. He glanced at his watch and frowned. Could she be giving him time to sneak into the secret place behind Cofa's Tree? That hadn't been their plan, but it was an opportunity he couldn't pass up.

Ditching his leather jacket, Nash pulled a hoodie out of the storage compartment located under his bike seat. Slipping the sweatshirt over his head, he kept the hood up to hide his hair and his face. He hurried inside the Baby Boutique, the store that shared one of its walls with Cofa's Tree. After checking the price tags of a baby swing, and a newborn-sized leather jacket, he moseyed to the back. The girl behind the counter, who had to be about nine months pregnant, was about halfway through ringing up a stack of clothes for a customer.

With the stealth that came naturally to him, Nash slipped past them and out the store's back door. One clunky old white two door sedan with a car seat in the back was parked next to a dumpster, which conveniently butted up to the fence separating their alley lot from the secret garden. Standing on the trunk of the car, he peeked inside the bin. It was full of flattened stroller boxes, tied trash bags, and a couple crib mattresses. *At least the refuse would provide a soft landing if he fell,* he thought, hoisting himself up onto the metal edge. He inched along the perimeter toward the fence, pausing only a moment to survey the garden. It was getting dark, so he couldn't see much, but he thought he saw movement in the trees.

"I need to know," he whispered, and jumped over the fence.

Chapter 37

Mira couldn't resist. She snapped a couple more shots of the magnificent Tanger. Would she even be able to capture the full effect of the aura he inspired? She'd get an A on her project if she did.

"I'll head down to the water," Tanger said. He ambled down the stone steps to the water's edge. He kicked off his shoes, then unzipped his jeans.

Suddenly shy, Mira turned the camera toward the lake to snap a few pictures of the rising moon. She heard the clunk of his belt hitting the rocky ground. She wanted to look, but she didn't.

"When I get into the water, yell down my instructions, okay?" Tanger's voice was laced with a smile.

"Okay," she said, busying herself with taking the pictures of the moon's reflection. After a moment, she heard the splash of water accompanied by a loud sigh.

"The water is nice. Tell me you'll join me after the photo session," he called out.

She glanced down at him from her perch. His hair was wet, his bare chest glistening. Wow! "Maybe I will. Maybe I won't."

"It's better than a no," he said with a grin. "So what are my instructions, sweetheart?"

The endearment made her heart sigh. "Um…you're already at about the right depth of water, but you need to turn so that your back is to me."

He did as she requested. "Anything else?"

She stared at his broad muscular back for several seconds before answering. "I need you to reach up toward the moon with your right arm."

He lifted his arm, his open palm facing the moon.

She snapped a couple of shots, but after a quick look at the camera's display window, she wasn't impressed by what she'd captured. Something was missing. "Maybe we need to wait a little bit. Maybe the moon isn't quite right."

He looked at her over his shoulder. "The moon will be too high in the sky if we wait much longer. Describe to me what you *want* to see."

She didn't know where the words came from, but she said, "Depth of feeling."

He nodded to her and turned back around. "Goddess moon, let my heart be open to a deeper song. Draw our souls together." His fingers spread wide as they stretched heavenward. It was almost as if power flowed through them.

"That's it," she whispered, snapping picture after picture, amazed at the energy he roused within her. After what seemed like a hundred shots, she took a moment to check out a few. The one right after he'd said those words was *the* one. It was exquisite. It was potent. And it drew her into its magical essence with a fascination that awakened her awareness of mysteries yet to be discovered.

"Did you get a good shot yet? It's getting kind of lonely down here."

She smiled at him. "Yeah. I got a great shot. In fact, I don't think we'll need to do another photo shoot."

"That's unfortunate," he said with a laugh. "Do you plan on painting it, or will you turn in the print?"

"Neither. I'm actually going to do something different." The idea had just popped into her head. "I'm going to print it and then paint over pieces of it...to symbolize a life in the process of creating its own reality."

"Overachiever." He laughed.

"Hardly." She had her perfect shot, but she wasn't ready for the evening to end. Laying the camera beside his discarded shirt, she made her way down the stone steps as elegantly as her high heels would allow. As she approached the water's edge, her stomach coiled.

"Join me," Tanger said, holding out his hand.

She wanted to, yet her resolve wavered. "I don't know," she said. The bright moon made a shadow on the water, but it wouldn't shadow the imperfections of her body – nor would it hide her unease.

"I think you *do* know. Just let yourself feel the natural beauty all around us, Mira. Absorb it." He turned around slowly, making a full circle. "Be part of it." His smile encouraged her. "It's how we are meant to live."

Maybe he was right. Maybe her hesitation was actually the source of her restlessness. Maybe it was why she felt so out of place in Pillar. Maybe it was holding her back from becoming her true self. "Okay," she said, slipping out of her shoes. Tanger didn't comment, but his expectant gaze spoke volumes. It made her anxious. "Turn around," she said.

"Seriously?"

She nodded.

He smiled softly. "Anything for you, doll." He turned so that his back was to her.

Swallowing past the nervous lump in her throat, she slipped the jumper off her shoulders. It dropped into a clump at her feet. The air was cool against her warm skin, so she hugged her arms around herself and stepped out of the pool of cloth to wade into the water. She gasped. "I thought you said the water was nice!"

He only chuckled. Then he asked, "Can I turn around?"

"Not yet."

When the water covered everything but her shoulders and head, she said, "Okay. You can turn around now."

He swung around and with long, water-logged strides, approached her. She wished she knew what he was thinking. Now standing less than an arm's length away, she looked up at him.

Tanger grinned as he reached out to give her bra strap a slight tug. "Well, it's not exactly the toss-convention-to-the-wind move I'd expected, but you're making progress."

She frowned at his chest. "Did you think I'd be someone who'd just throw off my clothes and frolic around whenever with whomever?"

"I'm not whomever." His wet fingers tilted her chin up so that her gaze met his. "And I expect a risk taker. You were one, once."

"I'm still a risk taker," she said, putting her hands on her hips. "I've started businesses, I've started a relationship with you and joined a group I know very little about...I even did the lucid dreaming stuff."

He let his hand drop to his side. "But you limit yourself," he said softly.

After she'd had that nightmare about Kya, she planned on scrapping the lucid dreaming. But other than those limits, she was bold, right? "I do not."

"You do with me."

She frowned up at him. "What about last night?" If that wasn't taking a risk, she didn't know what was!

"You're holding back a part of yourself." He brushed the pad of his thumb across her bottom lip. "I want all of you." He dipped his head so that their lips were only a breath away.

His challenge tempted her and his roguery enticed, yet she was torn by something inside that just wouldn't let her trust him with the abandon he was requesting. "I..." she said with a swallow.

"Mira," came a hushed whisper like an echo in the mists.

She jumped and swung around toward the sound, but no one stood on the upper flat. "You heard that, didn't you? You heard someone say my name?" Mira asked. After the doll and the dream about Kya, she was beginning to question her sanity.

He nodded. "I'll go check it out." Tanger hurried to the bank and started up the stone steps.

Mira wasn't about to be left behind. Frantic eyes scoured her surroundings as she waded into shore and slipped on her jumpsuit. It clung uncomfortably to her wet skin and underclothes as she climbed the steps. When she reached the outcropping, Tanger, already in his jeans and t-shirt, approached her.

"I didn't see anyone."

"What do we do next?" She shivered.

He sent her a reassuring smile as he took her hand. "I'll take you back to Cofa's Tree, then I'll come back to get a better look." He kissed the top of her head. "I'll make sure you're safe, Mira."

She didn't doubt that Tanger could protect her. "It just gives me the creeps," she said, looking all around, seeing moving shadows everywhere.

Tanger picked up his camera and slung it over his shoulder. "Yeah," he said. "Me too."

She didn't like hearing that! "Do you think it could have been Kya's murderer?" Mira could easily be the next on their list!

"It's a possibility, I guess." He took a flashlight out of his camera bag and, as he led her into the densely treed area, he switched it on. Swinging it back and forth, he said, "Looks clear so far."

But there are a lot of places to hide, Mira thought, clutching her shoes in her hand.

He must have thought the same, because he kept their pace quick.

The trek back seemed much further than she remembered. Her body was tense, her teeth chattering, and her feet throbbed. Neither Tanger nor Mira made a sound, except for their heavy breathing, as they entered the Enchanted Garden. Though it glowed with its wax lanterns, it didn't bring her any comfort.

Tanger marched her across the garden with determination. Opening the sliding door for her, he followed her inside Cofa's Tree. The warmth washed over her, comforting her - as did Vashti's presence. The store owner sat in a recliner, reading a book with a gauzy looking cover. It was entitled "Finding the Right Spirit Guide" *Great bedtime reading*, Mira thought, although something like that would probably help to redirect her thoughts of their evening visitor.

"Oh hi, kids. How was your outing?" Vashti asked, dog-earring her page.

After a quick glance at Mira, Tanger said, "I'm sure she got some great pictures." He handed her the camera and stepped back through the sliding door. "But I think we might have left something down by the water."

"Yeah. I think you're right," Mira said. "Thanks for checking, Tanger."

He nodded as he closed the door behind him, not one wisp of playfulness in his demeanor remained. Mira nibbled on her thumbnail, watching him until the darkness swallowed him.

Vashti set her book on the coffee table. "You look worried," she said.

"It's nothing a good night's sleep won't cure," she said with as bright of a smile as she could muster. Mira wandered toward the stairs.

"Well, goodnight then."

Mira turned. "Goodnight, Vashti."

Vashti studied her a moment before picking up her book again. "Let me know if you need someone to talk to, or need some guidance." She smiled softly and straightened the flap on the page.

"Thanks," Mira said. "I'll let you know." Right now, all she wanted to do was find something to barricade the window and door of her room while she reviewed her pictures. After all that had happened, she'd just die if one of the pictures didn't turn out like she wanted.

Chapter 38

Nash swayed as he latched onto the fence's wooden slats. It took him several tries to get back over it, and when he finally did, he found himself amidst garbage bags filled with what had to be dirty diapers. He lay there a few moments and tried to stop the dizziness. Reaching under his hood, he felt the tender spot on the back of his head. It was wet with blood.

"Time to move, Montgomery," he whispered. Whoever had pummeled his head would probably be looking for him, and unless it was Mira, he didn't want to be found.

Mira...he'd heard her voice, and Tanger's too. "What about last night?" she'd said, to which Tanger had responded, "You're holding something back. I want all of you." What had been her answer? He didn't know because someone had come up from behind and had knocked him on the head. But he still couldn't forget. Their words kept looping through his brain.

Nash sat up slowly and reached for a box that poked up out of the debris. Using it for leverage, he got to his feet. Knee deep in the garbage, he grasped the edge of the green metal pod. Although he felt like puking, he managed to maneuver himself out of the bin. When his feet hit the ground, he paused a moment to regain his equilibrium. Swiping the sweat from his brow, he forced his feet to move. As he hobbled along, he managed to control his walk, but not the direction of his thoughts. How had Mira moved on so fully and so quickly? Had she never really loved him? In his throbbing brain and aching heart, there was a battle going on. One side wished Mira wouldn't fall for someone like Tanger who he just knew would cause her grief. The other side wished she'd hurt as much as he did right now.

When he got to his bike, he noticed a piece of paper sticking out from beneath his gas cover. Twisting it off, he grabbed hold of the note. The strong smell of gas tickled his nose and made him even woozier, but he managed to read the neat print with the light from his phone. *Dear Nash – I went back to my apartment to get a bag of clothes. I signed up for a week's stay at Cofa's Tree and if I want to extend it, I can. I'll come by early tomorrow morning so I can change back into Tory and open your store. Hopefully I'll have some information to share. Stay safe, Love Tory.*

Nash supposed staying there would put her in a good position to find out details, if Mira didn't recognize her and squeal on her. His stomach curdled at the thought of something happening to Tory, or something happening with Mira that he didn't want to hear about. It was best to know the truth, he guessed, no matter how ugly it might be. He pulled off his sweatshirt, and after wiping the gash on his head with it, he stuffed it into the storage compartment. Slipping his jacket back on, he jumped on his bike and headed toward home…at least it would still be home for a few more days.

Chapter 39

Mira tried to lock her window, but the latch was broken. She tied a string around it instead, satisfied it would buy her time should someone try to break into her second story window. She double-checked the door. It was still locked. The doll remained secured inside the trunk in her closet, too, which was good. She didn't want to chance a visit to the dumpster with it in the dark of night after what had happened.

Grabbing a pair of sweats and a sweatshirt from her dresser, she quickly changed into them. As she hung her wet clothes over the rocking chair, the muffled sound of music wove its way beneath her door. The song was one of Nash's. Being with him seemed so long ago, and yet she found herself missing him again. Even though her current situation was dramatically different and her horizons seemed as limitless as she could ever want, she didn't feel like she was any closer to being the woman she wanted to be.

Ignoring the regret that wiggled its way inside, she wandered to her nightstand and picked up her phone. She'd had several calls from her mom and dad. For some reason, she really wanted to hear their voices, so she listened to their messages, twice over. They missed her and would love to catch up and see how she was doing before they left for Enab. Should she? She wanted to, and yet what if they could see beneath her façade? Would they see her fear, her failure, her guilt? Would they delay their trip? She couldn't let that happen. She needed to power through this – and it started with passing her art class.

Grabbing Tanger's camera, she muttered, "Well, let's hope this is as good as I think it is." She smiled, envisioning a grand revealing of her novel artwork – a piece that captured individuality bursting free in power and light. "Maybe it'll end up showcased in Divinya's classroom. Or maybe I'll have my own art show, displaying my photo-art." The more she thought about it, the more excited she became. The possibilities were endless!

Holding the camera's small screen in close, she flipped through the pictures until she came to the one she thought held the most promise. She stared at the lines of Tanger's body, softened by the moonlight, yet still appearing in sharper focus than if she had carved him. The moon's reflection on the water made it seem as if it was an opulent silver, like it held a promise of a rich life if a person drank it in. Tanger's image seemed so dynamic, it was almost as if he *was* the water…he *was* the moon…and he *was* everything in between. She couldn't wait to develop the picture!

Mira glanced at the door, wondering when Tanger would return. Maybe they could go tonight to Knack Photo, the all-night-photo shop, and get the picture developed. She wasn't going alone, not after what happened to Kya, and not after what had happened tonight. She shivered, hoping it was nothing to worry about.

Laying the camera down on the desk, she went to her dresser and grabbed a warm pair of socks and slipped them on. She sat down on her chair, crossing her feet at the ankles. Where *was* Tanger? She pursed her lips. How much time should she give him? She glanced at the clock. It had been an hour already. Blowing out a breath, she padded to the door. Her hand paused on the lock. "Don't be silly, Mira. Vashti is downstairs reading, people are chilling to music in their rooms. You're perfectly safe!" But was Tanger? She unlocked the door and poked her head out. The hall was empty, and Tanger's door was closed. She hurried across the hall and knocked. He didn't answer. She knocked again. "Tanger? It's me." Only silence answered.

Was he still at Wormwood's Water? Was he downstairs? She went to the top of the stairs to listen. She heard nothing. No conversation most likely meant Tanger wasn't with Vashti. Not wanting to talk to anyone but Tanger, Mira wandered back to her room. Curling up beneath her covers, she tried to relax, only sleep evaded her. What if something happened to him?

Sometime later, she heard a knock on her door. She looked at her clock. It was two in the morning. "Who is it?"

"Tanger."

Relief filled her as she jogged to the door to let him in. She fell into his arms and hugged him tightly. "I was so worried about you."

"I'm fine." He nudged her, putting a space between them. "I just came to tell you that I'm heading out of town for a while."

She frowned. That was *not* what she'd expected him to say. "Why?"

"It's a retreat of sorts," he said.

"What kind of retreat?"

His shoulders lifted slightly, his eyes cast down toward his rugged boots. "It's to restore my inner harmony."

What a wonderful thing they could do together. "Can I come with you?"

"No. It's more of a solitary quest. You understand." He reached down to where a paper covered frame was leaning against the wall. "I need you to turn my project in for me."

He needed to be away from her to restore his inner harmony? "I *don't* understand," she said, not taking the picture.

"It's just something I need to do," he said, not pretending that she was referring to anything but his leaving.

"Like a spider on a string, right?" Her stomach churned, her legs felt like they would only be able to hold her up for one more minute before they gave out.

He smiled weakly, but didn't respond to her observation, which verified that she was right.

"Will you turn this in for me?" he asked, holding the picture out to her again.

She couldn't believe this was happening. "You'd trust me to turn it in after this?"

"I helped you so that you could pass the class. Now I need you to help me."

She owed him? Was that what he was saying?

His slow smile widened as he looked her straight in the eyes. "Besides. I know that heart of yours," he said softly. "You'll help me."

A tiny bit of pleasure wormed its way into her heart, but it wasn't enough to make her feel any better. He was leaving without her. She thought about refusing again, but instead held out her hand. He placed the picture in it. As she propped it against the wall next to her door, he said, "Thank you, Mira."

She reminded herself that she hadn't made any promises. The project might never make it to the professor's desk. "Whatever," she said and slammed the door closed…only his booted foot stopped it.

"Wait," he said.

"I don't have anything more to say to you," she said through the door. Why had she even let herself hope?

He shoved the door open anyway and slipped inside her room. "You're welcome to use anything in my room while I'm gone."

"I don't want to use anything from your room. I don't need it. I don't need you." She was so confused. She hated to be confused. And even more than that, she hated to be tossed away.

Tanger frowned slightly, then before she could block him, he swooped in for a kiss. It was soft, yet filled with passion. Then he broke away.

"I don't get it," she spat.

"Just follow your heart and you'll be fine," he said, although at the moment, it didn't seem like he quite believed his own advice. It was impossible for her – her heart was full of want, sadness, hate, revenge, fear. What was she supposed to 'follow'?

"Just…go," Mira said. She wanted to be alone so she could think…or not think.

With one last look that she couldn't begin to decipher, he was gone.

Mira glared at the closed door, her insides squeezing painfully. Why did life have to be so difficult? Heart heavy, she wandered across the room. Slouching down on the bed, she stared across the room at the paper-covered artwork he'd left in her care. Just this past morning, she'd wanted to peek at it in the worst way. Now she wanted to rip it to shreds. What was it about her that everyone wanted to leave?

Chapter 40

Nash let himself into his apartment. Grabbing an icepack from the freezer, he pressed it against the gash on his head. He sucked in through his teeth, the coldness shocking him before it seeped through his entire body. At least the throbbing had lessened. Pacing through the kitchen area, into the living room, and then back to the kitchen, he tried to erase the picture in his head of Mira and Tanger together so that he could go through the details of what happened and analyze the facts. But it was impossible. The facts were clouded in a haze of emotion he couldn't withdraw from the situation.

If he'd kept his LifeChip, this wouldn't be happening. But although he longed for the peace he'd known with the calm perspective of having the chip, he also knew how much better, fuller, and more complete life could be. Or at least he thought he did.

Nash blew out a long breath and tried replaying the scene again. Could it have been the killer that had knocked him on the head? No, he couldn't assume that. But what purpose would the perp have to knock him out? What would be the motive? His intuition told him that it had to be someone that *wanted* Tanger and Mira together.

He frowned as he wound his way to the couch. Sitting on the slightly caved in cushions, he propped his feet on the coffee table. Who would want Tanger and Mira together? Taking out a piece of paper and a pencil, he began to make a list. NOT ME, he wrote in bold letters, then added names of everyone he could think of that would possibly want them together, no matter how extreme the reasons could be. Tory, Daphne, Vashti, Porsche and maybe even Houser. Or maybe Tanger had hired someone. And what about Eleanor and her husband Elroy?

Nash closed his eyes, trying to make sense of it all, but his excruciating headache wasn't helping. Leaning back, he told himself the situation would be clearer in the morning. But then a thought popped into his head. What if he had a concussion? What if he didn't wake up? Nash went to his desk and grabbed an envelope and a notepad. He took it back to the couch and began to write down all the information he knew, what he suspected, and he even wrote a letter to Mira. He poured out his heart in those words. And when he stared down at the papers through his tears, exhaustion struck him like a sledge hammer. He curled up on the couch and let it take him. If he didn't wake up, so be it.

Chapter 41

With the sun hot on her back, Mira paused in front of Knack Photo. Life-sized prints covered the glass entrance – one of a guy with a camera in hand as he looked off into the distance, the other of a woman holding a single flower, ready to pluck the last petal from its stem. Mira couldn't help but stare at the woman's sad expression, at the pile of petals at her feet, at the solitary petal left that would end all hope, but she refused to let it get to her. It didn't matter that Tanger had left without giving her a timeframe of when he'd be back. No promises had ever been made between them. She told herself that it was a good thing. It left her free to do what she wanted. Only what *did* she want?

Trying to shake off the gloom by focusing her thoughts on how spectacular her final project would be, Mira slipped into the photo shop. As she approached the counter, she became as jittery as if she'd had caffeine for breakfast and lunch. Would the photograph be as awesome as she envisioned? She needed it to be. What would it be like to see Tanger in print as she had seen him that night? Would she still feel the connection? Would it make his leaving hurt worse? It didn't matter how she felt about it. This was her last hope for a passing grade in her art class.

Tucking her hands into her pockets, Mira said, "Hi Leigh. Is my picture done?"

A petite girl with straight black hair smiled brightly at her. Her eyes squinted prettily, lighting up her entire face. "Yep." She went to the bin behind the desk and flipped through the orders. "Sorry it took so long," she said, pulling it out of the bin. "But to get high quality for this size print, I had to send it out."

"I understand. I'm just glad I got it before my final project is due."

"When is it due?"

"Tomorrow."

"Just in time, then." Leigh held out a package wrapped in a cardboard envelope the size of a poster. "You want to look at it before you pay?"

Mira took it and loosened the top flap to peek inside. Shoving away the feelings just a glimpse provoked, she scanned the print for defects. It didn't appear to have any – no graininess, no fuzziness, no flaws. Why couldn't her life be that way?

"It looks like a winner," Mira said with the semblance of a smile. After a glance at the total on the cash register's digital display, she leaned the picture against the wall. Taking out her wallet, she handed Leigh exact change.

"Thanks," Leigh said, stuffing the money into the register. "It's a great photograph."

"Yeah. I think so too." Hopefully it was good enough for her to get a passing grade in her class. Mira took the receipt from Leigh and picked up her purchase. As she swung around, the over-sized envelope smacked into the customer behind her, someone she hadn't even realized was there.

Mira gasped, looking from the bent corner of her print up to the person she blamed for it. "Nash?" His name came out like a gust of wind.

"Mira." He touched the edge of the package, but kept his eyes trained on her. "I hope it's salvageable."

"Me too," she said with a frown. After their last meeting at his apartment last week, seeing him felt awkward. Her twist of emotions wouldn't allow any words to come out.

"Here," he said. "Let's take a look at it and make sure I didn't ruin everything." Though his words seemed laced with hidden meaning, he gently took the print from her and laid it on the counter next to the cash register. As he began to unfold the top, reality struck. She grabbed his hand. She didn't want him to ask questions about the photograph, about Tanger, about them. She just didn't want to deal with it right now.

"No. That's okay. I'm sure it's fine." She tried to remind herself that he'd chosen his career over her, but his hand exuded warmth and his eyes were warmer still. Why couldn't her heart let him go? Would it be the same if Tanger were still around?

"Is this your final project?" he asked, folding the cardboard flap back into place.

"Yeah."

He smiled. "I'm glad you got it done." He lifted the package and handed it back to her.

"Me too. I just wish I knew what I should do next."

He looked at her thoughtfully. "No plans for the summer then?"

She shrugged. "Nothing set in stone, but I have a lot of options." She intended to list a few to prove it, but couldn't think of anything that didn't sound lame. "A lot of options," she repeated, softly this time.

"I'm sure you *do* have a lot of options." He stared at her for a moment, looking as if he was trying to think of something to say. Would he ask her to go with him again? Should she consider it?

"I, um, wrote you a song," he said, his words like a choked whisper.

It wasn't what she'd expected him to say, nor did her tangle of emotions allow for anything more than a generic response that would give them away. "That's nice," she said.

"Yeah, that's me. Nice." He shook his head. "I'll mail you a recording of it when I get the music part of it done."

The picture in her hands suddenly felt very heavy. "Why would you do that?"

With a lift of his shoulders, he said, "The reasons don't really matter I guess." He tucked his hands into his pockets. "I'm leaving tomorrow to go on tour."

She'd known it was coming, but it still made her sad. "I'm sure you'll be a huge hit and will have a ton of fun doing it."

"Yeah." He paused to look down at her. "Are you heading back home with that?"

"I'm going to Cofa's Tree, yes."

"Can I walk you there?"

Tanger was gone and Nash would be tomorrow. She let her guard down. "I guess that would be okay."

Nash smiled, though it did nothing to erase the sadness from his eyes. He took the package from her and opened the door to let her pass through. As she wandered outside, she bumped into Houser, who was on his way in.

"Hi, Houser." She looked away from his perceptive gaze.

"Hi, Mira. Hi, Nash." He glanced down at the package Nash held. "Is that a poster for your tour?"

"No. This belongs to Mira," Nash said.

Houser smiled. "Good." He lifted the memory stick in his hand. "Because I was hoping *I'd* be the one bringing Porsche the perfect poster pictures."

Nash smiled. "I'm sure she'll approve."

The posters added to the reality of Nash's tour – and the finality of their relationship. Mira's stomach turned sour. "I need to get back," she said and bolted down the sidewalk.

About halfway down the block, Nash caught up with her.

"I thought it was okay that I walk you back to Cofa's Tree? Why did you leave me?"

"Because you're leaving me." The blurted words betrayed her.

Nash began to say something, but snapped his mouth shut. After taking a deep breath, he said, "I don't want to think about yesterday or tomorrow, but I do want to tell you what I plan on doing tonight." His eyes had taken on a playful, yet intense look.

Mira was curious. "Tell me."

He smiled, and for a moment, the heaviness smothering her heart lifted. "I'm going out on a mission of sorts tonight," he said.

Though she knew she shouldn't ask any more, she couldn't help herself. "What kind of mission?"

"I did some digging and I think I have a lead on Kya's murder."

"So what does that have to do with me?" She felt a thrum of excitement.

"I want you to come with me to investigate," he said simply.

He wanted her to come with him.

"It's just for tonight. I'm not asking for any commitments other than that. Please come with me, Mira."

It would give her something to do, something to think about other than her own misery. And being with Nash while working on the murder case would be exciting for sure. Man, she'd love to see Kya's killer rotting in a cell! But what would spending more time, close time, with Nash do to her heart? Would his leaving be more painful? *You are overthinking this Mira*, she chided herself. *You need to live in the moment and for the moment.* Only her mind continued to argue with itself until they got to Cofa's Tree.

"So what do you say? Will you come with me?" Nash asked.

Throwing caution to the wind, she said, "I'm in. What's the plan?"

Chapter 42

He'd only had time to tell Mira to dress in black and meet him at the band shell right after dark before Vashti had come out of Cofa's Tree, interrupting their conversation with a request for Mira's help with the customers. It was just as well, Nash thought. Letting the mystery build had been a part of his plan, anyway. Only now he needed to kill time before he met up with Mira. His bags were already packed, and he'd done all the research he could do. So he set out for a ride on his bike.

He cruised around town, loving the hum of the machine beneath him, but with each passing moment, his nerves began to pop. Why did it feel like his happiness hinged on tonight? Maybe it did, maybe it didn't, but he needed to talk to someone he trusted before he went crazy. After parking his bike in his friends' townhouse driveway, he strode up the sidewalk between the budding and blossoming flowers that lined it. Their fragrant smell reminded him of the first time Mira had introduced him to nature as a chipless person. The memory hit him sharply and dug in until he ached with regret. He rang the doorbell, hoping Hayes would be able to help him. Mel opened the door.

"What a lovely surprise," she said with a bright smile.

Nash managed to smile back. "Is Hayes around?"

She nodded. "Come on in and help yourself to some tea and I'll get him for you."

Nash followed her into the house as he had so many times over the past year. He always felt so welcome here. It sounded corny, but that's how he felt.

Nash went to the kitchen and poured himself a glass of the best iced tea he'd ever tasted. He didn't know what kind of tea she used because she wouldn't tell him her secret. She always said that if she told him, he'd have no reason to come back and visit her. He sat down by the table. As he took his first sip, Hayes came into the kitchen, his arm wrapped around Mel's shoulders. "Hi Nash. How's it goin'?"

"Fine I guess."

The couple sat across from him. "What's up?" Hayes asked.

Nash took a drink of the cold liquid. "As you know, I'm leaving on my tour tomorrow." Reaching into his pocket, he pulled out a copy of his tour list and slid it toward them.

Hayes glanced at the list then up at Nash. "Looks like a full schedule."

"Yeah."

"Is it what ya want?"

Nash pursed his lips, looking down at the schedule that would be his life for the next year. "Yeah. It's what I want."

"So what's buggin' ya then?" Hayes asked.

Nash twisted the drink around and around. "Well, leaving Mira with a murderer on the loose bugs me," he said, resting his hands atop the table. "Actually, leaving Mira bugs me, period."

"Why leave then?" Mel asked.

He frowned. "My music is my passion…my career. It's who I am." He looked up at the pair. "I want Mira and I want my music career. I don't see why I can't have them both."

"How are you going to accomplish that? Last I heard you were on the outs," Mel said frankly.

"I invited her out tonight to convince her that we are good together and that she should come with me on tour." He hoped the investigation tonight would reawaken what Mira had felt for him during their quest for the Enchiridion, but he knew better than to tell Mel and Hayes that. They would try to persuade him to leave it to the authorities.

"Does that mean you plan on getting married before you leave tomorrow?" Mel asked.

Marriage? He wasn't nearly ready for that! "No," he answered, pressing his fingers back so that his knuckles crackled. "But having her on tour with me will be a good way for us to know if we are truly compatible."

Mel went to the counter to pour herself a glass of tea. "No two people are actually compatible," she said.

Nash frowned deeply. "You two are compatible."

Hayes laughed. Leaning forward, he said softly, "Get it out of yer head that there is a person that will fulfill ya and make ya "whole" and happy. That person doesn't exist."

"But…"

Mel moved to stand behind Hayes, glass in hand, an arm draped over his shoulders. "We have found a deep love and joy in our marriage, but it was a journey of two souls that made a choice and a commitment to love, and to change, and to sacrifice," she said. "Shacking up with Mira on a bus is only going to lead to heartache."

But it was better than no Mira! Logic told Nash that moving her on the bus with him was the perfect solution, and yet he couldn't disregard what his friends were telling him. Mel sounded so sure, and they were living proof of the relationship he wanted to have for himself. "I still don't see what harm it could do."

Mel sat down on Hayes' lap. "Let's put it this way. You will find temporary benefits, but human nature is a selfish one, and it's one that will lead you *both* to continue to look for someone perfect who will fill all your desires."

"So what am I supposed to do then? It's not like she'd marry me, even if I asked."

"Pray about it," Hayes said.

Nash exhaled a quick, disbelieving breath and shook his head. If there was a God, he hadn't been hearing any of *his* prayers. "Any other advice?"

Hayes gently shifted Mel off his lap and went into his office, a room adjacent to the kitchen. After a few moments, he returned with a book. Handing it to Nash, he said, "Start with this."

Nash looked at the beat up book titled *Cold Case Christianity*. It's cover pictured stacks of paper-filled folders and handcuffs.

"It was written by a detective named Wallace," Hayes added.

"I leave tomorrow and this is your advice?"

"Yep."

Nash picked it up, grateful for his friend, but not so grateful for his advice. "But I need to make this happen now!"

Hayes only smiled. "Just like hitting a fastball or writing a song that will speak ta the hearts of millions, a person has ta learn the craft and then put in time and effort ta make it work. It's the same with love."

Though it wasn't the reassurance he'd been hoping for, Nash tucked the book under his arm and stood. "I don't get what Christianity has to do with love."

Hayes laughed aloud. "At the heart of Christianity is love, my friend – Jesus *is* love and He's our perfect example ta learn the craft from."

"Yeah, yeah. So you say." Nash made his way to the door. "I might not read this, you know."

Hayes shrugged. "It's yer choice." He opened the door for Nash and added, "I hope it goes well for ya and Mira tonight. I really do."

"I know." Nash rubbed the back of his neck. "I keep trying to look at the world as if it makes sense, and yet it doesn't. Times like these prove how illogical it is. Like why, after pushing me away, would Mira want to even join me tonight?"

"All we can do is keep searching for the truth," Mel said.

"You think you know the truth, don't you?" Nash asked.

"I'm certain of it." Hayes' bold stare met Nash's. "In fact, I've staked my life on it."

"I suppose you have." Nash hugged them both. "I don't know if I'll see you before I leave, so I'll say good-bye now just in case."

"Take care and God bless, Nash." Mel smiled. "I hope you find what you're looking for."

So did he…so did he.

Chapter 43

Mira dried the last plate, put it in the rack, and hung the towel over the hook near the sink. The group who had come by for a lite dinner of veggie wraps and chickpea salad had been a welcome distraction. A glance at the clock, though, told her she still had an hour before she met Nash at the band shell. Her mind buzzed with ideas and scenarios. She couldn't wait!

"Care to join me? I have some good reading material," Vashti said, sitting in the chair, a book on her lap.

Too fidgety to read, Mira said, "No. I think I'm going to swing by and visit my parents. I haven't seen them in a while."

"Sounds good." Vashti returned to her book. "Have fun."

Racing up to her room, Mira stopped first at her final project, which was propped against her dresser. She turned off the fan and skimmed her fingers over the gloss finish covering. It was almost dry. Eyes grazing the majestic and mysterious print, she realized she was proud of herself – of how the details she'd added with her oil paints had brought with them soul-deep emotions promising pleasure and freedom. She stared at the painted image of herself, now a reflection on the water. It was as if the moon's light glimpsed her standing on the water's edge and implored her to reveal her true self. The water seemed to welcome her to drink of its life-giving sweetness, too. She planned to do both.

Stashing a black zippered sweatshirt into her oversized purse, she slipped into black leggings and t-shirt. After donning her lace-up, knee high flat boots – the ones Tanger called gypsy boots – she propped her purse on her shoulder and strode into the hallway...and right into a girl she'd never seen before.

"Oh. Sorry. I wasn't paying attention to where I was going," the girl said, ducking her head so that her face hid behind the edge of her black hoodie.

"No worries. I wasn't paying attention either." Mira studied the girl. She had very white skin and black painted nails and a nose ring. "Are you staying at Cofa's Tree for long?"

The girl shrugged, edging away from her, never looking up. "I've been here over a week, but I might stay longer. We'll see."

Mira wondered what her story was – and why she hadn't seen her before now. "Well, welcome…what was your name again?"

"I didn't say." She cleared her throat and turned toward the room Daphne had stayed in. "But it's Flora," she said in a raspy voice – as though the throat clearing had had no effect.

"Well it's nice to meet you Flora. I'm heading out tonight, but I'm sure I'll be seeing you around," Mira said, making her way to the stairs.

"Okay," Flora said, and with shaky hands, shoved the key into the lock, then disappeared behind the door.

Strange girl, Mira thought, hurrying down the stairs. As she crossed the room and made her way to the exit, Vashti looked up from her chair.

"How late will you be?" Vashti asked.

"I'm not sure."

"In that case, go ahead and take the key from the till drawer so if you come back after I lock up for the night, you can still get in."

Oh yeah. That's right! No parents, no curfew. She grinned. How awesome was that!

"Thanks," she said. She retrieved the key from the till and slipped it into her purse. Then with a wave, she headed outside.

The sidewalk's heat seeped through her shoes as she walked, and the warm air felt cozy and smelled a little like exhaust and dead bugs, but it didn't lessen her anticipation. She ignored the people and businesses she passed, and zoned-in on her thoughts and feelings. In a short while, she'd meet up with Nash to investigate Kya's murder. She was curious. What evidence *did* he have? What would they find? Why had Nash looked at her the way he had? Had he changed his mind about leaving? The mystery of what might happen tonight awakened a flood of emotions. Whatever happened, she vowed that she'd allow herself the freedom to enjoy whatever experiences were in store.

Before she knew it, she was halfway up the hill to her house. For once, the view only brought on a fleeting thought of the man she'd believed was her father. His death symbolized the beginning of life for so many, and she hoped that the energy she felt at this moment would allow her to realize the same. Tonight could be a new inspiration, a new confidence of direction that would launch her into something good and vibrant in her own life.

Mira climbed the front steps of her childhood home, debating on whether to knock or not. She decided a surprise would be just the thing, and let herself inside. Being the first time she'd been back since she'd moved out, standing in the foyer seemed odd, like she didn't belong anymore. When she heard voices coming from the dining room, she listened.

"Please Lord, help Mira to understand who You are. Keep her safe, but lead her back to You, where she's meant to be."

Her mom's voice trembled with passionate sincerity, and for some reason, it totally bothered Mira. She considered leaving, but she didn't have anything else to kill the time remaining until she met up with Nash. And she felt she should visit her parents at least once before they left for Enab. Now was as good a time as any, so she squared her shoulders and marched into the dining room like she still belonged there.

"Sorry to interrupt," she said, but she wasn't really. She didn't want anyone praying for her. She'd do her own praying, if she chose to do so, and to whom she chose to pray.

Her parents got up from the table, smiles of welcome on their faces. Mira almost felt bad for her negative thoughts about them, but she shoved the useless feeling away.

"I'm so glad you're here!" her dad said, giving her a big hug.

Her mom followed suit. "We were just finishing up with our study of one of the Enchiridion's passages. Would you care to join us for some dessert? I made coconut custard."

"Sure. I'll have a piece."

"Good." Her mom smiled, then disappeared into the kitchen.

Vaughn closed the Enchiridion and replaced it on the center shelf of the bookcase. "So what brings you by?" he asked.

"I can't just come for a visit? I thought I was welcome anytime." She felt so agitated, but wasn't sure why.

"You *are* always welcome," he said. "Have a seat. I'll pour you some coffee."

She sat down, but felt a sharper uncomfortableness than being in the foyer. Vaughn placed a coffee mug in front of her and poured a full cup from the carafe. The aroma helped soothe her.

"We've missed you around here. How are things going?" her dad asked as he took a seat at the table.

She didn't want to tell him that it hadn't been all that great. Her mistakes were her own and she didn't want to hear I-told-you-so. "Things are going brilliantly!!" Her overly bright statement made Vaughn's brow twitch. She'd have to be more careful.

"Here we go," Mira's mom said, placing the perfect piece of pie in front of her. She didn't waste time digging in.

"Mira was telling me that things are going great for her," Vaughn said.

"I'm happy to hear that." Her mom sat in the chair across from her, one next to Vaughn. "Tell us what's been going on."

She swallowed the bite in her mouth. "Well, I've met some really nice people who care about the things I care about. They're so…unique and have awesome perspectives." Her mom and dad exchanged looks, which irritated her. Feeling like she had to defend her statement, she added, "Their encouragement helped me get my final project done. Awesome, right?"

"The people or the project," Vaughn said, and took a sip of his coffee.

"Both."

"Did you turn your work in yet? Can we see it?" Her mom looked hopeful.

Mira took another bite of the delicious pie. "I don't have it with me and I need to turn it in tomorrow. You'll have to wait to see it until I get it back from the professor."

Her mom took a sip of Vaughn's coffee. "We'll look forward to seeing it later, then. I know that God gave you a lot of artistic talent. I can't wait to see what you do with that talent."

"So you say," Mira muttered. Swallowing a bite of pie, she added, "You wouldn't believe how happy I am. I have so many friends. I'm really beginning to figure out who I am."

"How are you doing that?"

Her mom's pained and disbelieving look torqued Mira off. "Why do you always have to question everything I do? Why can't it be enough that I'm happy?"

"We are only asking because we care." Vaughn reached for her mom's hand, his eyes taking on a sheen that only enhanced their blueness.

"Whatever." Mira shoved away the last bite of pie. "I'll see you around." She couldn't escape fast enough. For some reason, the positives she had been trying so hard to focus on looked stark and weak when she was with her mom and dad. She didn't like the feeling at all. As she took off down the hill, she had to admit that they hadn't really said anything bad, but she could *feel* their judgment of her.

As Mira headed over to the band shell, she wished the sun would set so she could forget what had just happened – so she could forget what had happened with Tanger too. She wanted to feel that rush of life with Nash tonight. And she couldn't wait.

Chapter 44

The band shell stage wasn't a comfortable place to sit, although no place would be, given the agitated state Nash was in. He glanced at his watch. It was meeting time. Would she come?

He closed his eyes a moment, trying to calm his nerves, but they refused to be calmed. So much was riding on what happened tonight! He peeked at the time again. Where was she? He frowned, knowing he had to look up and face the hard facts. Slowly, he lifted his eyes…and there she was, walking across the lawn toward him! Elation stole his breath, realization stole his heart. What they'd been through together came back in a flash and he knew at that moment he really wasn't ready to let go. But he had to play this right.

"Hi Mira. I'm glad you came," he said, offering her his hand. She took it and he pulled her up onto the stage.

"I told you I would," she said as she sat down beside him.

Legs swinging over the edge of the stage, they sat for a moment looking out across the grassy expanse.

"Do you remember coming here on our six-month anniversary?" she asked, disrupting the silence.

He gazed into her beautiful eyes, feeling his love for her all over again. "I remember," he said, reaching up to brush his hand against her cheek. "I remember the kiss we shared that made me believe in forever with you."

She leaned away from his hand. He let it drop to his lap, although maybe he should've pressed it against his chest to keep his heart in place.

"So much has happened since then," she said, "and yet…"

She still loved him. He knew it from the depth of his soul. He just had to get her to realize it.

"I feel like I don't really know you."

He hadn't expected those words at all. "You know more about me than anyone, Mira. And I know *you*."

She shrugged. "That person doesn't exist. I'm a new person now."

Ah. She was going to play that game. He'd play along for now. "Well, I'd love to get to know this new person. What do you say we start by staking out the Prophet House?" Later tonight, he'd ask her to come with him on tour, when the moment was right.

Mira's brows lifted. "And why are we going to do that?"

"Because Kya had paid them a visit the morning before she died. Because I found wigs in the master bedroom…black-haired wigs made of synthetic fiber. Because I've been watching the place over the past several nights. Did you know that Elroy leaves for a hike every evening and doesn't return until around three in the morning?"

"I didn't know that." Mira grinned, but then sobered. "Have you told the police?"

"Not yet. I don't really trust them with something that is so personal to me. I'll…we'll gather more evidence until the case is locked. Then we'll go to the police."

"Sounds great to me." Mira opened her bag and slipped on her dark sweatshirt, zipped it to her chin, and put up the hood. She looked over at him. "Ready?"

Already dressed in black head to toe, Nash jumped to the ground and nodded. "This way." He helped Mira off the stage and led her to his cycle.

"Is this yours?" Mira asked, her stare at the machine one of appreciation.

"It is."

"Are you…" She shook her head. "Never mind. Tonight is tonight." She slid her leg over the bike, then looked at him with a smile. "What are you waiting for?"

"Nothing." He slipped on to the seat in front of her. Immediately, her arms came around his waist and hugged him tightly. He paused to relish the feeling of momentary contentment and gratitude. On impulse, he turned and kissed her on the lips. It was so quick she didn't have time to respond – which was a good thing. He couldn't have handled a slap right at the moment.

Nash started his bike and eased it onto the road. As he rode through town, Mira's grasp tightened and filled him with hope. He almost took a roundabout way to their destination just to have the chance to enjoy it a bit longer, but he knew Elroy would be leaving for his hike soon.

They continued to the outskirts of town and turned onto the gravel road that would lead to the Prophet House. He took a left onto a side dirt road and pulled into his usual spot behind a freestanding garage. The house that had been attached to it had burned to the ground long ago, but the garage was still standing and had worked well for his surveillance efforts. Nash flicked the kickstand down with his foot and leaned over until the bike rested on it. He didn't get off the bike, though, because Mira hadn't let go of his waist and her cheek rested against his back. New Mira, old Mira…either way, he knew he was getting to her, but he had to be patient.

He felt like he could stay there forever, but that wouldn't help him reach his goals before he left town. "It's almost time for Elroy's hike. Shall we?"

She let go of him. "Absolutely," she said, getting off the bike.

He did the same. Resting a hand on her shoulder, he pointed at a clump of large stones about fifteen yards away. "That's my preferred stakeout area." He coaxed her softly in that direction. "Elroy should be coming out of the house," he glanced at his watch, "in forty seconds."

They advanced together through the trees to the rock formation.

"The best spot is up top. Want a boost?" He asked her.

"Yes." She turned her back to him and he placed his hands on her waist.

He loved the feel of her hips in his palms. He swallowed. He had to get control of himself. "Are you ready?"

"Yep."

He boosted her upward and she scooted onto the flat part of the tallest rock.

"This *does* give you a perfect view. I think I see him." She frowned. "No, maybe not."

Nash reached into the backpack he'd stashed between the rocks. Taking out a pair of binoculars, he handed them to her. "These should help."

"Thanks." She pressed them against her eyes, directing them toward the Prophet House. "I see him on his porch. Do you have any idea where he goes?"

"No." Nash leaned back against the rock, content to watch her. He already knew Elroy's routine. "I was waiting to do that with you."

She grinned a little. "Why?"

"Old time friends learning about each other in a new way?"

She let the binoculars drop and looked down at him. The smile on her face blossomed into something bright and beautiful. It took his breath away. She went back to her binoculars. "Hey. I thought you said Elroy wore a wig."

"He does." Nash did a quick perusal of the area, making certain they were still alone. "But he puts it on when he gets to the edge of the woods."

"Ah. You're right. He's putting it on now."

"And then he'll adjust it thirteen times – must be his lucky number – and then he sighs."

She chuckled softly. "You have him pegged." Mira glanced down at Nash again. "It's still hard to believe he could be a murderer. He's such a squirrely little guy and always seemed weird, but nice."

"Things aren't always as they seem, I guess," he answered. "Are you ready to follow him to find out what's going on beneath that wig – and in that brain of his?"

"I'm ready." She slid off the rock and gave the binoculars to him. Nash returned them to the backpack and slipped the pack onto his shoulders. He pointed into the woods. "We'll cut across that way. Shouldn't be hard to catch up to him, though we'll need to be careful. There are a lot of broken branches that if we step on them, they'll give us away."

"Gotcha," she said, and took off in the direction he'd pointed. But then she paused. "Can you still see well at night?"

"The old me or the new me?"

She whacked his stomach.

He laughed softly and took the lead, feeling even more hopeful than he had on the motorcycle. They followed Elroy at a distance. He was easy to spot in the moonlight with his bright silver coat and his swaying walk. But as he neared the top of a hill, he paused to look around. Nash reached out his hand to stay Mira. Both held perfectly still as Elroy put his hands on his hips and said in a high-pitched voice, "It's about time you joined me Belinda."

Nash scanned the area. Not seeing anyone, he glanced at Mira, who reached up on tiptoes to whisper in his ear. "Multiple personalities, do you think?"

"Maybe." They continued to watch the old man as he raced to the bottom of the hill. He stopped short at the door of an old shack. He went inside.

Nash and Mira took a circuitous route down the hill, one that hid them behind dense trees. By the time they looked through the grimy windows of the shack, Elroy was wearing a dress and tall red boots.

"Belinda, you're such a doll," Elroy said.

Then he answered in Belinda's voice. "Why am I so miserable then? I thought I'd feel better – whole, like I was really being me. Only I don't feel that way."

Elroy answered. "That's why we're meeting with Houser tonight. He'll help us figure this out."

"Are you sure you trust that Houser guy?" Belinda voiced.

"Yes," Elroy said. "I feel like he'd do anything for me."

"Let's go then," Belinda was back in full force. Elroy…Belinda…whoever he was…headed out the door toward Shanty Town.

Chapter 45

Mira couldn't believe her eyes or her ears. Why hadn't she ever picked up on Elroy's troubled mind? The idea that he'd killed Kya seemed a little more plausible now, but they definitely needed more evidence. Glad Nash could see well in the darkness of the treed area, Mira trailed after him.

"Do you think it's strange that Elroy…or Belinda rather, is meeting up with Houser?" Nash asked, moving swiftly, but leaving an ample amount of space between them and Elroy.

"Not really. Houser…he's a bit odd, but he is a really good listener." She thought about how he'd listened to her on that park bench when she'd been troubled by her situation – and he'd helped her find a solution to her dilemma and had helped her get into Cofa's Tree. "He seems to attract the broken-hearted," she added, but didn't want to admit to Nash she'd been on that list.

"Everyone has their talents, I guess," Nash said.

As they watched Elroy enter the bar on the edge of Shanty Town, she asked, "Do we follow him inside the Drink & Tinker?"

"I don't think we'll be able to find out anything from here, so yeah. But how do we do it without them recognizing us?"

Mira thought a moment, an idea coming to mind. "Do you think Elroy has more costumes in his shack?"

"I couldn't see much through the grimy window, but my guess is yes. The question is, will he recognize them?"

She looked up at Nash, his slight smile enhanced by a daring sparkle in his eyes. "I think we can take our chances."

His smile widened. "I'm with you, Mira."

Did he mean more than just the costumes? She didn't know and didn't ask.

They returned to the shack, thankfully not a far distance from Shanty Town. Nash, after a peek in the front window, opened the door. It creaked, but other than that, all was quiet. He flipped on the light.

Mira hugged herself against the sharp coldness as she stepped inside the drab place. The racks of women's clothing gave it a spark of life, though, with their dust-free, vibrant patterns and colors. But that's where the warmth ended. In the corner, stood a full-length mirror that was so hazy, a person could barely see their reflection. In the opposite corner was a table with three crumbling, twisted baskets. She wandered over to peek inside them.

"Cosmetics," she said, picking up an eyeshadow tray with more colors than the rainbow. "Wigs." She didn't touch those. "And art supplies." She glanced at Nash. "We better hurry."

"Probably a good plan." Nash rifled through one of the racks. "He has so much stuff in here, chances are he won't remember every piece of clothing, but pick a basic one just in case."

Not wanting to waste any more time, Mira snagged one of the few solid colored dresses. It was long and black, tight fitting, cut low in the front and high on the side. "This will be good...I think." As she peeled off her leggings, it became eerily quiet. She looked up. Nash was watching her, a leather jacket clutched in his hands.

Her erratic heartbeat pulsed heat throughout her body, a feeling she didn't have time to analyze right at the moment. "Turn around please."

He grunted, but obeyed.

Mira dressed quickly and went to the wigs. Who'd worn these? Were they full of nits? Although she hated to wear the scratchy things, she knew that her dark hair with its distinct cut would give her away no matter what clothing disguise she was wearing. She plopped a long blonde wig onto her head, then scraped some wild red lipstick across her lips. Glancing at her reflection, she couldn't tell if it was a realistic look or a dead giveaway. After slipping her boots back on - Elroy's feet were much bigger than hers – she said, "Okay. You can look. Does it work?"

Nash stared at her a moment, but all he said was, "That'll do."

She guessed it was good enough. As she slipped on her jacket, Nash, who'd already donned the biker's leather, plopped a curly red wig on his head and tucked his hair beneath it.

"You look ridiculous," she said with a chuckle.

"I'm sure I do." He grinned as he stuffed their clothes into his backpack and hoisted it over his shoulder. "Shall we go find ourselves a killer?" He held out his hand to her.

She took it, and again, that same thrill crept up her arm and went straight to her heart. "Why couldn't we have done this while we were dating?" she whispered as they left the shack.

Nash flipped off the light and closed the door behind them. Then he said, "Maybe we should consider ourselves officially dating…then we *will* be doing this while we're dating."

The idea was ludicrous, and yet it made her heart flip. Could this be a new beginning for them, truly? "I don't know how it would be possible for us to date when you'll be gone on tour for months. We weren't spending enough time together with you in town." And her longing to be with him wouldn't change. She knew that now. "Unless you're staying."

He stopped to pull her close. Ducking his head, he whispered in her ear. "You can come with me. Please come with me. It will be an adventure!"

Part of her wanted to say yes – to give in to the desire she still had for him. The other part didn't trust that he would ever have enough time for her – and she didn't know if her heart could take it. Before she could respond to his request, he said, "Just think about it."

Nash took her hand and led her out into the dark, mysterious night. It didn't take long for them to get back to the bar. As they stood outside its doors, he paused. "Last chance, Mira."

Did he mean last chance to accept his invitation to tour with him? Her heart was beating hard. "Last chance for what?"

"To back out of this. You know we could die in there. If Elroy's our murderer, he'll probably be crazy enough to kill us too."

Call it intuition, call it gut-instinct...whatever it was, it just felt right. "Let's do this."

He grinned. "After you, babe."

Chapter 46

After forcefully shoving his yearning for Mira to the back of his brain, his Reformer training came to the forefront. Nash stepped into the bar with Mira beside him. A hostess greeted them.

"Welcome to the Drink & Tinker. Thursday nights aren't as busy as most, so we have a wide selection for seating." The hostess tucked her order pad into the waist of the kilt she wore. "Are you familiar with how our place works?"

"No. We aren't," Mira said.

The young server reached for the pendant on her neck and swept it back and forth. Turning to give them a view of the various areas set up for the customers, she said, "Well, each table is a hobby table set up so you can create while you drink. We have a ton of choices…mechanics, art, music, gaming, cooking, brewing, forging - although a few people got burned in that section so it hasn't been as popular." The twist of her mouth transformed into a smile when she looked back at Nash. "You look so familiar."

"I don't recall that we've met." He added a rasp to his voice to disguise it. If his looks didn't give him away, his voice certainly could. "I'm sure the lighting is deceiving."

She shrugged. "So what hobby would you like to tinker with tonight?"

He quickly scanned the area. Elroy, or Belinda rather, sat in a booth with Houser, a container of paintbrushes between them. Nash pointed to a table kitty-cornered from them. "Is that one in the art section?"

"Yep." She grinned. "Good choice. That's right next to the cooking section and Chef Ricky just happens to be working on a new specialty tonight."

The server led them to the booth and handed them menus. "I'd just order drinks," she whispered, leaning over so they could hear her. "Chef Ricky always shares – and it's better than anything on the menu."

"Bring us the drinks that are the house special then," Nash patted her arm. "Thanks for the recommendation."

Her beaming face reddened. "The special is two frappes for three dollars."

"Sounds great," Nash said.

"Any flavoring?" Her pencil hovered over her order pad as she stared at him.

Nash looked at Mira, who was glowering at the server. Her spark of jealousy reminded him of her reaction to Deidre. Ah, Mira…such a passionate woman! "Do you have a preference, Mira?"

"Caramel, I guess." She leaned back and folded her arms across her chest.

"I'll be back with your house drinks in a jiffy, then."

As the server moved to the coffee bar, Nash peeked over at Houser and Belinda. They seemed deeply involved in their painting, not in conversation.

"This is what it would be like," Mira said softly.

He glanced at her. She was staring at the hostess, who was busy preparing their drinks. A sinking feeling took residence in his stomach. "What do you mean?"

"I mean…women will adore you. Even our server does and she doesn't even realize who you are. You'll be able to have any woman you want."

He reached across the table to grab her hand. "I don't want any other woman. I want you."

She frowned, then pulled her hand from his grasp to pick up a pencil and sketch pad. "Better get to work." She nodded toward the other sketchpad. "Our friends are starting to talk."

He grabbed the paper and a pencil and started doodling. It was as close as he could come to art – at least without something concrete to use as a model.

Nash could hear the soft whoosh of pencil against paper, and he was curious as to what Mira's swift strokes were creating. But he kept his eyes on his own page, knowing he had to focus on what Houser was saying.

"So what is troubling you tonight Belinda?" Houser asked.

Belinda frowned, the paintbrush hovering shakily over the canvas. "I thought I would like being Belinda, but something still doesn't feel right. I don't seem to be any happier than Elroy. I don't know what I'm doing wrong!" Belinda slashed the paintbrush across the front of the painting. "Now I've ruined it," she said, biting back a sob.

Houser took the picture from Belinda's hands, which gave Nash a glimpse of it. The self-portrait wasn't all that good in the first place, and the last smear of paint had crossed out the face, ruining it completely. Houser laid the picture down and took Belinda's hands. "Maybe it's because you feel bad about what happened before."

The hostess swept in with Nash's and Mira's drinks, blocking their view. "Here are your drinks, and," she laid down two plates, loaded with food, "Chef Ricky has to head out soon, so he said to distribute his creation now – seafood stuffed croissants." She licked her lips. "I tried a bite. They're delicious."

"Thanks," Mira said. Nash noticed she was trying to peek around the girl.

"Yeah, thanks," Nash seconded, wishing the hostess would move on. What had Elroy done that he felt bad about?

The girl hovered for a few moments, but then finally left, revealing something unexpected - Chef Ricky slapping cuffs on Belinda's wrists!

Nash glanced at Mira, who stared, wide-eyed at the scene unfolding. He grabbed her hand again and held it tightly. She didn't resist.

"Elroy Bilhan, you have a right to remain silent…" Chef Ricky's words droned on as Belinda looked on in stupefied silence

"What are the charges?" Houser asked, although he didn't look surprised at all.

"Murder of Kya Abernathy. Come on Elroy. Let's go." Chef Ricky, or detective Ricky…whoever he was…hoisted Elroy to his feet.

"My name is Belinda. Elroy did it. Not me! You can't do this," Belinda yelled out, then spit in Ricky's face.

He pursed his lips, but held onto his patience. As he dragged Belinda toward the exit, Ricky nodded to the guy who had been with him at his table. After stuffing the last of his food into his mouth, he went to Houser. Holding out his hand, he said something. The words were muffled due to the food stuffed in his mouth, but Houser must have understood. He reached beneath his shirt to pull off a recording device and handed it to Ricky's partner.

"He was part of a sting," Mira whispered to Nash.

"Looks that way."

She stared down at their now entwined hands. "I feel a little disappointed. I mean…" She frowned. "I'm glad they caught Kya's murderer, but I wish it would've been us who solved the case."

"I know what you mean." A little voice in his head suggested Nash change course. If he used his investigative abilities and became a PI, maybe he could talk Mira into working alongside him. He glanced at the pencil sketch she'd drawn. It was of Houser and Belinda. The details she'd captured amazed him and the expressions on the pair's faces were something Nash hadn't even glimpsed. "What did you feel when you drew this?" he asked. Suddenly it seemed important.

"I don't really know. I just felt like I had to draw it, and that followed."

Whatever she'd seen didn't matter now, really, except that it gave him enough hope, guts, and humility, to ask, "If I stayed in Pillar…opened a detective agency maybe…" he began, but she was already shaking her head. The constriction in his throat was painful. He scowled. "So you blame me for choosing my music over you, but when I offer two ways for us to be together…when I *choose* you over my dream…you shut me down." He tore his hands away and got up.

"You don't understand," she shouted.

"Really. Tell me what I don't understand," he said in a menacing tone, glaring at her, his heart breaking. Why had he even allowed himself to hope?

Her throat worked and her eyes turned glassy. "It's because I think you'll regret it."

His anger at her softened a little, as did his voice, but her stupidity on this rankled. What an illogical woman! But he wouldn't force her to stay with him. "I leave tomorrow morning to go on tour. You are invited to join me. If you show up by eight, I'll know you want to try again. If you don't come, well," he looked away from her trembling lips, "I'll know your answer." He turned and walked out the door. Even though she'd called his name, he couldn't endure a face to face goodbye. Hopefully she'd come to her senses. They belonged together. He knew they did.

Chapter 47

Her comfortable bed in her room at Cofa's Tree did nothing to help Mira sleep. The evening's events looped through her mind again and again until she felt like she was going to go crazy. *Should* she go on tour with Nash? She'd get to travel, experience new things. With Tanger gone, she had nothing holding her back…but what if he returned tomorrow or the next day? Besides, she'd begun to build new friendships and she'd become a part of a group in which she felt like she belonged. If she went with Nash, she'd have to give that up and she'd probably be secondary to his music…and also to his fame. Mira didn't know if she could handle all the girls flirting with him. And what if one of them piqued his interest and he ended up leaving her behind? If only she knew the right answer, but she was torn…and afraid she would choose wrongly.

"Argh!" Frustrated, she flung the covers on the floor and got out of bed. She grabbed her sweatshirt off the chair and slipped it on as she made her way downstairs, yet the cool, damp air caressed her still bare legs, causing a chill that seemed to go beyond skin-deep.

"I'm never going to be able to sleep," she grumbled. Seizing a blanket off the back of the couch, she plopped down in Vashti's favorite chair. The warm fleece, which she spread over her legs, made her feel a bit better. After a few moments of listening to the loud ticking of the clock, it began to irritate her, so she opened the end table drawer and snagged the topmost book. Propping it in her lap, she read the title of the first chapter. "Spirit Guides: the sure route to a happy life."

"Well, nothing else has helped," she muttered and read the introduction. "Hmm. Interesting." What a unique perspective. She didn't know if she believed it. They didn't have any proof, but she turned the page to read more anyway. As she continued on, hope blossomed. If a spirit guide could do all that for her, how could she go wrong? Mira poured over the words of each chapter, wanting to read the entire book before morning. After a while, though, the words began to blur and her eyelids drooped. She'd rest…just a little.

"Mira. Wake up. We have customers."

The words sank in as the warm hand nudging Mira's shoulder brought her out of her sleep-induced stupor. Eyes popping open, Mira looked around. Houser stood over her, grinning. Vashti was taking her caramel rolls out of the oven as Leigh from the photo shop waited by the till for her order.

"What did your professor think of your print, Mira?" Leigh asked.

Mira glanced at the clock. It was 8:45am! "Oh crap!" Her class ended at nine. If she didn't have her project turned in by the end of class, she'd flunk for sure! Tossing off the blanket, the book she'd been reading crashed to the floor. She left both in a heap and ran up the stairs to her room. Throwing on her clothes from the previous night, she grabbed her print and Tanger's project and raced down the stairs. As she dashed for the door, Vashti called out, "Houser's waiting in my car outside to take you to class."

"Oh. Thank you!" Mira said, surprised at the thoughtfulness and overwhelmed, too. She dashed outside, stashed the art pieces in the backseat and jumped in the front of the car with Houser, who immediately hit the gas.

"I really appreciate this Houser," she said, biting at a little jagged edge on her thumbnail.

"Glad I could help out." He glanced over at her. "You must have been pretty tired to sleep this late. You're usually up and gone before now."

"Yeah." Then she remembered. She'd wanted to see Nash before he left. "It's too late," she whispered, feeling warmth in her eyes.

Houser looked at his watch. "We still have ten minutes. And I can drive you right up to the door."

"I meant for Nash. He planned on leaving this morning at eight."

"Ah yes. I think I recall Porsche saying that. I take it you wanted to say goodbye?"

"Yes. No." She frowned. "I don't know." She always seemed to make a mess of things.

"Sorry Mira." Houser said softly as he stopped the car in front of the art building and shifted into park. "Let me know if I can do anything to help you." He pulled out a cigarette and put it between his lips.

"You got me here on time. That's enough." She got out of the car and grabbed the prints from the backseat. Tanger's scraped against the edge of the car door. "Thanks again, Houser."

"No problem," he said, lighting his cig. "It will all work out for the best. You'll see."

The gaping tear across the front of Tanger's project gave her a glimpse inside. It was a painting of her standing near the edge of Wormwood's Water, a glowing light behind her. Her image reflected on the dark lake, however, was different. The light was diffused and a shadowy hand clutched her shoulder. Tanger's perhaps? Although she wanted to get a closer look at the painting, time wouldn't allow it.

"I hope it works out to my advantage," Mira said, and with the prints tucked under her arm, hurried into the school.

Chapter 48

Nash listened to the quiet hum of the RV engine as it rolled out of Pillar. He had gotten a late start because he'd been procrastinating, just in case Mira would show up at his place before he left. Unfortunately, she hadn't. He wasn't surprised. Not really. He'd known in his gut there was more to their breakup than lack of time spent together. Staring out the RV's side window at the wide expanse of ocean, Nash wondered if that reason was Tanger. How deeply involved *was* she with the guy?

His hand pressed flat against the music composition notebook Tory had given him as a parting gift that morning. This had been his dream for so long! Nash knew it should be the most exciting time of his life, and yet, it wasn't. He glanced at the back of his driver's head. The guy, named Chad, wore headphones, his shoulders bouncing a bit to the tunes filtering through them.

Nash picked up his phone. After punching in Tory's number, he waited for her to pick up. She, at least, didn't disappoint him.

"Hi Nash. What's up?"

Her no nonsense tone soothed him. "We didn't have time alone to talk before I left," he said. "Did you find out anything more at Cofa's Tree?"

"Well, I found out my disguise worked. Mira didn't recognize me."

"That's helpful." He nudged the notebook side to side. "What about Mira and Tanger?"

"I haven't seen Tanger around at all, so I can't help you on that front."

"Hmm." He sat up straighter. "Have you gotten into the Enchanted Garden?"

"Not yet. I overheard them talking about a group meeting being held there tonight, so I'm working on getting an invitation to it."

"Good girl. Anything else going on? Anything unusual?"

"Well, I looked up the history of the place, and when it was a sanitarium, some really crazy people lived here. Not that I believe in ghosts or anything but…"

Her pause prompted him to ask, "But what?"

"I had this freaky dream that I can't seem to shake." Her strained chuckle spoke volumes of the effect this dream had had on her.

"What was the dream about?"

"I dreamt I went into the basement of Cofa's Tree. Following a sound, I opened a door." She paused. "Behind it was something," she swallowed, "something otherworldly." Tory cleared her throat. "But the dream isn't important. What *is* important is that when I went down to get something good to read in order to get rid of those thoughts that had gotten trapped in my psyche, I found Mira asleep in the main room with a book on her lap."

He could picture her, sleeping in a chair and doing just that. He smiled with longing. "Nothing wrong with that."

"What if the book was about Spirit Guides?"

He'd seen a book about spirit guides in the end table drawer. Nash sat up straighter in the captain's chair. "Spirit guides are hogwash," he said, but he couldn't escape the niggling feeling creeping up his spine that told him otherwise.

"Agreed. But that doesn't mean *she* won't believe in them."

"True. What do you think we should do about it?"

"Honestly? Nothing. And I, for one, will be happy to move back to my own place."

If he did nothing and something happened to Mira, he'd never forgive himself. He hoped Tory would be able to talk some sense into her. "You can get out if you want. We don't have a murder case to solve anymore," he said, knowing she'd find out sooner or later…probably sooner given the fact that she was a suspect.

"What?"

"Kya's murderer was arrested last night."

"No way! Who did it?"

"Elroy Bilhan."

"That squirrely little guy? Who would've thought he was Kya's secret admirer? Isn't he married?"

"He is married...but it appears as though he has some serious mental issues. I'm just glad Mira is safe from that lunatic. Only..."

"You mean you're glad we're all safe from him."

Nash winced. "Yeah, but I'm still worried about Mira."

"So you want me to stay and spy on her for a while longer." Tory sighed. "Am I right?"

This could be his opportunity to cut all ties, right now, for good. He shouldn't care what Mira was doing or who she was doing it with because *she'd* cut him off with an effective, heart-bleeding slice when she didn't come to see him that morning. And yet, he couldn't let it go – couldn't completely let *her* go. "Yes. You are right. Will you stay, at least until you attend one of their meetings in the Enchanted Garden?"

"She's moved on, Nash. You need to let her go."

He pinched the bridge of his nose. "I know. But will you do this for me? Please."

She paused. "Okay. I'll do it, but you owe me Nash Montgomery."

"Agreed," he said, and disconnected.

Chapter 49

Mira's day had drug on endlessly. She'd gone for a walk. She'd shopped at the secondhand store until she'd run out of tip money. She'd tried painting, which turned out to be a big fail even though she'd surrounded herself with the artistic atmosphere of Tanger's room. It had only raised more doubts about Tanger, about herself, about life. She'd tried talking to Claire, who kept turning the conversation back to herself. Even Vashti had been too busy with customers to talk. So here she sat alone in her room, rocking in the listing chair, a knot of misery building in her gut as she tried to turn her thoughts to the positive. But negative thoughts continued to hound her. Tanger had disappeared, Nash had started the tour he'd dreamt about, and she was left restless, without any idea of where to go next. Who was she anyway…her essential self? And what was she going to do with her restless energy that only seemed to be getting stronger?

A knock sounded on the door of her room. "Yeah?"

"Hi, um, it's Flora. I was told there's a meeting in five minutes at Wormwood's Water. Are you going?"

She didn't know how she'd feel about attending the meeting without Tanger, especially because the still full moon would remind her that her hopes and dreams where Tanger was concerned were not going to be her reality. Besides, she didn't want to get trapped in another conversation with Claire.

"I hadn't planned on it," Mira said, opening the door.

"Oh."

The poor girl seemed so dejected Mira almost changed her mind about going. Almost. "Are *you* going?"

"I want to." She looked down at her shuffling feet. "I just wish I knew more about the meeting – and what the group is like."

Mira leaned against the door jamb. Because Flora had been invited, she saw no reason not to confide the little she knew. "From what I've picked up so far, this group is supposed to show us a powerful spiritual path that allows us to transform our reality and ourselves to match our choices."

"Supposed to?"

She smiled, but inside she felt a twist of sad hopelessness that she couldn't seem to shake. "It's complex, so I guess I probably need more practice." She shrugged. "Hopefully I can figure it out. Who wouldn't want to be empowered by nature's forces to shape and bend their world to get what they need and want in life, right?"

"Sound good to me," Flora said, taking a small notebook and pen out of her pocket. "So what are the rules? How does it work?"

"Well...there are no set rules really." That was another thing she'd discovered in reading the Spirit Guide book. "What's right for me may not be right for you, so basically, we get to decide our own rules." Mira tucked her hands into her new-used secondhand store gauchos. Remembering a phrase she'd read in the Spirit Guide book, she repeated it. "In essence, we are the artists of our lives."

Flora wrote *we create our own world, we have no rules.* "This looks like something I want to dig into further. You sure you don't want to come with me to the meeting?"

Mira shook her head. "Maybe next time."

"See ya around then," Flora said, walking toward the staircase.

She thought again about going with her. Maybe it would refresh her spirit. But the other side won out...the one that wanted to have a pity party for herself, at least for a little while. "Let me know if anything crazy happens?"

Flora paused at the top of the steps. "*Will* something crazy happen?"

"Without rules, it's probably likely, wouldn't you think?"

"I'm sure you're right." Flora tucked her hands into her pockets. Without turning around, she said, "Do you really believe what they're telling you?"

She thought about that. She did and she didn't. "I like to keep an open mind. Besides, they all seem to know what they want and how to get it."

"What if it isn't true?"

Mira didn't want to think about that. "What is truth, really, but our perception of the things around us?"

"But…" she glanced over her shoulder. What pretty eyes she had. "Never mind. We'll talk later," Flora said, and hurried down the stairs.

The door at the bottom slammed shut, leaving a silent emptiness in its wake. Mira went to her nightstand and, shoving aside the envelope from her mom, took out a notebook. "If I want to create my own life as an artist would a painting, then I better get to work on figuring out what that will look like."

She sat back down in the chair. Her pencil scraped across the page until her self-portrait came to life, glowing, powerful, and happy. But that wasn't all. The scene surrounding her image was filled with landscapes she didn't recognize. Bodies and hearts wove throughout it, blending into trees and water. Did this mean she wasn't supposed to stay in one place? Only she didn't have the money to travel. Should she have accepted Nash's proposal? Was there a way to find him?

Mira tore the sketch out of the notebook and taped it on the wall beside her bed. It would be the last thing she saw at night and the first thing she saw in the morning. As she looked at the details of the drawing, she said, "Now, I just need to figure out how to shape my world to get what I want."

Chapter 50

Nash walked beside the various styles and sizes of boats, feeling the slight shift of the dock's weathered boards beneath his feet. The smell of fish didn't bother him as it had when he'd first gotten to Whynot almost three weeks ago. What *did* bother him was the conversation he'd had with Tory about what was going on at Cofa's Tree.

Strolling down the end row where all the yachts were docked, Nash pulled out his phone and rang Hayes' number. Thankfully, he answered.

"Nash," Hayes said with a smile in his voice. "How's it goin' my friend?"

"Oh. Alright." Nash glanced across the expanse of blue ocean to where the sun had settled on the horizon.

"Sounds like somethin' heavy is weighin' on ya."

"Yeah." Nash wandered to the stone path that would lead him back to the RV campsites. "Tory has been staying at Cofa's Tree for the past several weeks…in disguise," he said, getting into his golf cart. "And she found out some things that, although I think they're probably harmless and totally ridiculous, I can't get it out of my head."

"What kind of things?"

"Well, the group that meets there doesn't really have rules or standards of right and wrong, but it does seem like a religion because they have some sort of ritual with the moon."

After a momentary pause, Hayes asked, "What else do ya know?"

Nash punched on the golf cart's accelerator, the nearly silent hum creating a strange mix with the sound of crashing waves. Neither soothed him. "I know that Mira is trying to figure out how to become the artist of her own life by bending her reality. It sounds crazy, right?"

"Bending her reality? Wow."

"She was also reading a book about spirit guides – even quoting from it."

Hayes whistled softly. "Any power from the wrong source isn't a power she wants ta play around with."

Nash knew Tory had a "what we see is what we get" kind of philosophy, one built on logic, but her extended stay at Cofa's Tree had shaken even her a bit. She had begun to entertain the possibility of the existence of things beyond the material, natural world. It still surprised him. "How do you know there's even a source at all?"

"Ya have ta investigate ta find the truth."

"But spiritual truth can't be found, Hayes. There isn't any physical proof. It's just something our mind conjures…a result of social construct." Which would make what Mira was dabbling in harmless. Only why did he feel, deep down, that she *was* in danger?

"Do ya have physical proof that it's something our mind conjures?"

"No, but I have seen research concerning spirituality and the brain. One fact is if a person prays, over time, their brain actually changes. This evolutionary process could have begun with someone feeling better after having prayed to a God they had invented."

"Do ya have physical proof of that?"

"Well, no. But it makes sense."

"Through an evolutionary lens, maybe. But what if God *does* exist and He created our minds ta transform and feel good when we talk to Him?"

Nash shook his head. "None of it can be proven."

"Not in a lab-type setting, but we can use the method historians, scientists, and detectives use by following the effects - such as those we can observe in the brain - back ta the most likely source. If we take into consideration *all* the possibilities, we can find truth beyond a reasonable doubt."

He and Hayes used to have all kinds of discussions about God. Their differences never bothered him before. Why did it irritate him so much now?

Jaw clenched tight, Nash pulled the cart into the air-conditioned garage stall. "I don't want to argue about it right now."

"I used ta think it was arguing, that it was my beliefs against others' beliefs, but someone reminded me once that we are all in this together."

Shoving the golf cart key into his pocket, Nash wandered out of the garage. Halfway to his RV, he stopped. "Yeah. Whatever," he said, pausing to stare out at the ocean.

"Just hear me out for a minute," Hayes said.

Nash didn't want to listen, but he *did* want Hayes' help. Clenching the key in his pocket, he muttered, "I'm listening."

"Good," Hayes said. "Imagine for a moment we are all on a jury and we need ta decide if God exists or if He doesn't. We also need ta decide if Christ's claims ta be our Savior are true. Are you picturing it?"

"Yes," Nash ground out.

"Good. Now, we jurors can listen ta all the evidence from the prosecutor, the defense, and the witnesses in order to obtain our verdict, or we can listen ta only part of the evidence and hope that we are judging rightly."

Nash leaned against the RV, the heat of the sun-warmed aluminum heating his back. "I suppose, but what does it matter anyway?"

"It matters because our lives are at stake! If God exists and Jesus' claims are true, then our decision will determine the place we will spend eternity. If God doesn't exist, or Jesus' claims aren't true, we are to be pitied for wasting our only life on earth."

"I hadn't thought about it like that before," Nash said quietly, but he had thought about death, about the nothing he would become. He didn't like it, but he didn't want to be fooled by imaginary wishes just to make himself feel better, either.

"We are all on that jury, Nash, and we all need ta make a choice. My hope is that none of us are afraid ta hear and study the evidence, because eventually, when we die, the truth will be realized."

Nash cleared the sourness that his stomach had shoved up into his throat, and tried to turn his mind back to his safe logic. "So what about Mira?"

"If she's dabblin' in the spirit world – she's on a very dangerous path."

Mira's vision about the abyss popped into his head. He could picture clearly the place she'd painted. Love didn't exist there, but a heart-wrenching, soul-consuming loneliness did. It wasn't something he wanted to think about. Nash shut out the images, but helplessness still managed to weave its way around his desire to protect her. "I asked Tory to hire her to work at the music store. I wanted her to offer Mira my place, too, so that she could live there while I'm gone. Tory won't do it."

"Why not? Sounds like a good plan."

He tapped his fist against the aluminum RV panel. "She says Mira is fine where she's at," he said. "Even if it's crazy, she thinks I need to leave Mira alone to live her own life and focus on living mine."

"There are times ta let go, and times not ta," Hayes said firmly. "This is not a time ta cut and run."

Nash felt like he *had* cut and run. "Could you maybe talk to Mira – or maybe have her parents talk to her?"

"Her parents left for Enab yesterday, but maybe Mel and I could have her over ta the house."

"That would really put my mind at ease. Thanks, Hayes."

"Glad ta help." There was a long silent pause, which wasn't like Hayes at all.

"Hayes? You still there?"

"Yep." He cleared his throat. "You remember Elroy, right?"

"Like I could forget Kya's murderer."

"Yeah, well, I've been meetin' with him almost daily since he's been in prison."

"Why in the world would you be visiting that scumbag?"

"Because I wanted ta let him know that God's design for him and his life was wonderful, and that he had a purpose. I wanted ta point Elroy ta a way ta change his heart."

"He's a murderer…" Nash shook his head. "I don't know if a murderer's heart can change."

"God's forgiveness extends even ta murderers."

Nash wasn't about to start in on a philosophical discussion or another spiritual one, so he said, "I suppose you're going to tell me he had some spiritual transformation."

"He did, actually. He'd been reading the Enchiridion and doing a Bible study ta help him understand it correctly. He'd taken up guitar lessons, had been taught ta use his painting in a therapeutic manner, and he'd been taking a college class. Elroy was transformin' right before my eyes."

"*Was?*"

Hayes cleared his throat, but when he spoke, it hitched with anguish anyway. "Elroy was found two mornings ago, strung up by his sheets in his jail cell." He inhaled deeply. "They also found a portrait of him in that exact hanging position, with the painting propped right below his dangling feet."

Elroy had left a painting, just like he had with Kya. "I told you that you can't change the heart of a murderer."

"But he *had* changed!"

Even though he didn't believe Elroy had truly changed, Nash felt bad for his friend. "I'm sorry Hayes."

"Me too. Weird thing is that only a handful of people got ta see the portrait he'd painted."

Nash's Reformer beacon went up. "Can you get ahold of it?"

"Nope. It's locked away in the evidence room. Not even Detective Richards has seen it."

"That *is* weird. But maybe it's for the best. I imagine the gruesome portrait would cause more than one person to have nightmares."

"I suppose yer right." Hayes sniffed loudly then blew his nose right into the phone. "So on a much lighter note…how is everything else goin' for ya? I hear you're a big hit everywhere ya go."

"Oh, this music gig is great," he said, overemphasizing it a bit too much. He shook his head. "I mean, I've been really busy with rehearsals, concerts, interviews and with the fans. It's exhausting, but it's good." That's what he kept telling himself. Nash glanced at the view from his RV lot. "Not many people have a place to live with a private beach, overlooking the ocean. I even have an attendant who does everything I want him to – he cooks, cleans, runs errands, and drives me around. It's awesome."

"Good for you! Maybe Mel and I can come for a visit sometime."

"That would be great!"

"Send me another copy of yer tour schedule and I'll talk ta Mel. Hey…I have another call coming in that I have ta get. We'll touch base again, soon, okay?"

"I'll be sure to send out a copy tomorrow. Bye Hayes." Nash tucked his phone into his pocket. As he stared out at the ocean, he was filled with a sudden sense of awe at its power and its magnificent beauty. He also felt an ache deep down – one that said he wanted more than this. It wasn't logical - he had everything he could ever want – but the feeling remained nonetheless. With a long drawn out sigh, he made his way into his RV.

Chapter 51

Sitting at her desk, Mira put an x over today's date. It had been over five weeks since she'd moved into Cofa's Tree. Tanger had been gone for almost four weeks, and Nash for nearly that long. And her parents had left for Enab over two weeks ago. Several other items filled in the calendar's squares – new things she'd tried, outings and adventures she'd embarked on, and leisure activities, too. But the full calendar didn't fill her heart.

"This is where and who I *want* to be," Mira said, but the reminder of her responsibility to create the life she wanted only served to paint a grim picture of herself. She felt like a failure because she wasn't any closer to finding her purpose. She wasn't exactly happy either. Perhaps if she lived somewhere else, or had someone to share life and love with…

Mira glanced out her window. A couple walked by, talking, laughing, holding hands. She wanted love like that! But on this front, again, she had failed. Maybe if she viewed her relationships from a different angle, she wouldn't feel so hopeless. Yet no matter how hard she tried, she couldn't seem to look at what she'd done with Tanger as an experience to treasure. Deep down, something wouldn't let her. She ached with regret, feeling more like a treasure that had been thrown overboard than someone treasured or cherished or special. In fact, she felt like a piece of herself had been stolen and then had been tossed away.

Mira looked around her silent room, feeling lonelier than ever before – like it was squeezing the life out of her. *I have a job and new friends…I am fine!* But no matter how many times she told herself that, it was not enough. *She* was not enough.

Reaching into the desk drawer, she pulled out the sealed note from her mom. What could it hurt to read it? Besides, she wanted to be open-minded.

Slipping her fingers beneath the tapered seal, she worked the flap open. With shaking fingers, she pulled out the two folded sheets. Straightening them on the desk, she began to read.

I stand alone on the shores of Enab past.

it's midnight and the light of the moon and stars surround me.

I imagine I am not alone.

it makes me feel better for a time.

if only it wasn't so cold!

I dance as I hug my arms around myself —

pretending they are the arms of my lover, my friend.

it doesn't satisfy for long —

only makes me more aware of how alone I really am.

I begin to wander —

feeling, hoping, determined to find my tribe.

the ground crunches beneath my feet,

my puffed out breaths mingling with the frigid air.

I feel free -

yet as I walk, the cold seeps into my bones.

a tear escapes down my cheek,

warm at first, but leaving behind a frigid trail.

I swipe it away, angry at my weakness,

resolved that I will be great!

no matter where I end up...

it is all up to me.

I sit alone in the streets of Pillar present.

it's midnight and the lights of the city surround me.

though I am amidst a bustling crowd,

I still feel alone.

if only it wasn't so cold!

I have traveled the world to fill my heart with glorious experiences.

oh that I could hold onto those treasured feelings!

yet they escape me, as elusive as time,

like wisps of smoke drifting from a dying fire.

I wrap my arms around myself,

trying to ignore the aches of both my heart and my aging body.

I close my eyes in an attempt to grasp a different picture -

one encased in the memories I choose.

I try to convince myself it was all worth it — it is all worth it!

only right now, it doesn't feel like it's enough.

then I feel a slight breeze caress my face.

Its warmth is almost like a hug.

It tugs at my heart and soul and begs me to open my eyes.

but what if It isn't real?

Mira shoved the first page behind the second and continued reading, not because she wanted to, but because she felt she *had* to.

I lie alone on the hard hospital bed of my future.

it's midnight, and I gaze up at the fluorescent ceiling,

knowing that soon I will take my last breath.

I try to imagine that I am not alone,

that the stars I see through my window are my friends waiting to welcome me

or that I will return to live again and again until I get life right.

why doesn't either thought bring me comfort?

can we even know for certain what awaits our souls?

if only I wasn't so cold!

I curl into a ball and press a hand against my heart,

imagining that the ocean spreads before me...

that my bones and muscles don't ache...

that my friends and loves haven't moved on without me...

that the life, the Me I had created was all worth it...

but the evidence stands in stark contrast around me.

all I have left is the reality of what was, what is,

and my growing fear of what will be.

I cry out in agony, squeezing my eyes to shut out the despair

that has somehow woven itself throughout my being.

I cannot escape the feeling.

it overwhelms me...until I recall that magical moment of yesteryear.

that same Warmth once again caresses my face

begging me to look.

do I dare?

slowly my eyes open

through the window I see the Son rising on the horizon,

His light giving me a glimpse of a beautiful world

filled with unique people, their arms open wide,

their spirits warm and bright and beating in sync.

I want that world, I crave it, but my own creation hangs on like a leech

telling me that my life is what I make it

it screams, "don't let go of your freedom!"

only where has it gotten me?

I feel imprisoned by freedom's limitations —

like my power has only served to trap me in a place I don't belong.

I feel torn - like dark and light are fighting for my soul.

yet as I lay there, trembling, struggling for breath,

a life-line swings in through the window.

I sense it will drag me away from all that is me in the past

beep, beep, beep...the machine monitoring my heart is like a ticking bomb.

I need to decide.

i take a chance and latch onto the life-line

and hold on tightly as i am caught up in its amazing grace.

i am swung up into the welcoming arms of the giver of Life.

i have never felt such contentment, such joy, such hope, such love.

how can i do anything but dance, sing, create, explore and rejoice with every breath?

i haven't lost myself...i have found the Truth of who i really am.

and i have found my Way home, where my soul belongs.

Mira stared at the last section and felt anxiousness crushing her chest. She folded the poem back up, but not before one of her tears had found the page. It wasn't what she'd expected from her mom, but now that she'd read it, the words seemed stamped in her brain, haunting her more than the doll's cries, more than her nightmares. What if she was wrong? What if her mom was right?

Tucking the pages back into the envelope, Mira pulled another piece of paper out of her drawer, hoping it would give her the answers she needed. It was what she called her "dream-path picture". She'd agonized over the stupid thing for days after she'd drawn it. She'd studied it, contemplating what it could possibly mean. Oh, she'd come up with several ideas, only none were feasible and they had all seemed to fall flat the more she had thought about them.

Depressing, is what it was — and why it had found its home in her drawer. She looked at it again, though, trying to look deeper to find a remedy for her troubled and restless heart.

It was hard to admit she couldn't understand her own art, but desperation — no, a shift in perspective — was why she'd decided to ask Vashti to interpret it. Clutching the envelope from her mom and her dream path piece, she headed downstairs. The dinner crowd had gone and Vashti stood behind the bar, cleaning up. Mira wandered over to the barstool closest to the window and sat down, the picture and poem both on her lap.

"Mira. What a nice surprise," Vashti said. "How are you?"

"Good, I guess."

Vashti tilted her head as she looked at her. "You don't sound like you believe it." She finished drying a copper mug and put it on the shelf. "Maybe you should come to the meeting tonight. You haven't been to one in a while."

Mira sighed, her fingers running across the page resting on her lap. "Oh, I don't know."

"Have you been avoiding us because of Tanger?"

"Maybe." Mira frowned. "Is it usual for him to disappear, or is it just me?"

"He's been known to drift." Vashti leaned toward Mira, resting on her elbows. "I'm sure he'll be back soon."

If that was true, Mira didn't want to be around when he showed up. There would be no pining woman waiting for him to return! But where would she go? And how? She had very little money saved.

"I wanted to show you a couple of things. First this." Mira handed Vashti the letter from her mom.

Vashti showed little expression as she read it, although Mira could've sworn she'd glimpsed a slight flaring of her nostrils and a clenching of her jaw. When Vashti finished, she shoved it back into the envelope.

"Well, what do you think?" Mira asked, her insides twisted, mournful, and worried.

She cleared her throat. "It's a charming piece, well written and all that."

"But do you think it's true?"

"It came straight from your mom's heart, so it's true for her. You know all good writing and personal truths come from a person's heart, right?"

Mira *didn't* know that. "So what actually comes after death is all based on what we believe in our hearts?"

Vashti nodded.

Mira was skeptical. Believing something is true doesn't necessarily make it true. What about a child put into a timeout for doing something wrong? She might believe with all her heart that her parent didn't love her, but did that make it true? It was more likely, actually, that love was the reason for the punishment. And what about a person in the desert? Maybe they saw water in the distance, and they believed with all their hearts it was there. If it was a mirage, they wouldn't get the water they needed, and they would die. Yet instead of saying this to Vashti, Mira locked it away for later. Right now, she wanted answers for her life, answers she *wanted* to hear.

"Here's the second thing I wanted to show you." Mira laid her drawing on top of the bar and slid it toward Vashti. "I call it my dream-path picture." Would Vashti blurt out what in meant without her asking? Mira hoped so!

Vashti took her time examining it. "Looks like your intuition is talking."

"That's what I thought, too."

Vashti slid it back toward her. Mira stared down at it. "Um, ah, do you know what it's saying?"

The corner of Vashti's lip curled. Was she amused at Mira's ineptness? Before Mira could react, though, Vashti pulled it back in front of her. Pointing at the people's bodies woven into the trees and water, she said, "This suggests that you travel." She traced one of the hearts. "And this indicates that you'll find love."

Mira smiled. Love was what she was missing! She knew it in her heart. "But can you tell from the picture where I should go?"

She slid the drawing back toward Mira again. "I think that's a good question for your spirit guide."

Mira had read a few chapters of the book on spirit guides. All she really remembered was that they were at varying levels of consciousness and energetic frequency, whatever that meant. "I don't have a spirit guide."

"We all have spirit guides," Vashti said. "We have one main spirit guide that is with us from birth to death along with other ones that pop in and out to help us on our journey." She came around the bar to sit beside Mira. "In fact, spirit guides are a powerful source for us to call on for help. They're devoted to guiding, supporting, and nudging us so we can gain clarity and insight and dramatically improve our quality of life."

"Seriously?" Mira leaned in, her restless anxiety begging for relief. "How does it all work?"

Vashti wound her arm around Mira's shoulders. "If you want to realize your truth, and if you want to find answers on how to enjoy life and well-being, you *must* improve your intuition and revere your inner-knowing."

Revere her inner-knowing? *What?* "And how would I go about doing that?"

"Well, you need to clear your head so you can hear the whispers, for one."

Clearing her head would be tough. Even resting, her thoughts zipped around like tireless bunnies in a garden. "Anything else?"

"Find a peaceful space to connect with your spirit guides. Ask their names in the form of a prayer and then with conviction, tell them you want to build a closer relationship with them."

Had Tanger done that? Had his spirit guide sent him packing? "I guess I could give it a shot." Mira took her drawing and headed toward the stairs.

"I also think intuitive writing would work well for you."

Mira frowned over her shoulder at Vashti. "I'm not the best writer," she said.

"No need to be a good writer, dear," Vashti said, a sparkle in her eyes. "You only consult your spirit guide in letterform and ask for help, clarity, insight, direction…whatever it is that you feel your soul is searching for."

Writing to some entity she knew nothing about seemed ludicrous. "Is that what you do?"

"I have."

Mira thought about Vashti, how she always seemed so sure of herself. "So will the spirit guides write back the answers?" Her life would be so much easier if they did.

Vashti chuckled. "They can. Or you might feel the answers coming through your fingertips and feel you have to write it. At other times, you'll need to look for signs - coincidences, lines from songs, people's words, or TV shows…that type of thing. If something repeats, your guide is sending you a message. The more you do it, the deeper the connection with your spirit guide, and the greater your intuitive insight will be." Vashti grabbed a small bag from the end table. "You want to give it a try?"

She'd probably enjoy trying to connect the dots – and if it got her out of this funk, it would be worth it. "I do," Mira said.

Vashti handed her the bag.

Mira's curiosity on high alert, she peeked inside. Before she could ask what to do with the rocks and the candle, the door to Cofa's Tree opened. Mira looked over at the customer who'd just stepped inside. "Hayes," she said with a grin and hurried over to him. She gave him a quick hug. "What are you doing here?"

"Since when can't a person stop by ta see his friend?"

Her happiness at seeing a familiar old friend warred with her itch to try something new - connecting with her spirit guide. She glanced at the clock. Maybe she could spare a few minutes. "Can I buy you a coffee?"

"I actually wanted ta invite ya over tonight for a game of cards."

If he would have asked before she'd talked to Vashti, she would've been jumping at the chance. "I hate to miss out on Mel's tea, but I have plans." She clutched the bag tighter.

"I'll accept your offer of coffee then." He grinned.

"Okay," she said, setting the bag on the table then going for two large mugs. "Want cream or sugar?"

"No thanks." He lingered at the door, his gaze traveling around the establishment before coming to rest on her. "Care if we drink it outside?"

Something in his voice stirred up her worry-radar. "Is there something wrong with Nash, Hayes?"

"He's fine." His smile reassured her. "It's just such a beautiful evening, I hate to waste it."

"Sounds good to me. I'll meet you out there."

He nodded and went out the front door to sit on the bench.

"Oh shoot. The coffee pot is empty," Mira said, grabbing the coffee beans from the tin on the shelf. "Would you tell Hayes it will be a few minutes?"

Vashti grabbed the tin from Mira. "How about I brew some coffee for you and bring it out." She shewed her with a flick of her hand. "You go spend time with your friend."

"Thanks Vashti." Mira opened the door. "For everything."

Vashti nodded, and went to work on the coffee.

"Coffee will be ready in a few," Mira said as she stepped outside. The heat from the sidewalk seeped through her flip-flops as she made her way to the bench – the same bench that she'd first met Tanger. Pushing him to the back of her mind, she sat down beside Hayes. "How's Mel doing?"

"She's great." Hayes positively glowed when he talked about her. "She's busy working on printing up the Enchiridion in a variety of languages." He handed her a warm leather bound book. "Here's a fresh copy for ya. It's in English," he said with a proud smile.

"Thanks," she said, setting it aside. She leaned back against the bench. "How about you? What have you been up to?"

"More of the same," Hayes said with a shrug. Then he grinned. "But lately, I've been feeling this tug ta get into missionary work."

Mira thought about the tug he'd mentioned. Could that be his spirit guide? "Would you want to go to Enab and work with my parents?" She missed them all of a sudden.

"No. I have another place in mind. It's a town called Ezilli."

"What does Mel think about it?"

"She's on board, but it's more of a future goal than immediate." He twisted around on the bench so that he faced her. "Enough about me. How are things going with you?"

"Great." Or they would be maybe after she consulted her spirit guide. "I'm getting things figured out."

Hayes rubbed his hand across his five o'clock shadow. "How are ya going about getting things figured out, exactly?"

She frowned. "Why? Did you hear something about me?"

"Oh, nothing really, except for some rumors about what goes on at Cofa's Tree."

"Rumors?" She rubbed her stomach, wishing she'd had a bite to eat.

"Yeah." He looked at her with concerned eyes. "Dabbling in the spirit world is really dangerous Mira. Don't do it."

"Don't do what?" Vashti asked, two steaming cups of coffee in her hands.

Hayes turned his gaze on Vashti, his expression inquisitive, yet laced with a spark of challenge. "Nothing you need to worry about miss."

She shrugged. "I wasn't worried, but I like to make sure my renters and my friends aren't being bullied."

With a snort, Hayes took the mug from her. "You don't know me woman, but you kin save yer breath. There's no bullying going on here." He glanced at Mira. "Ain't that right, Mira?"

She nodded, taking her own cup of coffee. "Hayes and I are friends from way back," Mira said, remembering the first time she'd met him…how he'd held a knife to her neck, but ended up saving both her and Nash. "You don't have a thing to worry about."

Sipping the hot brew, Mira watched a skeptical Vashti disappear back into Cofa's Tree. "Vashti is a nice lady. I'm not quite sure what got into her."

"Maybe we're on opposite sides."

"Opposite sides? The war is over."

"There's a spiritual war still ragin'," Hayes said. "Don't listen to her babble. Follow the truth, Mira."

The truth for Hayes was different than her truth, right? That's what she wanted to believe. "I will," she said.

Before he could continue, his phone rang. "It's Mel." He glanced at Mira. "Is it okay if I take this call quick?"

"Only if you tell her hi from me."

He answered his phone. "Mira says to say hi." He twisted the phone so that the mouthpiece was away from his mouth. "She says hi back." He pressed the phone back into place. "So what's up? Ya sound a bit out of breath."

Hayes listened intently, leaned forward, then sat up straighter. Eyes widening, he said, "Yer serious?" Then he ran his hand through his hair. "When do we leave?"

Hayes stood up, looking heavenward. "I'll talk to ya in a few minutes, babe." He slipped the phone into his pocket.

Standing up next to him, Mira shoved her hands into her pockets. "Let me guess…you won a vacation somewhere and you leave tomorrow."

He shook his head. "We got a call from Mission Matchup. They want us to bring a load of the new translation we just printed up…and then they want us ta stay ta teach their people about Jesus."

"That's awesome Hayes." Again, Mira wondered if his spirit guide had led him to this. She was more and more excited to get in tune to hers so that she, too, could find a clear path to live out her dreams and be happy.

"Well, I suppose I better get movin'. Mel's packing up the Enchiridion translations as we speak. I'm tasked with packing up our things." He made a face then bent to give Mira a hug. "I'd ask ya to move into our place while we're gone, but Mel said she already has our house rented out."

"Must be divine intervention, huh?"

He smiled. "Exactly." Pulling back, he reached into his front pocket. "Think about what I said, okay?"

"I will."

He pulled out a key on a key chain that had a mini Enchiridion dangling from it. "We're not going ta need a car in the town we're going ta. Would ya mind taking care of mine while we're gone?"

Was this a sign from her spirit guide? It had to be! She took the key and clutched it in her hand. "I would love to take care of it." She peeked up at him. "Do you mind if I put some miles on the car?"

He chuckled. "Not at all…as long as ya take care of it – and take care of yerself."

"Thanks, Hayes." She gave him a hard squeeze. "Be safe and give me a call when you get there."

"I'll try, but I've heard reception isn't very good there." Hayes kissed her forehead. "God loves ya, Mira, and He has big plans for ya. Never forget that."

She nodded, a lump forming in her throat. Another goodbye to a friend from her past. In fact, the only one left from their group still in Pillar was her – another sign it was time for her to move on.

She watched as Hayes walked away. The spring in his step was unmistakable. That vibrancy would soon be hers, too. She only had to get in touch with her spirit guide…after she got a sandwich.

Chapter 52

It had been a week since Nash had gotten a recorded message from Hayes about Mira — a message that had left him hopeful, but he needed more details. He stared out at the rolling waves as he punched in Hayes' number again. Just as it had been doing all week, the call went right into voicemail. Nash licked the salt from his lips, tapping the phone on his thigh. *Tap, flip, tap, flip.* He needed to hear Hayes' message again. Leaning back against his RV's warm fiberglass, he entered his code.

I talked ta Mira, warnin' her not ta dabble in the spirit world. She wasn't defensive or anything, and she accepted my gift of a freshly printed Enchiridion. Both are good signs. While we were talkin', I got a call from Mel, telling me about an offer ta do some mission work...so Mel and I are actually leaving tomorrow mornin' for Ezilli. I think Mira is okay, but just in case, I gave her my car ta use with the permission ta take it on a trip. Gettin' her away from Cofa's Tree will get her away from Vashti's influence. I have a bad feelin' about that woman. Anyway, take care Nash. Hope ta connect soon, but it might be a while since the cell phone coverage in the mission camp is sketchy at best.

Non-existent was more accurate. Scraping his windblown hair back, Nash opened the door to his RV. As he stepped inside, he heard music filtering from his bedroom. Mira? Maybe Hayes had given her the updated tour schedule he'd emailed to him after he'd arrived in Whynot. Nash's heart lurched. Closing the screen door softly behind him, he made his way to his room and peeked inside. He frowned, his heart dropping in disappointment. "Tory? What are you doing here?"

She made a dog-ear on the page of the book on her lap. "What kind of greeting is that?" She stood, laying the self-help cover on the bed.

"One of a person irritated with a friend who wouldn't even try to persuade Mira to get out of Cofa's Tree."

"You can't argue with stupid," Tory said, walking over to him.

His eyes narrowed.

Tory raised up her hands. "Sorry, but it's how I feel. How about we start this hello over with a hug?"

Nash stared at her new haircut, the lack of glasses, the slim fitting clothes. He flicked a lock of her hair, trying to push aside his irritation with her. "Is this what happens when you read a self-help book?"

She chuckled. "Maybe." She swept in to give him a hug. Even though he wanted to stay mad at her, Tory was Tory, and he had to admit the hug did feel good. "I ordered pizza, if that makes you feel any better," she said.

"I guess, as long as it isn't that healthy vegan crap you told me you started eating."

"It's half veggie, half pepperoni." She stepped back and let her gaze float around the RV. "This place is more awesome than I thought it would be," she said.

"Porsche insists on only the best - granite countertops, leather furniture, and every electronic luxury one could imagine. I even have a pool and a hot tub in a screen room that's right out these doors." He pointed at the sliding doors off his room.

"Already peeked out there," she grinned. "And I think I'll fit quite nicely into the swimming suit that was left floating in the pool."

"Party in the hot tub last night," he explained.

"Sounds like fun." Her eyes sparkled.

"It was." Or at least he thought it had been. He didn't remember much of last night. "So why are you here…really? And don't give me any of that self-help crap."

Tory moved past him and made her way to the kitchen. She poured herself a drink, which was odd in itself because Tory didn't drink. She sat down. Nash followed suit, watching her carefully.

"Can't I visit a friend that's been gone over a month just for fun?" she asked.

He stared at Tory for a moment. "Not you. It just doesn't make logical sense."

"Well, I've changed a little." She smiled slightly, which sent up more warning flags.

"You might as well spill it."

After inhaling deeply, she said in a breathy rush, "There's been a busy arson in Pillar this past week. The Prophet House was burned down."

It had been an old house, but Nash wondered if the fire had anything to do with Elroy. Payback maybe? Or maybe an effort to hide evidence? What if Elroy was innocent and the real murderer had come after him in his jail cell? An uneasy feeling settled in Nash's gut. He had to get his hands on the painting from Elroy's cell…if it hadn't been destroyed.

"I have to go back to Pillar," he said, thinking about how he could shift his schedule to make it happen.

"Um…you really don't have anything to go back to."

His stomach dropped to his toes. "Did something happen to Mira?"

"Why does it always come back to her," she spat. "Nothing happened to her except your precious Mira has left town to follow her new dream…whatever that is."

A little spark of hope ignited in his heart. "So what *do* you mean then?"

"Well," she pressed a hand against the base of her neck as she looked down at the floor. "Your music store burned down. No one was injured, but it's gone…all of it."

Nash forgot to breathe. "No!" he managed to rasp.

She looked up at him. "That's not the worst part."

"What could be worse?" A deep pit had settled in the bottom of his belly.

"Your insurance company declared bankruptcy two days ago."

"So you're saying I have nothing." Shock held him perfectly still. Now he truly had nothing to fall back on.

"You have your career, your RV. You have me," she said, grinning at him in a way that looked silly coming from Tory.

"Well, I'm glad you're safe." He frowned, twisting the drink glass on the table, an expanding liquid puddle surrounding it.

"Me too. And actually, I'm glad it happened."

He scowled at her.

"I mean, not glad it happened, but glad that it's gotten me to think outside the box…outside of Pillar." She finished the remaining liquid in her glass. "I need a job and I need you. That's why I'm here."

Nash got up to pace between the kitchen cupboards and the table. "I don't do the hiring."

"I already talked to Porsche. She said she'll find a spot for me."

"You went behind my back? Unbelievable."

Tory smiled softly. "I know the idea will take some getting used to, but think about it." She stood and placed a hand on his arm. "We'll be great together."

"It's not going to happen," he said, removing her hand.

She looked as if he'd slapped her. "I thought you'd be happy about it," she said, her eyes narrowing on his face. "You think she's coming back to you, don't you!"

"Yes, no, I don't know."

"This is ridiculous." Hands on her hips, she said, "You need to make the decision to let her go. It's time to start living your own life rather than waiting for something that's never going to happen."

"So you keep saying. Is that another bit of garbage advice you picked up from your stupid book?"

"The book isn't garbage, and it's plain to see you're letting her destroy your happiness – even still."

Maybe she had a point, but he refused to believe it. "Or maybe it's because Mira and I actually belong together."

She snorted. "You just want what you can't have."

The thought had never crossed his mind. Could that be why he was feeling this way?

Tory grabbed his hand in hers and moved in close. "Give me a chance, Nash…a real one."

He was going to say that he just didn't think it was possible, but before he could utter one syllable, she planted a kiss on his lips – one filled with passion and desire.

A knock sounded on the door, his security guard's voice clearing as he popped his head inside. "I have a pizza here for you," he said.

Nash was thankful for the interruption. It would give him time to get his thoughts together. He peeled himself out of Tory's grasp and went to get the pizza. "Thanks, Chad."

"Need anything else?"

Nash glanced at Tory who was staring at him with a soft smile. "Not right now," he said.

Chad nodded and disappeared, closing the door behind him. Nash took the pizza to the table and sat down.

"Aren't you going to join me?" he asked.

She looked disappointed, but she sat down, too, across from him thankfully. As she opened the lid of the pizza box, she said, "You know, I think we should give it a trial run." She handed him a slice of pizza.

He took it, but set it down to cool. "What do you mean by "it"?"

"Me working with you…being with you. We'll be a great pair – you'll see, if you just give it a chance."

An empty feeling settled in his stomach, one that wouldn't be fed by pizza – or her ideas. He got up. "I need to go for a walk…clear my head."

"Okay. I'll get my bags unpacked."

This pushy Tory, he didn't much care for…and having her as a manager *and* shacking up with him? "Don't."

A flash of hurt crossed her face, but she washed down her bite with another splash of her drink. "You'll warm up to the idea on your walk. Go," she said, waving her hand toward the door.

Biting back his retort, he stepped out of the RV. Taking out his cell, he punched in his security guard's number. As Nash slipped into his golf cart, Chad picked up. "There's a woman I need you to remove from my RV. I'm going for a drive in the cart. Have her gone by the time I get back."

"Right boss."

He was taking the coward's way out and he knew it. And even though he felt a twinge of guilt, he really didn't even know if he liked this new Tory at all. He certainly wasn't ready to live with her. And he absolutely didn't need anyone telling him how to think or what to do. "Be as nice about it as you can, Chad. Tell her I need time and space and that I'm sorry." He paused. "Oh, and give her a hundred for her troubles."

"Consider it done."

Nash glanced back at the car Tory had driven all the way to see him. Her proposition had taken guts and planning, two qualities that assured him she'd be fine without him. As he pulled his golf cart up to the docks, he turned it off. Leaning his forehead against the steering wheel, he could hear the waves lapping against the docked boats. The realization that he didn't have anything to go back to…no Mira, none of their friends, no music store, and no apartment to call home, hit him hard. He'd never felt so alone in his life!

Chapter 53

Mira showered quickly, trying to ignore the mold infused into the caulk of the tub surround. The Crossland Motel on the east side of Bolinbroke had been such a welcome relief last night. She'd been so tired after driving all day. Only now that she could see the room more clearly in the morning light...yuck! She swallowed back the acidic taste that had settled in the back of her throat. "Life is what I believe it is," she whispered, and repeated the phrase a few more times for good measure.

Rifling through the items in her suitcase, she snagged a pair of leggings and a short-sleeved shirt long enough to cover her butt and put them on. "This is a *great* hotel," she said, "and I'm on the adventure of a lifetime." She repeated this phrase as she walked across the towel path she'd made to cover up the carpet that was more stain than not. After running a quick comb through her ink black locks, she carefully applied some makeup. If...no when...she reached the place her spirit guide was leading her, she wanted to look her best.

Satisfied with her hair and her makeup, she reversed her route back to her suitcase. Grabbing her shoes, she put them on while standing. Now that she got a good look at the bed, she really didn't want to sit on it. She stuffed last night's clothes into her suitcase. After zipping it up, she grabbed it and her purse and headed out the door. The fresh air was a welcome relief, and it put a spring in her step as she hurried to her car. She set the suitcase down and hit the unlock button on the key fob. That's when she noticed the tire.

"You have got to be kidding me!" she said, staring at the flat. "This can't be happening!" She kicked it hard, ignoring the resulting throbbing pain from her crunched toes. "Now what?" She looked around the parking lot. Only one other car was in it, and the car looked as if it had been abandoned there for many years. Muttering under her breath, she tossed her purse into the front seat and her suitcase into the back. She popped the trunk and dug inside it to find her spare tire, hoping she'd be able to figure out how to put the thing on.

"Need some help?"

Mira started, whacking her head on the trunk lid. A sharp pain spliced through her skull, and she cried out. Suddenly, it all seemed too much. Tears flowing, her shaky hand reached for the tire iron. Grabbing it, she swung around.

The guy put up his grease-infused hands. "Whoa. Just wanting to help out."

Though she could see his powerful biceps flex beneath his tattoos, she didn't have the energy to keep the tire iron lifted. Still keeping it at her side, though, she swiped at her tears and sniffed. "I'm just a little on edge this morning." She worked up a watery smile. *Life is what I make it*, she repeated in her head. "And I'd really appreciate some help." She'd never owned a car, so her experience with changing a tire was zero.

"I'd be glad to help. What do you want me to do?"

"Whatever one does to change a tire," she said with a tiny chuckle that hinted at her building hysteria.

"That, I can handle." He moved to the trunk and pulled out the spare tire and the jack.

"The tire iron will come in handy, too," he said, holding out his hand. His kind brown eyes met hers. They matched his soothing voice...which didn't match his appearance...at all.

After a moment's hesitation, Mira handed him the tool. Taking a small step back, she crossed her arms over her stomach and watched him work. His movements were quick and practiced. He knew what he was doing.

He'd slipped the jack beneath the car and already had the flat tire off the ground. "You have a kid?" he asked, reaching for the tire iron.

"No. No kids."

"I just wondered since you have a doll in your trunk," he explained as he worked to free the hubcap.

"The doll is a symbolic thing." Vashti had insisted she take along - that it would symbolize her spirit-led journey…taking the doll on a journey it couldn't have done alone was just like the spirit guide taking her on a journey she couldn't do alone.

"I'm not sure what that thing symbolizes," the guy said, glancing up at her as he loosened the tire's bolts. "But I'm glad it isn't for a kid. That thing would cause nightmares for sure." He winked.

Mira smiled for real this time. "That's why it's in my trunk."

The guy chuckled as he pulled off the tire and replaced it with the new one. He lowered the car back down, and Mira sighed with relief when the tire held.

Standing up, the man brushed his hands on his jeans. "The spare is a full-sized one and it looks like it's in okay shape, so it should get you to where you're going." He looked at her in a wondering way, but she wasn't going to share the fact that she didn't actually know where she was going.

"Thank you," she said, tossing the flat tire into her trunk.

He replaced the other tools. "You should get the tire fixed, though, just in case you have another flat."

"I'll make sure to do that." She reached into her purse for a ten. "And thank you so much for your help," she said, handing it to him.

He tucked his hands into his pockets. "You keep it," he said, "I'm glad I could help." He smiled in a way that made her forget her initial fear of him. "Besides," he said, "I can change a tire in my sleep, so it was no big deal." He nodded toward a tow truck parked along the side of the café across the street. On its back window it said, "Just a tow away…". Mira's gaze fell to the car hoisted behind it, its windows riddled with bullet holes.

"Can I at least buy you breakfast?" she asked.

He stared at her a moment. "Why not?"

Mira smiled. "Good."

"The Hideout Café okay with you?" he asked, pointing across the street.

The café's sign hung at an awkward angle atop the grey and peeling shake shingles that ended about halfway to the ground. A metal bin, stamped with the word ICE, stood on one side of the front doors. On the other side was a rack of split wood for sale. The place didn't look much better than the motel, but Mira reminded herself that it was just breakfast. "Is the food good?"

"The best."

"Let's do it, then," she said, grabbing her purse from the car. "Lead the way."

As they walked together across the parking lot, he asked, "Where are you from?"

She saw no reason not to tell him. "Pillar."

He looked both ways before crossing the nearly deserted street. "Heard that's kind of a wild place," he said, peeking over at her.

She glanced up at him. "And this place isn't?"

"Hopefully that will change soon," he said. "I'm working on it."

She wondered what his story was. "Have you lived around here long?"

They approached the front door, which he opened for her. "A little more than six months."

Mira stepped inside, thinking it looked even worse than the outside. Mismatched chairs stood around tables covered with tablecloths that could easily hide leftover food and crumbs. It smelled like grease and smoke, which made her stomach churn. "And you like it in Bolinbroke then?"

"Like is a strong word," he grinned, coming in behind her. "But I've become quite fond of the people here. They are good-hearted."

The door closed, cutting off the fresh air. "Good-hearted people shoot out car windows?"

He didn't pretend to not know what she was talking about. "Some are misguided, some are *not* good-hearted, but this is the place I need to be for right now."

Before she could pry further, a server approached. Her navy apron was dusted with flour and a smear of mustard. As she grabbed a couple of menus, she asked, "Booth okay today Percy?"

His name was Percy? Mira never would've guessed that. He looked too tough and rough around the edges to be a Percy. "A booth would be great, Zee."

They followed her to the table in the far corner that overlooked the front parking lot. Zee laid down the menus and asked, "How's Charlie doin'?"

"He's great. He just started t-ball, and loves it!"

"My Noah is into soccer this year, but I'm thinking it might not be his sport. He's so sweet that he likes to give everyone a chance to kick the ball…even if they are on the opposing team." She chuckled.

"He sounds like a winner to me," Percy said.

Zee beamed. "Can I get you both something to drink?"

"Coffee," they said in unison.

"Cream or sugar?"

"No thanks," they said – both at the same time, again.

It was weird, but as she looked at the stranger across the table from her, she felt a connection. Not the crush type, but one of kindred spirits.

As the server left to get their drinks, Mira glanced at her menu. "Do you have a recommendation for me?"

"The French toast bake is good. But if you don't want sweet and are more adventurous, try the Omelet Surprise." He closed his menu and laid it on the table. She laid hers down as well. As if on cue, Zee came by. She laid their coffees down in front of them.

"Let me guess. You want this week's omelet surprise," she said to Percy.

He nodded. "I hope it's as good as last week's."

"Mixed results on this one," she said, scrunching up her nose.

Zee turned her attention to Mira. "What can I get you dear?"

"I'll have the egg and cheese omelet."

"You're playing it safe, huh?" Zee commented.

Mira reminded herself that she was the creator of her own life – and she wasn't here to play it safe. "I changed my mind. I'll have the omelet surprise, too."

The server's dark brows lifted. "You sure?"

"Why not?"

"Well alright then. I got it down."

As Zee hurried back toward the kitchen, Percy said, "I apologize for not introducing myself earlier. I'm Percy Thurman."

"I'm Mira," she said.

He smiled. "Nice to meet you, Mira." He raised his coffee to his lips and took a careful, but none-too-quiet swig. "So what brings you to Bolinbroke?"

"I'm just passing through."

"That's what I said six months ago." He reached into his pocket and pulled out a card. It said, "Thurman Towing…just a tow away".

She glanced at it before sliding it next to the salt and pepper shakers. "I know you said that you like the people here. Is that why you decided to stay?" She paused to look around.

"That's a big part of it." His hands folded together on the table in front of him. "Where is your final destination?"

"I'm not sure yet," she said. She took a sip of her coffee. The robust flavor didn't sit well in her stomach. Maybe she needed to eat something before drinking it. The smell of the place wasn't helping either, unless one enjoyed the scent of month old deep-fat-fried foods and ashtrays. "I guess I'm looking for a place where I can really be me." Whoever that was.

"What does that place look like to you?"

There was no censure in his eyes, only warmth and understanding. "I'm not sure about that yet, either, but when I find it, I'll know."

"I believe it."

"You do?"

He nodded.

Zee arrived with their plates. The omelet's steamy fragrance didn't mesh well with the other smells in the place.

"If you'll excuse me for a minute…I need to use the restroom," Mira said.

"Care if I start eating?"

The question caught her by surprise. "No. Go ahead." Mira hurried to the bathroom, but when she opened the door, she turned her head with a groan. "Yuck." The whoosh of smell from inside the restroom was more nausea-inducing than outside it. She'd have to hit a cleaner bathroom on her way out of town.

As Mira turned to go back to her breakfast, she spied rows of pies spinning in a circular, yellow-glassed display. A bulletin board hung on the wall beside it. She took a few moments to look it over while she tried to tell herself that she felt healthy and spry and that it smelled like a field of honeysuckle.

Scanning the ads on the board, she saw Doberman puppies for sale, a truck - with tires taller than Percy - for trade, a cleaning service offering a free week trial, and a church advertising their upcoming banquet dinner. The poster taking up the middle portion of the corkboard promoted a band called 4HIM that would be playing in the city of Whynot this coming weekend at a bar called Dreamer's Club.

The city name stuck out…hadn't Percy just said why not when she'd offered to buy him breakfast? It had to be more than a coincidence! Vashti's words resounded in her head. Repetitive words were one way the spirit guide would speak to her.

Feeling a flair of hope, Mira went back to the booth. A woman stood there, talking to Percy. Her eyes sparkled, and the interesting cut and color of her hair emphasized her multiple tattoos. She was pretty, in a way, but the skin on her neck seemed like it was scarred or burned maybe.

"Mira. I'd like you to meet my friend Francine. Francine…Mira."

"Nice to meet you Mira," she said, but she quickly looked back toward Percy. "I'll see you tomorrow night at the show?"

He grinned, his face radiating with warmth. "I wouldn't miss it!"

She beamed back at him and walked away.

"Francine is one of the reasons I stayed here," Percy said softly.

Mira took a tiny bite of her eggs. "She's your girlfriend, then?"

"No. She's just a good friend." He ate the last bite of his omelet.

"How did you meet?" Mira managed to take another bite of her omelet.

"Just as I arrived in Bolinbroke, I came upon a horrible accident." He laid his napkin over his plate. "A car had hit a median and had flipped onto its top. Fire shot out from its engine, but I could still see the trapped driver through the smoke. I bolted over to the car, reaching in through the driver's window to cut the woman's seatbelt, but she shoved at my arm, screaming, 'Get away!'" He ran his hand across his mouth and his eyes took on a faraway look. "She said she wanted out…not out of the car but out of life." He frowned. "I kept working at pulling her out anyway, but she kept fighting me. 'Just back away and sing to me,' she'd yelled. I did sing to her, only it was as I pulled her out of the car." His mouth curved into a half-smile. "She was so angry!"

Mira frowned. "Then how did you end up being friends?"

He took a swig of his coffee. "Well, I decided I couldn't just leave town until I knew she was okay, so I checked into the hotel right across the street. And every day, I went to the hospital to see Francine."

"How did she take that?"

"Pretty well when she was on the heavy pain medication to help with her burns. Not so much when they were weaning her off them." He smiled as if in remembrance, his warm eyes so expressive, Mira couldn't look away.

"So what happened?"

"During my first visits, I didn't say much of anything. But then her ex-boyfriend came by, and I found out a little of Francine's story." Percy's face took on one of pain – a pain over another's experience. "Not only was I angry, but I was determined to make her see the truth. She'd almost thrown away her life, her potential, because of this abusive jerk."

"She didn't know he was a jerk?"

"In her heart, she knew." His brows pinched together. "But like so many of us, Francine didn't know who she was in God's eyes. I had to let her know she was loved by God more than she knew – and that He created her with a purpose."

Mira guessed some would appreciate that view, but she was on the road to create her own purpose and carve out her own life. "Did Francine buy into that?"

He looked at her strangely before continuing his story. "It was important for her to know the truth, so I started reading to her out of the Enchiridion of Emmanuel. It soothed her most of the time, but when she really got agitated, I turned the words into a song." He chuckled. "It wasn't until much later that she told me I was a crappy singer."

Mira's thoughts turned to Nash. Where was he singing now? Did he miss her at all? "I'm not much of a singer, either, but I do enjoy music," she said.

"Then maybe you could go hear her sing. She's in a band called 4HIM that's performing this weekend in Whynot."

"That's the group I saw on the bulletin board." Hearing Whynot again *had* to be a sign. "Who knows? Maybe I'll be around Whynot to hear her perform."

"She'd like that."

"Will you be there?"

"Yeah. Wouldn't miss it."

Zee came over with the coffee pot. "Want me to top off your coffee?"

"No. I need to get going," Mira said. "Could I get the bill please?"

"It's already been covered." Zee looked down at Mira's nearly full plate. "Although I should probably comp that meal. Did the cook put too much salt on it or something?"

"It was fine," she said. "But this was supposed to be my treat." She looked at Percy, who had stood up.

"Meeting you was *my* treat. I am happy to buy a friend breakfast." He grabbed his business card off the table and held it out to her again. "Don't forget this."

After only spending an hour with her, he'd called her friend. It seemed strange, and yet, she somehow knew he was the kind of person who *would* come to help her if she needed him. Percy wasn't just a likeable guy…he had a genuinely giving and loving soul. "Thanks Percy. I'll keep it handy," she said, slipping his card into her purse. "It was nice meeting you."

"Godspeed Mira." Instead of shaking her proffered hand, he grasped it in both of his. "I hope you find what your heart is truly looking for."

She felt that all too familiar twinge of longing. "I do too," she said, and headed to the exit, Percy following.

His phone rang a second later and he answered. "Just a tow away…Percy here." He opened the café door for Mira while he listened to his caller. As Mira stepped outside, Percy put a hand on her arm. "See you this weekend," he mouthed.

She nodded, not wanting to tell him no.

He grinned and waved before jogging to his tow truck. She heard the rumble of his engine as she made her way to her own car.

Mira felt a tug of sadness as she watched his truck speed down the road. Writing it off as 'some people are easy to connect with, some aren't', she jumped into her car. She turned on the radio as she headed to the edge of the parking lot. Right or left? She reached into her purse and pulled out the map she'd picked up in the motel lobby.

As she scoured the many towns that had popped up after the LifeChip had been destroyed, the announcer on the radio said, "It's a lovely day in the city of sunshine. Why not take advantage of it?"

Whynot…those same words kept coming to her over and over. She studied the map and zoned in on an area ten hours away from where she was. Her fate was sealed. "Whynot here I come," she said, and turned left.

Chapter 54

Instead of going back to his RV, Nash headed downtown on foot. He tried to direct his thoughts to his music…to his next stop on the tour…to the girl he'd met that past week. Although she'd seemed very nice, he couldn't even remember her name. Without permission, his thoughts shifted back to Mira. He felt better knowing she'd left Pillar, that she'd be away from the murderer – if Elroy wasn't their man, as Hayes believed. She was also out of that crazy Cofa's Tree. But where had she gone? Was she meeting up with Tanger somewhere? The thought rankled.

"Enough, Nash. It's time to think about yourself!" Yet as he approached Whynot's main street, he found it hard to dredge up much enthusiasm. On paper, his life seemed perfect…fun, lucrative, exciting. In reality, though, it felt like it was missing something – a big something - and he found himself wondering more and more each day, what the purpose was in all of it. Plunk away at life until he got to the end of it? It seemed so pointless, even with a sprinkle of happiness here and there along the way.

He stepped onto the sidewalk of the street they'd termed "Music Row". The quietness surprised him. Just a few people walked about and the only music he could hear was the tunes piping out of a couple of bars down the street. When Nash approached the corner of Prime and Paramount, he slipped into the "Dreamer's Club", the bar he'd played in this past weekend. Dimly lit, it took a moment for his eyes to adjust. Once they did, he checked out the room. Over in the corner, a young woman hung seductively on an old guy. In a booth near the pair, two ladies leaned toward each other, deep in conversation. And the bartender, Jeremiah if he remembered correctly, stood behind the bar, drying a glass.

Nash walked over to him. "Slow night, huh Jeremiah?"

He smiled. "Yeah. After Revel Week, I think everyone needed a detox day." Jeremiah wiped a white towel across the bar in front of Nash and laid out a napkin. "What can I get for you?"

"Anything with alcohol. Surprise me."

"Okay." Jeremiah began the process of mixing a drink. "So how are things going? You had an awesome show the other night."

Nash shrugged. "It's going okay, I guess."

"Trouble in paradise?" Jeremiah asked as he set the drink down in front of Nash.

Nash cupped the tall glass with his hand. "I'm starting to think that paradise isn't attainable."

Jeremiah chuckled. "I think I can help you with that." He leaned forward onto his elbows.

Picking up his drink, Nash said, "By giving me a lifetime of alcohol?"

"That's not even close to true paradise, even though I think alcohol will be available in paradise," Jeremiah said with a grin.

"You're talking about life after death. There's no concrete proof of that."

"But that doesn't mean it can't exist." He leaned against the bar. "Maybe think about it this way...what if our longing for perfection is a longing to return to a perfection we once knew – a place our souls actually belong?"

"Interesting philosophical concept, I guess, but I lean toward logic and science." Except for where Mira was concerned...there was not much logic in how he felt about her!

Jeremiah filled a glass with water and put it in front of Nash and handed him a menu. "So you're saying we just "are"...that our lives and our world have no meaning but to exist and die."

Nash's heart twinged. "It's unfortunate, but yes."

"How do you explain, then, that even during our recent LifeChip era, we had many who couldn't be stifled, who rebelled and broke out to find meaning and purpose?"

Mira came immediately to mind – her passion, her drive, and her dreams that made her yearn for a changed and vibrant world. Why *would* that urge thrive in a world that had used science to obliterate it? "I don't believe there's any reason to speculate beyond the universe of matter and energy because there is nothing beyond it."

"Can you prove that scientifically?"

"No," Nash admitted. Before he could make a case, a guy, about thirty-five in age, came barreling into the bar. He was full-out dancing – every part of his body including his eyes. He rushed around the bar and picked Jeremiah up in a bear hug. "She's cancer free, Russel. She's cancer free!! Can you believe it?"

Russel?

"I believe it," the bartender said. "I told you. Prayer is powerful."

The guy released Russel and grinned. "God was listening, like you said, and," he looked upward, "This is so unbelievable. Thank you Jesus! She just had a scan and she's cancer-free."

Russel slapped the guy's back. "I am so happy for you."

"Thanks Russel…for everything. We'd lost all hope before talking to you and now…" He swallowed back the emotion, but couldn't contain the tears that had formed in his eyes. "You're the first one I told, so I better get moving and spread the word."

"Well, give my love to Gina."

"I will," he said as he moved from behind the bar. On his way past Nash, he pressed a hand against his shoulder. "You should listen to this guy…or rather to what he has to say about God – not about fashion."

Russel threw a bar rag at him and he laughed. "I'm fashionable and you know it."

"Polka dots with stripes, socks with sandals, vests over baggy t-shirts…should I go on?"

"If you think it's important," Russel said with a grin.

"Actually, I don't care one whit. I just feel like I'm going to burst."

Russel flicked his hand toward the door. "Just don't do it on my floor."

The guy laughed and hurried out the door.

"So what's his story?" Nash asked with a smile, the guy's happiness contagious. "And why didn't you tell me that Jeremiah wasn't your name?"

The bartender grinned. "What you called me wasn't important at the moment. I know who I am, so it's no big deal." Russel nodded toward the couple in the corner and began pouring two more drinks. "And the guy that just came in? His name is Jack. His wife's name is Gina. Several months ago she was diagnosed with cancer, but the treatments weren't working and the hospital sent her home to die. They'd given her a few weeks to live – a month if they were lucky." Russel wound around the bar with the freshly poured drinks. "I'll be right back."

As Russel tended to the other customers, Nash took a swig of his own drink. How horrible that would be…to find out you, or your wife, had cancer and only had a short time to live. It seemed so unfair, so cruel. Nash hoped he never had to deal with that, but he supposed everyone wished the same thing.

The bartender returned, only this time he sat on the bar stool next to Nash. "I met Jack on the day he was to take Gina home to die." Russel shook his head. "The depth of his pain was so visible, so real, it broke my heart. But I had a hope that he didn't."

"What hope was that?"

"That prayers are powerful. That God listens. That miracles happen."

Nash snorted. "There isn't any proof there's even a God, let alone that He performs miracles. These flukes in nature are nothing more than coincidences."

"I beg to differ," Russel said as he pulled a piece of paper out of a drawer. After writing something on it, he handed it to Nash. The word he'd written was HELP. "If you saw this in ten foot letters dug into the sand on the beach, would you believe it more likely that some person wrote it with a purpose in mind, or that the words had been formed randomly by the natural forces of water and wind?"

"That someone wrote it is obviously the answer."

"Then it's perfectly logical to consider that not everything is random, that there very well might be an intelligence behind the creation of the world."

Nash took another drink. "But say you gather a group of monkeys to type random letters. Given enough time, they can actually create a Shakespearean work."

"Even if that is a possibility," Russel said, "when searching for the source of the manuscript, we also have to consider what is probable, and what is most likely. So even if it's possible for the monkeys to create the manuscript over time, it is much more likely that Shakespeare wrote it."

"I guess." Nash ran his finger along the top of the glass.

"And if you think about it, someone would've had to provide the monkeys with the typewriters, with the letters and the language already in place...kind of like God with our DNA and RNA."

Nash shifted on his seat and took another drink. "I suppose it might be possible for a higher being to exist, but that has nothing to do with miracles."

"Yet what if a God - powerful enough to create our cosmos, who exists outside our natural system - can reach inside our system to change the orderly way in which things work?"

"You're saying a miracle would result instead of it being a random coincidence."

Russel grinned. "Exactly."

There was logic and rationality to Russel's reasoning, but Nash didn't really know if he could buy into it. God-given miracles just seemed too easy of an explanation. But then of course, random coincidence came off as a simplified and convenient explanation as well.

"Still not convinced?" Russel asked.

Nash shook his head, although he wondered if he'd been too quick to write off any possibility of God.

"You might be when you hear the rest of Gina and Jack's story. Do you want to hear it?"

Nash nodded, curious.

"Jack came in the night Gina was diagnosed. I told him about God, about His Son, about His Spirit – and about prayer. Jack accepted it as truth and shared it with Gina. Together, their faith blossomed – and they prayed with all their hearts. I prayed with all my heart, too."

"So you're saying that through your prayers, God chose to heal her from cancer."

"The doctors had said there was no hope – that she would never be cancer free and that she would die within weeks. But she hasn't died, and the cancer is gone. I say it's the only reasonable explanation that makes any logical sense."

The proof was right there. Or had there been a misreading of the scans? Or was Jack delusional?

"You can look into it further, keep track of her progress, that kind of thing…if you want to make sure it's really the truth."

"I might just do that." Could the guy read his mind? "Either way, though, Jack and Gina's story does give me something to think about." Nash laid cash for his drink on the bar. "Thanks for the drink…and for the talk."

Chapter 55

Mira rolled into Whynot at 10pm. With bathroom breaks, her ten-hour trip ended up being twelve hours – a long trip, but she'd made it.

She turned onto the main drag and pulled up in front of the first place she saw, Halal Grill. She turned her car off and listened as her engine gave a tiny gasp as if it was relieved. "I am glad to finally be here, too," she said, patting the dash.

She got out, and in the space between door and car, she took a moment to stretch her aching back and to look around. The dull streetlights didn't give her a clear view, but she did get a feeling. The handful of diverse people on the sidewalks made her curious and sparked a tingle of excitement in her belly. "Is this home?" she whispered.

Trying to imagine herself fitting into this place, she wondered what to do next. Find a place to stay? Find a place to eat? Walk around?

She wasn't all that hungry, but she was thirsty. Slipping her purse strap over her shoulder, she locked her car door and stepped up onto the sidewalk to scan the menu taped onto the lit windows of the Halal Grill. A woman swept past her, her unique scent leaving a trail. Mira's eyes followed the woman who had 'that look', one that oozed confidence and originality. She crossed the street and disappeared into a bar called Dreamer's Club. That's where Francine would be playing on Friday! Mira smiled and hurried across the street, deciding now was a good time to check it out and to get a drink.

Inside the joint, she spotted the perfumed woman sitting in a booth, surrounded by several people, all laughing and joking around. Should she walk over and introduce herself? Mira wondered. "Why not?" she answered herself with a tiny chuckle. Yet as she wandered toward the group, the bartender stepped in front of her, menus in hand.

"You must be new here."

She nodded and smiled. Obviously he knew his customers.

"I have an open seat for you on the end." He pointed over his shoulder toward the bar. "And that spot comes with a free drink."

"Seriously?"

"Yeah."

Free, right now, was something she couldn't pass up. After a quick glance at the vibrant group of friends, she said, "Sure." Besides, the bartender could probably give her some tips on what to do in Whynot. "Thanks."

The bartender grinned, his teeth bright white against his dark skin. As he walked with her over to the bar, he said, "I'm Russel, by the way." He held out his hand. "Welcome to Whynot."

Mira shook his hand. "I'm Mira. And I'm glad to be here."

He pulled out the bar stool for her and then scooted her in. "What can I get for you?"

"I'll have a seltzer water." The bubbles seemed to settle her stomach.

"One seltzer water coming right up."

As he moved behind the bar, she turned to watch the group that had captured her attention. One of the guys had a long scraggly beard and a shirt splattered with paint. The woman sitting next to him had silver hair weaved with gold and copper, clipped on the side. Her lips were extra puffy and she held a sculpture of this ugly figure with one long arm and one short one.

Mira squinted, trying to get a better look. It appeared as though, on the figure's back clung a creature of some sort. It was ugly, but interesting at least. Across from the one holding the sculpture was the woman Mira had followed inside. Next to her sat an attractive man sporting man-bun, one that allowed a portion of the rest of his hair to hang down his back. He had a close-cropped beard and wore only a pair of shorts. As he rubbed his flat stomach, Mira noticed his calloused hands. *I knew there was a reason I was drawn to the group…they have to be artists…and perhaps they are just the community of friends I am looking for!*

Russel returned with her drink.

"So what brings you to Whynot?" he asked, leaning sideways against the edge of the bar as he dried a wine glass.

"Adventure…a band called 4HIM…," she shrugged, "a number of things. I guess I'm just going where life leads me."

His black eyes studied her, but it was a curious look and nothing else. "Do you know the band well?"

She shook her head. "I only met Francine earlier today," she said, glancing back at the artist group, hoping they wouldn't leave anytime soon.

"Do you know the group you keep staring at?"

"No," she said, feeling her face redden as she turned her attention back to Russel. "Enough questions about me. Tell me, what's Whynot like? What do you like about the town?"

He put the wine glass on a shelf. "Whynot started rebuilding a month after the global reformation. A businessman moved in, and so did his ideas." He grabbed another glass from the dishwasher rack and ran the towel across it. "Turns out, this guy really loves the arts – music, art, theater, libraries – that type of thing." He smiled. "So if you like the arts and entertainment, Whynot is your city."

Now *that* sounded like a place she could fit in! And she couldn't wait to get started. "Sounds awesome to me."

"It is." The bartender leaned in. "But it has its downfalls."

"I don't want to hear about downfalls," she said. "I'm all about positive thinking and living life to the fullest."

"Ah." He studied her a moment. "I guess you must be staying at the Heaven Hotel then? It's the most inspiring place in town with its architecture and its landscaping. Great friendly service too."

It sounded like a place she couldn't afford. Scrunching up her nose, Mira said, "I don't really have a place to stay yet."

"Well, I hope you can get one. All the hotels book up fast here. We have a lot of tourists."

"Oh no," Mira said, and pulled out her phone, only to look up when she saw the skin…and abs of the bare chested guy from the table. He stood right next to her, and he was even more attractive up close.

"What can I get you Sam?" Russel asked.

"An Irish Red." He turned to look back at the group and shouted, "We'll just see about that."

Russel filled a tall frosted glass with an amber colored liquid and handed it to Sam. As the guy turned to walk away, he slipped a folded piece of paper into Mira's palm. She tried to glance at it discreetly, but the small print was impossible to read without bringing it out into the light. Instead, she watched Sam walk back to his table. As he sat down, he smiled at her.

"Watch out for that group, Mira." Russel's softly spoken words startled her.

"Why? They seem like fun."

"I am sure they can be fun, but…" He paused and went to the till. He pulled out a little packet filled with papers the size of business cards. Handing it to her, she peeked inside. A ticket to the 4HIM concert? A phone number for a free night in a houseboat? Free lunch at The Docks restaurant? A gift card to Paramount Discount? There had to be a catch. "Way are you giving me this?"

"Because I can," he said without a hint of a smile.

"How much do you want for these?" She reached into her purse.

"No money. Just a promise."

Ah…it came with a condition. "What's the promise?"

"That you'll stay away from that group."

He was totally serious. "You're sure concerned about them."

"They have a different way of looking at and living life. I've tried to…" he shook his head. "Just be careful."

"I will," she said, her interest in the group all the more piqued because of his warning. They sounded like just the kind of people she was looking for – ones that wanted to live life their own way and have fun doing it. Mira stood up. "Thanks a ton for these!" She tucked them in her purse. "And for the drink."

"My pleasure, Mira."

As she walked the length of the bar, she could feel the bartender's eyes on her as well as those of the group's. The note burned hot in her palm, but she wouldn't look at it yet. She wouldn't look at any of them, either.

When she got outside, she hurried to her car and slipped into the driver's seat. She flipped on the light. With shaking fingers, she held the note up. It said, *I am drawn to you like a melody to a song. I live at The Grotto on the east side of town. Stop by sometime — the sooner the better. Sam*

He'd left directions. "Why not?" she said with a grin as she pulled out of the parking space. "Grotto Sam, here I come."

Chapter 56

After finding Paramount Discount, grabbing a few groceries, and then freshening up, a couple hours had passed. The next thing on Mira's list was to find The Grotto. It was late, but she wasn't tired, and she really wanted to do this. So, she drove out of town, carefully following Sam's written directions. Her clammy hands gripped the steering wheel as she pulled into the circular gravel lot. It was surrounded by a rustic wooden fence, like he'd mentioned, but where was the grotto? She could see the campground, with tents spread out on the sandy grounds to her right. Off to her left, a little dirt pathway wound its way through dense trees. And directly in front of her was a small beach area with its waves curling up onto its empty shoreline. Not a grotto in sight!

Part of her was relieved, and she seriously considered turning around, but the challenge to live life fully in the present urged her to continue her search. Putting the car into park, she rechecked the directions. This *was* the place Sam had marked. Getting out of the car, she slipped her purse over her shoulder. "If I were a grotto, where would I be?"

Scanning the area, she zoned in on the dirt pathway. Her gut said to follow it, so she did. About ten feet from the parking lot, she saw him. The glow from the tip of his cigarette and its accompanying trail of smoke had given him away.

"Hi, beautiful." The man continued to lean against the tree as he watched her.

Her heart started to beat erratically, but she ignored it. "Sam?"

"I've been waiting for you." He approached her, his smile visible now that he stood close. "It's kind of hard to see your way on this dark path, but I know it by heart, so no worries."

Self-preservation hovered at the edge of her senses. "The path leads to The Grotto?"

"Yes." He took one more drag on the sweet smelling stick, tapped the end of it against a tree and shoved the remainder in his pocket. "It's a great place."

Sam seemed calm and happy and not in the least threatening, but she reached into her purse to check for her knife anyway. The cold metal reassured her. "What exactly *is* The Grotto?"

"It's mostly a place we get together to do our art, but you won't be able to get the feel of the ambiance or for the community without seeing it firsthand." He tucked his hands into his shorts pockets. "You want to see it, right?"

She hesitated, Russel's words hovering on the edge of her mind. "Will you just point the way? I have to do something first and then I can meet you there."

"In the daylight, I'd say yes, but at night without a guide, you'd probably get lost."

Obviously finding it herself wasn't an option. "Maybe tomorrow would be better."

"Or I can just wait for you to get back, if you want. By the way...if you need a place to stay, there's a spot for you there."

"Oh." She hadn't arranged to stay at the houseboat yet. "If you'll wait for a few minutes, I should have my answer."

"Fair enough," he said, and took the smoke out of his pocket, relit it and went back to leaning against the tree.

Mira hurried to her car. Pulling the candle and the notebook out of her backpack, she took them to the sandy beach. After rushing to create a circle of stones around her, she lit the candle. Flipping the notebook to an open page, she wrote, *Oh Wyze Woman, I am thankful for all you do – for getting me to this place that challenges me to find out who I am. Give me clarity as to my next step.* Mira stared at the candle as she listened to the soft ripple of waves curling onto the shore. She listened intently for direction, trying to clear her mind so that it could be filled with the wisdom of the Wyze Woman spirit guide. *Anju...*the word seemed to settle in her mind, and was accompanied by a slight buzzing in her ear. Mira didn't know what it meant, but she wrote it down. Tamping down her nervous excitement, she closed her eyes and visualized herself in a sacred space…a grotto. She smiled. Yes, a grotto…she could feel safe and wonderful there, captured in an historical and romantic time. Inside the grotto, it began to glow, then a woman appeared out of the mist. She looked like an angel with magical transparent wing panels similar to a Glasswinged butterfly. "Speak to me, Anju," she said. "Tell me, should I go to The Grotto?"

If Anju answered, Mira didn't hear it over the noise that had erupted in the nearby tent area. She squeezed her eyes tighter, trying to ignore it and clear her mind again. But the conversation grew louder and louder. Just when Mira thought she could no longer stand another second of the annoying distraction, someone said, "Yes. Yes. Yes."

Mira's jaw dropped, her eyes popped open. There was her answer! Now sure of her next step and anxious to experience The Grotto, she blew out the candle, gathered it and her notebook and left the beach. She strode past the group, granting them a smile. They all smiled back and wished her a goodnight.

Jogging to her car, she replaced the candle and notebook, then took her purse and backpack in hand. Eyes focused on the dirt path, she wandered along it until she came to the spot she'd left Sam. Where was he? "Sam?"

"Over here. Just taking a pee."

She turned and spotted him, the top half of his white butt cheeks clearly visible. She turned away.

"It's something we all do, babe. Nothing to be shy about."

She forced herself to turn back toward him to show that she wasn't inhibited. "Just watching my step."

He grunted. "You coming to The Grotto with me tonight, then?"

"Yeah," she said.

"Good." He zipped up his pants. "Follow me."

She hurried along behind him. His bare feet seemed to miss every stone and stick. His head weaved so as to miss every low hanging branch.

Not so with her. "You seem like a covert operative," she said, stumbling along.

"I was once," he said. "But I don't talk about it," he added before she could even ask anything.

"What's your name, by the way?"

"Mira."

"Mira what?"

"Sam what?"

He chuckled. "Sam Logos."

She didn't want to tell him her real name…she wanted to be free of her past as well. "Mira Anju," she said, using the word that had come to her on the beach.

"We have an Anju in our group. First name, not last. It means one who lives in heart. So your name means wonderful one who lives in heart. Nice."

It did have a nice ring. "What does your name mean?"

He laughed aloud. "It means a lot of things. The one I prefer today is sun child."

His skin was tan enough – especially compared to his butt cheeks. She could easily imagine him as a child of the sun.

"Well here it is," he said, leading her into a clearing. A stone-like structure stood before them, lights and voices filtering through its open windows.

"Is it a castle?"

"That's the look we were going for." His work-roughened hand patted the stone wall. "Love this part of history."

She didn't know quite what that history entailed, but it certainly looked romantic.

"Come on. I'll show you inside."

Mira followed Sam into The Grotto. The walls were stone on the inside, too. The area had a compartmentalized look, each tarped area unique. The segments sported sculpting, painting, metalwork, glasswork, and more. Only one artist remained, though - the silver, gold, and copper-haired woman. Her hands molded a ball of clay as she stood in front of a blood-red tapestry with an eye in its center. She looked up at Mira and Sam as they approached.

"Anju…was I right or was I right?" Sam grinned at her, clearly pleased.

"You were right," Anju said with resignation. "What type of art are you into dear?" she asked, directing her attention to Mira.

"Um…I used to paint, but I'm not sure which medium I want to get into now." Although, she did have her camera along – and according to Divinya, she had an eye for it. Perhaps she'd focus on that.

"Let me know if you want to give sculpting a try," Anju said, going back to the mug that now had an ugly face sculpted into the side of it.

"Thanks," Mira said, although she didn't really think she'd like to learn from the woman called Anju. Her style was a bit creepy in Mira's opinion.

Sam continued down the long hall to another door. He opened it. "This is where I work…and sleep."

The room had walls, but no ceiling. Several torches burned, illuminating the area. She approached one of the stone pieces. "You're a stone mason," she said, running her hand along the carved cello.

"I am. And this is my musical sanctuary – where I work, eat, sleep, and find peace." He sat down on a chair made of logs.

"Your work is beautiful," she said.

"I hope it makes me famous someday."

"I think it will." She moved onto the next piece…a saxophone. It was sleek, sexy, and seemed to cry out its own melody. "Do you have stories to go with each piece?"

She could feel his eyes on her as she moved to the stone guitar.

"Yes."

"Maybe I could write out the stories to accompany the art," she said.

He stood up and walked slowly toward her. "It might work," he said softly. "But those stories are so much a part of me, they will be hard for me to share."

His honesty was humbling. "Maybe it will make the pieces more relatable, and powerful."

"Maybe." He nodded. "Do you need something to eat?"

"Sure."

Going to a shelf stacked with various goodies, he said, "How about an apple?"

"That would be great."

He tossed it to her. "Thanks," she said, rubbing it across the fabric of her leggings.

"I know it probably seems weird to you that I invited you here," he said, leaning back in his chair.

"I guess," she said, waiting for him to continue.

"When you came into Dreamers, I saw something in you I still see in myself and I thought maybe you were the one I've been waiting for who can help me find it."

"Find what?"

"The song to my melody…the answer to my longing…" He rubbed his hand across his face. "It sounds crazy. I'm crazy I guess."

"No," Mira said. "I get it." She took a bite of the apple. Wiping the juice off her chin, she added, "And I suppose the only way to find our answers is to search for them in many different ways. The answer has to be *somewhere* we can find it, don't you think?" She took another bite of apple.

"I keep hoping," he said, slapping the tops of his legs and standing up. He moved over to the wall opposite of the food, and adjacent to his chisels and other tools. "This is where I sleep – or at least try to sleep." He pointed to another rock ledge, which was located across from his. "And you can sleep on this one."

"Thanks." It was only one night, Mira told herself as she finished her apple. She threw the core over the top of the wall.

Sam didn't say anything about it, but as he climbed onto his rock ledge to lay down, he said, "So tell me a little about yourself…whatever you want to share."

Mira went to her own rock ledge and laid down. Tired of trying to stay positive and sick of pretending she had her life figured out, she decided it would be a good thing to share her story. Maybe it would lead to Sam sharing his, and maybe they'd make a tremendous artistic pair that would soothe each other's hearts and free them to love fully.

"It all started with a dream," she began.

Chapter 57

Mira awoke to the sound of chiseling. Laying there a moment, she rehashed the discussion she'd had with Sam last night. She'd blabbed her entire story, and now he knew more about her than anyone. She knew quite a bit about him, too, yet why had she told a stranger her every secret? Running her hand down her face, she bit back a groan. At least it had brought about a trust between them — and a pact to let the past stay in the past and not let it define who they were. Only why did her past keep creeping up and getting in the way?

Scooting to the edge of the slab, Mira sat up to watch Sam work on his newest piece. To imagine him as a small boy, locked in a cellar broke her heart. No wonder he liked living in an area without a roof! The nightmares of his past still haunted him. She knew this was true, not only because he'd told her, but because his cries and fitful sleep during the night had proved it. That she'd laid by his clammy, trembling body for a while to comfort him had helped, but it didn't erase the pain from his eyes.

She got up, grabbed an extra sweatshirt from her backpack, and slipped it over the one she wore. The chilled air didn't have the same effect on Sam, whose bare chest glistened with sweat. As she approached to get a closer look at how he worked, she glimpsed the danger in his eyes. It seemed locked onto the stonework and nothing else.

"Good morning Sam."

He didn't say anything, only continued his rhythmic chiseling.

She tried not to feel hurt. *Don't take it personally*, she said to herself. He's only zoned in on his art. Taking her bag and her purse, she wandered through the deserted place. The art intrigued her, but she needed a bathroom. After a quick look and finding none, she slipped out the back door. Heading the opposite direction of the path they'd taken last night, she slipped into the treed area to find a spot hidden, yet close enough that she could still see her way back.

"This should be good," she said into the crisp morning air. Squatting down, she relieved herself, then dug into her bag for a fresh set of clothes. After a hasty look around to see that she was still alone, she stripped down to nothing and then as quickly as she could, put on what she'd brought – an asymmetrical tunic top, leggings, thigh high boots, and a zippered sweater.

Tucking the dirty clothes back into her bag, she started back toward The Grotto. As she approached, she noticed Sam standing against the stone wall, dressed in faded jeans and snug fitting grey hooded sweatshirt with cutoff sleeves. Had he been watching her? If she asked and he said no, she'd be embarrassed for accusing him. If he said yes, she'd be embarrassed that he'd watched her. So she said, "Good morning, Sam."

He smiled, but the circles beneath his eyes told a story all on its own. "Good morning, Mira." He stepped closer. "Would you like to come with me and meet a few of my friends? We're having coffee together this morning at Beans & Leaves."

"I'd love to," she said.

"I'm glad." Sam offered her his hand. "It's clean. I promise."

It wasn't the cleanliness she was worried about, but she took his hand anyway. It felt cool and callused. He led her down a path that ran right by the area where she'd changed her clothes. "This is the way to the coffee shop?"

"Yep." He chuckled. "It's a well-used path that goes from the campground where you parked your car to the Bay Street Market." He winked at her. "But don't worry. I kept watch for you."

She could feel her face heat up, but she managed a smile despite the awkwardness. "Thanks."

His eyes turned a bit glassy before he looked away from her. "Thank *you*," he said, his Adam's apple working up and down.

"For the show, or what?" she asked, even redder than before.

He laughed. "No, for helping me last night." He looked down at her.

"You're welcome," she said, feeling good that she could at least be a little comfort for him.

Neither said anything else until they arrived at a little coffee shop that overlooked the bay. A few people sat outside, but Sam led her inside to a table where two other people sat. One was Anju. The other was the second guy who had been at Dreamer's last night.

Sam introduced her to Finn before asking the whereabouts of the rest of their group.

"Sylvia has an art show, so they went to check it out," Anju said.

Sylvia? The Sylvia that had stayed at Cofa's Tree? Before she could ask what the woman looked like, the pair started talking about Sylvia's art.

"It's pathetic, I think," Anju said, "I mean, there isn't much originality to the pieces."

"You should see Danby's stuff then. *That's* original, but no one would want it." Finn shook his head.

"Well, I'm about ready for my big showing. Then we'll see who the true artist is," Anju said. "People will love my art because it's real, soul deep, and relates to our inner eye."

Ah…that's what the eye on her tapestry was all about.

"We should only be true to ourselves," Mira said, thinking back to a conversation she'd had with Vashti. She didn't know if it actually worked in the conversation, but Sam looked at her and smiled.

"Oh yes. You have it right, dear," Anju said. She took a drink from a cup labeled matcha green.

"Do you want something to eat or drink, Mira?" Sam asked.

"I'll have whatever you're having."

Sam nodded and went to the counter.

"Bold and brave woman," Finn said.

"Why? Does he have bad taste?" Mira asked.

He shook his head.

Anju laid her hand atop Mira's. "You must just have a special touch with our dear friend Sam. He's a bit of a wild one."

Mira didn't see Sam as wild. She saw him as vulnerable and talented, albeit a bit on the quirky side.

Sam came back over with a wooden number, which he put on the table. He sat down again beside Mira.

Anju leaned in and whispered, "Did you hear that Van got ousted from his place?"

"Why this time?" Sam asked.

"Well," Anju sniffed, "He was renting it out to a bunch of people to, you know, make some money on the side. Apparently that wasn't following the rules, according to the landlord."

"Poor Van," Finn said.

"*Was* it against the rules?" Mira asked.

"Yeah, but they're dumb rules – all on the side of the landlord, in my opinion," Finn said. "Where'd he move to?"

"Not sure. He called to ask me to help him move, but I'm sick of moving stuff." Anju leaned forward again. "I just moved my art studio out to The Grotto...what a bunch of work that was!"

"I can imagine," Mira said.

The barista showed up with four scones and two drinks labeled cortado. Suddenly starving, Mira picked up one of the biscuit-like cakes and took a bite.

"So what do you think of Sam's art?" Anju said.

"It's some of the most expressive I've ever seen," she said truthfully. "I hope he decides to market it someday."

Sam took a drink of the cortado, his eyes connecting with Mira's. "I will someday...when my story finds its happy ending."

"Sometimes the journey is a story worth telling – as is revealing it piece by piece," Mira said, thinking about her own story that had yet to find a happy ending.

Finn clapped his hands together. "She's brilliant."

"And she came to *me*," Sam said, and took a bite of his food.

"It must be fate, then," Anju said, wringing her hands.

For a moment, all was quiet. Anju interrupted the silence by clearing her throat. "By the way, we're having a little get together tonight. Would you and Sam like to come?"

"What kind of get together?" Mira asked.

"Dancing, celebrating life and love and feeling free to express who we are," she explained.

"Sounds interesting," Mira said.

"It's great fun," Finn said.

Up for some fun, Mira glanced at Sam, a twinkle of challenge in her eyes. "What do you think, Sam? Shall we go?"

"I'm in for a little dancing tonight," he said, "if it's with you."

Joy and hope at his words radiated from within her heart. "Mind if I take my camera?"

Anju chuckled. "We love cameras dear. And we're so glad you'll be joining us."

Chapter 58

Nash strode, barefoot, to his private beach cove. He sat down on his lounge chair and kicked back. The soft fabric covering made of wicking material helped to keep him cool and comfortable. Crossing his feet at the ankles, he sighed. "This is the life," he said. Taking a drink of his Pina colada, he gazed across the ocean. If his words were true, then why didn't he feel anywhere close to content right now? Maybe he needed to appease his creative nature and write a song or tune.

"I *did* tell my band and managers that's what I'd come here to do," he said. Even though he didn't really feel like it, he pulled the notebook out of the backpack he'd brought and flipped through the pages. When he got to his last entry, he read the scribblings. It had been the last time he'd talked to Hayes. As he read his questions, the emotions that had grabbed at him then, grabbed at him now. "How can we discover truth?" he'd written, his mind even now scrambling for answers to that. "When is it time to let go?" Nash's heart began to ache. He rubbed it as his eyes traveled down the page of his written thoughts. The last question struck him hard. "Change of heart…is it real?" Nash didn't know if he'd been referring to God, to Mira, or to Elroy, or all three, but it invoked a deep desire to get the answers.

His hands started to shake as he pulled the drink up to his lips. The ice-cold beverage tasted good, but his throat ached from the shaved ice pieces he'd swallowed. The Reformer in him insisted that the true murderer still lived and begged him to take on the challenge of finding the truth about Elroy. The man in him begged him to find the truth about Mira, even if he didn't like it. The heart in him begged him to find the truth about a Savior. The logic in him begged him to forget his past and the whole lot of them, follow his own path, and make money doing what he loved to do. His inner struggle seemed to be getting worse.

Nash jotted down a few of these thoughts, knowing that often, at the most difficult times, his most powerful music came to life.

The ring of his cell phone interrupted his sentence. Pursing his lips, he tossed the pencil into the sand, point down, and grabbed his phone from his backpack. He didn't recognize the number. He didn't usually answer if he didn't know the caller, but for some reason he did. "Nash here."

"Sorry if I'm interrupting anything," came an apologetic male voice across the line.

Nash took a calming breath. "No problem. What can I do for you?"

"This is Russel, from Dreamer's and I was wondering if you could help me out. We have a bit of a dilemma."

"What kind of dilemma?"

"The band that plays on Friday night…their guitarist's mom is really sick and is in the hospital, so they're looking for someone to take his place. I know you're busy with your own gigs, but I was hoping you might be able to help them out."

He could hear the desperation in Russel's voice – and he felt sorry for the guitarist and his group. "I don't have a gig until Saturday night so I guess I could help out. What's the name of the group? And when are they practicing?"

Nash could hear the relief ring through Russel's tone. "The group's name is 4HIM, and they won't be here until right before the gig."

"I'm afraid I don't know any of their songs."

"I have a practice CD for you. If you want, I can drop it by your place."

"That would work."

"I'll run it by after work tonight, then."

Nash gave him his address and tucked his phone into his backpack. Taking a swig of his drink, he retrieved the pencil and jotted down a few more lines.

Chapter 60

Instead of joining Sam at The Grotto until it was time for Anju's get together, Mira had decided to spend the day arranging her lodging and exploring Whynot's beaches with her camera. She was really glad she had! Not only did she have an amazing place to spend the night, her heart felt refreshed, too.

Mira stepped up onto the dock, unable to get one image she'd captured today out of her head. An old man in a tattered and worn hat had been sitting on a piece of beached driftwood, his hairless thin legs made white by a layer of sand. He'd worn a captivating expression as he'd looked out at the lowering sun in the horizon. Why was that picture imprinted in her mind? And why did it affect her so much? The more she thought about it, the more she was convinced it wasn't the perspective after all. It was the combination – the sunset, the man as the beholder of the sunset, and the powerful connection between them. *That* made it beautiful and real. And it somehow just seemed to soothe her soul. It also made her want to pursue love. After all, what good was love without someone to love?

Breathing in the salty air, Mira headed toward the small boat where she would spend the night, thanks to Russel. She paused at the gate to make sure this was the right one. When she spotted the unique bright fish symbol on the boat's cabin, she smiled and moved onto its deck. Small pots of plants filled one section of the large space, a grill, a small table, and two chairs covered the remainder. She wound around the table to the door that led into the cabin. The studio style suited her – cozy, but with an expansive view of the ocean from her bed. What could be better than that? She checked her phone messages. She had only one – from Houser.

"Hi Mira. Houser here. A package addressed to you showed up at Cofa's Tree today. Do you want me to send it on to you or hold onto it? Let me know.

I hope you're having a great time, wherever you are, and that you are finding the happy home you were searching for. Hope we can catch up soon. Bye now."

Saving the message, she headed to the shower. She'd deal with the package later. Right now, she had to get ready for Anju's party. Stepping into the mini-bathroom, she crowded in between the toilet and sink. She grabbed the handheld showerhead and quickly washed from head to toe, watching as the soap bubbles disappeared down the drain in the middle of the floor. She wondered where the water went, but she supposed it didn't really matter.

After a quick hair rub with the towel, she wrapped herself up in the soft terry material. She opened the bathroom door to clear out the steam. Swiping her hand across the fogged up mirror, she messed with her hair. "Swept up, hanging down, curly, straight?" She settled on the tousled look. Her makeup, she went for bold, using white shadow along the edges to make her eyes pop out and bright red gloss to accent her sultry pout. Satisfied with her "night look", she went to her bed. Opening the suitcase she'd taken from home, she ignored the doll she'd tucked inside and dug through her things. Nothing seemed dance worthy. Nothing spelled sexy, or mysterious, or even confident.

"This will work," she told herself, slipping on a long tank top and flip flops. But as she wandered outside, it just didn't feel right. Too plain, she thought...at least for tonight. A rhythmic tap of heels against wooden decking turned Mira's attention to the stylish woman, probably in her forties, walking by the boat.

"Excuse me...miss?" Mira called out. "I'm new around here and I was wondering if you could recommend a good place for me to buy some new things for my wardrobe."

The woman stopped and offered her a bright smile. "Actually, you're in luck." She dug into her clutch-purse and pulled out a business card. Handing it to Mira, she said, "I just opened The Exchange here last month."

"The Exchange?"

"It's one of the fastest growing businesses in the country." She pointed to the card. "On the back is a scratch and win bonus. You might even get some new clothes for free."

"Awesome," Mira said. "Thanks!"

"I hope you enjoy Whynot. It's a great little city," she said, and with a wave, went on her way.

Mira grabbed her purse and phone and headed across the dock to where her, or rather Hayes', car was parked. She checked the business card for the store's address, and typed it into her phone. Fortunately, it was only a few miles away, and with the light traffic, Mira drove up to The Exchange in less than five minutes. The store sat between a restaurant/bar called Shifty's and a four-floored building with a giant sign that said, "Leasing For Events."

Mira parked on the gravel lot between The Exchange and the event building and hurried into the store, ready to power-shop. She had little time before the party started.

A clerk approached her with a broad smile. "Welcome to The Exchange," she said, handing her an electronic tablet displaying pages of clothing.

"Can't I buy things here?" Mira asked the young attendant snapping her gum.

"Yep, but first you have to pay a small fee to join."

So that was the catch! "Really?" Mira wondered why the woman hadn't mentioned a fee.

"It's actually a good deal," the clerk said in her sprite's voice. "You can barter and buy using a point system once you join the club, which is really sweet." She handed her a brochure that explained how The Exchange worked. "If I were you, I'd try out the silver membership first and go from there."

She could read about it, but asking was faster. She'd read about the details later. "Okay. Say I bought a silver membership...what happens next?"

"You bring in things you want to exchange. Each item receives a number, signifying its value. These numbers go into an account and you can use them to "buy" from the online store or from here." She splayed her hand across the maze of closets and mirrors that filled the place.

Interesting - and worth a shot. Mira handed the girl the required membership fee, and also the business card the woman had given her.

"Sweet," she said, and scratched off the back. "Looks like you have thirteen free points. You have any clothes to trade?"

Mira shook her head.

"You can probably find something for the thirteen points, but keep in mind, your account can accumulate points you can keep for later if you don't find what you want now."

Glancing at the numerous choices even just within the store, Mira asked, "What kind of stuff can I buy with this?"

"Anything…accessories included…as long as it adds up to thirteen points or less."

Because she only had a half hour before she met up with Sam, she asked, "Do you have any suggestions for me? I'm going to a dance party tonight and I want to look…well, I want something that will make a statement."

The girl grinned. "I have just the area for you to start looking for that perfect ensemble." She led Mira over to the far corner. A rack of clothes stood on her left, shoes and accessories on her right. "Have a look and let me know if you need more help," the girl said, and drifted away.

Mira laid the electronic tablet on the tufted gold and wine-colored bench and flipped through the rack of clothes. Several pieces caught her eye, but they were tagged for more points than she had…and she, in the very least, needed shoes to accessorize. Her old flip-flops weren't going to make the statement she wanted. She continued to search through the stuffed clothing rack. Then she spotted a dress that jumped out at her – and it was only five points!

She grinned as she grabbed it off the rack and held it up. Made of Chantilly lace, the soft sea-foam green spilled into a deepening color of nearly black along the dress' tiered-hem. The bodice looked slightly fitted, the neckline accentuated by a cross-cord, the sleeves were three-quarter length. She took it into the fitting room.

"I hope this fits," she said, quickly disrobing. Although a little shaky, probably because she was nervous about tonight, she managed to get it on in record time.

She twisted from side to side, liking how it looked. It was very flattering, actually. She stepped out of the dressing room to check out the shoe rack. As she slipped on a pair of spiky half boots, which were five points and awesome, she heard a soft whistle. She turned around.

"Sam?" She tried not to let her surprise show.

"I was next door and spotted your car," he said as he approached her. "You look beautiful." He stopped in front of her to hold both of her hands. "Tell me this is what you're wearing tonight."

"That was the plan," she said, stepping back from him. Wary after what happened with Tanger, she paused. Sam wasn't Tanger. And hadn't her intuition and her spirit guide led her to Sam? She took a step closer and kissed his cheek before quickly heading to the crowded rack of jewelry. "I have three points left for earrings. Care to help me pick them out?"

"I'm not sure how good I am at picking jewelry," Sam said, "but sure." He came to stand beside her, his rough fingers looking even more masculine against the dainty jewelry. "How about these?"

The earrings he held out to her had heart-shaped moonstones at the top with graceful streamers of polished silver flowing from them. She read the tag accompanying them. *Intuition and heart entwined, flowing deeply and forever.*

"These are perfect." She smiled and glanced at her watch. Just in time! "I'll pack up my other clothes and have the clerk cut off the tags for me. Then we can head to the party if you want."

"Sounds like a plan," he said.

Mira shoved her tank top and flip flops into her oversized purse then went to the sales counter to settle up with the clerk. Tags clipped, earrings in, she offered Sam a bright smile. "Ready to go when you are."

"Well alright then," he said. Taking her hand, he led her outside. "As fate would have it, our party is right next door." He pointed to the four story building on the other side of her car.

"What a coincidence," she said with a smile. Not that she believed in coincidences anymore. Everything seemed to happen for a reason.

"The party is up on the fourth floor," he said as he escorted her into the building. The hall was nondescript, but as they stepped into the red and gold walled elevator, a mystical sort of feeling enfolded her.

"Is there food?"

"Yep."

As the elevator climbed its slow ascent, Sam's hand seemed to get warmer as it rested on the curved spot of her lower back. With each second, her nervousness and her anticipation grew. "I don't really know what to expect," she whispered.

"That's half the fun," he said.

"I suppose you're right." The elevator dinged, signaling the opening of its doors.

Sam ushered her into a hallway that had windows that overlooked the bay. He paused for a moment. "Amazing, isn't it?"

She stopped to look. The wooden planked pathway located behind the building connected to marinas dotted along the bay. About three marinas down, she glimpsed a purple luxury yacht – just like the one she walked past to get to her own boat. There couldn't be more than one of those, right? She could've easily used the walking path to get here. Oh well. "It's nice," she said.

"Nice?" He looked askance at her, a half-grin on his handsome face.

She shrugged. "It just seems to be missing something."

"Perhaps you're right," he said, his hazel eyes filled with promises as mysterious as this party. "Shall we head inside and get this party started?"

She could hear the loud thrum of music blending with many voices behind the door at the end of the hall. "Most definitely," she said. She straightened her shoulders, telling herself she was ready for a new adventure in the next chapter of her life. And she was going to have a great time doing it.

The merriment increased in volume as they approached. From the door hung a sign: Welcome To The Love Lodge.

Love Lodge? "Is it like a speed dating kind of thing?"

He opened the door. "Not exactly."

Unease kept her feet in place. She frowned.

"Having second thoughts?" His eyes sparkled with challenge.

"No," Mira said. The intensity of the place as she stepped inside hit her like spiked punch on an empty stomach. The room was long, with a buffet table on one side, a bar on the other, and tables in between. People milled around the food, some stacking their plates high, others, stealing a piece here and there and popping it into their mouths – or someone else's mouth. At the far end of the room was a stage where a singer belted out an obscenely high note. Mira squinted toward her.

"Is her outfit made up of body paint?"

"Yes," Sam remarked simply.

Mira felt Sam studying her as she absorbed her surroundings, but he said nothing – just seemed content to let her look her fill.

The area between the stage and the eating area was a dance floor. On the buffet side, there were three doors. Two were bathrooms. The door just past the bathrooms had a sign posted in front of it that said, "For Bold and Beautiful Adventurers".

"Do you want to check out the B&B room…or save it for later?" Sam asked, pointing at the sign.

Curiosity almost made her say yes, but not knowing and holding off suddenly seemed more…fun. "I'll leave it for later, let it tease me all night until I finally give in and check it out."

Sam laughed. "I like your style, Mira." He swept her into his arms. "And I like you!" His eyes sparkled with life and desire, making Mira feel amazing inside and out.

"Shall we dance?" she asked.

"That's music to my ears." He pulled her out onto the dance floor and wrapped her in his arms. "You're my soul's song…my heart's rhythm…the harmony attached to my melody," he said with a grin.

She giggled. "We're not talking in music speak all night, are we?"

He shrugged as he twirled her around, his rough hands scraping gently over her body. "Don't see why not."

Why not…the phrase popped up over and over. And yet this connection to music was difficult. It reminded her of Vaughn…and of Nash.

"Don't like that look you're wearing," Sam said, and grabbed her close. "You're thinking about the past again. Let it go."

He was one to talk! He managed to let it go during his waking hours, but asleep, his past haunted and terrorized. She decided not to mention it and make waves that might ruin their evening. "I'm working on it," she said.

They continued to dance, song after song, their bodies truly working in harmony. She melted into his arms, not thinking about anything but the rhythm and how her body loved to move to it. But after five songs, her right shoe gouged into her little toe and her bladder was stretched to capacity. "I need a break," she said, a little breathless.

"Can I get you something to eat or drink?" he asked, leading her to a table close to the buffet.

"Maybe just water for now." She put her boots on one of the chairs. "I need to use the bathroom," she said. "Be right back."

He looked over his shoulder and gave her a thumb's up.

Mira slipped into the bathroom. The empty room cooled her sweaty skin. She took her time in the stall, her thoughts filled with Sam, with possibilities for them, for her. Perhaps she and Sam would build something special. Maybe she'd have an art show with her photographs that captured the world through people's eyes. Hope filled her heart.

Putting her sweat-dampened clothing back into place, Mira went to the sink. As she washed her hands, she looked at her flushed face in the mirror. Her eyes glittered with happiness and she felt more carefree than she had in a long time. It had been the right choice coming here. Drying her hands on a paper towel, she went out the door, ready for another round of dancing. Only the door didn't open into the dance room, but rather the B&B room. She hadn't realized that the bathroom had two doors — nor had she even imagined that the other room would be like this!

She took a step back but couldn't seem to tear her gaze away from the assembly of people gathered there. They sat on loveseats in a circle that surrounded a pillar with a massive lit candle in the middle. In various state of undress, some people grouped in pairs, and some were doing things she'd never imagined possible.

"We're embracing our natural freedom and beauty. There's no shame in it — only life and balance. Want to join in?" the woman nearest to her asked.

Mira hadn't considered it that way and as she absorbed the emotion flowing freely around her, a reactive heat spread through her body. "I'm not sure," she said honestly.

Hands came to rest on her shoulders as Sam's voice brushed across her ear. "I see you decided to check out B&B without me."

His warm body pressed against her back. "Not on purpose." She plastered a smile on her face as she glanced up at him.

He smiled back and put his arm around her waist to lead her closer to the group. Swinging her into an embrace, he proceeded to dance with her around the circle. She could feel every nuance of his body as every eye seemed to be drawn to them.

"Take it in, babe. Go with the flow of energy you're feeling," he said. "It's exciting and fun – and anything goes here, Mira. You're free to really be yourself – to entertain your true desires, to be a free spirit unencumbered by the restraints society has put on us."

She closed her eyes a moment. "Yes. Yes, I feel it." She felt his hands scrape across her body, but she shoved them away. Opening her eyes, she grinned at him. "Let me do this my way." As she reached for the top button of her shirt, she couldn't hold his gaze. Looking away, she caught the gaze of another.

"Tanger?" Mira stared at the guy she'd believed could be her soulmate. Two women sat on his lap. Pain, sharp and deep, struck her heart, wiping out the power and freedom that she'd felt just moments before.

"Mira."

She thought she heard Tanger say something more, but her mind screamed over his words...*Get out!*

She listened and darted out of Sam's arms. In her flight, she didn't stop for her shoes, only ran through the dance room, past the buffet, and escaped into the hallway. She punched the elevator button like a woodpecker against cedar, but the doors remained shut and Sam's voice calling out to her got increasingly louder. Abandoning the elevator, she raced around the corner and slammed open the exit door. The cold, clammy stairwell only heightened her terror, but she had no choice. She dashed down the steps, clutching the rail because she kept tripping. When she reached the bottom floor, a tiny bit of relief worked its way into her trembling nausea. She was almost free! She swung the door wide, hoping to see her car and make a quick escape, only it wasn't the parking lot but rather the planked path. After a moment of panic, she recalled that it would take her back to her boat. Should she run?

The door on the side of the building opened, so she tucked herself behind a bush to listen. Sam spoke first. "Do you see her?"

"No," Tanger answered. "Maybe she's hiding inside."

"Maybe, maybe not." Sam's voice was laced with amusement. "Didn't realize you were the same dude that loved and left her," he said. "Not judging you for it, but why'd you do it?"

Mira held her breath even as tears of intense emotions formed in her eyes.

"Can't believe she told you that," Tanger spat, "and it's none of your business, you crazy ass." Tanger thumped his fist on what sounded like a car hood. "You know where she's staying?"

Sam's chuckle was his only answer.

Tanger growled, which was followed by the squeak of an opening door. Silence followed. Had both guys gone back inside? Mira hoped so. She didn't want to see either of them. After waiting a few more minutes and hearing nothing, she bolted away from her hiding spot and hit the dimly lit path at a run. She could taste the salt of her tears as she cried out in a hoarse whisper, "What am I? Junk?"

No answer came, only a despairing cloud of unworthiness. Her emotions raw, she blubbered pitifully, her bare feet smacking against the wooden path as she ran. About halfway to her place, she slowed to a jog. She had to. It was all she could manage between her hyperventilating gasps of breaths. When she finally reached the dock that would lead her home, she leaned back against the first post she saw. She closed her eyes and tried to create a reality she didn't feel. "It's not you, Mira. It's not your fault."

After several moments, she managed to calm herself. "This was a good thing tonight," she told herself. But her words were not at all convincing, nor could she come up with any silver lining at the moment. There had to be one, though, right? Her eyes again filled with tears as they scanned the docks for a sign of her boat, her haven. But she couldn't see it. Again, that feeling of desperation and loneliness threatened to suck her under.

"Can I help you miss?"

Mira twisted around. "Russel?"

"Mira?" He closed the distance between them. As soon as he saw her face, he opened his arms wide. She didn't hesitate to fall into them. They were strong and comforting and just what she needed at the moment. Russel patted her back and whispered who knew what, but it soothed her. Soon, her tears subsided.

"Are you going to be okay?" he asked, running a hand down her hair.

She sniffed and nodded, backing away from him.

He tucked one hand into the front pocket of his jeans. "Want to tell me what happened?"

He'd think she was totally stupid if she told him what had just happened. She took a deep breath and blew it out. "I'm just confused, tired. I really need to relax."

He studied her a moment. "Is there anything I can do to help?"

"Walk me to your friend's boat?" She didn't have a clue where it was right now. Her brain seemed to be in a fog and the docks looked different in the nightlights than in the sunlight.

"I can do that." He rested his hand softly on her back, and keeping space between them, led her down to the last row of docks. Steering her to the left, they continued on in silence until he stopped in front of the one with the yellow fish. "Well, here we are," he said, reaching out to open the gate for her.

"Thanks Russel," she said, stepping through it.

"Are you sure there's nothing else I can do for you?"

"Get me another night's stay on this boat?" She worked up a smile that probably looked more miserable than anything.

His soft smile was comforting. "I can do better than that." He took out his phone, and typed something into it. A message came right back. "I can get you a month. Will that work?"

Some of the heaviness in her chest eased. Her smile was real this time. "That would be perfect." As long as she could avoid Tanger…and Sam, too.

He texted his friend again. "It's yours for this month then," he said when the reply came in. Then he laid his hand over hers, which was resting on the top of the gate. "And tell you what…I'll have some groceries delivered to you later tonight, too…unless you're going out again."

"I'm not going anywhere." She looked into his dark, concerned eyes. "Why are you being so nice to me? You don't even know me."

To that, he grinned. "But I know someone who does."

She frowned. "Who?"

"You'll have to stop by Dreamer's sometime and I'll tell you more." Lifting the CD he held in his hand, he said, "Right now I have to get this to a friend who's filling in at the 4HIM concert on Friday. You're coming to the show, right?"

Russel had been so generous and kind, she couldn't say no. "You gave me a free ticket. Of course I'll be there."

"Happy to hear it." He started to walk away, but stopped and turned around. Pointing at her with the CD, he said, "See you Friday."

Mira nodded then watched him until he disappeared from sight. She let herself inside the cabin and collapsed on the bed. Her head throbbed, and she felt exhausted. She was so ready for this day to be over!

She didn't bother taking off her dress, only curled up beneath the covers. The slight sway of the boat soothed her a little as did the lapping of water against the dock, only her mind refused to rest. The night replayed in her thoughts – each step, each song, each person. Why was Tanger in Whynot? Why had he come after her tonight if she meant nothing to him? And how did Sam fit into all this? She rubbed her temples with her fingertips. Maybe she needed to focus on her own life and forget about men altogether. Yet as she tried to convince herself of that, her heart refused to agree. It only pounded with a soul deep ache of loneliness.

Mira twisted to her other side. Why couldn't she have a loving relationship like her mom and Vaughn, like Mel and Hayes? She just had to try harder to make her intuition and her heart work together. But how?

Mira's eyes opened to the silver reflection of the moon on the water. Her stomach twisted, leaving a sick feeling in its wake. Placing her hand across her belly, she willed it to settle, but it wouldn't obey. Her lips tightened and she sipped in small breaths. The feeling got worse! She bolted upright and slammed open the window. Poking her head out, she puked over the side.

Chapter 61

The parking garage where Nash left his bike was a block and a half away from Dreamer's. With his guitar slung over his back, he walked down the concrete ramp to the graveled alleyway. Flanking him as he walked the quiet path were several second story apartments, their balconies and fire escapes made visible by a few streetlights. The dark area seemed lifeless except for a cat that had scampered behind a dumpster.

Nash approached the back door of Dreamer's. He'd come through this door less than a week ago, the star of the night, his band and fans all vying for his attention. But tonight he came alone – as just a band member. And even though he'd had the music down after a few days of practicing with 4HIM's CD, he didn't know anyone from the band, and their lyrics weren't something he really believed in. He felt out of his element, like a circle being jammed into a square opening.

"It's just a gig," he told himself, and went inside, plastering a confident smile on his face.

A tall woman with purple hair, loads of tattoos, and a thick banded scar across the base of her neck, hurried over to him. "Praise the Lord, there he is!" With a warm smile, she held out her hand for him to shake. "You must be Nash."

He nodded, wondering what had happened to her. It looked like she'd been hung by fire-heated barbed wire or something.

"I'm Francine, lead singer of 4HIM," she said, "and we are so thankful you are helping us out tonight."

"Nice to meet you, Francine." She wasn't anything like he'd pictured. She didn't seem to match her music.

The rest of the band crowded around. "This is Jax, our bass player," Francine said, nodding at a girl who was about four and a half feet tall.

Jax gave Nash a hug around his waist. "Welcome, mate."

Francine pointed to a guy who had a scar on his face from ear to chin. "Donny is on drums."

Donny slapped his back. "Good to have ya on board tonight."

A slender man was next to be introduced. He had such dark skin, Nash imagined it would be hard to see him in a dark room – unless he smiled like he was doing right now. "And this is Ty," Francine said. "He's our keyboardist."

Ty shook his hand. "Couldn't do the show without you, my friend."

"I'm glad I could help," Nash said, "Although I'm not sure how we'll blend – especially since we haven't practiced together."

"No worries, mate. We got someone looking out for us," Jax pointed upwards. "Whatever happens, God will be able to use it."

The words made Nash uncomfortable. He changed the subject. "How's your guitarist's mom doing?" Nash asked, setting his gig bag on a table.

"BB's mom is improving," Francine said. "Thanks for asking."

Jax handed him a water bottle. "We'd actually planned on practicing for an hour here beforehand, but," she pulled out the ticket and handed it to Nash. "It turns out there was a typo on the ticket." She chuckled. "Our show was supposed to start at eight, but the ticket says seven."

She was laughing about it? "That's in ten minutes," Nash said, quickly taking his guitar out of his bag. He was glad he'd tuned it right before he'd come.

"It'll work out," Francine said with a genuine smile.

Their positive attitude was catchy. "No worries, right?"

Ty gave him a bright white smile and a thumbs up.

"Gather up, everyone," Francine said.

The group huddled in a circle, Francine dragging him alongside her. Arms over each other's shoulders, Francine prayed, "We thank you Lord for watching over BB's mom and pray for her continued healing. We thank you for getting us here safely, for the blessing of Nash, and for the opportunity to play at Dreamer's tonight. We know You put dreams in our hearts for a reason and only You can show us what that purpose is and how our story fits in with Yours. May you work powerfully through our music, our words, and our actions tonight. In Jesus' name we pray. Amen."

"Amen," the band chorused, then proceeded to cheer and give each other high fives. "It's going to be an awesome night," Donny said, twirling his drumsticks.

Francine gave Nash an extra one-armed hug. "We *are* truly grateful for you, Nash," she said. "Should we do this thing?"

"Absolutely," he said. Even though the entire pre-show meeting seemed strange to him, he was glad to have had a chance to experience their unmistakable bond.

Francine smiled, which made her look very pretty amidst all her 'extras'. "Here's your connection to the receiver and amp." She clipped a transmitter box onto his guitar strap. He hooked its cable into the output jack on his guitar. "And here's your mike." She handed him a headpiece and put on one of her own.

She glanced at her watch. "Okay…let's roll friends."

Francine led the band out onto the stage. Nash looked at the swelling crowd as he took the open spot beside her. He wasn't in the spotlight, but he still felt a rush - one he didn't really understand. But he was going to roll with it.

"Hello friends," Francine called out. "We're the band 4HIM. If you don't know us, you will after tonight," she said with a laugh. The crowd cheered. After introducing the band, some of whom she promised would share their stories before the end of the night, Francine lowered her tone, which was already low and raspy.

"We all have our stories and the awesome thing is that tonight, our stories are intertwining." She gave the crowd a thumb's up. "After my LifeChip was removed last year, I became, shall we say, a passionate person. Actually, I was an adrenalin junkie. The more things I tried, the more dangerous and risky things I needed to do in order to reach that high." She stepped ahead so that her toes touched the end of the stage. "Each of my tattoos tells about the many things

I've done," she said, running her hand along her arm. "Almost every inch of my body is covered. And yet even after all those...let's call them adventures...I couldn't fill up on the inside." She walked to the right side of the stage where Ty stood beside the keyboards. "I could tell you the horrible, shameful things I've done...but I'm not going to. Instead I'm going to tell you about the end of that girl and the beginning of a new one - one who has purpose, one who is filled to overflowing, one who knows she is loved beyond compare."

She paced to the other side of the stage, and again, went to the edge. "The first song we're going to sing is the one I wrote when I was in the hospital. It's had many revisions, but it's based on a turning point in my life - when a guy named Percy sang to me as he pulled me out of a burning car." She shaded her eyes to look over the crowd. "You out there Percy?"

"Wouldn't miss it," a big guy in the corner called out, waving and smiling.

She held a hand to her heart and with a big smile, said, "The song is called, "Out of the Fire and Into the Light."

Nash watched Francine for his cue to start the song. When she nodded, he began to pick the solo that, now that he knew the story behind it, seemed eerily powerful and beautiful at the same time. The crowd must have agreed. The insanely quiet crowd was awe-inspiring rather than uncomfortable or stifling. They seemed to be listening to each melodic tone as if it was the key to their next breath. As he reached the end of his solo, Francine and the rest of the group came in like a storm at the end of a quiet gust of wind. The passion that was manifested in their song shot right to the heart and spoke to his own.

As they continued without pause into the next song, Nash followed along, strumming the easy, yet poetically appealing, shift of chords. He looked across the crowd and saw someone he hadn't expected. It was someone he didn't like.

Chapter 62

With the exceptions of an outing to retrieve her car and another to go to Paramount Discount, Mira had spent the past few days hiding out on the boat, feeling sorry for herself. Neither Sam nor Tanger had sought her out, but Russel had been true to his word, sending a girl out with groceries for her. Mira glanced at the small plant he'd also given her. It had several buds ready to flower and a note attached to the terracotta pot. It said, "The Lord will guide you always; He will satisfy your needs in a sun-scorched land and will strengthen your frame. You will be like a well-watered garden; like a spring whose waters never fail."

Mira sat down at the table, staring out across the ocean. She thought about her prophetic dreams of the past. Even if the Lord was no longer directing her through her dreams, was He using her spirit guide to show her the way?

A voice in her head chimed in. Where is your spirit guide getting you? The outcomes are real...you don't feel satisfied. You're lonely and miserable. Admit it! She was miserable, but it was probably her own fault for not being better at listening. Her spirit guide cared about her, right? It would make sense, then, that the path would lead to something great. Only it didn't feel so great right now. Not at all.

Mira toyed with the small box on the table in front of her. Intuition had pushed her to buy the test from the drugstore. Intuition was telling her to look inside and read the results. She lifted the cover and peeked inside. Her heart dropped to her stomach.

"I'm pregnant," Mira gasped. Even though she'd guessed it, she still couldn't quite believe it. She pressed a hand against her lower abdomen. What was she going to do? She had no job or source of income. She only had this houseboat for a month. And what about her adventure? How was she to find her true self with a baby around?

Her eyes squeezed shut for a moment as her mind scrambled for a bright side. A baby might be the answer to her loneliness, she told herself. A child would need her, would always be around to love her. Only, she didn't know the slightest thing about babies. And her mom was on Enab building a new church, so she couldn't count on her to help. This was *not* where she'd expected this journey to take her!

Arms snuggly pressed against her stomach, she allowed her despair to take over. She should get out of the tank dress, forget about the concert at Dreamer's, and forget about her dreams. Her life was ruined!

She sniffed loudly and grabbed a tissue to wipe the stupid tears off her face. The concert ticket Russel had given her sat on the table beside the flowers. She'd promised him she'd go tonight – and she felt like she owed him, yet the thought of facing him made her feel ashamed. And going to the concert meant she'd be surrounded by music and gaiety and she'd be reminded that she was nothing but a wretched stranger. The tears kept coming, and she let them. Exhaustion began to take hold and lured her gaze to the bed. "No. I'm not going there," she said firmly. "It's time to stop the pity party."

She grabbed her phone and dialed the last number that had come in. Houser.

"Hello."

"Hi. It's me. Mira."

"You sound upset. What's wrong?"

Houser had always been such a good listener, but still the whole truth wouldn't come out. "I'm just having a bad day. Nothing I can't handle."

There was a pause on the other end. Then Houser said, "What can I do for you then?"

She cleared her throat. "I, ah, I was wondering if you could send that package to me."

"Sure. Where do you want me to send it?"

Mira gave him the address for Dreamer's.

"You're in Whynot?" Houser's voice held a tinge of disbelief.

"Something wrong with Whynot?"

"No." He chuckled, but it seemed a little off. "I'd like to spend some time there myself. I've heard that Whynot is a city of opportunities."

"Opportunities and disappointments," she mumbled.

"What was that?"

"Oh, nothing. Just being grumpy," she said. "You're welcome to come and visit me." Although she didn't know how she felt about him staying on the boat.

"I might take you up on that," he said. "Why don't you give me a call when you get the package, and we'll talk more about it then."

"Sounds like a plan."

"Good. Take care, Mira."

"Thanks," she said, and ended the call. Hoisting herself up off the chair, she went to the cupboard where she'd stashed her candle and several stones. Gathering them in her arms, she brought them to the dresser that sat next to her bed. After placing the candle in the center and arranging the stones in a circle around it, she lit the candle's wick and whispered the words Vashti had told her to use. She was desperate for answers – about the baby, about Tanger, about her life.

Mira cleared her mind, waiting to hear, to gain direction. A movement right outside her window caught her attention. She peeked over just in time to see a bird dive into the ocean for his food. Instead of looking at it as an annoyance, she chose to look at it as a sign. Her interpretation? She needed to feed herself when the occasion arose, and she needed to be as free as a sea bird. What that meant with respect to her situation, she didn't yet know. She ended her prayer to a goddess who seemed as abstract as beauty or spirituality. If only she could see things more clearly! But that, too, would come in time, she hoped.

Feeling a bit better and more determined to fix her life, she redid her hair and makeup and went outside. "Everything is going to be great!" she exclaimed, trying very hard to believe it as she went through the gate and out onto the dock. She kept her steps unhurried and controlled, but it still didn't take her long to get to the parking lot where her car waited. Unlocking her car door, Mira got into the driver's seat. As she slipped the key into the ignition, her phone rang.

"Hello?"

"Hi Mira. This is Claire."

"Claire…." That she'd called surprised Mira. Any other day, she might have welcomed it, but today, she wasn't in the mood to talk to her. "I'm kind of in the middle of something. Can I call you back?"

"No…I just wanted to run a business idea by you."

She gritted her teeth, trying to hold onto her patience. "You're starting a business?"

"Yep. It's called All4You. My motto is; gypsy soul, hippie heart, fairy spirit, boundless body – your freedom awaits. What do you think?"

Mira recalled a verse from the Enchiridion of Emmanuel that mentioned heart, soul, body, and mind. It was similar to Claire's motto, only Claire's didn't include the mind. "It sounds interesting. What will you do, exactly?" Mira asked, starting the engine.

"I'll help people tap into the paths they should be walking on this planet by going into their homes and giving them advice," Claire said. "It will mostly focus on how to be true to oneself."

Mira checked the rearview mirror. "What kind of advice would you give, say, to someone who had relationship problems?" she asked, backing out of her parking spot before shifting into drive.

"It's individual, of course, but really what it comes down to is that if a situation or a relationship doesn't help them be their best, I'll tell them to get rid of it," Claire explained. "After all, we are the creators of our lives and if we get rid of the negative, it frees us up to live out our journey in the manner that releases the boundaries of our bodies and that speaks to our gypsy souls, hippie hearts, and fairy spirits."

Was this her spirit guide sending her this information? Mira wondered. Claire calling out of the blue hadn't happened before. And her words…Mira totally connected with them. She wanted the negative out of her life. She wanted a gypsy soul unbound by others. She wanted a hippie heart, free to love whomever she chose. And she wanted a fairy spirit – a magical one filled with power over her world. Mira pressed a hand against her belly, wondering just what boundless would mean for her. "Where did you learn about this stuff?" she asked, wondering if there was at least a book she could read to further her insight.

"I'm self-taught," Claire said. The sound of shuffling papers came over the line. "And I think people are going to love this business, don't you think?"

"I'm sure of it, Claire," she said. "Just talking about it has helped *me* figure a few things out."

"Can I get a written testimony on that?"

Mira would have to see how it turned out, first. "I'll work on it, okay?"

"Perfect. Let me know if you need any more of my services."

"Will do," Mira said. "Goodbye Claire."

"Bye Mira."

Mira drove the rest of the way to The Dreamer's Club, deep in thought. She saw no open spots in front of the bar, so she parked a few blocks down. The silence in her car felt like a funeral, so she cracked open her door to the sounds of the busy streets, and flipped on the overhead light to jot a few things into her notebook. "Now all I need is another 'coincidence' or two to give me a clear answer to my...dilemma."

Feeling a little more positive, Mira got out of the car. She stared at the toes of her shoes as she made her way to the club, anxiousness twisting her stomach the closer she got. As she neared the door, she paused. The loud music perforated the club's walls, walls that held numerous people she didn't know if she cared to interact with at the moment. She thought about the advice she'd discovered through her spirit-guided 'coincidences'. Was she really coming here for herself, or was it because she felt she owed Russel? When she considered it, she realized that she didn't actually want to be there and it was freeing to know that she didn't have to feel obligated or bound by other's wishes.

As she turned to leave, though, the door opened, the music blasting out, no longer muffled by walls. A song was coming to an end, but the pleasant melodic riff held Mira in place. And it actually made her smile.

"And now for a special song requested by our fill-in guitarist here," a miked band member said. "Nash...you want to tell us what drew you to this song?"

Mira clapped a hand over her mouth. Stepping aside, she collapsed back against the outside wall of the building. Nash was playing at Dreamer's? The entrance door closed behind a group of people just as Nash began to speak. She could hear his voice, but could no longer make out the words. Part of her wanted to run inside. Part of her wanted to run away. "Gypsy soul, hippie heart, boundless body, fairy spirit," she said, quoting Claire's business motto. She realized that she wanted to see him. "Whynot," Mira said with a shaky smile.

Letting herself inside Dreamer's, her eyes immediately went to the stage. Seeing Nash made her heart ache with longing and desire, even though she didn't want it to be that way. A flicker of hope made its way to her heart as she watched his fingers caress the strings of his guitar. Her eyes drank him in - every part of him - from the thick hair that hung over his intense eyes, to the half-smile that lit his handsome face, to the twitch of flexing forearm muscles, to the booted feet that tapped out a rhythm that matched her heart's. Yet still, she thirsted for more. She felt a strong urge to touch him, to talk with him, to hold him close. But that would involve admitting she'd made a big mistake...no, many of them. And she didn't even know if he'd forgive her, let alone consider any sort of relationship with her. The continual draw to him, though, was something she couldn't deny, no matter how hard she'd tried. She wandered over to a table in the corner and sat down. A server came by and asked if she wanted anything to drink, so she ordered a water. Clutching her purse against her stomach, she listened as the song's chorus played again. "There's hope in this place, surrounded by love and grace."

Could Nash be thinking about her as he sang? Whatever he was thinking didn't really matter because a glimmer of her own hope sparked to life for real this time. Everything was going to be okay. She just knew it.

Chapter 63

Nash unplugged and walked over to the amp where he'd left his towel. Running the soft cloth across his neck and face felt good. Francine giving him a thumb's up and a smile after the set, felt good. In actuality, he hadn't felt this powerful of an emotion since he'd removed his LifeChip...and since Mira. His eyes scanned the dimness of the crowd as he stepped off the stage for the break. That's when he saw her – or at least imagined he saw her.

He took a moment to catch his breath, the words of the previous song floating through his brain. There's hope in this place...but could he dare hope where Mira was concerned? Should he? He didn't know how he felt exactly, but he couldn't take his eyes off her. What was she doing in Whynot? Why was she at The Dreamer's Club?

"You coming to the back room with us for break?" Donny asked him, signing his drumsticks and handing them to a young woman who kept squeaking between giggles. "Russel brought in some wood-fired pizza and we have plenty of cold water still in the coolers," he added.

"I think I'll pass for this last break," Nash said. "I see someone I want to talk to."

"See ya in a few, then," Donny said with a smile, and disappeared into the back room.

As Nash made his way to the front of the club, he made sure not to make eye contact with anyone. He heard someone say "great job" and another say "great set." A few reached out to pat his arm. He only offered them a brief smile and a nod, not daring to slow down. Nash took a deep breath as he neared Mira's table, his mind scrambling for what to say. She looked amazingly lovely. Should he start with that? He sidled up to the table, a huge lump in his throat. Grabbing the chair next to her, he finally managed to say, "Mind if I sit here?"

Her eyes swept up to meet his and he was immediately lost in them. The chemistry between them remained as strong as ever, sparking like water on an electric fence.

"Nash," she said, her tone breathy, and way too alluring.

He sat down next to her. "I'm glad you made it to the concert."

"I, uh, didn't know you played with 4HIM," she said, looking down at the glass in front of her.

He rubbed a hand against his aching chest. "Just filling in for tonight."

"You all sound great," she said, taking a drink of what looked to be water.

"Thanks. They're a lot different than I expected, but they, and their songs, have really grown on me."

"That's nice," she said.

An awkward silence crept up between them. Nash frowned. "So what brings you to Whynot?" Even though he knew he shouldn't wish it, he hoped that she'd gotten hold of his schedule and had actually sought him out.

"Fate," she said simply.

He grinned. "Care to explain that?"

She smiled back at him and the rush he felt from that spoke volumes. In his heart, he'd never truly let her go.

"No explanation necessary," came a strong, deep voice through the dimness.

Mira immediately stood up. "Tanger," she said, her voice now high and shaky.

"After the party at the Love Lodge, I'm surprised you had the guts to show up here, Mira."

Nash had heard of the place and the wild parties and functions that went on there. He guessed he shouldn't be surprised, given the stuff she'd gotten in to at Cofa's Tree, but it made him feel sick inside.

"What are you doing here?" she asked Tanger.

"I saw your car. It took me a while to find you, though," Tanger said. "We need to talk."

"Yes." She blew out a long breath. "Yes, we do." She slipped her purse strap over her shoulder. "I'm sorry Nash," she said, her eyes regretfully somber, yet seemingly resigned.

Nash wanted her to say she'd be back, that they needed to talk, too. Seeing her made him realize just how much he missed her – and yet it looked as though she'd truly moved on, even if he hadn't.

She followed Tanger to the door. With each step, Nash's heart ached more and more. Why did he keep letting her do this to him? "Don't leave with him Mira," he called out as he raced toward the door.

"Let her go," a woman said, catching his arm. "You have more pressing issues to deal with." Nash swung around, ready to lambaste the lady for butting in, but when he saw who it was, the words locked in his throat. "Porsche? What are you doing here?"

His manager glared at him. "You signed a contract, Nash, and that includes not singing with any other band." She yanked him toward the side door. "Come with me. Your night is done."

He set his feet and yanked his arm from her grasp. "You don't own my time. I didn't have a gig tonight."

She nodded toward a guy standing next to her, who pulled tri-folded papers from his suit jacket pocket. "Doesn't matter, but the contract you signed does," Porsche said as the guy handed him a copy of Nash's contract. "You come with me now, or you're in violation and will owe me big time."

The beautiful, business-minded woman suddenly looked evil to him. "What if I want out of the contract?"

"I'm afraid that isn't possible."

On impulse, he tore the contract into pieces.

She only laughed. "We have several copies." She yelled over her shoulder toward the bar. "Russel, your band will have to play without a guitarist." Then she nodded to two over-sized thugs who came to stand on either side of him. "Nash, if you don't comply, I'll sue Russel and this stinking little band, too."

She was serious. Nash clutched his hands into tight fists. He hadn't felt this much hate in a long time.

"What's going on?" Russel said, his voice coming from somewhere in the crowd who'd gathered to watch the scene.

"Mind your own business, dear," Porsche called out.

Russel popped into view and squeezed in beside Nash. "I'm here for you," he said, putting a solid hand on his back. Another man came up on Nash's other side. "I'll second that."

That a stranger wearing a Thurman Towing t-shirt, and a bar manager Nash had just met would stand by him in this situation was no small thing. Not only were two giant thugs flanking Porsche, Porsche herself spelled disaster. She had so much power, not just in the industry, but in the city of Whynot. Going against her could easily mean the end of either of their businesses.

"I appreciate that more than you know, Russell and Mr. Thurman." Running a hand across his mouth, Nash tried to come up with a solution. There was only one. "Would you tell the band that I'm really sorry? I didn't know my contract didn't allow me to play with them – and I feel really bad about cutting out, but..." he glanced at Porsche. "My hands are tied."

Russel looked him in the eyes. "You sure?"

He wasn't, but he didn't want his mistake to cost Russel his business – or 4HIM their band. "Yes."

"Okay." Russel looked up, his gaze taking in the gawking crowd. "One free drink on the house," he announced.

A cheer went up as the group followed him to the bar.

The thugs took Nash's arms. He gritted his teeth, "Call your flunkies off me. I said I'd go, and I'm going."

She nodded to them and they let him go. Nash stormed out of the bar toward the back alley to where his motorcycle was parked.

"No. We'll give you a ride home," Porsche said, pointing to the awaiting limousine.

He stood still for a long moment, then, pursing his lips, stomped over to the car and got inside. Jaw clenched, arms crossed, he fought for control. But as they drove away, the entire situation swirled in his head until he snapped. Nash struck the window again and again and curses flew from his lips just as harshly and just as swiftly. For several miles, his hate-filled verve drove his savage rant, yet as they turned the corner that would take them to the last stretch home, his energy failed him. It was like he'd been zapped by an electric current that had left his body an uncontrolled mess of energy, but the residual effects had left him paralyzed. Hand now pressed against the glass, his eyes blurred as misery creeped up to settle in his heart.

"Glad you got that out of your system," Porsche said. She nudged his shoulder.

He looked down at the drink she held out to him. He took it and downed it in one swallow. At least it would help him forget for a little while.

Chapter 64

Mira sat on the park bench next to Tanger, her heart beating hard, her mind creating a hundred conversations she could have with him in the next few minutes. She hated him for leaving her, but he needed to know the truth. She tried to relax, digging her feet into the still warm sand. Her houseboat sat down the row of docks off to their left, which gave her some comfort. She didn't know why Tanger had picked this place to talk, but its privacy suited her, especially because of its nearness to help, if she needed it.

Tanger twisted on the bench so that he could look at her.

"Why did you come to Whynot, Mira?" he asked.

The question irritated her, as did his almost accusatory tone, but she was too tired to play games. "I felt like I needed to get out of Pillar, and this is where I was led."

He looked at her strangely. "Led by whom?"

Doubt stabbed a knife into her confidence. She fiddled with the edge of her dress. "My spirit guide," she said.

Tanger clasped his hands together. In the moonlight, his eyes sparkled as much as the blonde strands of his hair. "That surprises me."

She frowned. "Why?"

"Because it was my intuition telling me to run here...*away* from you."

"I don't understand," she said, feeling hurt all over again.

"Back in Pillar, I felt drawn to you...almost too much." He leaned back against the bench seat. Running a hand through his hair, he continued, "Wanting you like that made me uneasy." Propping his foot up on the bench, he wound his arms around his bent knee. "So I reached out to my own spirit guide who said you were dangerous, that you would lead me away from everything I value."

"I'm hardly dangerous," she said, confused. "And I had only hoped we could journey through life together."

He glanced at her. "But what if we are on alternate paths?"

He was totally serious! "What makes you think we might be?"

He snorted. "Well, for one, you were at Dreamer's listening to a band called 4HIM."

Did he know she couldn't watch Nash perform without feeling drawn to him all over again? "What does that have to do with anything?" she asked, picking at a loose thread on her hem.

"Do you even know what that band stands for?" He shook his head. "They're spreading a religion that focuses on serving and loving others."

Her stomach flipped. "So you don't believe in loving others?"

Tanger looked at her like she was crazy. "While love is great for what it brings a person, what's more important is our individual freedom. I don't know about you, but I want to be lord of my own life, not for anyone else to be lord over me." He ground his heels into the sand. "I mean, if I don't feel like I want to do something, why should I do it?"

She understood wanting freedom, but she wondered how far that freedom went with him. Did it include wandering whenever and wherever the wind blew? Did it mean they could have other partners? She felt her shoulders droop even though she tried to keep them confidently straight. Was it a freedom to do whatever they felt was right at the time – like leave when the other person might need them most?

They sat in silence for a few moments.

"I can't deny I still want you," Tanger said.

Mira's heart hung heavily with the secret she had yet to share.

"So, I was thinking, why don't we spend some time together while you're here?" He wrapped his arm around her shoulders and gave her a little tug. Instead of feeling comforted, she felt confused, stifled, frustrated.

"But you're not making any promises for any more than that, right?" she asked.

His arm around her slackened. "I *can't* make any promises and I don't expect any from you, either. You understand, right?"

She did and she didn't. "Would that change if I told you I'm pregnant?"

He froze. "Are you?"

She stared at him a moment then nodded.

He turned to face her. After a quick glance at her stomach, he looked her in the eyes and asked, "Is it mine?"

The words slashed her heart, even though she reminded herself that he didn't know her all that well and that he was involved in a world of different standards than she was used to with her own family. "Yes. It's yours," she said firmly, but wished that it wasn't true.

Tracing the edge of the bench with his fingers, his thoughtful look transformed into an excited smile. "I have a solution."

She tried to push away the lingering guilt by hanging onto the certainty in his tone. "You do?"

"I know this woman named Jadis I met a while back in Pillar. She lives in an apartment over the pet shop and she's a pro with potions. She'll work some magic and take care of this problem for you."

Problem for ME? Why not for both of us? She stared at him, a stranger and yet a part of her. Her hand touched her belly. "Are you saying you want me to abort the baby?"

"Of course. It's not a big deal – one quick visit and you'll be free again." He leaned over and kissed her slightly parted mouth. She pulled away.

"It *is* a big deal for me. This is a baby's life we're talking about here."

"Not really." He clasped his hands in front of him. "I believe a soul enters a body at first breath and if deity wants a soul to be born, it would be with a woman who wanted to have it. If a woman chooses abortion, deity already knew she would because we are all connected. It gives you the freedom to choose what serves you best."

She frowned. "But then why put it there in the first place, if deity knows if it will be aborted anyway?"

He shrugged. "Maybe the mom can learn from having to go through the process. Just like anything in life - even if it is hard, we learn from it and it helps us grow."

"How do you know this is true?"

He shrugged. "It's what I believe to be true."

She wanted to believe that what he said was right, but something inside her wouldn't allow it. The salty, humid air felt suddenly suffocating.

"Hey," he said with a shake of his head. "It's what's best for everyone." He sent her a bright smile. "Just ask your spirit guide and you'll know I'm right."

Was he right? Could it be best for everyone? Conflicting thoughts jumbled Mira's mind, the warmth in her belly drawing her hand to cover it once again. "I'll have to think about it," she said. "Do you need a ride home?" she asked, wanting to be alone.

"That would be great," he said. He stood up and offered her his hand. She didn't know how she felt about him right at the moment, but she took his hand anyway, and together they walked to the parking lot. No one spoke until they got to her car and Tanger looked down at her feet.

"You forgot your shoes again," he said, with a chuckle.

She wasn't in the laughing mood, and didn't want to think about her escape from the party, either. "I'll get them later," she said. And hopefully by then, she'd know the pathway she should be on.

Chapter 65

Nash collapsed onto the park bench, staring at the abandoned shoes beside it. He knew who they belonged to...he'd seen Mira and Tanger sitting on this bench only moments ago. He hadn't been able to pick up all of their conversation, but he'd heard enough. She was pregnant with Tanger's baby. Taking a big swig of whiskey, he welcomed the burning feeling as it slid down his throat. He waited for it to numb the ache in his heart, but it didn't.

How had this happened? He and Mira were supposed to be together forever, to have an unbreakable bond. Until now, he'd held out hope that eventually she'd make her way back to him. But after what he'd heard, he knew that there was no place for him in her life and never would be.

With a growl, he picked up one of Mira's shoes and flung it away from him. It landed on a swing, jarring the rubber strip into a twisting dance. Back and forth, back and forth it finally slowed to a stop. He took another drink and realized he'd almost drunk it all. Lonely desperation, resentment, bitterness...they all wove together like a three-stranded cord, one he didn't know how to unravel, one that threatened to choke him.

"I hate you, Mira Kinneson!" Nash whipped her other shoe across the playground. This one landed on the far side of the garbage cans. He shoved himself off the bench and walked, stumbling across the sand to the docks. Polishing off the last of his drink, he tried to convince himself there was a good side to all this...but he couldn't see it. All he could see was misery. He didn't even care about his music career anymore.

He continued across the wooden planks until he got to the dock's end. There, he plopped down with an inelegant thump. The weathered slats dug into his legs while the water of the bay soaked into his jeans. He hung his head, his eyes filled with tears, his arm banded across his chest to keep his heart from shattering. What in the heck was he going to do now?

"Nash?"

Slowly, he turned toward the sound. He blinked back his tears. Was he imagining her? No. Mira walked, barefoot, in his direction. *Look away! Look away!* Shifting his attention back to the water, he forced himself to stay still, even when he felt her standing behind him.

"Nash?"

Her soft, familiar voice made his heart ache all the more.

"Did you come back for your shoes?"

"Uh…yeah. You okay?"

"No." He tossed the empty bottle, the water splashing out around it before it settled to a bob.

After a long silent moment, she asked, "Is there anything I can do to help?"

He reached back and snagged her hand, pulling her down to his level. He glared into her eyes, caught between want and hate. "You are a bitch, and a whore," he spat, choosing the anger…the safer emotion.

Her eyes widened, her mouth dropping open.

"The only way you could help me is if you could remove yourself from my memory."

Now on her knees, her eyes narrowed into a piercing glare. Yanking her hand out of his grasp, she swung. Her palm connected with his cheek in a resounding clap, leaving his ear wringing and his skin tingling.

"I've made mistakes," she growled, "but you don't know my story, Nash." She staggered to her feet. "You don't know what I've been through, what I'm going through," she sucked in a deep breath, "and yet you have the audacity to judge me from your self-righteous, drunken perch. You," she pointed her finger right into his face, "are the one I want removed from *my* memory."

She stormed, shoeless, away from him and away from the park – the last he'd probably ever see of her. Good riddance, he thought, and yet a deep dark pain threatened to suffocate him. After several moments, he decided he needed more to drink. He hoisted himself to his feet. A sudden shift of the dock knocked him off balance, lurching him to the side. He overcorrected, and swayed to the other side, creating a zig-zag that made him dizzy, but eventually, he managed to get off the docks. With one last look at the bench he'd seen Mira and Tanger on, he took off at a run. But he couldn't outrun the image – or the words.

Finally, he arrived at his RV and stepped inside, winded and longing for something to ease the pain. As he looked around his place, though, he only felt an aching emptiness that would not be soothed. Grabbing his backpack, he slammed item after item inside…miscellaneous clothes, toiletries, a wad of cash, jerky, and a bottle of wine. He staggered to the coffee table to retrieve his mp3 player and the book Hayes had given him. As he stashed them in his bag, he noticed what had been beneath them - the song he'd written for Mira. "I need some fresh air," he rasped, feeling sick.

Tossing his backpack behind the chair, he grabbed another bottle of booze and made his way to the door. Throwing the screen open, he stumbled through it, scraping his shoulder on the frame. "Shit!" He rubbed the spot with his booze hand, spilling a goodly amount of liquid on his back and the RV steps. After an accusatory glance at the offending door jamb, he swung the bottle back to his lips and stalked over to the limo. His chauffeur, Chad, with his impeccable tux and stylish hat, was nowhere in sight. Nash slumped into the driver's seat and rested his forehead against the steering wheel. His head spun and his clammy skin stuck to the leather seat.

"Ahhhh," he growled out, looking desperately for relief…physically, mentally. That's when he noticed Chad had left the car keys in the cup holder. He reached for the key fob, staring at them as they dangled from his fingers. The drive to escape crept into his mind and wouldn't leave. He aimed the fob at the ignition. *Click…click…click.* After three tries, he remembered he only needed to push a button for the car to start. Tossing the keys back into the cup holder, he stabbed the ignition button with his index finger. The engine rumbled to life.

Nash took another swallow of the burning liquid and shifted into gear. As he drove out of the Luxury RV Park, he turned left, toward the mountains, instead of right, toward town. It wasn't the best choice, he discovered a few minutes later. The curvy roads were really doing a number on his stomach. He pulled off to the side, and cracking open his door, puked on the shoulder. It smelled like recycled appetizers and booze. He propped his forehead on the arm of the door, waiting for the sick feeling to pass. Only it came back with a vengeance. Once more, he spewed out the contents of his guts. Gasping for breath, he swiped the slime from his lips and spit, over and over again to get the taste out of his mouth. After a few moments, the nausea subsided.

He sat back in his seat and, rolling down his window, he started out again. The cool, crisp air whipped across his face as he drove. Although the wind at first sparked life into him, the lull of the engine and the emotional upheaval of the day soon drained his energy. His eyes drifted shut. A warm calm covered him, his mind floating into an unconscious state he relished. But then that click between sleep and wake jarred him back to reality. His eyes shot open. A bright yellow sign, blaring a warning of a sharp curve ahead, catapulted his heart into overdrive. "Holy crap!" he screamed as he slammed on his brakes and cranked right.

The back end of his car swung wide in an uncontrolled arch. As it lurched around the corner, Nash caught a glimpse of a man hoisting a car onto a tow-truck. "Nooooo!!" he screamed as his car slammed into the man, crushing him against the tow-truck. A shrill cry weaved through crunching of metal and glass, the horrific sounds exploding in Nash's ears just as the powerful thrust of airbags whipped his head back. And then there was a sickening silence.

Chapter 66

Mira sat beside the kitchen table, watching out the window she'd opened last night. The vibrant wildlife outside carried on as usual, but her own life could not do the same. She'd awoken that morning with a heaviness in her heart, a heart that felt crushed by Nash's treatment of her. Not only that, but the cold hard reality of what she could expect from Tanger left her feeling empty and sad. What was she going to do? Her nausea reminded her of the huge decision she had to make. Even though she'd called on her spirit guide and the answers had come in three – the sea bird, Claire's call, and Tanger's suggestion to visit Jadis – a strong, uneasy feeling inside still held her back.

Deciding to stay in her sweats and sweatshirt for the day, she wandered the two steps into the kitchen. Breakfast didn't sound all that appealing at the moment. "I could definitely use a cup of coffee, though," she said.

After grinding the Harmony Blend coffee beans that she'd brought along from Pillar, she emptied them into the filter basket. She poured the water into the coffee maker and hit start. It sparked to life, the gurgling sound as it filled the pot reminding her of her time at Cofa's Tree. Within moments, the aroma, like a dusting of incense, permeated the slightly briny air. This too, brought to mind her experiences of late – ones brimming with uncertainty. As she started to question if she even wanted a cup of the brew, she heard someone call out to her from the gate. She peeked out the window. "Russel?" What was he doing here? Quickly sweeping her hair up into a ponytail, Mira stepped outside.

As she approached the gate, Russel said, "I hope I didn't wake you."

"No. Just having a relax day," she said, reaching for the gate's handle. "Would you like to have some coffee with me on the deck?"

He smiled. "Sure, if you have some made."

"I do. Have a seat and I'll pour us some."

"Sounds great," he said, and headed toward the bistro table at the far end of the deck.

"So what brings you by," she called out through the window as she poured coffee into two mugs with blue anchors on them.

"Actually, I brought a package that was addressed to you. It came to Dreamer's."

A mug in each hand, she kicked the door open with her foot and headed toward her visitor. "I was going to let you know it was coming, but I didn't expect it to get here so soon."

"It was sent overnight. Must be important," he said, holding the package out to her.

She set the mugs down, the steamy scent of coffee pleasant in the fresh morning air. "I don't know how important it is, but thanks for bringing it over." She took the package and laid it in her lap, wedging her finger in the seal's gap to tear it open.

"No problem. I had a stop to make in the area anyway." Russel took a swig of his coffee. "So what did you think of the concert last night?"

She'd managed to open the envelope, but decided not to look inside until her guest left. "The little I heard was good I guess," she said and took a drink of the coffee. The liquid was hotter than she'd thought and scalded a path down her throat.

"I noticed you didn't stay long."

She shrugged, wishing she had some cold water. "Things came up."

Russel tilted his head to the side. "How well do you know Nash Montgomery?"

Her gaze snapped up to meet his. She could hear her own heartbeat as she answered. "We have a history. Why?"

"Well, I saw you talking to him – and saw you leave with another guy."

"I did talk to Nash, and I did leave with someone else," she paused to glance down at her fingers tracing the mug's handle. "A friend. Why?"

"Just seeing if I can fill in some details a detective wanted to know."

Again, her eyes met his. "Did you say detective?"

Russel's eyes took on a dark sadness that made her hold her breath as she listened to his next words. "The car Nash is typically chauffeured around in was in a horrible accident last night."

"What!?!" she gasped, her hands clutching the chair edge beneath her. "Is Nash okay?"

"We're not sure. No one was with the car at the accident site. A search crew scoured the area around it. No evidence of Nash or his chauffeur has been found."

Her heart sank to her toes. "Was anyone else at the scene? Anyone injured?"

He nodded. "The car crushed a guy against his vehicle. The doctors predict that he'll live," Russel inhaled deeply. "But he's in a coma right now...and he's paralyzed."

Had hers and Nash's confrontation last night pushed him over the edge? Where was he? "That's horrible!" Her hand shook as she took another sip of a brew that tasted harsh and bitter.

Russel nodded somberly as he took another swig of his own. "I don't know what your situation is with Nash, but after I saw you together last night, I thought you probably knew him...that you'd want to know what happened – and that maybe you would know where he is."

"I'm sorry. I don't."

He stood up and put his hand on her shoulder. "Well, if you do see him, could you tell him the police would like to talk to him?"

She looked up at Russel, tears in her eyes. "I will."

"Thanks," he said, and walked slowly toward the gate. "And thanks for the coffee."

"You're welcome." She held up her package. "And thank you for bringing over the package...and for telling me about Nash."

He nodded and with a wave, he was gone.

Mira stared at the swells of water crashing in their steady way against a neighboring boat's hull. Had Nash been driving that car? Where would she even start looking for him? She picked up her phone and tried his number.

"Pick up," she whispered. But it went right to voicemail.

"Hi Nash. This is Mira. I, um, I just wanted to tell you that I'm really worried about you and that I'm…I'm sorry." She took several painful breaths. "Come back so we can talk, okay?" She hit end and laid the phone on the table, staring at it as she envisioned his lifeless body lying somewhere in the trees. She'd know in her heart if he was dead, right? She reassured herself that the search crew would have found him. But where was he then? Her keys…she needed to get her keys!

Grabbing the coffee cups and the envelope off the table, she hurried across the deck. As she swung the door to the galley open, the envelope slipped out of her grasp. It crashed onto the wood-planked decking, its contents spilling out.

"Crap!" Mira put the coffee cups inside then hurried back to pick up the mess. One of the items was a second envelope. It was sealed and had her name on it, with the Cofa's Tree address below it. There was no return address, but it was rubber-stamped with Whynot's post office information. Could it be from Nash?

With shaking fingers, she managed to get it open. Inside was an invitation to an event called SRF: Self-Realization Fellowship. "A place to bring all your burdens and cleanse the mind of its negative energy," she read. "A place to learn breathing techniques to merge body and spirit, and to transfer energies to find the perfect balance." She glanced at the address. The event would take place right outside of Pillar in just a few days. It piqued her interest, and yet she couldn't even think of leaving until she talked to Nash.

Then she noticed something stuck against the back of the brochure. She peeled it away. It was a picture of Nash and Tory kissing in what looked like a top-of-the-line RV. Mira swallowed hard as she took the three steps to the boats edge. Why would someone send her this? *Who* would send it? Tory maybe? Or was it Nash, sending her a message – one she couldn't misinterpret? As she stared at the intimate photograph, a big, fat, ugly tear dropped onto Nash's face. Even though it warped the perfect lines of his image, she felt she could see him much more clearly. "The why and who don't really matter," she sniffed. "I'm h-happy this happened because now I know I can finally cut all ties with him without regret." Even with that decided, she couldn't dredge up one spark of joy, and the burden of it all threatened to suffocate her. With a loud growl, she shredded the picture into tiny pieces.

"I release you from my life…from my thoughts…from my heart," she said with as much confidence as she could muster. She tossed the segments into the water, only instead of dispersing, they hovered around the houseboat, floating, taunting her. What a depressing reminder that her own life was in shreds and that her heart wouldn't be forgetting him any time soon, no matter how she might wish it!

Mira slipped back inside the houseboat and slammed the door shut with her foot. She marched over to her dresser and set up her altar. It was time she took charge of her life and her destiny.

Chapter 67

Nash caught a whiff of the stage clothes that still smelled, despite his dip in the ocean last night. The Reformer in him warred against his plan, but the sour smell of puke, sweat, blood, and booze reiterated his need for new attire. He watched the truck driver cart another box of clothes into The Exchange. He'd have six minutes, give or take thirty seconds, before the guy returned for another load. Time to go!

Nash crept from his hiding spot behind the garbage bins and jumped into the back of the delivery truck. The morning light would allow him to find what he wanted, but he'd also be easy to spot. He'd have to move fast.

Several large boxes remained in the load, each marked with size and style. As Nash wove through the rows to scan the labels to find something to wear, the smell of cardboard mixed with exhaust…plus his own smell, made him nauseous. "Come on," he whispered. "Where are the men's clothes?" He climbed over a stack of two boxes to the next row. *Women's lingerie, women's shoes, women's jewelry, women's skirts…men's dress wear.*

Nash grinned, barely holding back a whoop. With jittery hands, he unfolded the flaps and dug in. He was almost to the bottom before he found something close to his size. He pulled it out. "Perfect."

Stripping down to nothing, he shoved his old clothes into a bag he'd found in the dumpster. He slipped on the clean pants, then the button down shirt. Leaving the buttoning for later, he shoved his arms into the jacket. He took a hat from a nearby box and plopped it onto his head. Grabbing the lapels of his jacket, he smiled slightly. At least it would buy him some time.

Quickly shoving the mountain of clothes back inside the box, and slapping the folds into place, Nash skirted around it and headed toward the open back door. Only as he jumped from the trailer, the driver returned with his wheeled cart.

"Hey. What are you doing?"

Nash took off, his bagged, soiled clothes still in hand. He glanced over his shoulder. The guy hadn't pursued him, but he did have his phone pressed to his ear. Nash ran around to the other side of The Exchange, where a woman had just opened her car door.

"Will you give me a ride to the hospital," he asked, breathing heavily from his escape and from the adrenalin pumping through his veins. He shoved the hat low over his eyes. "My brother was in a car accident, and I need to get there now!"

She looked at him only a moment. He must have looked desperate enough because she said, "Get in."

More than happy to oblige, he got into the passenger seat. She asked a few questions, but he only gave her minimal answers. The less she heard his voice the better. On the five-minute ride, he buttoned his shirt, and tried to calm himself.

She pulled the car into the hospital parking lot and drove him right up to the front door.

"Thanks," he said. "You're a life saver."

"I hope he's okay," she said.

"Me too," Nash said, and shut the door. He pulled the bowler hat down as low as he could without inhibiting his vision. He took the stairs up to the intensive care floor. Although he'd cut his hair short and he wore a formal suit, it was risky coming here. But he needed to be here. He had to see for himself what he'd done. Had he really paralyzed a man named Percy who had a towing business and a family?

Nash rubbed his stiff neck as he surveyed the waiting room. The bright walls sported prints with inspirational sayings like "This is where the healing begins." The oversized windows provided an ocean view almost as amazing as the one from Nash's RV. And yet, given all that, the waiting area seemed totally depressing. Flip...flip...flip...flip...a woman with a zoned-out stare turned the pages of a magazine. A man walked over to the coffee counter to refill his extra small Styrofoam cup, then, with one hand in his brown trouser pocket, proceeded to pace across the room as he sipped. An elderly gentleman sat in the corner, reading a leather bound book, his teeth worrying his bottom lip. All seemed to be in different states of distress, waiting for news that would either bring joy or despair.

Trying to breathe past the constriction that had overtaken his lungs since reading the morning paper, Nash fought the terror inside him. He didn't want to go to jail, didn't want to be responsible for ruining someone else's life. And yet, he *was* responsible – and torn between running or owning up. Seeing Percy with his own eyes would end the insane war inside his head, right?

Nash slipped through the doors that opened into the ICU hallway. He approached room number 1540. The door was ajar. A voice - a very young and innocent voice – drifted through it...and right into Nash's heart.

"When will he wake up mommy?" the child said.

"He has a lot of owies," a woman answered. Though her voice trembled, it was purposefully soft and soothing. "And the medicine he's getting makes him very sleepy." She cleared her throat. "It won't be too long and he'll be able to talk to us."

"Can he come to my t-ball game?"

"Not the one tonight."

Nash felt the warmth gather in his eyes.

For a moment, there was silence. Then the boy whispered, "Can he hear me?"

"Yeah, I think so."

"Can I sit by him?"

"I'm sure he'd like that. Want me to help you up?"

"No. I can do it."

Nash inched forward to peek inside the door. A young boy of about five curled up against an unconscious and pale man named Percy. He was the man that had stood up for Nash at Dreamers, the one wearing the Thurman Towing t-shirt! Nash felt like throwing up, yet he couldn't leave. He needed to know more.

After a few moments, the boy sat up on his knees and put his hand on his dad's cheek. "I picked some flowers for you, daddy. Mommy put them in a cup by your bed."

Nash glanced at the small jar holding wilted dandelions and felt another surge of guilt.

"Mommy said you would like them, and the picture I drew, too." Reaching into his pocket, he pulled out a folded piece of paper smudged with chocolate. Unfolding it, he held it up close to his dad's face. "See. I drew you and me and mommy at the beach. And there's the sand shark, just like we made last time."

The rhythmic sound of Percy's heart beat monitor was his only response. It did nothing to distract Nash from the sound of the woman's stifled sobs.

The boy kissed his dad's cheek. Percy's heart beat a bit faster. The boy then looked upward, his hands clasped. "Dear God, please help my daddy get better. Amen."

Unable to watch any longer, Nash backed away from the room. Leaning against the wall, he fought for control. He'd done this! He'd destroyed their family! Guilt filled every pore until it seeped out his eyes in scarring strips. He knew he deserved to go to jail for this. He deserved to lose his career, his fame, his prosperity…his very life. And yet none of those things would fix Percy or what he and his family would have to endure.

"It's time to go get ready for your ballgame," Nash heard the mom say.

Knowing he couldn't let her or the little boy see him, he escaped down the hallway to the nearest exit and high-tailed it outside. Seeing a therapy bench landscaped with bright flowers and a quietly burbling fountain, Nash walked over to it and sat down. Head in his hands, he whispered, "What am I going to do?" Nothing he thought of came close to making the pain in his chest go away.

Nash's phone buzzed in his pocket. He hesitated, then reached for it. It was Porsche. He let it go into voice mail. After it buzzed again, signaling the end of her message, he dialed in to listen to it.

The first message was from Mira. His heart ached even more at the sound of her voice. He refused to talk to her, though, despite the longing he felt, despite the need he had for a friend right now. Mira had made her choice, and it wasn't him...it wasn't them.

His finger hovered over the four to delete the message, but at the last moment, he hit seven to save it. He listened to the next message.

"You need to get in touch with me, pronto." Porsche's firm tone demanded a response as much as her words did. His teeth clenched. "I can't fully cover up for you unless you come out of hiding. You look damned guilty, which I know you are. The only mistake Chad made was to leave the key fob in the stinking car." Her intensely loud volume dropped to a harsh whisper. "He'll take the rap if I tell him to, but I need you out and performing like you're innocent. Do you understand what I'm saying?" She gave a loud sniff. "Meet me at the Love Lodge, ten o'clock tonight, to sign the new contract and to memorize the story we've constructed to absolve you of all guilt. If you don't, you'll regret it."

Chapter 68

"Go." It's the word Mira had heard after calling on her spirit guide. And she'd seen the green lit stoplight that the neighboring boat had put up on its dock. Both were 'coincidences' that reinforced what she needed to do. So she'd packed up yesterday and headed out of Whynot. Now, after another night's stay in her same room at the Crossland Motel in Bolinbroke, here she was, a spider on a silken string, floating where the wind would take her...which was to Pillar just in time for the event.

As she drove into the city she'd grown up in, she glanced in her rearview mirror, envisioning all she'd left behind. Her feeling of dissatisfaction was as strong, if not stronger, than when she'd left Pillar, she realized. More depressed than she cared to admit, she whipped past the COO building that sported the blossoming tree. Her gut cinched tighter as her failures hounded her mind and dragged on her emotions. She tried to push the negative thoughts away.

"This event is going to be spectacular and it will be just what I need," she said and tried to work up a smile. The smile, though she'd managed to put it on her face, didn't go any further than that.

Mira continued on the main road. The familiar copse of trees on her right formed the barrier between her old house and the city. Had it been only a little over a year ago she and Nash had escaped through these trees in search of the Enchiridion? Mira pulled off to the side, clutching the wheel as memories washed over her. They'd been through so much together. Oh, how she missed that special time with him and the rare connection they'd shared from the beginning. She closed her eyes, trying to wash it all away so she wouldn't have to feel so much, only it was still there – every last memory. Oh, how she wished she could redo this entire past year. But that wasn't possible.

Teary, Mira dug into her purse and pulled out the brochure - her only hope right now. She laid it on her seat and wiped her tears before starting down the road again. "This is going to lead me to true love," she sniffed, "and happiness." And she would find a place where she felt satisfied with who she was and what she was doing. The solutions to her inner cravings existed, and she would find them...this weekend!

The road adjacent to Pillar took her out past the southern city limits to where the trees grew sparser. She recognized the area – the once abandoned place she and her mom had escaped to that first night they'd taken on the challenge of following Mira's dreams of finding the Enchiridion. "I'm here because of my dreams, but my dreams are different this time," she said, though the fear of the danger they'd faced long ago still clung to her. Like mud on her boots, she couldn't shake it, yet she continued. Presently, the space had a more uplifting aura with its large sign on wooden posts that announced the temporary community that had been erected for the event.

"SRF: Exploring artistic self-expression and identifying human reality" it said. She turned down a dirt road to where an area had been carved out to accommodate the conference. Driving into the lot, she parked near the road, beside a purple electric car. Several vehicles filled the section marked off for parking. On the opposite side of the car lot stood various tents, different shapes, sizes, styles, and colors. Between the tent area and the wide stretch of beach loomed a giant tent, probably for the speakers the brochure had advertised. Adjacent to that stood several smaller tents, each with a banner or signboards. These were set up in a circle and butted up to the cliffs that once housed Freetown. Even though the rebels that had hidden there had disbanded after the Obliteration Movement, she couldn't help but shiver at the flashback it sparked. Burt Guyver – evil, powerful, a man still showing up in her nightmares – hadn't been seen since he'd taken the key from the pocket of the Benefactor. Could he be hiding in this area? Or incognito maybe?

"I'll be safe with all these people around," Mira said, shaking off her fear. She grabbed both her purse and suitcase as she got out of the car. After spotting the check-in table where two ladies sat, she headed that way. As she got closer, she recognized them both...Vashti and Divinya.

"Hi, Mira. I didn't know you'd be coming to this event," Vashti said.

"Oh...you know," Mira shrugged, "where the spirit leads." She glanced over at the lodging tents. "How does this work?"

Divinya shoved a paper in front of Mira. "The fee is on a sliding scale," she said.

"I'll cover Mira's," Vashti interrupted.

Mira's gaze swung over to Vashti.

"I'm just glad to have you here," she explained with a shrug and an encouraging smile.

"Well, thanks," Mira said.

"Anywho," Divinya said, "this contract is one everyone who attends signs. It states you will keep this event confidential. Whatever goes on here, whoever is attending the conference, and whatever anyone does is all kept private."

As Mira stared at the line that called for her signature, she wondered if they had something to hide. Unease swept through her.

"The privacy clause is only set up to allow us to leave our inhibitions at the door and explore who we really are without fear of condemnation," Vashti said. "It's a worthwhile event. That, I can promise."

Divinya handed her a pen. "I thought you were the kind of person who was always up for an adventure."

She had been, but that part of her had become less and less visible. And yet, maybe her increased reluctance to take a chance was the wall keeping her from the place she'd feel whole and fulfilled. She took the pen from Divinya and signed on the line.

"And here's the guest list to sign, too," Divinya said. "Most everyone who signed up for the event is here already."

As Mira signed her name, she perused the other names on the list. Most she didn't recognize. But she did notice a few people that she was acquainted with - Sam, Houser, Claire, Hunter, Finn, Anju, and Amaryllis. Tanger's name wasn't on the list, which she had mixed feelings about. Yet she wasn't going to worry about it.

"So now what?" she asked.

Vashti handed her a paper that had times and locations for each individual event. It also had a few common sense rules like throw away garbage and so on. "I'll show you to your tent so you can rest up before dinner and the opening event." As they walked toward the lodging area, Vashti said, "Our speaker tonight is Sylvia. She's the one running this whole show."

Sylvia was the one who'd brought the bikini girls to town. Mira hadn't seen their names on the list, thankfully. "Sylvia, huh?"

Vashti smiled. "I think you'll enjoy it." They approached the tent on the far edge of the last row. She opened the flap. "Sorry it's so far from everything, but it's first come first served."

"I understand," Mira said, ducking inside the tent. There was a bed, a lantern sitting on a small table, a chair beside it, and a full-length mirror stood in the corner. The area was better than she'd thought it would be. Laying her suitcase on the bed, she said, "Is there a bathroom nearby?" She had to pee a lot lately.

"We use the back forty," she said with a smile. "That's one bonus to you being on the end. The field is right behind you."

"Just what I wanted to hear," Mira muttered.

Vashti chuckled and patted her shoulder. "I'll let you get settled. Let me know if you need anything else."

"Thanks Vashti…for paying the fee for me, for welcoming me here."

"I'm just glad you could join us, Mira." Vashti disappeared behind the flap, leaving Mira alone. She sat down on the bed, her hands pressed together between her knees. Seeing Sam after their last encounter at the Love Lodge would be uncomfortable, but hey, whatever happened here, stayed here. Besides, she had nothing to prove to anyone.

She got up and opened her suitcase, only to hear a quiet rap on her tent flap. "Vashti?"

"No. It's Houser. I saw you drive in and thought I'd come by and say hi."

She opened the tent flap with a smile. She said, "Come on in, Houser. I'm glad to see you."

He glanced at her face, his eyes tiny slits of observance. "You look like you haven't slept in a week. Did you get your package?"

"I did. Thank you for sending it to me."

"Sure." Hands tucked into his back pockets, he said, "I hope the package isn't the cause of your sleepless nights. I'll feel bad if it is."

She sat down on her bed with a sigh. "It is, and it isn't." She glanced at him. It had been so long since she had someone to talk to — really talk to without worrying. "It included pictures of Nash and Tory together."

He took a seat beside her and rested his hands on his knees. "I take it that bothers you?"

"It hurts more than I realized." Tears swelled in her eyes, but she brushed them away.

"I'm sure everything will work out," he said.

She snorted through her stuffed up nose. "That's what I keep hoping, yet other crap seems to be waiting for me around every corner."

Houser tilted his chin down and looked her in the eyes. "I think this event will change this negative road you're on." Houser said, "And if not, we might have to get a bit more creative."

She didn't know what he had in mind, but his confidence reassured her. "Thanks, Houser." She swiped at the remaining dampness on her cheeks. "I feel better already."

He stood up. "Oh hey. Is that the doll I gave you?" he asked, pointing to the tuft of hair sticking out behind the folded leggings in her suitcase.

"Yeah."

He smiled as he brushed a hand down his pin-striped vest. "Did you know each of those dolls has a history?"

"Vashti mentioned it." She pulled the doll from the suitcase. "What's this one's story?"

"Her name is Nadya, which means hope. She was made by a gypsy whose daughter died in prison. It's said the girl's spirit lives on in the doll." He glanced at the freaky looking thing with fondness. "I'm glad you took her on your adventure. Gypsy's like their freedom."

"You actually think her spirit lives in the doll?"

He nodded. "I'm surprised she actually let you lock her away in this suitcase without putting up a ruckus."

His words sparked her memory of what happened in her room at Cofa's Tree - the doll crying, the mysterious way it had gotten out of the locked trunk. She shivered. "Why don't you just take her back with you?"

He glanced at Mira. "When your adventures are just beginning?"

"I'm having a hard time taking care of myself," Mira admitted.

"She seems content so far." Houser picked up the doll and, stroking her hair, brought her to the table. When he propped her into a sitting position on the hand-scraped wooden surface, Mira spoke up.

"Could you please take her?" Mira would freak out if the thing cried during the night or even if she just sat on the table and stared at her.

"You sure?" Houser took the doll and carefully tucked into the crux of his arm like one would a real baby. "She's given me powerful dreams in the past – ones that have led me to live freely while being confident in who I am."

Houser was eclectic, but he also seemed so sure of who he was and how he lived. Mira rubbed her forehead with the tips of her fingers. Maybe the doll had provoked the dream she'd had about Kya. She had no clue what it was supposed to mean, though perhaps it had been something as simple as a scare tactic to prompt Mira to get out of town. "I have so much to think about, Houser – so much incoming information that keeps confusing me." And she knew that with the guest speakers tonight and her spirit guide being more active, there'd be a lot more to consider. "Right now, I need to simplify, okay?"

He nodded abruptly. "I understand."

"Thanks Houser." She smiled, but it was a pathetic attempt.

"I'm here for you," he said, his expression shifting to one of somber resolve as he exited the tent.

Chapter 69

Thankful for the cover of night, Nash approached the Love Lodge. He'd thought long and hard about coming here, but what else could he do? Being a fugitive wasn't a situation he'd ever thought he'd be in. He was a rule follower, for heaven's sake! Only he'd broken the rules…big time, and now he had to pay with his freedom. Jail, being a fugitive, or living under Porsche's thumb…any of those choices put him in shackles. Porsche's alternative, however, was probably the best he could hope for.

Nash went inside the building. One of the guys who had escorted him home from The Dreamer's Club that fateful night was there to greet him.

"Right this way," he said.

Nash followed him down the hallway and into a large, office-like room. Wall-sized mirrors covered three of its four walls. Porsche sat in a leather chair behind a polished wooden desk, a red cloche hat tilted on her dark hair. This beautiful, powerful woman looked as though she was used to getting her own way.

"Have a seat, Nash." With the confident look of one in charge, she pointed to the other chair.

Although he balked at her ordering tone, he sat.

"You can leave us now," she said to her hired man. He nodded and left the room.

"You look good in a suit," she said, her eyes raking over him, her cherry red lips drawing up into a flirtatious smile.

Nash didn't respond.

"I'd have thought you'd be more…grateful for my help, but you're not really like other men, are you dear?" She chuckled. "That's why I wanted to sign you, you know."

"I thought it was because of my talent and potential," Nash ground out.

She waved a hand. "Plenty of people have talent – and they're really eager to have an opportunity to use it, especially after being stifled by the LifeChip for so long."

He didn't really care why she'd picked him. It didn't matter at this point. "So what story am I bringing to the police?"

She met his stare as she tapped her long fingernails against the table. After a few moments, she answered. "That you were upset at being dragged away from your little concert so you had Chad drive you off to a place in the woods where you like to camp."

"Okay. What about Chad, then?"

She shrugged. "He fell asleep at the wheel on his return to town. That's when he ran into dear Percy."

Her smugness irritated him. "Don't you care at all about what happened to Percy?"

She shook her head slowly. "Only in how it affects me and mine." Her eyes turned hard. "Crap happens, Nash."

He swallowed, knots forming in both his throat and his stomach. "What will happen to Chad if I go through with this?"

"I'm not entirely sure about the judge they've assigned him to…silly judge has a strong will to do what is right. But I have a lot of influence in the courts." She used the pad of her index finger to dab at the corners of her lips. "You don't need to worry about Chad."

The one thing that Nash had confidence in was that Porsche had the power to pull things off – and he believed she could do so with Chad, too. He couldn't do anything about Percy and knowing that Chad most likely wouldn't have to suffer for his untruth helped to make his decision. "So what do you want from me in exchange?"

She looked at him with a smug glimmer in her eyes. "I want your soul, of course."

He frowned. "Come again?"

She laughed until she was brushing tears from her cheeks. "You should've seen the look on your face."

"Not funny. What's in the contract you want me to sign?"

"Oh…just a few more years of commitment to me." Still smiling, she got up and walked around the desk. Sitting on the edge of it, she crossed her legs, allowing a good portion of her thigh to show over her tall boots. "Just your signature here, and you'll be back on the path to fame and fortune." She nudged the pages toward him and handed him a pen.

"I'll have to think about it," he said, standing.

Her smile dropped as her eyebrow raised. "You can't be serious?"

He'd signed a contract without reading it thoroughly before. He wouldn't do it again. "I am *very* serious." Nash walked away, perusing the contract in his hands. When he got to the door, Porsche stood in front of it, blocking his path.

"I need your answer. Now."

"You're not going to let me think about it?" he asked, feigning a confidence of his own.

She searched his eyes. "Not until I give you a little *more* to think about." She yanked him close and kissed him full on the mouth. After several moments, she released him. Running a finger down his chest, she said, "If you sign the contract, I promise it will be worth your while, Nash." When he didn't respond, her eyes turned from fiery lust to a burning threat. "And if you don't…there will be hell to pay."

Chapter 70

Mira made up her mind. She'd dress for adventure – like a woman ready to take on the world and make it her own. Thanks to The Exchange, she now had several choices at her disposal. She snatched up her midnight black weskit, which was tailored with a fitted bodice and peplum that reminded her of pirate wenches of the past. She tightened the grommetted, cross-laced front so that her breasts pushed up enticingly. Her short and sassy skirt was a deep red that seemed to melt into dip-dyed black toward the bottom. Her ankle boots had flame-buckled straps and crisscrossed front lacing bound in bronze hardware. She glanced at herself in the mirror, thankful her stressful past few months had at least led to weight loss. She looked sexy and powerful, especially because the makeup hid her tiredness. As she swiped her hand down her still flat stomach, she was reminded of the fact it wouldn't be that way for much longer, unless she visited Jadis like Tanger had suggested. Pushing it to the back of her mind, she marched out of her tent into the salt-infused, balmy evening air.

About halfway to the tented area where the first meeting would take place, Mira noticed Finn and Anju only a few steps in front of her. She considered slowing up so she didn't have to make small talk with them, but changed her mind. "I am bold and confident in who I am and what I have to offer," she said softly, picking up her pace.

"Hi, Finn. Hi, Anju," she called out.

They peered over their shoulders. "Oh hi, Mira." They both smiled as they made room for her to walk beside them.

Mira felt more optimistic just walking between friends. "So where's Sam?"

They exchanged a look. "He had an attack on the way here. We took him to the Remedy Shack for a ceremonial sauna. It's a great way to purify, heart and soul."

Before she could ask details, Finn said, "Did you hear about my art show?"

Mira shook her head.

"It was great exposure, but I don't know if I'd do it again. It's a ton of work."

"Did you sell some of your pieces?" Mira asked.

"I didn't sell a thing." He flicked his hand in the air and shook his head. "People don't understand my work. I'm thinking about moving down the coast to where people are more open-minded."

Mira had thought those at The Grotto – those who participated in things like the Love Lodge – would be open-minded enough for about anything. "What was the theme of your show?"

"Authenticity."

"Do you have a favorite piece?"

"Yep." He smiled and pulled out his phone. Handing it to her, he said, "This one's called The Villain Within."

Mira looked at the picture of his favorite sculpture. A man had two parts to his face. Half of it looked normal. The other half appeared as if his skin had been peeled away, revealing a vile looking creature. "Interesting perspective," she said, trying to hide her revulsion as she handed the phone back to him.

"Finn says we all have evilness inside us, and that we need to embrace and celebrate our true selves, but I don't agree," Anju said with a slight pout.

"And Anju thinks that we only need to open up to the powers of the universe and that the power living inside us will enable us to create our perfect selves," he said, glaring at her.

She popped him on the shoulder. "Well, my art reflects my views – *and* it sells."

He harrumphed. "You've only sold a few, and only to simple-minded people - none of whom seek the advice you're trying to sell, I might add."

She raised her chin. "People love to hear what I have to say."

"So you keep telling us," he muttered.

"Hey," Mira said, interrupting. "Here we are at the tent. Just look at all these people." She scanned the crowded area. "I, for one, can't wait to hear the information they'll share with us at this event."

"I'm looking forward to the food, too. I'm starving," Anju said, her momentary pique disappearing as she hurried toward a booth that had a line of about twenty-five people.

"Well, after dealing with her, I'm heading over to the drinks," Finn said, "That woman drives me crazy!"

"I thought you were a couple," Mira commented.

"Yes and no. We have a relationship with no boundaries," he said as he edged backwards toward the drink booth, which was twice as long as the food one. "Care to join in?" he asked, his eyes sweeping down the length of her and back up again.

For a moment, his handsome face dropped its pretense, revealing something else, something truer – and at that moment, Mira could see Burt Guyver, the guy she'd first met in the Cords' cave, the guy that always seemed to be lurking around when evil was present. "No thanks. I'm going to find a good spot to sit," she said.

He nodded. "Maybe I'll see you around later."

Or not. The look of promise in his eyes was not a promise she wanted to be kept. She scurried away from him toward the east-most side of the tent near one of the exits. Eyeing a spot three rows from the front, she picked up one of the brochures stacked on a stand at the end of the aisle and sat down.

The chairs filled up quickly, and even though people still lined up at the booths, Sylvia came on stage and started her speech

"Hello, fellow travelers. Welcome to the first annual Self-Realization Fellowship Conference. I am so excited for this event. Not only will we be transformed heart, soul, body, and mind, but we will be able to transform the world around us. Can't you just feel the energy of our life force?" Sylvia lifted up her hands.

"Yes," the crowd shouted.

"If you look in your brochure, you'll see we have plenty of activities in store for you this weekend. Tonight, after my introduction, the Wellness Market will be open for you to peruse. There are a variety of vendors, and if you look on the back of the brochure, you'll get an idea of what each one offers."

Mira glanced at the many opportunities on back of her pamphlet. There were places selling food, potions, clothing, books, and jewelry. There were shops that provided services…massage, fortune telling, Reiki treatments, a worship center, crystal healing, and chakra balancing.

"Until three in the afternoon tomorrow, we'll be offering meditation and yoga classes as well as the yoga sutras of Patanjali for the more advanced."

Mira read the description under yoga sutras. It said that Patanjali was an ancient sage they didn't know much about, but his oral tradition had been handed down and fitted into sutras of wisdom that most likely came from God to help people figure out their human selves. Mira was curious as to what they'd found as proof for those claims. Perhaps the bookshop would carry more information on this Patanjali.

"The shops will open again in the late afternoon. And after a fabulous meal Saturday evening, we'll all head out to the beach for a celebration of community for the pleasure of all participants."

The crowd cheered. Sylvia grinned. "Each of these items that takes place during this event is for a purpose…and that purpose is to tap into the power and energy of Mother Nature and also within ourselves as we celebrate the art of radical inclusion and the outpouring of creativity and artistic self-expression." She strode with obvious self-assurance to the opposite side of the stage. "We are on a journey, one in which we'll learn more about ourselves and how to view our mistakes as simply a beautiful opportunity to grow. We'll learn to control our mind's fluctuations," she tapped her head, "to create inner stability as we embark upon a spiritual quest that will renew our passions and bring energy and peace to our lives."

Mira didn't understand how it all worked, but after looking around at the flushed excited faces, she felt a rush of her own. The answers to her soul's longings might truly be found right here, this weekend. Hope built inside until it was a powerful glow.

Sylvia ended her speech with a thank you, and encouraged them to check out the market and to get to know each other as well. Determined to give it her best shot, Mira followed the crowd outside to where the vendors had set up shop. The sparkly tent sitting off to the side caught her eye. Fortune Telling…just what she needed – and there wasn't even a line!

Mira marched over to the temporary structure made of dark fabric, glittering with stars. She breathed deeply and stepped inside. A set of Taro cards sat on the table, the hands of the reader placed lightly beside them. The woman looked up.

"I thought you'd come," Vashti said with a sure smile. "Have a seat Mira."

Strangers telling her fortune was one thing…Vashti doing it was another, but Mira swallowed her pride and sat down. A fortune was a fortune, she supposed. "So how does this work?"

"All you need to do is listen."

"Alright." Mira rubbed her sweaty hands on her skirt. "I'm ready."

After a moment of studying her client, which made Mira squirm in her seat, Vashti flipped over the first card - the number eighteen and a picture of the moon.

"The moon is powerful," Vashti said. "It controls the tides and also seems to bring out people's wild side." She smoothed her hand over the card. "The mysteries of the moon are eternal, and unveiling its secrets are enchanting, but…" she lifted her index finger, "the moon is also associated with illusions. What is seen by its light is not necessarily your reality." Vashti looked at Mira. "This deception can be inside yourself or it can come from another. But new information *will* come to you, possibly in a dream or a vision, that will expose the truth to you."

As she tried to decipher Vashti's words, a sense of foreboding crept up Mira's spine.

Vashti covered her hand with her own. "Accepting the darker, wilder side can free you and bring you peace. Denial will only bring you chaos. Dealing with the truth, even the truth within ourselves, is imperative."

"Okay," Mira said, a bit afraid of what her inclinations and dreams might tell her. She also wondered if she was deceiving herself – or if someone else was deceiving her. Time would tell, she supposed. "I'll deal with it."

Vashti smiled and flipped over the second card. It was the number zero. "This is the card of the fool and it means you must make a leap of faith, taking only the baggage of your past that will benefit you. You need to go beyond your boundaries," she said, twirling her hand, "and you must not allow your fears to hold you back. And most of all," she wagged her finger, "you have to believe whole-heartedly that anything is possible."

Mira thought about what that meant and realized she didn't even know what her dreams were anymore. She'd have to think long and hard tonight.

Vashti turned over the next card, the number twelve. It had a picture of a man hanging by a rope. Mira gasped, remembering her nightmare about Kya.

"This doesn't mean you're going to die, if that's what you're thinking," Vashti said.

Relief whisked through Mira.

"What it *does* mean is that your situation may be improved by letting go. For example, you might need to sacrifice something you love if it is in your best interest." Vashti looked at her. "Are you holding on to something that will get in the way of you finding love, enlightenment, and life of infinite possibilities?"

Immediately, Mira thought about the baby. Who would want her if she had a baby – and a baby body complete with saggy skin and stretchmarks? And with a baby, really experiencing all life had to offer wouldn't happen. She'd seen it happen to so many in Pillar.

"Here's your last card," Vashti said, carefully setting it next in line with the others. It was the number six and portrayed a picture of lovers. "A decision may be weighing heavily on your mind." She looked at Mira.

"I do have a decision to make," she admitted. "A big one." Her hand cupped her stomach, feeling warmth but nothing else there.

"This card also tells me you need to mend fences, or you need to separate yourself from a relationship that cannot be salvaged."

Nash and Tanger both came to mind. "What if I don't know if a relationship is repairable or not? How do I know what to let go of and what to try to mend?"

"That's when you look to your heart, and decide what it is you truly desire— what you need to make yourself whole."

Nash's face flashed into her thoughts. No matter how hard she tried to forget him, to move on, something connected her to him on a deeper level, one she didn't understand. But was being with him again even possible? The picture of him and Tory came to mind. It made her stomach ache, but for some reason it didn't make her want him any less. Why couldn't she just let him go?

"I have some thinking to do." Mira stood up and edged to the tent flap. "Thanks Vashti."

Vashti nodded. "Just remember…within a circle, there are no absolutes - no rights and wrongs to shackle us to a powerless life. You have the power to change your life, Mira."

"Got it," Mira said, giving her a thumb's up as she slipped out the doorway and passed the crowd that had gathered there.

Chapter 71

Nash wandered across the small paved parking lot toward the beach. He was surprised to see a car parked there at this time of night, but he didn't see anyone around so he continued on. Stopping at the edge of the boardwalk, he took off his shoes, and then peeled off his socks. He walked across the wooden bridge, and took a moment to let his feet sink into the silky sand.

"Hey, dude. It's pretty dark for a swim."

Nash started, casting a quick glance toward the voice. "True."

The guy sat cross-legged on the sand, his surfboard propped vertically behind him. "You wouldn't have something to eat, would you?"

"Not on me." The cogs in Nash's brain began to turn. "Do you live around here?"

"Yeah dude. Here, and in my car." The kid pointed toward the parking lot.

"Would you like to make a deal? You can use my RV, and you can eat all the food I have in it."

He brushed aside his long, scraggly hair. "In exchange for what?"

"For the use of your car." He tucked his hands into his pockets.

"Sure." The guy got to his feet, unzipped the front pocket of his board shorts and dug out his keys. "When will I get it back?"

"I'm not sure. If you don't hear from me in a month, go ahead and sell the stuff inside the RV and get yourself a new car."

The guy looked at him carefully. "You in trouble?"

"Yes."

"Been there myself." He approached, holding out his keys.

Nash took them before giving him the key to his RV. Then he told him the address. "If anyone questions you, just tell them that you're Nash Montgomery's cousin and that you were invited to come for a visit."

"Got it," he said, shoving the key into his pocket. "Anything else?"

Nash thought a moment. "Actually, yes. There's a backpack behind the chair in the living room area. If it hasn't been confiscated, wear it out on a walk and as discretely as possible, stash it behind the dumpster at the end of the road."

"Easy enough." He raised a brow. "This place nice?"

"You won't be disappointed."

"Sweet." He turned to leave, surfboard in hand. About halfway across the boardwalk, he looked over his shoulder and said, "Good luck, man."

"Thanks," Nash said, and watched the guy disappear from view.

Instead of going to the car, Nash wandered closer to the shoreline, the cooling sand encasing his feet with each step. Pausing, he gazed across the moon-lit ocean. It was the same spot he'd stood when he'd first gotten to Whynot. He'd been so pumped to have access to so many amazing views of the ocean. The ideal surroundings fit right in with the perfect life he'd envisioned for himself. Yet although the majestic scene still created a powerful image, he couldn't erase the one of the little boy with his small hand against his dad's cheek. It haunted him, and he didn't know what to do about it. If going to jail would absolve his conscience, he'd check himself in right now, but he feared the solitude, the time to think about what he'd done. It would be torture.

Nash followed the stretch of shoreline to where an outcropping of jagged rocks stood like bleak, yet intimidating, shadows in the moonlight. Climbing to the topmost point, he sat down and wound his arms around his knees. The unyielding surface beneath him dug into his butt and the dampness of the sea-sprayed rock began to infuse his black dress pants. The keys in his pocket, while offering him a method of escape, gouged against his thigh, adding to his misery. The lump in his throat and the ache in his heart wouldn't go away. He hung his head, barely hearing the incessant crash of the waves against the solid stone, barely feeling the droplets speckle his skin. The cool breeze brushed across him, causing a swell of goosebumps he couldn't ignore. But the uncomfortableness he felt on the outside was nothing compared to the unbearable pain inside. Never had he felt more alone than now – or more helpless.

He looked up. As he watched the blanket of brooding ocean that concealed the danger lurking beneath its surface, he felt it call to him, like blackness calling to its matching soul. Yet his instinct to survive was too strong and he had other options. None of them were perfect options, but at least he hadn't been left paralyzed, without choices. Signing the contract from Porsche would mean his career would continue to flourish as if nothing had ever happened. Disappearing with the surfer's car would allow him to start over…a new person with a new life. Logic said either one of those two options were reasonable and better than admitting guilt and going to prison for who knew how long. What was holding him back? Whatever it was pulled at his heart like a magnetic orb of moral conscience that told him he knew what was right, but it was still his choice to choose.

Climbing down off the rock, Nash slowly made his way to the parking lot. Signing the contract would allow him to continue to pursue his dreams instead of always looking over his shoulder as a man on the run. And yet, he knew Porsche wanted to control him. Her tactics were really not all that far off from the ones the previous government had used to do the same. And he'd worked so hard to be free of their LifeChip! Could he bear to lose that hard-won freedom? Nash continued to the car. Unlocking it, he slipped into the driver's seat. He started it up. "To second chances," he said, and shifted it into drive.

Chapter 72

Mira wandered toward the beach that sat at the edge of the conference grounds. Swallowing her pride, she tried Nash's number again. This time, his mailbox was full. She leaned against an eight-foot stone that, with others its size, created a private fenced-in cove between the open beach and the Freetown cliff. As she watched the water churn, she heard a noise drift on the wind past her ear. She strained to listen. The sound came again, like a cry someone tried to stifle. It seemed to be coming from behind her.

Mira wound around the stone wall into the sheltered area. Tucked within its towering walls sat a large flat stone, with Anju atop it. Her head hung, and her soft sobs sounded even more pitiful up close.

"Mind if I sit down?" Mira asked.

Anju looked up and with a long sniff, said, "Only if you promise to not tell anyone about this."

"Tell anyone about what?"

"About me crying and hiding away like the pathetic imposter that I am."

"I won't tell anyone. I promise."

Anju made room for her and Mira sat down. "So what's going on?"

"I thought I was on my way to figuring everything out, but I'm not."

The excited hope that had built in Mira's heart just moments before slipped a notch. "Did something happen?"

Anju's eyes squinted as they studied her. "You have to swear to secrecy, Mira."

Whatever it was, it had to be heavy to ask again for her to keep things private. "I swear," she said.

Crossing her arms over her stomach, Anju said, "I've been doing some magic – have been for quite a few years now. It was supposed to lead me to true love, but nothing is working out like I want it to."

"Maybe it just needs time," Mira suggested, thinking the same for her own situation.

"Yeah. Sure," she snorted. "Have you read Amaryllis' book about the three H's?"

"No, I haven't."

"What she says in the book is that to find true love, we need to have our three H's aligned…our hearts, our heads, and our hoo-has. I follow the rules to a T, do my magic spells that guarantee love, and do you know what keeps happening?"

Mira shook her head.

"I go through men like I go through my herbal tea." Anju put her face into her hands. "I think I want out, Mira."

Placing a hand on Anju's shoulder, she fought against her own doubt. "Are you sure?"

She glanced at Mira, frowning. "Yeah." She sniffed. "Yeah, I am. But I don't know where to go from here! What else *is* there?" The last came out as a wail.

"There's the Enchiridion of Emmanuel." Mira didn't know where the thought had come from, but the words had popped into her head and she'd said them.

"But that's so…infantile, so…jejune," she said, and started to cry again.

"I don't know what to tell you," Mira said, feeling Anju's desperation begin to dig its hooks into her own positive, hope-filled plans. She had to get away from her and her negative energy. Mira stood up, and after awkwardly patting Anju's back, she said, "Maybe a good night's sleep will help."

"I've heard that a million times. It changes nothing." She looked up. "But thanks for trying."

With a nod, Mira escaped the weeping girl, telling herself that she wasn't going to let it affect her. Anju wasn't the same person as she was. Yet as Mira approached her own tent, she couldn't get Anju out of her head. The girl's situation had left a heavy cloud hanging over her, one that prompted her to rethink her situation. What if she did all the things she was supposed to do – like Anju had – and ended up just as miserable? Maybe Anju had done it wrong. Yeah. That had to be it.

As Mira stepped into her tent, her foot collided with something. She jumped back, hoping it wasn't alive. She glanced down, immediately recognizing what it was - the doll Houser had taken with him. He must have dropped it. Picking it up, she brushed the dead grass out of its hair and brought it inside. She'd bring it to Houser tomorrow. Right now, she had to connect with her spirit guide.

Chapter 73

Nash pulled the surfer's car into the Crossland Hotel that sat on the edge of a town called Bolinbroke. The town's name sounded familiar, but he didn't recall why. Maybe a fan had lived there, maybe it was one of the places on his schedule to perform. Whatever it was, its hotel was a welcome sight.

He parked in front of the lobby. Adjusting the bowler hat so that it sat low on his forehead, he got out. For a moment, he stood and breathed in the fresh air, but it didn't make him feel any better.

Closing the car door, he headed inside. The man at the counter watching TV barely spared him a glance.

"I need a room," Nash said.

Without looking away from the news on the screen, he slid a printed out form in front of Nash. "Cash or credit?" he asked.

"Cash," Nash said, signing on the dotted line.

The attendant finally looked away from his show. "Bastard needs to pay," he muttered.

"Come again?"

He pointed his thumb over his shoulder at the TV. "Over in Whynot, some rock star smashed into one of the nicest guys to ever live in our city."

On the screen, they showed Percy rescuing Francine from a burning car. Acid lurched into the back of Nash's throat. He swallowed, but couldn't get rid of the taste – or the feeling.

With another glance at the screen, the attendant's fingers began to curl like flexible grappling hooks. "If I get my hands on him, I'll kill him," he said with a shake of his head. "No, I'll torture him first, then kill him." His eyes glittered and the corner of his mouth curled up into a sneer. "Unless the chauffeur driver killed prince Montgomery and threw him in a ditch somewhere. Then I'll have to go after the driver."

At the hate resonating from the man, Nash stepped back, his legs trembling, his heart hammering. He glanced at his vehicle through the barred window. Leaving Bolinbroke now might make the guy suspicious, and he'd have no chance of escape then. Besides, he hadn't been recognized so far. But the sooner he got out of the lobby and away from people, the better. "How much do I owe you?" Nash asked, reaching into his jacket for his wallet.

"Two hundred dollars," the dude said, flicking a key card onto the desk.

The hotel looked like rats would second-guess staying there. "I just need one night."

"That's the price today. I'm in a bad mood. Take it or leave it."

Nash flipped the cash onto the counter and grabbed the key. As he headed to the door, the guy called out, "Room twelve. Enjoy your stay."

Nash nodded and escaped outside. He got back into his car and moved it down the row, parking it directly in front of his room. There were no other cars in the lot, except for an abandoned one. No big surprise there. Two hundred dollars? Ridiculous!

Grabbing the backpack he'd retrieved from the dumpster before leaving Whynot, he let himself into his room. It smelled a bit like mold. The bed was unmade, and several towels lined the floor as if making a path from the bathroom to the bed. It was a good idea, but obviously the room hadn't been cleaned. He wasn't about to request that it be cleaned – or to request a new room. It was too risky. And another run-in with the motel maniac wasn't the first thing on his list of things to do. He did value his life, after all!

Tossing his bag on the bed, he unzipped it and reached inside for the wine. As he pulled it out, though, memories of the accident pounced like vivid predators. He threw the bottle into the trash. Wanting a distraction, he wandered over to the pillow that still showed signs of a head lying upon it. On impulse, he picked it up and brought it to his nose. It smelled a little like bleach and something else. He sniffed it again. His stomach flipped. It smelled like Mira. He rang the office.

"Did you happen to have a young woman staying in this room last night...dark hair, pretty?"

There was a short pause on the other end of the line. "We don't give out information like that."

So it was a possibility at least, Nash thought as he put the pillow back into place. "I understand." He hung up the phone and, after changing into his sweats, laid down in the spot Mira could've lain. Staring up at the water-stained ceiling, he let his memories of her wash over him. He remembered the time they had first kissed, and the day they had shared the dreams of their hearts. He ached for her as much now as he had then, – strike this! in a different way but it was no less powerful. But it was like a thirst that would never be quenched.

Nash closed his eyes. The memories brought him no comfort, only terrorized him, judged him, accused him, and sentenced him to a lifetime of an anguished soul, one that was haunted by loss of love and a searing guilt at the destruction of Percy and his family's lives. Pressing his hands against his head, he growled out, but there was no relief.

Taking a deep breath, he sat up. He grabbed the remote and flipped on the TV, only to see his face pasted on the screen. A reward was being offered for any information that would lead to his arrest. Porsche must have realized he'd taken off. Fear clawed its way to the surface, intermingling with the loathing he had for himself. He got up and went to the desk. He had to write...to compose...to relieve some of the burden that was blocking the air to his lungs. He ground the tip of the pen against the tiny pad of paper. Nothing came to mind...not a word...only an unbearable feeling. His head dropped and tears came, but they offered no relief and only managed to wash away the last vestiges of his hope that this could somehow be resolved. He had to end this misery!

His mind scrambled for answers. The first thing he needed to do was leave behind the truth. He'd write to Percy, tell him how sorry he was. He'd write to the authorities, and tell them what he'd done to prevent Chad from paying for his mistake. And…he'd write to Mira and tell her he truly did love her.

As he began to write his first letter, though, he realized the pen didn't work. He tossed it across the room. Desperate for another, he whipped open the drawer. Rummaging through it, all he found was an old tootsie roll wrapper and a fresh copy of the Enchiridion of Emmanuel. He stared at it a moment through his tears.

"Open it." Nash looked around. No one was in his room, yet he swore someone had said the words.

"Open it." The words came again, more insistent this time.

Nash opened the book, recognizing the copyright mark inside the cover. It was an Enchiridion that had been copied and donated by Hayes' and Mel's company. Wiping the wetness from his cheeks, his shaking fingers turned the page. A quote was written in red ink. It said, "The burden of sin, erased by the blessedness of forgiveness, brings the greatest joy." He could sure use some forgiveness!

On the adjacent page was another quote. "The Enchiridion of Emmanuel – the Bible. Many have opposed it. Many have tried to disprove it. Many have tried again and again to erase its existence from the world. Yet it lives on." Nash thought of Mira, how they'd worked so hard to recover it. Oh, how he wished he could turn back time! He swallowed past the lump in his throat as he continued to read. "Those who believe in its truths have staked their lives on its words…words that infuriate the unbelievers and the power wielders…words that encourage and motivate the less fortunate and the broken to overcome obstacles by faith while God's glory shines brightly through them." Well, he definitely qualified as broken! Nash gripped the book, staring at its numerous pages. Could he truly believe the words written inside were inspired by God? His eyes shifted to the following line. "Why does this book invoke so much passion?" Yeah. Why would it, if it was merely a book? He read on.

The Bible contains the mind of God, the state of man, the way of salvation, the doom of sinners, and the happiness of believers. Its doctrines are holy, its precepts are binding, its histories are true, and its decisions are immutable.

Read it to be wise, believe it to be safe, and practice it to be holy. It contains light to direct you, food to support you, and comfort to cheer you.

It is the traveler's map, the pilgrim's staff, the pilot's compass, the soldier's sword, and the Christian's charter. Here too, Heaven is opened and the gates of Hell disclosed.

Christ is its grand subject, our good its design, and the glory of God its end. It should fill the memory, rule the heart and guide the feet. Read it slowly, frequently and prayerfully. It is a mine of wealth, a paradise of glory, and a river of pleasure.

It is given to you in life, will be opened at the judgment, and will be remembered forever. It involves the highest responsibility, rewards the greatest labor, and will condemn all who trifle with its sacred contents.

Wow! Hope and wonder began to simmer inside him. He had to take a closer look. A slip of paper marked a page, so he turned to it. Psalm 32. He began to read. What did he have to lose?

Chapter 75

Mira sat beside the table in her childhood home, only it didn't look quite like her house, even though it had the exact same view. She sipped the drink she held in her hand as she watched Nash enter the gate that would take him to her front door. He was so handsome – and seemed so in tune to her melody that he looked up. When their eyes met, he smiled, and the warmth of it went straight to her heart. He was coming back to her, where he belonged. He tore his gaze away and jogged toward her front door. Seconds later, the doorbell rang. She thought she might keep him waiting a little while, to build the anticipation, but *she* couldn't wait. She rushed to the door and flung it open. His outstretched arms begged her presence and she immediately melted into them. "I knew it was a lie…a nightmare. You're mine…always have been, always will be," he said. Her heart cried yes, but still, she had a bit of trouble speaking it out. Finally, she managed. "I haven't been with anyone. There's no baby – nothing to stop us from being together." His hand brushed down her hair and her back. "I love you Mira."

Mira rolled over, her movement dislodging her covers, the cold night air of her tent immediately bringing her out of her dream-filled haze. She tugged the quilt back up under her chin, relishing the after effects of the dream she'd just had. Love was right around the corner. She could feel it. And after connecting with her spirit guide – and after the telling dream she'd just had – she knew that her next step would be one leading to love and fulfillment. The dream also told her that her pregnancy wasn't part of the plan. She needed to call on Jadis. Figuring a visit to her in the middle of the night would surely help her to keep her secret, Mira jumped out of bed.

Not really knowing how it all worked, she donned black leggings, a black sweater, and her favorite old comfortable boots, then put the rest of her things into her suitcase – except for Nadya, which she left sitting on the chair. Even if the doll had something to do with her dream, she still thought the thing was creepy. With one last survey of the tent, verifying she had everything she needed, Mira escaped outside.

Instead of taking the path in front of the row of tents, she snuck behind them. As she approached the endmost tent, her foot caught on one of the ropes that tied the tent to a stake in the ground. She tumbled forward, landing face first on the prickly grass. For a moment, she laid there, listening for the laughter of someone that might have seen her fall. But all was silent, so she rolled up onto her butt. Thankful that she hadn't blown her cover, she picked up her suitcase and got to her feet. More careful this time, she made her way back to her car.

It didn't take long for her to drive into town. Pillar was still hopping, but thankfully, the partiers tonight didn't extend past the dance studio. She'd be able to visit Jadis undetected.

As Mira turned into the alleyway toward Jadis' place, a huge billboard came into view. It pictured an ultrasound image of a baby in utero. Beneath it, it said, "At the moment of conception, an explosion of creation occurs, and a baby's DNA is fully determined. At 3 weeks and 1 day after fertilization, the baby's heart begins beating." Her grip grew tighter on the wheel and her palms began to sweat as she drove on.

A half a block later, another sign came into view. This one quoted Psalm 129:13-16. "For you created my inmost being; you knit me together in my mother's womb. I praise you because I am fearfully and wonderfully made; your works are wonderful, I know that full well. My frame was not hidden from you when I was made in the secret place, when I was woven together in the depths of the earth. Your eyes saw my unformed body; all the days ordained for me were written in your book before one of them came to be."

"Stop it, Mira! A fetus is merely tissue, not formed with a design in mind. This is not a big deal! You are doing what's best for everyone."

Her argument sounded flat to her own ears, but she didn't want to think about it anymore. Shutting out the arguments in her head, she decided parking beside Nash' music store would be the way to go, because if anyone *did* come around, they wouldn't give Hayes' car being there a second thought. Feeling calmer, she flipped off her lights and continued down the final stretch. As she approached her destination, Mira gasped.

Shifting into park, she turned off the car and got out. The gravel crunched loudly under her boots as she slowly made her way to Nash's Music Store. His store's back door was now a large hole in the wall, charred black and smelling of strong smoke. She pressed her hand against the edge of it and took one step into the dark space. Rubble, half-burned instruments, and lights hanging by a web of wires seemed to be the only things that remained. Mira felt sick inside. Who had done this? Even if it was an accident, it was heartbreaking. Nash had worked so hard to build his business. Straightening her shoulders, she told herself that it was only a building, that it didn't signify anything about hers and Nash's relationship.

"Everything is still going to be okay," she said. Turning back around, she glanced at Jadis' back steps, steps she had yet to climb - the ones that would seal her decision. A coldness swept over her, like she'd been locked in a freezer. The sharpness of the frigid air pricked her skin and seeped through her pores. She forced herself to step outside, wanting to escape the feeling. As she walked toward Jadis', she spotted someone coming down her steps. Fighting back a squeal, she scrambled back into the music store and out of sight. She huddled against the crumbling wall, watching, listening, waiting. Maybe she should come back later. She took a hesitant step toward the door, but paused when a bright light like a watery illuminated cloud spilled out of the glowing metallic disk lying on Nash's floor. "Go to Jadis before it is too late," a voice said. "Hurry, before they stop you."

Mira froze. The cloud darkened to a color blacker than the darkness that surrounded her. "Do it!" The voice was sharp instead of sweetly coaxing now.

Still, she couldn't move, and the terrorized scream in her throat came out as a pitiful mewling.

The cloud amassed into swirling gauzy scarves, each shrieking in their dissonant tones. "Go. Do it now!"

Mira grabbed her ears as they chanted, but she couldn't look away. They twisted together faster and faster until they blended into something that looked like a face - her spirit guide! But her angelic Anju's pleasant appearance soon melted into hideousness, eyes gleaming with possessive cruelty. Horror imprisoned Mira, shackling her feet to the floor as she watched the once lithe figure of her spirit guide began to molt and leave behind the image of Burt Guyver with his predatory sneer. His craggy skin was now marked with vile deeds that radiated like neon prizes. Desperate to escape, Mira's frantic mind howled, "Someone help me!" Immediately, her feet released, as did her voice. She screeched at the top of her lungs and ran for the door. As she burst through it, she heard a loud crack and the sound of evil dissonant laughter right before a beam struck her on the head.

Chapter 76

As Nash approached Whynot's city limits, his palms began to sweat. He wiped at his dry, gravelly eyes. He'd spent hours last night reading the book Hayes had given him - Cold Case Christianity. It had helped to reassure his logical mind so his reading of the Enchiridion of Emmanuel could connect to his heart. He'd also spent several hours praying. Although he was quite sure he hadn't done it correctly, and that his pathetic attempt to reach out to God was laughable, something had changed…inside him. He didn't know how or why exactly, but as morning approached, Nash knew in his heart he needed to turn himself in. He needed to tell the truth, no matter the consequences. His first stop was the hospital.

Nash pulled into the parking lot. He'd decided to keep his identity hidden until he could talk to Percy and beg his forgiveness. Still dressed in his suit and bowler hat, he strode into the hospital. His stomach curled with anxiety, his heart beat at twice its normal speed. What if Percy wouldn't forgive him? It was a possibility he had to deal with. Nash took the stairs to the third floor, to the intensive care section. He continued on through the doors without stopping, knowing that if he did, he might put it off, or talk himself out of, what he needed to do. As he approached Percy's room, the door was closed. Instead of knocking, he quietly opened it and peeked inside. Percy's wife was asleep in the chair, their son also asleep, tucked in her arms. Percy was still hooked up to all his machines, his heart a strong rhythmic beep of constancy in the background.

Nash took a deep breath and stepped inside. No one woke up, so he went to the side opposite of Percy's wife and son. Moving the rolling table packed with flowers and balloons, Nash knelt down on the floor beside the bed. The smell of antiseptic overpowered the smell of flowers. The tile beneath his knees was cold and hard. None of that mattered – only this family did, right here, right now. Nash looked upward and whispered, "Help me say the right thing Lord." Nash didn't know if it would help, if God was even listening, but he still felt the driving need to forge ahead. Grasping Percy's warm, calloused hand, Nash rasped, "Percy. I don't know if you can hear me or not. I hope so, pray so. You don't know m-me." Nash tried to take a deep breath but it felt like a car was being lowered onto his chest. Hot tears formed in his burning eyes. "I am the one who…" his voice had risen three pitches higher, "the one who…" Tears began to flow freely now, but he didn't wipe them away. "I'm the one who was driving the car that hit you." He squeezed Percy's limp hand. "I wish I could take your place, undo what I've done, but I can't and I am so very, very sorry." Nash could feel his hand trembling as it held onto the man he'd hurt so badly. "I know that's meaningless, that it doesn't change what you're going through, but I want…" Nash frowned, the pain of it almost too much to endure. "I want to beg your forgiveness…and the forgiveness of your family." Nash leaned his forehead against Percy's hand. "God forgive me," Nash cried out.

"I forgive you."

Nash heard the words, but didn't know where they had come from. Maybe he was dreaming. He looked up at Percy. His eyes were open, filled with his own tears.

"I forgive you," he rasped.

The extreme pressure in Nash's chest eased just a little. "Really?"

He nodded. As slight as the motion was, Nash had seen it. The overwhelming rush of gratitude brought a gush of warmth and a wealth of tears. "Thank you. Thank you!" he cried between his sobs. That's when he noticed Percy's wife and son. His wife brushed Percy's hair from his forehead as his son climbed up beside him on the hospital bed.

Nash stood up slowly. "I don't deserve forgiveness from you or your son – or from any of you, but I am truly sorry." He reached into his pocket and took out the bank card with his account information on it. "I've already called them and transferred it to an account set up in your family's name." Thankfully, the teller had been a fan of his, and after explaining what he wanted to do, she'd willingly overridden the freeze on his account. As he handed the card to the tearful woman, she opened her mouth to speak. Nash interrupted. "Do whatever you want with the money. It's yours." He took his hat off, and twirling it nervously in his hands, he added, "My next stop is the police station, so I'll just say goodbye now because there's really nothing else to say." Nash turned to walk out. Just as he stepped out into the hallway, he heard Percy's wife say, "We all need forgiveness." And then he heard a tiny laugh through her tears. "Thank you for bringing my husband back to us Lord. He's awake, Charlie. He's awake!"

Percy had just woken up for the first time? Nash hadn't known. Filled with a sense of awe and thankfulness he couldn't explain, he hurried out of the hospital. As he jogged toward his car, an ambulance raced toward the emergency room doors. Even though it was a different city, different *everything*, Nash remembered when Mira had rescued him from the hospital where his next stop would've been the Stint – or even worse, Enab. But she wouldn't be rescuing him now.

Nash got into his car and drove out of the parking lot. He took his time, absorbing all that was coming to life in Whynot at the dawning of a new day. It could quite possibly be the last daylight he'd see for a long time, but he could handle it. A surge of anxiety swelled in his chest as he remembered how close he'd come last night to ending it all. Oh, the gift of a non-working pen! Even though he felt freer than he had in a very long time, he still had a nagging fear. He was afraid of what he'd have to endure, terrified to lose his hard won freedom. But he was still resolute in his decision.

Nash pulled into the fifteen-minute parking area in front of the police station. He paused for a moment to watch the woman who would be the first to hear his confession. She looked mean, if her constant scowl was any indication. "Help me do this Lord," he said. Even though it felt weird saying it, he'd made a commitment to trust God last night, and praying was part of the deal. He got out of the car and headed into the station. "Hi," he said, resting his arms on the counter that stood between him and the clerk.

"How can I help…" her eyes widened when she noticed who he was, "you?"

He smiled, though it wobbled as he spoke. "I'm here to turn myself in."

She looked over at Detective Ricky Richards, who headed toward them alongside another detective. "Another murder in Pillar, Marge…the girl's name is Anju and she's from this area," the local detective said. "Her killer left a painted…" Both detectives noticed Nash at the same time and stopped short.

"I'm here to turn myself in for the accident I caused," Nash said.

Detective Ricky looked at his associate, hiding a small grin.

"Unbelievable!" The local detective slapped the folder he held onto one of the desks. Sitting down sideways on the edge of it, he growled, "Unfortunately, the victim called a few moments ago and said he isn't pressing charges."

Nash wanted to believe it, but it was unbelievable. "Could you repeat that?"

Marge butted in. "What about the city? Can't we press charges?" The accusatory squint of her puffy eyes made her look mean enough that Nash wouldn't want to even ride an elevator with her.

"Can't do it," the detective growled. "Boss already said it would be bad publicity – especially because the victim is already making headlines with his story." He folded his arms across his chest. "Pisses me off."

Detective Ricky's smile had blossomed into a wide one, which lifted the hope in Nash's heart. "So Percy really dropped charges? I am free to go? I'm really free?"

"You are," the local detective snarled. "But don't think I won't be looking for something to charge you with, jerk."

Nash didn't care that he'd been threatened or called names. He was free. Praise the Lord! Grinning, he plopped his hat back on his head and skipped outside. The air smelled so fresh, so wonderful. The unexpectedness of the tremendous gift Percy had given him made him pause. Now what? He'd planned on being locked up for years.

Detective Ricky came through the station's door and walked toward Nash. Shifting his tan trench coat over his other arm, Ricky asked, "Got a minute?"

Nash smiled. "I've got more than a minute, thanks to Percy."

The detective looked at him. "I'm glad."

Nash wondered why but didn't care enough to ask. "Thanks. Me too."

"I'm in a bit of a bind, Nash," all hint of his smile gone.

"How so?"

"You heard detective big mouth talking about our newest case, right?"

"Another murder in Pillar...I can't believe it!" Nash's elation at being free was suddenly dampened by the news. At least Mira was safe in Whynot.

"I know you'd worked on Kya's case, and I know you used to be a Reformer. Would you consider coming back to Pillar to assist me on this case? I'm at my wit's end." He glanced at Nash, his expression pleading. "I know your music career is more lucrative and the compensation from this case would be small, but I could really use your help."

Any money would be good because Nash had just given away everything in his account and he'd need to use his savings to fight his contract with Porsche. Even so, he didn't know if he wanted to go back to being a Reformer, nor did he want to leave Percy and his family until he knew he was well on his way to rehabilitation.

"I wasn't planning on going back to Pillar," he said.

"I was afraid you'd say that." Detective Ricky, who looked haggard and pale today, despite his earlier smiles, pulled out picture and handed it to Nash. "Recognize this girl?"

Nash glanced at the picture and felt his heart swing into erratic action. "It's Mira Kinneson. Why?"

"How well do you know her?"

"Very well. What's going on detective?"

"Mira was the last person to talk to Anju."

Nash's stomach dropped to his toes. "I thought Anju was killed in Pillar."

"She was…at a convention."

The sinking feeling worsened. "You think Mira's involved?"

He met Nash's wide-eyed gaze. "No. Actually," he pinched the bridge of his nose, "Hayes sent me here, hoping these buffoons had managed to track you down, so I could, uh, borrow you for a bit to, ah…"

Ricky looked quite uncomfortable. "Spit it out."

"We want to question Mira as soon as she wakes up, but her doctor says that when and if she comes out of the coma, the police aren't allowed to talk to her until she's well. I don't have that kind of time." He turned to Nash with pleading eyes. "If you can be a friend and sort of official at the same time, maybe we can track down this killer and get the son-of-a-bitch."

"She's in a coma? What happened to her?"

"Are you in on the case then?"

"Yes," Nash said.

The detective clapped him on the back. "I'll fill you in on the details on the way to Pillar."

Chapter 77

She felt trapped. Where was she? What had happened? Mira struggled to escape her confines, but she couldn't move her arms or legs – not even her mouth. And she couldn't open her eyes! She felt the warmth of a tear in the corner of her eye. It hovered there, waiting for something to set it free.

"When will she come out of the coma?" Mira heard the tremble in her mom's voice as she asked the question.

"We don't know if she will. Brain injuries are complicated," the man who had been discussing her case said.

"Will she have brain damage?" Mira's dad asked softly.

"We can't be certain about that either." She heard a sound like papers shifting from one hand to the other. "But we have a brain scan scheduled for later today."

They were talking in very soft, low tones from a far off place, but Mira's hearing was exceptional. She could hear someone chewing gum, and even though music came through a speaker off to her left, she could still hear someone approach. It was a nurse, the one that smelled like lilies, antiseptic, and curry.

"We're going to take your blood pressure again now," the nurse with a calm voice said. Mira felt the tourniquet tighten on her arm. "Your pressure is good, sweetie."

Mira felt a pat on her arm and tried to say thank you, but she couldn't get the words out.

Someone sat down on the bed beside her and reached for her hand. "We shouldn't have moved to Enab," Mira's mom said, her voice wavering. "None of this would've happened." She sniffed.

None of what?

"You're going to be okay, honey." Her dad's voice sounded so strong, so resolute, she almost believed him. "Do you remember when we were sent to the Stint?"

She searched through the doors of her mind, grasping onto a vague recollection of a chair that had imprisoned her – and an Amender Bug that had tried to erase her memories. Neither had succeeded. She felt her muscles twitch.

"I think she can hear us," her mom said, clutching her hand more tightly.

"You were always different, Mira...a fighter, and you never gave up. You aren't giving up now, either," her dad said.

She didn't want to give up, but she was so tired. Letting her mind relax, the sounds of the room began to fade away. Her eyes opened to something much different than her parents in a hospital room. *Wormwood's Water*. Which one was real? She didn't know, but she liked being in the second reality better than the first. Standing beside Wormwood's Water, she lifted her hand and smiled. "I can move!" And she could speak, too!

"Then why don't you move on in and join me?"

Mira blinked. The dark rippling water revealed Tanger, who stood facing her, a full moon behind him. He was so handsome and his welcoming smile and outstretched hand enticed her. "I'm not sure, Tanger," she said, fearing the blackness of the water that separated them.

"You have nothing to fear and everything to gain. I can fulfill your every longing. Come to me my love."

His allure pulled at her heart. She stepped into the water. It was cold and had a weird smell, but she trudged ahead. With each step, though, the brightness of the sky grew dimmer. She couldn't see Tanger very well at all.

"Hurry, before they come to get you," he said.

She turned around to see who "they" were. All she could see was a bright light holding something that looked like a sword. She looked back at Tanger.

"Come to me. You're mine for good this time," he said.

That he wanted her made her feel loved and treasured. As she forged ahead, the water began to thicken. "Tanger?"

Tanger's image suddenly dulled, like a dark cloud had formed between them. "Keep moving, Mira. Hurry!"

She took another step, only to have something swoop by her head. She looked up to where several formless creatures wore flexible screens on their backs, each displaying a picture. "This is your future," one said. She glimpsed scenes of her and Tanger kissing, of her with a child, of her strolling through an art studio with people lined up to buy her work.

"Yes!" She reached for the images, yet every time her fingers brushed against them, they disappeared, leaving her desperate for just another glimpse. "Why can't I touch them?" she asked, glancing up at Tanger. Only Tanger had disappeared from her view.

"No!" She frowned, confused, and took a step back, and another. As she took a third step back, a flash of lightening shot down with a tremendous boom, illuminating the water that surrounded her. The formless creatures...the pictures...they were gone! A scream escaped her lips as she tried to flee the swirl of the vile looking demons that now filled the waters. But they slithered around her body, trying to latch onto her clothes while they chanted. "We will give you all these things. Come with us." She swatted at them as she lunged toward shore, but something had latched onto her back. She screamed, glancing over her shoulder at a shadowy hand – one that belonged to a demon. He clutched her like she was his prey. Tanger's painting...it wasn't what she'd thought! Had he known? Had it been a warning? The cold, sharp teeth of the creature sank into the flesh of her neck, sucking the life from her veins. His claws dug deeper into her shriveling skin. Mira cried out, grabbing at the creature to rip him off her.

"Hold on," came a voice from the shore. "God is stronger. Believe, Mira. Believe I can save you. I am your Savior."

Help...help had come. "Please save me!" Mira reached out toward the light hovering on the shore. The demon's death grip released, freeing her, leaving her gasping and incredulous. Wormwood's Water faded from her vision. She was back in the hospital with its rhythmic beeping and its soothing music. Her mom's lips pressed against her forehead while her dad whispered a prayer for her healing, heart, body, soul, and mind.

"She's settling down now," her mom said. "What happened to her? Why was she so agitated?"

"Sometimes patients get overstimulated with too much going on around them. Maybe you should leave her for a little while," the nurse said.

But Mira knew it wasn't that…and she didn't want them to leave, but unlike in the dream, here, she still couldn't speak. She felt a hand – her dad's hand, give hers a squeeze. "Everything is going to be okay," he whispered.

Mira didn't know if she could believe him.

Chapter 78

"So do you want to go over the latest evidence surrounding Anju's murder again?" Ricky asked Nash as they rolled into Pillar.

"No. The bits and pieces keep circling like vultures in my head so I can't even think straight," Nash said, looking out the window toward the towering Center of Operations. It seemed like a lifetime ago, and yet here he was again...trying to save Mira.

"Want to talk about something else?"

Nash sighed. Pinching the bridge of his nose, he said, "Thanks for helping with the paperwork at the station."

"No problem. I wanted you to have time to visit Percy and his family before we left." He tilted his head toward Nash. "Sorry I had to rush you."

"I had enough time to return the car I'd borrowed, and to hire a lawyer to deal with Porsche. And Percy said he'd stay in touch, so it all worked out okay." Except for Mira being a prime suspect in what was being termed, *The Canvas Killer.*"

As they approached the block where the hospital stood, Nash's stomach twisted with the breakfast he'd eaten. Even though evidence pointed to her involvement, he kept picturing Mira lying dead in that alcove.

"Why do you think Mira was even at that event?" Nash thought, the question nagging him.

"The group is Satanic, manipulative...many people fall for it," Ricky said, pulling into a parking garage.

"I thought the group she'd joined is the Wiccana-Way."

"It is." Ricky drove through the rows, looking for a spot. "Anything opposing the one true God is on Satan's side."

"You believe that – the supernatural, I mean?" It all seemed imaginary, more like people playing super heroes and villains.

Ricky pulled into an opening on the third level. "A person can't work a job like mine without believing it." He shifted into park. "If you'd seen what I have…" he tugged at his neck tie as if it was too tight. "Yeah, Nash, there are definitely demons among us."

Nash didn't know if it was true or not, but because of Mira's involvement in something thought evil by the police force, he wasn't going to reject the idea. "I'll keep that in mind," Nash said, releasing his seatbelt.

"I'll wait here for a bit so no one can connect us together." Ricky reached into his wallet and pulled out a twenty. "Here's some cash for a taxi for later."

"Thanks." Nash stuffed it into his pocket.

"I know you care about her Nash, but keep in mind, she is linked to all three of the murder victims – Kya, Elroy, and now Anju."

"I won't forget." He opened the door.

"You have that list of questions, right?" Ricky added.

Nash patted his chest. "In my pocket."

"I'm heading over to talk to forensics shortly to see if they came up with anything more. Keep me posted, okay?"

"I will," Nash said, getting out of the car.

"Thanks Nash," Ricky said, tilting his head to look at him through the passenger door. "Good luck in there."

Nash nodded, then quickly strode past the rows of parked cars to the stairway, which he took to ground level. Once outside, he hurried to the hospital's front doors and slipped inside. He waved at the valet before heading down the long stretch of hallway that had floor to ceiling glass on each side and allowed the sunshine to brighten the space. At the end of it, he turned right and passed the lobby that had been converted from its rundown and utilitarian state to one of warmth and creativity. He barely spared the bold artwork covered walls a glance as he marched to the neurological intensive care unit. A nurse with long dark hair weaved with grey sat beside a desk, checking her computer.

"I'm here to see Mira Kinneson."

"Are you family?" she said, looking up.

He nodded.

She studied him for a moment, at the flowering herbs Ricky had insisted he bring.

"Mira and I aren't family exactly." He swallowed hard. "We're together."

Her wary look transformed into a smile of recognition. "I thought that was you, Nash Montgomery." Her smile slipped a little. "I'd heard you two broke up before you went on tour."

"We reconnected," he said, trying to smile.

"That's good to hear. I always liked you two as a couple." Eyes lighting up, she said, "I bet she'll wake up now that you're here."

"I hope so."

She looked around to the monitoring area, then leaned forward. "I'm really sorry that she lost the baby," she whispered.

He tried not to let his shock show. Looking down at the plant, he said, "Yeah. Me too. How's she doing today?"

"She's about the same."

"Can I see her?"

"Actually, she's down in diagnostic right now, getting a brain scan. She should be back in a half hour or so."

"Okay. I'll just put this in her room and wait, then."

She pointed to a room located right across from where he stood.

"Thanks," he said. He went to the door, and after knocking on the doorframe, stepped inside. The bed was empty, the table beside it sporting two vases of flowers. He checked the cards held by the plastic prongs poking from their bright plumes. One bouquet was from Mira's mom and dad, the other, from Hayes and Mel. Nash sighed, glad that neither were from Tanger. He was a complication he didn't want to deal with right now. Nash put his herbs next to the flowers, and after a glance at the clock, decided to take a walk.

Nash stepped back into the hallway and once again, approached the nurse. "Hey, could you point me to the cafeteria?"

She handed him a map instead. "Since this hospital has had so many additions, it can get kind of confusing," she explained.

"Thanks." He took the map and studied it as he walked. The cafeteria was on the main floor, right below where he stood, but because of the way the hospital was constructed, he would have to go through the west wing, take that elevator to the second floor, wind back and take another set of elevators to the main floor. Well, he had time to waste before Mira returned from her testing.

Nash headed toward the west wing. As he turned the corner, he discovered a long row of windows that gave him a view of the intensive care nursery. He stopped, mesmerized. One of the tiny babies under the bright lights of his transparent tomb flailed his arms, crying out with his piercing voice. He had patches over his eyes. The wires protruding from the pads stuck to his chest connected him to a machine that, every time he moved, went into a beeping frenzy. As the nurse reached into his cage-like crib to soothe the lonely child, Nash wondered if music might help.

Drifting away from the heart-rending scene, Nash couldn't help but think about the baby Mira had lost. Even though it hadn't belonged to him, it pierced his heart. Wanting to put the dismal thoughts behind him, he took the elevator down to the second floor and wound back through the west wing. As he approached the set of elevator doors that would take him to the cafeteria, he saw a sign for the diagnostic area. On a whim, he decided to check it out. Mira had to be close by.

Tension clenched every muscle as he moved quietly down the hall, listening and watching for any signs of her. Muffled voices mixed with the hum of machines through closed doors, until he came to the last one in the row. This door was slightly ajar.

"What I want you to do now, Mira, is imagine you are playing a tennis match if you want to answer yes. If you want to answer no, I want you to imagine that you're roaming the street alone," a woman said and after a few seconds, asked, "Is your name Mira?"

There was a long pause followed by the clicking of keys, then the woman asked a second question. "Is your name Isabelle?" There was another slight pause before she gasped. "Woah. This is unbelievable!"

The click of the keys accelerated as she mumbled, "Different neural patterns appear when the patient is asked certain questions. It is likely she hears and it appears as though she can communicate."

A chair scraped back. Nash chanced a peek inside the room. A single technician stood next to a curved opening that Mira laid beneath. "Did you grow up in Pillar, Mira Kinneson?" The tech glanced at the imaging screen and smiled. "Looks like that's a yes."

Nash checked the screen, how the neural signature map made a bright orange orb-like pattern.

"Did you help locate the Enchiridion of Emmanuel?" the technician asked.

The resulting brain pattern was the same.

"Was your father's name George?"

Mira's brain pattern changed and so did the color. The orange was now blue.

The woman patted Mira's leg then quickly typed in the results. "I'm going to get the radiologist to verify my findings. I'll be right back."

Just as the technician came out of the room, Nash slipped around the corner to stay out of sight. He listened to the woman's retreating footsteps. When all was silent, he dared a peek into the room. Mira was alone. Without time to waste, he snuck inside. Taking out the list of questions he'd gotten from Ricky, he asked the first one that was a yes/no question. "Were you with Anju two nights ago on the beach near Pillar?"

The pattern lit up. Her answer was yes.

"Did you see her murderer?"

A different pattern showed on the screen. "Mira, did you see her murderer?"

The pattern changed to one he recognized. Her answer was no.

"Did you have anything to do with the murder?"

Again, her answer was no.

Not that this was something they could use in court, but relief washed over him as he scanned the remaining questions. None of them could be answered with just a yes or no. Glancing at the clock and then the door, he went to Mira's side. Placing a hand on her bare shin, he felt tears gather in his eyes.

Even though he didn't want to ask it, he felt he needed to. "Do you love Tanger?" He glanced at the screen. *No.*

He managed a wobbly smile. "Do you know who I am?"

Yes.

"Do you know why I am here?"

No.

"Can you feel my hand on your leg?"

Yes.

He frowned, his heart aching. Running his hand along her leg, he whispered, "Are you afraid?"

Yes.

"You're a fighter, Mira, and you have a lot of people fighting for you. You're going to be fine."

Her brain pattern changed to one he couldn't decipher, just as Nash heard voices coming closer. "I have to go. I," he paused, not knowing quite what to say. "I love you Mira...always have and always will." He escaped out of the room only a spilt second before the technician and radiologist entered. As he walked away, he heard the technician say, "She's shaking." Nash heard the whir, and figured they had pulled her out of the tunnel. The woman's next words confirmed it. "She's crying."

With a knot in his throat, Nash escaped down the hall and stepped into the bathroom. Going into the only stall, he took several deep breaths, fighting his own tears. He felt so helpless! After a few moments, he sent Ricky a text.

Mira isn't the murderer and didn't see the murderer. That's all for now. I'll explain the details later. He hit send and rolled out of the bathroom, just in time to see the technician push Mira down the hall. They disappeared into the staff elevators.

Before he could follow, a slow-moving elderly lady crossed his path. Her hair was short and tightly curled, her lips ruby red against her pale wrinkled skin, her lobes hanging with the weight of her oversized pearl earrings…but her eyes oozed compassion and confidence as they looked up at him.

"Is there something I can help you with, son?" she asked.

He ran his hands through his thick hair. "I don't think there's anything anyone can do but wait."

She smiled. "Oh…there's always something."

She looked so entirely sure of herself, Nash found himself curious. "Oh yeah?"

"I was there, young man."

He frowned. "You were where?"

"Within sight of Mira when she was hit by the beam."

"What? How?" He shook his head.

"I woke up in the middle of the night with a pressing feeling that I needed to confront Jadis, my granddaughter who has caused our family a lot of heartache. I got dressed and drove over to her place. The front entrance to her apartment was locked, so I took the back way. On my way up the stairs, I saw movement in that burned down music store. For some reason, I felt I needed to check it out, so went back down the stairs. That's when I saw the beam crash down on that young lady." She pointed to the elevator they'd disappeared into. "She should've been dead, young man, but something – someone - was there protecting her."

"Who?"

She leaned in closer. "A presence deflected that beam. I can't explain it in any other way than that."

"I wish that presence could've protected her fully."

She shrugged. "Only God knows the reasons. Maybe in time we will know them as well."

"I guess, but that means we're back to waiting."

She grinned and pointed to a room with a sign over it. *Chapel.* "While waiting, when you're troubled, when you're hopeless and helpless…pray. Prayer changes things."

Her confidence was contagious, her witness of the scene inspiring hope that God was out there and working. Patting the woman's shoulder, he walked into the chapel with her.

Chapter 79

Mira heard music…Nash's voice blending with the soothing strum of his guitar.

Each time she heard it, it became more real, yet so did her fear. Would they all leave her again once they found out how stupid she'd been? Her baby was dead…Anju was dead, just like Kya…and Mira's life was still a meaningless mess, haunted by the evil she'd seen in the choices she'd made.

The song drifted over her thoughts, warming the edges of her anxious heart. *I can't do this,* her mind argued, begging her to succumb to the darkness she used to escape. *You can…because I'll be with you,* came a voice that sounded like the waves of an ocean. And as if she was surrounded by the wave itself, it dragged her toward the shore. She opened her eyes, blinking rapidly at the sudden brightness of the hospital room.

Nash's hand stopped mid-strum. "Mira?"

Tears ran down her cheeks at the sight of him. "Nash," she rasped, her throat raw.

Propping the guitar in the corner, he went to her side and sat down on the bed next to her. Tears filled his eyes as he grasped both of her hands and studied her face. "You look like you're really awake this time."

She tried to frown but it hurt. "This time?"

"You've been drifting in and out for several days. That you're talking now proves you've crossed the line to the living," he said with a wide grin. He stared at her and shook his head as if in disbelief. "This is the best day of my life," he said, then looked upward and whispered, "Thank you, Jesus."

Something twinged in her heart. "Where is…" she swallowed hard.

He held a cup with a straw to her lips and she took a drink of the cool delicious liquid.

"Everyone else went out for lunch," he said quietly. "I'd call them, but I'm greedy and want to spend some time alone with you before they swarm in." He smiled and wiped the tears from her cheeks, but let his own fall. "I've been waiting for this moment to come, and now that it's here, everything I'd planned on saying seems trivial."

She took a moment to just look at him. His hair was a mess, his eyes weary, his face scruffy, but he was so incredibly handsome and familiar that she ached for him to be closer. "I'm glad you're here," she said, the sound of her voice no louder than a breath of wind through trees.

"That makes two of us." He reached for her hand and squeezed. "Do you even know what happened to you? The accident? That you were in a coma?"

She nodded once, but the motion made her cringe. "I could hear everything," she croaked. "How long?"

"A week, but it seemed like an eternity." He brushed the bangs away from her eyes. "Does your head hurt? Does anything hurt?"

Everything hurt, including her heart. "My head," she said softly.

He reached for the nurse's call button, but Mira blurted out, "No. Not yet. I'm tired of being fuzzy headed."

He laughed at that. "Worse than a LifeChip, I'll bet."

"Much worse. So when can I get out of here?" She reached for the tubes attached to her arms.

"Woah there, oh impulsive one." Nash pressed his palm against her hand to stop her from yanking them out.

Her throat felt thick. "But you love me anyway, right? I heard you say it...or was it just because you thought I wouldn't survive?"

"You really *did* hear everything, didn't you?" He leaned over and kissed her cheek. "I meant it. But we have a lot of things to talk about."

"Like Tory? And your music tour?"

"Tory?" He looked confused.

"I got a picture in the mail while I was in Whynot. It was of you and Tory kissing." Her head began to throb as the events of the previous week began to unfold like very clear photographs in her mind.

He looked perplexed, but he said, "I'm not sure when that could've been taken, but Tory and I...we parted ways. And I'm working on getting out of my music contract."

A tiny bit more hope wheedled its way into her heart.

His dark brows knit together. "What about you...what about Tanger?"

She was suddenly too tired to think of how to explain it, let alone voice it, so she shook her head ever so slightly.

"I'll take that as he's out of the picture." He grasped her hands tightly in his and pulled them to his lips for a kiss.

She took a moment to study him. Focusing on his face seemed to help keep her eyes open and her mind alert. "What does this mean...for us?" She had to know.

"I wasn't going to get into any of this until you were well."

"I'm well enough," she said, pulling back her shoulders.

He stared at her, then glanced over his shoulder at the door. "I suppose our private time is limited, so..." He inhaled deeply through his nose. "I need to ask you some questions before I can answer yours." He looked deeply into her eyes.

Her heart began to gallop. "Okay."

"The first question has to do with the case I'm investigating. Anju's case."

The reminder of her murdered friend made her sick inside. She didn't want to go there – ever again. "What does that have to do with us?" she asked with a painful swallow.

"Maybe more than you realize." His look was one she'd seen back in his Reformer days. "How involved are you in the Wiccana-Way?"

The vivid images of demons in her dreams...or had those demons been reality?...sent terror to her limbs. "I'm done with their lies," she rasped, shuddering.

His intense stare relaxed. "I was hoping you'd say that." He squeezed her shoulder reassuringly. "We searched the music store where the old woman had found you. We were looking for evidence of foul play in case the murderer was after you, too, but the beam that hit you hadn't been tampered with. We *did* discover the contents of your suitcase strewn all over the floor. And we found several doll hairs on your clothing. Can you explain why that would be?"

"I'd left my suitcase in the car. The doll had been in my suitcase, but I'd left it in my tent at the convention." She tucked her hands beneath the sheets so he couldn't see them tremble. "You don't think I had anything to do with her murder, do you?"

"No. Your accident happened around a half hour before Anju's murder, if her autopsy report is accurate."

Tears welled in Mira's eyes. "I should've stayed with her!"

He studied her. "Why didn't you? Why did you go to the music store, Mira?"

Mira knew why…she'd chosen to abort her baby and had intended to hide there until the woman on Jadis' stairs had gone. But if she confessed her secret, what would he think of her? She couldn't bear to lose him now that she had a chance to put things back together. She'd lost her baby, a truth that made her feel sick, guilty, and empty, yet it left her with another option - Nash wouldn't have to know any of it.

"Mira?"

She licked her dry lips. "After talking to Anju, how her magic had only brought her misery, I decided to get away for a while." She took a few moments to catch her breath. She was suddenly very tired.

"What happened then?" Nash asked softly.

"I drove by your music store and decided to go check out the damage."

His stare seemed to go to her very soul. "Are you sure that's all there is to it?"

Did he know something more? No one else knew why she'd gone there. Nash *couldn't* know. "I'm sure. And I'm also sure that that part of my life is done." She recalled the demon-filled room and shivered.

Nash released her hands. Standing, he picked up a blanket folded in a tight square beside her feet. He opened it with a quick flick and laid it across her body. After tucking it over her shoulders, he slipped his hands into his pockets. Even with the additional blanket, Mira felt strangely cold.

"Now tell me the truth about that night, Mira."

Chapter 80

"It *is* the truth," she said.

He didn't believe her. "All of it?" he asked.

She glanced at him, then looked down toward her toes. "When I'd driven into town, I'd been thinking a lot about you. That's why I went to your store. And when I got there, I was shocked to see what happened. It hit me really hard, Nash."

His hands curled in his pockets, his heart sinking with each of her lies. "Yeah. That hit me really hard, too."

"Did you know the blackened shell reminded me that the same had happened to all our dreams? A store can be rebuilt. Can our dreams be?"

Anger flared, but he tamped it down. After all, her mind might not be all that clear after the trauma she 'd been through. He'd give her one more chance. "That will depend on you," he said. "Do you trust me Mira?"

"Yeah. I do."

"Then tell me, is there another reason why you were in the neighborhood?"

She paused for a moment. Inside, Nash begged her to answer truthfully.

Finally, she said, "No…that was the only reason."

His heart felt like it had been smacked by resuscitation paddles – the sharp jolt followed by a painful beat. "What about the baby you had planned to abort?"

Her mouth dropped open and her eyes filled with tears. "I…I…"

He raised a hand to stop her excuses. "Relationships need to be based on truth. And no matter how much I love you, without honesty, we have nothing."

"I'm sorry, Nash," she squeaked out between sobs. "Please give me another chance!"

He would *not* feel sorry for her, nor could he bear to be around her right now. "I forgive you," he said softly through tears of his own. "But I cannot trust you." He grabbed his guitar, holding it by the neck. "Good-bye Mira."

Nash had had so much hope for them, for starting over. But she was not the same person he'd come to love. The realization crushed him and he needed air. As he escaped the room, he ran right into Houser, who had a package tucked underneath his arm.

"Nash...how's the patient doing?" Houser asked.

"She's awake now," Nash said as evenly as he could.

"Talking?"

He nodded.

"Good. How's she seem?" Houser asked.

Nash snorted and shook his head. "See for yourself," he said, and hurried to the elevator doors that would get him to the fresh air he needed.

Chapter 81

Mira carefully yanked the IV out of her hand, which prompted an annoying beep — one she didn't want the nurses to hear. She hit the machine's silence button, then pressed stop for several seconds. The machine turned off. Good. Throwing off the blankets, she stood shakily on her feet. For a moment, she closed her eyes to let the wooziness pass. When she opened them, Houser was there, standing right in front of her.

"Looks like the patient is ready to fly the coop," he said with a smile.

She looked into his compassionate eyes and started to cry. "I don't know what to do anymore. Help me Houser," she wailed, slumping against him.

He dumped his package on the bed and took her arm. The firmness of his grip stabilized her, helping to keep her on her feet. "I take it you didn't find your answers at the event."

"No," she rasped.

"Care to explain?"

She didn't want to upset him, but she didn't have the energy to get into details. "No."

"Doesn't work for everyone," he said with a shrug. "So what happened with you and Nash?"

A sob escaped her lips as she tried to eke out the words. "He hates me. *I* hate me."

He patted her shoulder awkwardly. "Anything I can do?"

Nash would surely tell her parents and her friends what she'd intended to do, what she'd been involved in. They'd be appalled, and she couldn't bear to see the disappointment in their eyes. She was a failure in every sense. "You can get me out of here."

Houser looked at the door and then at her, his brows raised. "Are you serious?"

Her heart hammered, her body quivered, and her throat ached. So much pain! She couldn't stand it! "I don't know what else to do!"

With a gentle motion, he sat her down. "Do you know how much time we have before the others return?"

"I don't know," she sniffed. "I'd guess not much."

He stared at her a moment, then grabbed the package he'd brought. Going to the wardrobe, he pulled out her backpack and stuffed the package inside it. Snagging a zipper sweatshirt, a pair of Capri leggings, and her shoes, he knelt in front of her. He worked her feet into the Capri's leg openings, then slipped the shoes on her feet. Knees crackling when he stood, he gripped her elbow and pulled. She stood, wobbly, in front of him He yanked the leggings up to her waist, pausing only a moment before reaching around her to untie the back of her gown. She gasped as she scrambled to keep the gown in place.

"We have to hurry," he whispered, and with one hard tug, he flung the gown to the floor and kicked it beneath the bed. As he quickly slipped the jacket sleeves onto her arms, he explained. "Your hospital gown would give us away."

She calmed a little, saying nothing as Houser zipped up her sweatshirt. "I wish we had a cap," he said.

"There's one," Mira said, her voice trembling as she pointed to the corner where Nash's coat and cap sat in a heap.

Houser snatched it up, but with a very gentle touch, placed it on her head. "There."

"I'm so tired, Houser," she squeaked.

He wiped her tears with the pads of his thumbs. "I'll take good care of you, Mira," he said, hooking his arm through hers.

Mira took a deep, shuddery breath, glad to have someone take care of her. "Thanks."

"My pleasure," he said, ushering her out the door, her bag in his other hand, his coat draped over it.

Mira was shaky, but Houser was a stable presence beside her as they walked toward the elevators. As they stood side by side, waiting for them to open, she whispered, "What if we see my parents?"

"We'll say I was taking you out for some much needed fresh air."

Feeling a bit better now that they had a story, Mira watched as the doors opened.

"It's empty," she breathed with relief.

"That it is," Houser said, leading her into it.

As the doors closed them inside, Mira asked, "Where are we going? And please tell me we aren't taking your bicycle. I don't have the energy for that, nor would it be a comfortable ride."

He grinned. "We're taking a cab to my house. I have a place set up that will bring you the peace and clarity you need. All you'll need to do is to commit to the process."

She couldn't imagine it, and didn't know what process he was talking about, but she was desperate and he seemed so sure he could help her. "Is it built out of plastic bottles too?"

"No." He smiled. "That's just the outside of my house. The inside is something altogether different."

She was intrigued, and for a moment, she forgot how miserable she was.

The elevator continued down to the ground floor. When the doors opened, Mira spotted Nash through the glass front doors. He got into his car and raced out of the parking lot. It seemed so final and left her feeling empty and wanting something she knew she could never have. She grasped her heart to keep it from shattering.

Houser didn't say anything, only ushered her outside to where a bright teal colored cab waited.

"Are you sure you want to come home with me? I could take you out for ice cream or a movie or something instead."

She studied him through her tears. He had been her friend, really, since he'd given her the doll that had fallen from his bike. "Ice cream and movies are a temporary fix. I need to do something drastic – something that will last forever."

"I can help you with that," he said, opening the cab's back door.

Mira ducked inside and plopped down onto the neon flecked seat. Houser got in beside her and put her bag on the floor behind the driver's seat. "666 Dollhouse Road," he said to the cab driver.

"Got it," the driver said, and shifted into drive.

Mira leaned back, resting her head against the seat. Her head was throbbing, and nausea kept a constant vigil inside her. "Did you happen to take any of my medications with you," she said, her eyes closed.

"No, but I have something at my house that will take care of your pain," Houser said reassuringly.

"Good."

The car was warm and comfortable, the ride lulling. She dozed for what seemed like only a few minutes when Houser woke her with a gentle nudge.

"We're here."

"Already?"

He smiled. "Sleeping makes the trip go a lot faster," he said, grabbing her bag. He got out, then helped her out, too.

"Your house *is* really made of plastic bottles," she said, surprised.

"Yep." Reaching into his back pocket for his wallet, Houser leaned down to look through the now open front passenger window. "How much do I owe you?" he asked the cab driver.

"Oh, you know what I'll want."

Houser paused, but then tucked his wallet back into his pocket.

What was that supposed to mean? Mira bent to get a look at the strange cab driver and glimpsed only the grey stubbly hair covering the back of his head.

"We'll see you again soon, dear," he said, and as he shifted into drive, he looked over at her and grinned. He looked so much like Burt Guyver, a ragged scream gushed from her lips.

Chapter 82

Nash stared at the cup of coffee he'd just poured. The aroma was pleasant enough, but being in this dining room where he and Mira had sat together many times was not. Today, he regretted renting her old place. Not that their recent conversation would quit circling in his mind anyway. He pressed the heels of his hands against his eyes. He'd given her every opportunity to come clean, and yet she'd lied. Why? To cover up who she really is perhaps?

His phone rang. Pulling it out of his pocket, he'd half expected the number to be Mira's. It wasn't.

"Hi Hayes. What's up?"

"I put you on speaker. Is Mira with you?" Hayes' worried voice spoke volumes.

Nash clutched the edge of the table. "No." He stood up. "What's going on?"

"When we got back from lunch, she was gone. Did something happen between you two?"

"She lied to me, Hayes. I called her on it and told her I couldn't be with someone dishonest."

"Why did you discuss something heavy with her when she's just waking up? For heaven's sake, Nash. What were you thinking?"

"I…it started with a question about the case. I wanted to know if the killer could be after her too…and the rest just came out." He'd been so happy to have her back, he didn't want to waste time second-guessing…he'd wanted to start over fresh, then, and there. But that had changed when she'd repeatedly lied.

Hayes took a deep breath. "So how was she, exactly, when you left? And when did you leave?"

He glanced at the clock. "I left about an hour ago…and she was…distraught." Over the phone line, Nash could hear a woman sobbing.

"Anyone see her leave?" Nash asked, walking to the window.

"This is detective Ricky. No one saw her and the security cameras were put on a loop."

Nash frowned. "It was planned?"

"Looks that way."

"Any chance she was so upset with me that she escaped through the window?" Nash asked.

Vaughn's low voice was accusatory. "It's sealed shut on the third floor, to prevent suicide."

Nash gut twisted as he stared out the window toward Pillar, but he wasn't really seeing it. Then he remembered Houser. "When I left, Houser had just stopped by to see her. Happen to talk to him?"

"Didn't know about that," Ricky said. "I'll give him a call."

"Wait." Nash pressed his fingers against his temple, replaying the scene in his head. "He had a package under his arm."

Nash could almost hear the detective thinking through the line. "Was it the size of a doll?" Ricky asked.

"Yeah." Nash's stomach sank to his toes, his heart shifting to overdrive. "How quickly can you get a warrant?"

"I don't think we have enough evidence," Ricky said.

"There were synthetic hairs found at all the crime scenes. They didn't match any of Elroy's wigs. The hair we'd found with Anju's body matched ones we found in Mira's suitcase. Mira told me they were from a doll that she'd left in her tent at the event. I studied the list of event attendees. Houser was on the list!" Nash blew out a frustrated breath and raced for the door. "I can't believe I didn't put it together before!"

"I'll call you when I get the warrant."

"Okay," Nash said, disconnecting the line. But he didn't have any intention of waiting for the warrant. "Dear Lord, please help me find her!"

Chapter 83

Houser's hand clamped over her mouth as the cab drove away. Mira struggled to escape, but he held her firmly against his solid body.

"Calm down, Mira. I have you, now." His grip loosened. "You're okay."

She sucked in a deep breath through her nose and tried to relax, but she couldn't take her eyes off the retreating cab.

"You are acting like you saw a ghost."

She nodded, thankful that it had disappeared from view.

"No worries, dear. He's gone." He twisted her around so that she could see his house. "Even though it's built out of plastic bottles, it's surprisingly secure. You'll be safe here...with me."

She nodded again.

Slowly, he released her entirely.

"I'm sorry," she said, her voice trembling with the aftershocks of seeing who she considered the devil in human skin. "I recognized the driver...and I don't like him...at all."

Houser smiled. "He's not my favorite cabby either, but he's out of our hair now."

"Yeah." She glanced at the surrounding area. The heavily treed area created a beautiful oasis without a neighbor in sight.

"Well...welcome to my home," he said, swinging his arm wide as if presenting her with a gift.

The house was a work of art. "It's beautiful."

"That surprises you?"

"Actually, yes."

"You'll find I'm full of surprises. Come on, I'll show you around." He strode toward his front doors, her backpack in his hand.

Mira hesitated.

"I'm not the bad guy, here. I rescued you, remember?" He leaned against his door jamb, tucking one of his hands into his front pocket.

When she didn't respond, he shook his head and muttered "women" under his breath. He pulled out his cell phone. "I'll call a cab. Where would you like to go?"

She didn't have anywhere to go – especially as a hospital escapee. And she definitely didn't want to go anywhere with the cabby that looked like Burt Guyver! "I'd like to see your place, Houser."

He looked at her intently. "You sure?"

"Yes." Limping toward him, she looked more closely at the entrance. She had to admit - the ingenious architecture intrigued her.

Mira followed him inside. The foyer had curved walls, making it almost seem circular. The walls were dark, each framing a life-sized painting. The floor was artwork in itself, the small cemented-in stones creating a picture of a raven encircled by a snake. Its backdrop was a moon. She didn't know the significance, but it was well done. "Did you do the floor?"

"I did. It took me almost a year."

"Persistent."

"Persistence…patience…it all works to create something powerful," he said, leaning back against one of the wall paintings as he let her look her fill.

"What about the wall paintings? Did you do those too?"

"Yes." He smiled. "I'm still adding details to them, so I consider them ongoing, new life-inspiring projects."

How the paintings were new life-inspiring, Mira couldn't figure out, but she was accustomed to the interpretive art-speak. Many artists liked to create deep, mysterious meanings to the things they produced, so she played along. "I can see the despair of the women in this painting, and in the one behind you," She squinted to get a closer look. The figures were a sepia tone with soft lines that seemed to fuse together, but she could see clearly the change in their demeanor. "They appear very…still."

"Tranquility at its finest," he said, offering her his arm. "How about I show you my second favorite room?"

"Is the entryway your favorite, then?"

"No. I'm saving my favorite for last." He led her through doors made of scraped walnut.

As she stepped into the room behind him, she gasped. "It's like paradise in here," she exclaimed. The room was the size of the band shell and concert lawn combined, the ceiling a glass dome that looked like it could open. In the center of the area was an island supporting a large tree with various tropical plants surrounding it. Water flowed around the island, creating a sensational replica of nature, complete with stones and sand. "I can't believe this isn't your favorite!"

He chuckled as he laid her bag down beside a stone-carved lounge chair. "Care to join me for a swim?"

Even though it was breathtakingly beautiful, her head was throbbing. "I think I'll just sit for a while, if that's okay."

"Suit yourself," he said. Houser strode over to an inlet, ditched his shoes and squished his feet into the sand. Closing his eyes, he seemed to relish the small pleasure. Mira couldn't help but be impressed by the complexity of Houser. He was quirky, but he was a compassionate listener. He was extremely talented, judging by the home he'd built for himself, and yet he seemed humble enough to enjoy life's small joys.

I wish I were like you, she thought, the tears gathering in her eyes as she recalled all her failures. But she could learn from him, right?

As she watched Houser peel off his shirt, a bird came out of nowhere, squawking. It swooped in, narrowly missing her head. She squealed and ducked as it circled over her. She felt something warm and wet land on the top of her head.

"Oooh. Houser…your darned bird pooped on me."

He laughed, now waist deep in the water.

"Is there a bathroom I can use to clean it up? I'd like to change anyway."

Glancing over his shoulder, he paused, then nodded.

"It's down the hall," he said, pointing to a doorway, "the third door on the right."

"Thanks." She grabbed her backpack and wandered across the room. Stepping through the doorway, she followed the wood-planked hall to the bathroom. Even though she had bird poop in her hair, and she was totally exhausted, she was curious about what the bathroom would look like. Carefully, she pushed the door open.

The bathroom was huge. To her right was a small alcove with a toilet, to her left, a sink on a floating vanity. One by two foot ecru tiles covered the back wall and hanging on it was an enormous circular mirror with a sculpted swirl falling from the top and ending midway. It looked a little like a snake, but on further inspection - and because of how it was positioned directly above a coffee cup shaped tub - it appeared to be more like a waft of steam. The images etched into each of the mirrors reflected sparkles of light from the chandelier, lending to the dramatic effect. The bathroom was a masterpiece!

Mira smiled, but it slipped when she noticed something protruding from behind a curtain across from the tub. Dropping her bag, she walked over to it. Peeling back the silken fabric, she gasped at the camera sitting there. Beside it laid a developed photo of her and Tanger standing together in Wormwood's Water, Tanger's face partially scratched away. He'd been there…Houser had been the one spying on them!

Mira clamped her mouth shut to keep from screaming. She had to get out.

"Think, Mira, think," she whispered, clutching her hands against her aching head. For a moment, she couldn't do anything but sway back and forth, locked in her terror, but then a warmth came over her, a breath of something that reminded her of the wave-like voice in her dream. "I am with you," it said. And then an idea popped into her head.

She turned on the faucet and, as she crept out of the room, she locked the bathroom door behind her. Taking the direction opposite of the pool, she chose the door that she thought most likely to provide a way outside. Yet as she snuck into the room, she froze. A foot-wide ribbon of water flowed down a brick wall that had an old-world style partial plaster overlay. Displayed on either side of the waterfall was a shrine of dolls, thirteen of them, all with an accompanying painting.

"No." She couldn't believe what she was seeing. A painted image of Kya, lying dead in her tub, hung beside one of the dolls. A canvas portraying Elroy, hanging by a sheet in his prison cell, was pinned next to another doll. A third doll was propped next to a portrait of Anju's broken body, distorted on the sharp rocks of Freetown. When Mira saw the doll at the end of the row, she gasped. Heart tripping, she stared at Nadya, the doll Houser had given her. The painting next to it was only a vague shape and no face, but she knew in her gut whose face it was meant to be.

"No...no," she said, backing toward the door. She swung around, ready to run...only Houser stood, wrapped in a towel, blocking her path.

"I see you've found my favorite room," Houser said.

Chapter 84

Nash mentally went through the list he'd made. Houser in the cop car near Cofa's Tree...Houser talking to Elroy in the Shanty Town Restaurant...Houser working for Porsche...Houser renting at Cofa's Tree...Houser entering the photo shop where Nash had seen Mira before he'd left for his tour.

It all added up and instinct told him Knack Photo was his best bet to get Houser's unlisted private address. He wasn't about to follow the book on this one, and he didn't trust anyone else, especially the people at Cofa's Tree.

He parked his bike along the street and hurried into the store. He tried to keep his mind on what he needed to do instead of what could be happening to Mira that very moment. Only images like the ones of Kya and Anju haunted him as he approached the counter.

"Hi, Leigh. I was wondering if you could help me out with something?" He shoved his shaking hands into his pockets and gave her the best smile he could muster.

She beamed back at him. "Anything, Nash Montgomery. I love your music!" She leaned forward onto her elbows, gazing at him like the love struck teenager she was.

"Could you find Houser's address for me?" he asked.

She blinked. "Why?"

His mind scrambled for a believable reason, one that he wouldn't have to waste time explaining. "I want to stop by and see his...work. He's brilliant, I hear." The images flashed in his thoughts again, puke surging into the back of his throat. He swallowed it back down.

"He *is* brilliant," she said with a nod, "and he's going to help me with my photography. Isn't that awesome?"

"Yeah. Awesome. Can you get his address for me, then?"

After one more glance at Nash, she went to the register. As she clicked keys on the computer, his hands began to sweat, his feet shifted back and forth. It was taking too long!

"You wouldn't happen to have one of your new CD's on you," she said, writing something down on a scrap of paper. "I'd love an autographed one." She walked over to him and handed him the address.

He folded it in his hand and kissed her cheek. "You're amazing." As he raced out the door, he called out, "I'll get you a signed copy tomorrow."

Nash hopped on his bike. As he started it up, he glanced at the address. The trip would take him fifteen minutes and she'd already been gone for almost two hours. His heart sank, and his limbs felt heavy as he shifted the bike into gear. He willed himself to pull back hard on the throttle, but he couldn't help but think he was already too late. What would he find when he got there? His imagination was only too happy to provide an answer – a horrifying one. Helpless terror twisted inside him, threatening to choke him, but he couldn't let Houser win!

"God…if you're really out there, really listening, I need a miracle. Help me not to be too late!"

Chapter 85

"It wasn't supposed to be today," Houser growled, wrapping his broad arms around Mira, effectively locking her arms against her sides. "I wanted more time with you!"

"We still have time," she pleaded, fear making her tone high and weakly pathetic. How could she have been so wrong about him?

"Unfortunately, *I* don't have time. Not anymore." His arms cinched her in tighter, his tongue licking along her earlobe.

She kicked and wriggled, trying to break free, but he was too strong. "Don't do this, Houser," she begged.

"You are a gift," he said. "I can't say no."

Mira felt sick, his wet body behind her making her skin crawl with dampness as she struggled against him. "LET ME GO," she spat, swinging her head back. It connected with his nose, making a loud crunch.

"Stop," he said, capturing her forehead and smashing her back against him, tucking her head beneath his chin. "You have to understand." His hand on her forehead loosened, but only a little. "I've transferred twelve unredeemable, lost and broken souls into the dolls to make their world and mine a better place. See how peaceful they are now?" He tilted her so that she was forced to look at the dolls. "I had to do it this way…you *had* to be number thirteen, my lucky number."

"But why? I want to live!" The despair in her voice was unmistakable, his imprisoning hold on her driving terror into her very core. "Let me go Houser," she pleaded. "I'll do anything."

He was quiet for a long moment. Then he whispered in her ear, "When I first saw you in front of Cofa's Tree, I knew you had to be mine, in body *and* in soul. In order for it to be perfect, though, I had to take care of three more people to prepare the perfect place for you. It took careful planning - getting Nash out of the picture and allowing that son-of-a-bitch Tanger to lay his hands on you. Do you know how hard it was to watch you two in the water?"

Mira remembered that night in Wormwood's Water. She'd thought it was the beginning of a whole bright new world for her, but the world she'd found was fraught with the hopeless despair Houser preyed upon. "Tanger isn't here. Neither is Nash," she said, tears in her eyes. "You don't have to..." she glanced at the dolls, her throat constricting painfully, "transfer my soul to have it. I'm right here...with you."

"But I know what happened in the abandoned Spectrum Music building that night. It opened your heart to the light. I need to transfer your soul before I lose you." His arms cinched up tighter, and pain shot through her head, arms and ribs. "I don't have a choice."

"You do have a choice," she squealed.

"You were delivered to me. You're mine," he said. He picked her up, and as he carried her across the room, his towel fell to the floor. But he didn't trip on it, nor did her flailing cause him to miss a step. He was determined, powerful. She screamed with all her might, but there was no one to hear. Her shrill cries turned to wretched shrieks when he shoved her into the six-inch deep pool of water that gathered the falling water beneath the shrine. She grabbed for the edge of the pool, but it was too slick. She scrambled to get a better hold, but Houser climbed in and flipped her onto her back. Sitting on her stomach, he shoved her hands beneath the water and propped his knees on them. The water hovered at the edges of her face as he leaned forward, his left forearm pressed against her neck. She couldn't scream, couldn't breathe. Then she saw the dagger in his lifted right hand and she screeched out a pathetic mewling sound. His gaze locked onto hers. There was lust in his eyes...and something else...more evil than the Benefactor, more evil than Burt Guyver...and more real. Houser's pupils had transformed into something unworldly - an elongated star surrounded by an almost transparent color.

She had to do something now or she was dead! She shoved her hips upward, then kneed him in the back. He only grunted and pressed harder on her neck, his face inching closer. She cried out, desperation driving her frenzied movements. "Jesus…help me!"

Houser froze, his breathing labored, his eyes narrowed. "But you're mine!" The words came out as if spoken through a reverberating speaker.

She thought back to the words her mom had sent with her before she'd moved into Cofa's Tree, the ones she'd read to her in the hospital. "I am *not* yours!" she managed to eke out through her crushed windpipe. "I am a child of God's." As she fought for air, Houser snarled, but he shifted back ever so slightly, enough to allow her to speak more easily. "I was created by God for a purpose," she said, seeing the words on the billboard like they were the loveliest thing she'd ever laid eyes on. Her heart was filled with wonder and a soul deep regret for a life she might never get to experience. "And He loves me enough to die for me," she said as more tears fell, "and He's promised to help me live my life fully."

A deep growl emanated from Houser's throat until it crescendoed to a raucous roar. "NO!" He picked her up by the neck and thrust her out of the tub. She slid on her butt across the floor and slammed into the wall. Dazed, Mira clutched her throat, watching the scene as if it was a slow-motion film. Houser stood, water sloshing off his naked body, chest heaving with a ferocious rage, his hands clenching as he stepped out of the tub.

Mira tried to get up, but her feet slipped on the watery tiled surface and she crashed back to the cold floor. She glanced back at Houser. As he crossed the room with heavy, deliberate steps, his evil smile grew broader, and the dagger swung out from his clutched fist.

Mira got to her hands and knees and scrabbled for the door. She could see Houser's bare feet…close, so close. She lurched for the handle, but as she felt the metal beneath her palm, it slipped from her grasp. The door swung open. Mira looked up. "Nash!" And he had a gun!

Houser roared and lunged at the same moment Nash pulled the trigger. An earsplitting *crack* filled the room. Houser's and Mira's screams echoed through the room, then both faded to nothing as Houser's body crumpled at her feet. Blood spilling from his chest, he stretched out his hand to her, his eyes dulled with pain. "I can give you everything you want – all your soul longs for," he rasped.

"You're a liar…and an enemy of God." Nash kept his gun trained on Houser.

"Abaddon is the true king. You'll see," he croaked.

"The reason Jesus, the Son of God, appeared was to destroy Abaddon's work…your work – and the work of your friends." Nash must have decided that Houser was no longer a threat. Laying down his gun, he knelt on the floor beside Mira and gathered her in his arms. "And I'm going to destroy the Wiccana-way, because we are more than conquerors through Him who loves us." His even, confident tone began to soothe the sickening terror inside her.

"NO, NO, no, no." Houser's voice grew weaker with each no.

Nash pressed a kiss against her head and smoothed the wet hair from her face. Then he began to sing softly, a lulling tune, a balm to her aching heart. "And I am convinced that nothing can ever separate us from God's love. Neither death nor life, neither angels nor demons, neither our fears for today nor our worries about tomorrow—not even the powers of hell can separate us from God's love," he sang.

New hope filled her as the life completely left Houser's body. Mira whispered, "Do you really believe what you just said…what you sang?"

"Although the words came from the Enchiridion of Emmanuel, it took me a while to believe them," he said with a half-grin, "but I do." She could hear the conviction and wonder in his voice. And as she laid there in his arms, she could feel a powerful, warm love surround her. Only, when she caught sight of a doll floating face down in the water, everything came rushing back in one horrible, tormenting swoop.

"I don't deserve to live…I was pregnant and I was going to abort the baby…I don't know what I was thinking…I wasn't thinking…I deserve to be there," she said on a sob, pointing to the dolls. "I'm so sorry, so sorry, so sorry," she blubbered and then began to weep with all the anguish in her heart pouring out. "Jesus, help me…and please, please, forgive me!"

Epilogue

Nash held Mira's hand as they looked out the window of her childhood home. Her mom and dad were upstairs packing for their trip back to Enab.

"Tell me again," Mira whispered, tears gathering in her eyes.

Nash moved behind her, looping his arms around her. Resting his cheek atop her head, he said, "I forgive you and I love you, and we're in this together, so get used to it."

She smiled and leaned back against him. The guilt still poked into her mind and heart sometimes, but since she and Nash had begun to study the Enchiridion of Emmanuel together and she'd come to truly know Jesus, that feeling was getting less and less.

She reached for the teal colored glass of water that rested on the wide window sill. Holding it to her lips, she paused. Her love for God and for Nash were getting stronger and stronger – something she didn't know was possible or so marvelous, and yet, it was so much more than that. She was done journeying through life alone, floating along with each whim, drinking in the lies and false promises of Wormwood's Water, while thirsting for a life that would never satisfy. Now she anchored herself with a firm foundation she could rely on…the truth that, even though she could never be perfect, Christ loved her perfectly and for eternity. She adored life, each breath, each sunrise, each person, each twist of events, each challenge. And she was excited to see where God would take her next. Her *and* Nash.

Taking a swig of the clear, cold water, she rested it back on the ledge. "So how did the music session go in the intensive care nursery?"

She could feel him smile behind her. "Those little ones loved it."

She turned to face him. "And I love you, Nash Montgomery." It was a promise sealed with a kiss she didn't deserve, but welcomed as a gift.

Afterward

Thank you for reading *Wormwood's Water*! Just as with Mira and Nash, we are often faced with some tough questions and viewpoints. Some people will claim that because so much is known about how the universe works, God is simply unnecessary. Some will tell us that truth is relative (like an opinion) and that we should try on religions like we would clothes in a store to see which fits us best. Some will even say that it is impossible to know the truth – and sometimes we *do* feel like throwing up our hands because of all the information. But God, who IS truth, has provided a way for us to discern it. If we take the time to be on the jury (listening with an open heart and mind to the defense, the prosecution, the evidence, and the eye witnesses), we will come to find the truth of who we are, who God is, and what our purpose is…and that is an awesome place to be.

Caution:

Mira's journey takes her off the path of truth and love and onto a path of lies and destruction within the supernatural world. This world is real and it is dangerous, and it is in direct opposition to God. Although Mira got involved with this spirit world and was saved from its destruction, do NOT ever try anything that is opposed to God! There is *no such thing* as a good witch, wizard, or spell, a friendly spirit guide or spiritist, a simply-for-fun Ouija board or séance, a harmless meditation to find a higher level of consciousness or enlightenment, a good psychic or fortune telling, a safe lucid dream…the list goes on and on! God condemns sorcery and witchcraft, communicating with the dead, and participation in the occult. And the Bible strongly denounces these practices, warns us plainly concerning them, and advises us to resist evil, not to entertain it. (Deuteronomy 18:9-11, 1 Samuel 15:23, Leviticus 19:31, 20:6-7, and James 4:7) Scripture also tells us that the source of these practices is Satan (and his demons). They are set on deception and destroying us through these mediums, and in other ways, too. Their aim is to keep us from an awesome relationship with the God who loves us and came to save us. Thankfully, though Satanic supernatural power is real, God's power is stronger, and through the name of Jesus Christ, He can set us free.

Bible verse favorites for this book:

Revelations 8:10-11: "Then the third angel sounded his trumpet, and a great star burning like a torch fell from heaven and landed on a third of the rivers and on the springs of water. The name of the star is Wormwood. A third of the waters turned bitter like wormwood oil, and many people died from the bitter waters."

John 4:13-14: "Jesus answered and said to her, 'Everyone who drinks of this water will thirst again; but whoever drinks of the water that I will give them shall never thirst; but the water that I will give them will become in them a well of water springing up to eternal life.'"

Ephesians 6:12: "For our struggle is not against flesh and blood, but against the rulers, against the powers, against the world forces of this darkness, against the spiritual forces of wickedness in the heavenly places."

Song favorites for this book:

"Thrive" – Casting Crowns

"Beautiful" – MercyMe

"Nothing Is Impossible" – Planetshakers

Author's Note:

While researching for this book, I was confronted with an evil presence – a supernatural power that I had once disregarded. The supernatural world is real, and it is powerful, destructive, and deceptive, but God's power is greater, and even though evil skirmishes will continue until the world's end, the war for our souls has already been won through the sacrifice of Jesus Christ, our LORD and Savior. Find Him, get to *know* Him intimately – He is so awesome! Not only that, but He knows the you-iest you and He carved a sacred, magnificent combination of dreams and purposes right into your core. And if you trust Him and let Him transform you and lead you, I can promise it will be an amazing journey, one that will last forever.

Michelle Heisel

is the author of The Heart of it All series. Her passion is to bring love into a dark and hurting world while encouraging people to ponder, to ask questions, and to pursue the truth of who they are and why they are here. *Pillar's Fire* – the first book in the series – concludes with passion restored, but it's opened many doors to claims of truth that look good, sound good, and seem like they will answer the yearning of the heart. The second book in the series, *Wormwood's Water*, is a suspense-filled thriller that delves into this journey of the spirit where lies are exposed, and love, forgiveness, and the truth are found. The mother of three sons, Michelle lives with her husband in SD.

Go to **michelleheisel.com** to find out more about the author and to read an excerpt from *Magnum's Opus*, the third book in The Heart of it All series.